Meanwhile in the Middle of Eternity

Edited by Phil Giunta

Firebringer Press
Baltimore, Maryland

"So Hungry..." by Phil Giunta was originally published in the Bethlehem Writers Roundtable, Issue No. 50, October 2017. It is used by permission of the author, to whom rights have reverted.

"Take a Cue from the Canine" by Phil Giunta was originally published in the Bethlehem Writers Roundtable, Issue No. 59, January 2020. It is used by permission of the author, to whom rights have reverted.

Published by:
Firebringer Press
6101 Hunt Club Road
Elkridge, MD 21085

ISBN: 978-1-948178-03-7

March, 2021

Printed in the United States of America

Cover Art by Michael Riehl

INTRODUCTION

A little ambition, fortified by dedication and perseverance, can take you a long way. In this case, seven years, three books, and 43 stories to be exact. For me—as editor, contributor, and project manager—each trek into the Middle of Eternity has been unfailingly rewarding.

I'm particularly grateful to Steven H. Wilson, our esteemed publisher at Firebringer Press, for taking a chance on my wild idea for a speculative fiction anthology comprised, in part, of stories by as-yet unpublished writers. Every new writing project is an exhilarating experiment—be it short story, novel, novella, essay, vignette, even an introduction. Developing an anthology is no different. The moment I flipped through my copy of *Somewhere in the Middle of Eternity*, hot off the press in the summer of 2014, I knew that this experiment had been a success.

One that was obviously repeatable.

Among the extraordinary creators whose stories and illustrations fill these pages with wonder, there is a core group that deserves special recognition for anchoring this series since book one—writers Daniel Patrick Corcoran, Michael Critzer, Susanna Reilly, Stuart Roth, Steven H. Wilson, Lance Woods, and artist Michael Riehl, whose enchanting covers and interior illustrations grace all three volumes.

The indomitable April Welles, who joined us in volume two, returns here with a pair of engaging and diverse adventures, and we again expand our roster of prodigious storytellers with the additions of Sean Druelinger, Julie Feedon, Christopher D. Ochs, Peter Ong, and Bart Palamaro.

I met Sean in Rehoboth Beach, Delaware while on vacation with Steve Wilson and his family. At dinner, Sean mentioned a short aviation mystery he had written many years ago. I was intrigued by the premise and encouraged him to submit it.

Julie was introduced to me by my wife as the two had been members of a local chapter of STARFLEET, the international *Star Trek* fan club. I had the pleasure of reading a sample of Julie's writing, an excerpt from her horror novel-in-progress. I was impressed and invited her to send something wicked this way. Julie's atmospheric spine-tingler did not disappoint.

Peter has penned numerous articles for defense, maritime, and emergency vehicle publications, and was referred to me by April Welles. His knowledge of the aforementioned topics allowed him to craft an action-packed SF military tale for us.

I've known Chris and Bart for several years as fellow members of the Greater Lehigh Valley Writers Group, and first encountered their exceptional work in our group's annual (now biennial) anthologies. It was immediately clear that Chris and Bart are masters at conjuring spectacular and engaging tales, two of which I'm thrilled to present here.

We also welcome artists Laura Inglis, Tim Marron, and Cheyenne-Autumn Christine Reilly who, along with Mike Riehl, provided the interior illustrations for this volume. Laura and I have been friends for many years, having met through the Maryland SF convention scene, and I hired her to create the delightfully eerie covers to all three of my paranormal mystery novels. Tim Marron's mind-blowing digital art came to my attention through Steve Wilson, and I knew immediately that I wanted his work in our book. Steve also brought Cheyenne aboard to illustrate his werewolf story. As a student, she's just getting started in her career and again, helping nascent artists and writers is what this anthology series is all about.

If I seem effusive to the point of gushing about our third leap into the *Middle of Eternity*, you'll find out why soon enough. To that end, I shan't delay you any longer...

Phil Giunta

January 2020

IF THESE WALLS COULD TALK
By Christopher D. Ochs

Every part of Michael's body ached. The stitch in his side had relented, but his legs still burned from pedaling all the way from the downtown grocery store to Old Man Nikolaidis' mountainside cabin. Now his arms and shoulders complained as well, while he lugged two bags of canned goods up the slate footpath from the foothills' service lane to the cabin's spacious front deck.

He stopped a moment to gape at the size of the house—this was no humble hunting cabin. It splayed wider than any house in town and was fit for a magazine cover. Two stories tall, its thick timbers were bookended on either side by a garage and a greenhouse. Michael admired the tiny trees that sat in small decorative pots, gracing every window box and topping every railing post.

Tripping over the steps, he spun sideways to regain his balance with his top-heavy load clutched in both arms. He placed one bag next to the imposing door hewn out of thick wooden beams and searched for a knocker or doorbell. The only features on the door were a heavy brass doorknob and a lock faceplate sturdy enough to take a direct mortar hit. Michael frowned and took a deep breath that was zinged short by

his side stitch returning with a vengeance. He raised his hand to knock, when an argument filtered through the door.

"What's upset you this time? As if I couldn't guess," came a voice that might have been Mr. Nikolaidis'. It had a rolling accent like his but was much deeper.

"What you do to their bodies is an outrage," a female voice with the same thick accent trembled with anger.

Michael shook his head. *That* couldn't *have been what I thought I heard.*

"You've been using that same old saw for a hundred years, my love," said the man with inexhaustible patience. "Besides, what am I to do? It's the only way you allow me to make my living."

"And this unnerving desire to live in homes made of corpses—I'll never understand it," said the woman.

Michael gasped, and let slip a bag of groceries. It fell on the deck, splitting apart and sending a dozen cans rolling every which way. A rapid drumming of approaching footsteps replaced the voices, and the door flew open.

"Who are you?" demanded a man wearing a red-and-black plaid flannel shirt and carpenter's jeans with heavily soiled knees. He stood a foot taller than Michael, with a burly frame as weathered and rough as the cabin's exterior. His commanding figure was made all the more forbidding by his dire expression and authoritative voice. Though he had a strong resemblance to Mr. Nikolaidis, his face was framed by black hair punctuated by wisps of gray at his temples.

Hannah warned me something was weird about this place—but Christ!

Michael's gut twisted, urging him to turn tail and run, but his legs refused to budge.

"We don't want any," the lumberjack boomed as he stepped back to slam the door.

"I-I'm Michael," he squeaked, followed by a gulp that made his ears pop. "From Almstedt's grocery. I'm... delivering Mr. Nikolaidis' order?"

The man squinted harshly, drilling Michael with a withering stare. "You're late. And where's Hannah? She usually delivers my... the

groceries." The man held the door close to his side. He glanced with nervous surprise down the stone path.

"Hannah's my cousin. She's out with a bad case of mono, and she asked me to cover for her." Michael gathered the closest cans from his scattered flock. He whimpered as his side developed a new cramp. "Where's Mr. Nikolaidis?"

"He's... upstairs in his room."

"He has to sign for this," Michael groaned as he straightened with an armload of canned beans, pulling a receipt from the remaining bag.

"Wait here, I'll get it." The man tore the receipt and the bag from Michael's arms. He turned, shoving the door closed with his foot, but the door banged ajar from its frame, allowing Michael to peer inside.

A small slate open foyer stepped up into a large room paneled in knotty cedar. It was a spartan area, pungent with the scent of conifer and sparsely dotted with antique furniture. He craned his neck to see who might have belonged to the woman's voice, but the room was empty. He jerked back outside when the man returned, reading the receipt in his hand. He clomped past the bottom of a stairway separating the front room from an adjoining dining area paneled with the same knot-filled wood.

"Is that the whole order? It seems a bit short."

"There's one more bag of veggies on my bike."

"Okay, go fetch it," the man said, still wearing an expression that made Michael's heart quiver and palms sweat. "I'll bring this mess in myself."

Michael scurried down the walkway and retrieved the last bag, plodding back up the path a bit slower than his first load. He was halfway to the cabin when he spied the man collecting cans that had rolled off the front deck.

Michael stumbled to a stop—it wasn't the lumberjack.

Though he wore the same shirt and dirty denims as the first man, they draped loosely on his slight build. His profile sported an aquiline nose not unlike Old Man Nikolaidis, but where Old Nik was almost entirely bald, only the top of this man's head poked through shocks of white

hair. Michael always thought Old Nik stooped over so much, his back resembled a cooked shrimp, but this guy only showed a hint of an arch in his spine. He retreated into the darkness of the cabin.

Michael trudged the rest of the path to the front door. He deposited the grocery bag without a sound, hoping to skedaddle before anyone came back. The door flung open, and the lumberjack glared down at Michael.

"Here's your receipt. Tell Almstedt that I'll call in another order next week." He quickly added as an afterthought, "... for Mr. Nikolaidis."

"Okay, sure." Michael picked up the bag again with a feeble grunt, as his legs complained anew at their use. He tilted his head to one side then the other, hoping to catch a glimpse of the woman he heard, the white-haired man or perhaps Old Man Nik himself. "Are you having a family reunion?"

"None of your business," the brawny man snapped as he grabbed the bag. "Just be sure that Almstedt sends Hannah with the order. Only *Hannah*, got it?"

"But she *can't*. She's quarantined for another ten days."

The man's stern glower relented, replaced with a squinting curiosity. "You... you had no problem getting up here?"

"It was a haul to get three full bags up Cedar Road, and my legs..."

"That's not what I meant, kid. The access lane and the driveway were clear? No heavy brush or tree branches? Nothing blocking the way?" The man's strange intensity fixed Michael where he stood.

"Nope. The whole way was wide open." Michael stared open-mouthed at the eccentric lumberjack.

"Unusual... I mean, good." He scanned around the woods, peering through the forest canopy into dappling sunshine that angled through the cabin doorway. "What's your name again?"

"Michael."

"Here you go, Michael." He dug out his wallet and handed him a ten-dollar bill. "That's for your trouble. Make sure Almstedt sends you with my next order—only *you*. I... *we* don't appreciate strangers."

No kidding.

"And just leave the bags here on the porch, or in the garage. Not inside, got it?" Before Michael could respond, the lumberjack slammed the door shut in his face.

Michael strolled back to his bike, taking in the view from which his aching legs and side had previously distracted him. Between the lane and the sprawling cabin, the metal garage had one door rolled open. A flawless classic automobile glimmered within the dark recesses of the bay. On the opposite side of the cabin, movement behind the shining glints of the greenhouse drew his attention.

Thick verdant growth pressed against spotless glass. The building sparkled like diamonds in the sunshine that speared through wind-blown foliage.

Behind the farthest corner of the greenhouse towered an elm swaying in the breeze. The giant dominated its coniferous neighbors, its crown spreading out like a bell. It danced with the wind, glorying in the sunlight as it reached for the sky, with leaves so green their color seemed to bleed into every neighboring fir and cedar. Michael's gaze was riveted to the elm—deciduous trees were unheard of this high up. He left the enclave with the distinct impression the elm waved at him.

Michael rode back to town, glad to be away from the crotchety linebacker. When he pedaled onto the main road, he was overtaken by the notion that the farther away from Old Man Nik's place he got, the grayer and thinner the forest became. He took a deep gulp from the water bottle clamped to the spar under his seat. *This summer is really brutal.*

He didn't see anything remotely as green until he rode past the local home décor shop across the street from Almstedt's General Store. Two tiny trees just like the ones at Old Nik's were proudly displayed in a pair of storefront windows, for prices higher than all the money Michael hoped to earn this summer.

Michael stumbled into the grocery store, nearly kicking over a cardboard display hawking the latest snack food craze. He skidded to a stop, forced to cool his heels until Mr. Almstedt finished with a customer at the counter. He handed the receipt to Mr. Almstedt.

"Oh good, you got Mr. Nikolaidis' signature. I would've laid odds he would have spooked you off his land," the stocky bald man chortled as he wiped his hand on his apron.

Michael exhaled a scared little laugh. "Yeah, almost. But I didn't see him." A spark of recollection screwed up Michael's brow. *Wait—that guy didn't go upstairs; he came from the back room.* "Someone else signed for it. The guy looked like Old Man Nik's younger brother."

"Oh? That's strange. I didn't know Nikolaidis had family," Almstedt remarked. "Though Hannah told me he had an off-and-on groundskeeper. Other than that, he's lived alone up there in his cabin as long as I can remember."

"Well, he had a bunch of visitors today. The guy who signed for it sure looked like he was related. There was an older man with white hair, too. And I heard some woman with the same accent as Old Man Nik. It was weird, like something flaky was going on."

Almstedt stared at the receipt. "But this is Mr. Nikolaidis' signature. You sure you got things straight? He doesn't like visitors."

"Yeah, I'm sure," Michael countered. "The younger guy demanded that I'm supposed to bring next week's order—no one else."

"Now *that* sounds like Mr. Nikolaidis," Almstedt chuckled while he scribbled on the phone pad.

"Why are they all so grumpy?"

"Can't speak for the rest of his family, never met 'em. But Old Man Nik, he's been that way since... since I don't know when. He came over to America from Greece long before I set up shop—sometime after the war, I think. Been a pain in most everyone's neck ever since he got off the boat."

"Which war?"

Almstedt finished his writing and regarded Michael with an unsure half-frown. "World War II, I guess." He handed Michael another list, and two large paper bags, each with two cartons of smokes. "Here... fill this out and deliver it to Widow Akins."

"Aww, all the way up Cedar Road again?"

"Yup. This one won't be so heavy this time. She's out of dry cat food and cigarettes again. Then you can call it a day."

With a sullen whine, Michael snapped the bags straight and filled them with boxes of cat chow. *Why does every town have a crazy cat lady?* He paused with a half-full bag as his eyes were drawn again to the splotches of vibrant green in the décor shop window across the street.

"Nik's place was loaded with those little trees. What are they?"

Almstedt followed Michael's gaze. "They're called bonsai, and they're difficult to grow," he replied, while turning off the deli counter display. "Mr. Nikolaidis has a knack for it and makes a good living from it. His best pieces have been sold to arboretums across the country. Museums, too. *National Geographic* wanted to do an article on his work. They tried to interview him, but he turned them away." He stood, squinted at the ceiling and scratched his temple. "Or was it that they couldn't find his place?"

A tickle ran up Michael's spine as the strange lumberjack's words came back to him, *"Nothing blocking the way?"*

———

Michael rode his mountain bike up tortuous Cedar Road to Widow Akins', the bags in baskets on either side of the rear wheel. With each pump of the bicycle pedals, his legs swore oaths that he would pay dearly tomorrow for this second insult.

With the lumberjack's question still worming in his ear, the forest grew thicker and greener as he approached Nikolaidis' property. The shade quickly thinned and faded back to a thirsty brown when he rounded the switchback leading to the Akins' place. *Wait... how did I pass Nik's?*

A woman wrapped in a dough-splattered muumuu, with a burning cigarette hanging from her cracked lips, greeted Michael. A river of blue-gray smoke billowed out the door of the ramshackle cottage. Michael's nose crinkled at an odor that reeked like a gang of polecats had sprayed their marks on a burnt carcass.

"Here's your delivery, Mrs. Akins," he said between coughs.

"Come on in, Michael," Widow Akins said in a voice that rattled like aquarium charcoal in a coffee grinder. "Mr. Almstedt told me to expect you. I have a pen around here somewhere." She submerged into the blue fog of her hovel, all the while grating a soliloquy about the dry heat, a new recipe for snickerdoodles, and a stream of other topics that drowned in her endless hacks and ramblings.

Michael took a deep breath and marched into the gloomy den. A chorus of meows announced his intrusion into the murkiness, and Michael struggled to step lively around the gathering herd of purring ankle-rubbers. Every ashtray between the front door and the kitchen was rimmed with cigarettes that had burned their entire length while waiting to be picked up again.

He deposited the grocery bags on the last remnant of open space atop the kitchen counter. The defenseless bags were pounced upon by a half-dozen curious furballs. A breeze wafted through an open kitchen window. Michael exhaled, hoping he wouldn't yak on his next breath.

A cough drowning in phlegm and gravel announced that Widow Akins had found her pen. He snatched the signed receipt and using as little of his remaining air as possible, he machine-gunned out, "ThankzMizzAkinzGottago," before dashing out the front door.

Michael toed up his bike's kickstand, when Widow Akins chased after him, mincing along in tiny piglet steps, bearing a plateful of cookies. "Don't you want any, dearie?" she rasped, followed by a cough that sent her lit cigarette butt sailing out of her mouth onto a knot of dry grass.

"No thanks, Mrs. Akins!" said Michael. He rolled over to the grass and stamped out the smoldering ember, before the whiff of smoky, cat-flavored cookies made his throat slam shut. He pumped the pedals furiously, zooming past shriveled brown brambles into acres of green. So focused on wind-whipping the stink of the Akins dump out of his nostrils, he was startled when the overflowing forest gave way once again to brown scrub. *How the heck did I miss Old Man Nik's place again?*

———————

Michael was never so glad for an evening shower. Not only did it wash away the salty sweat and grit of the day's work, but it rinsed out the stench of cat whiz and tobacco that clung to his hair.

The next morning, the alarm clock blared far too early for Michael's liking. *How did Hannah ever manage this?*

He clomped downstairs in a half-stupor to breakfast, and climbed back up twice as slow, stumbling over his own sleepy feet. Dressing for work, his eyes popped open and his breakfast threatened to about-face when he put on yesterday's T-shirt and the reek of old cigarette smoke invaded his nostrils. He settled for his second favorite T-shirt—his dad's—with a giant bass thrashing on the end of a fisherman's line. Three sizes too large for his body, it hung on him like a garbage can liner.

Michael biked into town, his legs reminding him on every incline that they hadn't forgiven him for yesterday's hauls. When Michael entered the store, Mr. Almstedt was on the phone. Almstedt pinned Akins' receipt to the corkboard next to the wall phone and nodded his thanks while he cradled the receiver against his shoulder and scribbled on a notepad.

"Yes, Mr. Nikolaidis. I wasn't expecting another order until next week, but we can send that up by the end of the day." The two exchanged glances, Almstedt's garnished with a wink and Michael's accompanied by slumping shoulders and a whining sigh.

The explosion of flowers bordering the entire length of the driveway leading to Old Man Nik's place did nothing to brighten Michael's mood, or soothe his aching quads. *Why couldn't those Nat Geo guys find Nik's? And how did I miss something so obvious yesterday—twice?*

He trudged up the steps to the front door with a bag in either arm, one overflowing with vegetables and fruits, the other holding enough wrapped steaks, chops, and ground sirloin to give a mountain lion the meat sweats.

Michael kicked the door jamb as loud as he dared to get the attention of Old Man Nik, the lumberjack, or whoever else might be inside. "Hello? Mr. Nikolaidis?" He kicked the frame a second time and leaned his ear close to the door. Through the heavy planking, he could hear something that made his neck hairs stand on end—a murmuring of many voices. He called again, and the droning got louder.

When no one answered, he kicked the door, hoping it would be loud enough. The door swung open, and the voices stopped.

"Hello?" Michael stepped into the foyer. The aroma of fresh oil soap breezed around him. "Hello-o-o," he called again louder, looking for the source of the voices. Same as yesterday, the room paneled in polished knotty cedar planks was empty, save for an opulent rug and an overstuffed leather recliner sandwiched between a wrought-iron table and floor lamp.

No TV, so where did the voices come from?

"Mr. Nikolaidis?" he said as loud as he could without sounding like a scream. "Is anybody home?"

He shrugged his shoulders, and his tired arms paid him back with a twinge.

I better unload these before I drop them.

He couldn't leave them outside, as the lumberjack instructed yesterday. The raw meat would attract bears from every mountaintop, and raccoons would make off with the rest. *And guess who would be blamed for it.*

Michael pursed his lips and, holding his breath, took a step into the foyer. *No voices, no linebacker jumping out of the corners. So far, so good.*

The living-room table was too small to hold his cargo, and it would be an unholy mess if any of the wrapped meats leaked onto the chair or the rug. Michael lugged his armfuls past the staircase leading to the darkened upper floor. He tramped into the dining room, paneled in the same knot-filled cedar. A granite table, supported by formidable wrought-iron legs stood with a single matching chair, looking quite lonely. The bags pulled on his weary shoulders like they were laden with cement. He was more than happy to finally unload them on the table.

The nape of Michael's neck crept half an inch higher. He was being watched.

Surveying the dining room, it dawned on him the walls were bare—no pictures, no paintings. Michael's brow creased when he recalled that the front room also had no wall hangings of any type. The unsettling sense of being under a microscope grew when a pair of knots in the paneling caught his attention.

They were black as charcoal, and seemed to stare straight at him, as a tiger would its prey. Lines of woodgrain bunching around the eyes emphasized their unnerving intensity. The predator's eyes weren't alone— others were dotted throughout every stained panel.

The knots were always in pairs, in every shape from circular to oval, elongated to almond, and every irregular shape in between. Some looked sad, some were pensive, others were surrounded by drooping wood rings that gave them the semblance of crying. Some looked worried while others were angry, full of rage. A few seemed happy, but a twinge behind Michael's sternum insisted they were laughing at *him*.

Regardless of their shape or imagined emotion, Michael could not shake the impression that each pair of eyes was examining him.

He retreated backward, to the base of the stairway between the rooms. "Mr. Nikolaidis, are you home? Is everything OK?" he called up the stairs. A hushed chorus of murmuring floated down from the gloom.

"Everything is *exodos*," a woman's heavily accented voice reverberated from the front room.

Michael fairly jumped out of his sneakers, and the susurrus of whispers ceased. Once he swallowed his heart again, he poked his head into the room. It was empty, except for the austere furniture and the room's own set of wooden knotholes staring at him. Dozens of morose, gleeful, vengeful, suffering, and hungry eyes returned his darting gaze.

His brow and palms broke into a sweat. His lungs refused to fill, and his bowels wriggled. *I don't believe in ghosts, but this is too weird.*

The metallic baritone of an old car horn stuttered to life, then sang out with a sustained blast.

Michael could breathe again. He dashed out the door and down the front deck steps. Doubled over with effort, he took in several deep gulps of air before looking up.

Old Man Nik beckoned to him from just inside the garage door. He was in a near panic, his spindly arms flailing like a wounded bird's wings within his loose plaid shirt. Behind him was his immaculate Studebaker—by the look of its styling, probably only slightly younger than the old geezer. It sat inside the metal garage with its hood propped open, still shrieking out its obnoxious monotone shrill.

"Can you help me here?" Old Man Nik mouthed over the blare, waving him forward.

Michael took a few faltering steps toward him. He felt a twinge of trepidation, but the old man's tortuously curved spine and imploring smile overcame any uncertainty. Michael held his hands over his ears as he followed the old man to the auto's driver-side door. Nikolaidis pointed sharply, directing Michael's attention to the steering wheel.

"When I tell you," he screeched over the deafening noise, mimicking the act of beeping the horn. The old fossil shuffled to the front of the car and disappeared behind the hood. After a few heartbeats, the maddening howl stopped. The hood of the car slammed down, and Nikolaidis' silhouette stood out against the bright sunshine behind him.

"Now?" asked Michael.

Nikolaidis twisted around and brought down the garage door.

"What the—?" Michael sputtered. *Oh brother, not good. What kind of a creep is he?* He pushed the car door open until it groaned against its limit, keeping it between himself and the old man.

Nikolaidis advanced to the side of the car, standing next to its front whitewall. He held his palms face down at chest level, his disarming smile now replaced with a worried look.

"Don't be afraid—Michael, was it? I'm sorry if I scared you, but I had to get you away from her. This is the only place she can't hear us. Take your bike and never come back." He stopped to grab one garage door handle and grunted with effort as he lifted the door open the barest crack.

"What are you talking about?" Michael said. "Who's *she*? That woman I heard in your house?"

Nikolaidis spun around, his face ashen. "Oh God, you *heard* her?" He twitched and reapplied himself to the stubborn heavy garage door. He grunted in a spasm of pain, pressing his palm against his scrawny back. "Help me with the damned door, and just go, before she suspects."

Michael dashed to the opposite handle and whooshed up the garage door, its segments clattering like a machine gun as they sped past their roller guides. He ran to his bike, and zoomed down the slate path, not looking back. The slate gave way to the dirt service lane, twisting like a serpent coiling around its prey. He batted away fronds of dense brush and dodged leafy branches that drooped down into his path. His breath came in spurts, but he ignored his returning side stitch. The burning in his thigh muscles grew to a new crescendo, just as he skidded to a halt in a clearing.

Before him stood Old Man Nik's cabin. *How ...?*

Michael turned his bike around and peered up at the late afternoon sun. *West—head straight west back to Cedar Road.*

He pedaled across the clearing and went down the slate path a second time. *This* has *to be the way out.*

The tangerine sun neared the mountainous horizon, and Michael kept it in his sights. The service path veered away unexpectedly to the north. He ignored it and plowed his mountain bike into the scrub. Brambles scratched at his legs, and leafy tangles pulled at the handlebars. The vegetation thickened, but he sailed westward over gullies and moguls, never losing sight of the sun. The overhead canopy grew dark and ominous, but soon parted. The trees and scrub thinned out, finally giving way to a footpath wide enough for his bike. Michael rode frantically toward the reddening sun, until he came to another opening.

He skidded to a stop in a cloud of dust by the rear of the garage. Beyond the cabin and greenhouse loomed the enormous elm tree, the last traces of the blood red sunset shimmering on its highest leaves.

Old Man Nikolaidis shuffled around the corner of his garage. His shoulders slumped in defeat as he regarded Michael with sad eyes. "I'm sorry. I'm so sorry," his voice trembled. "She insisted I bring you back today."

"What happened?" Michael screamed between pants and gasps. "How did I get here? West—I went west! I *know* I did. Followed the sun all the way."

"I'm sorry—so sorry," Nikolaidis repeated, putting his shaking hand to his forehead. "I tried to warn you. I should have scared you away the first time you came here. Now she won't let you go."

"Warn me? How could you? I didn't even see you yesterday. You were upstairs when I met your..." Michael stared slack-jawed at Old Man Nikolaidis, dressed in a baggy pair of soiled carpenter's jeans and a black and red plaid flannel shirt that hung on his body like a deflated hot air balloon. "That was you? No, that *couldn't* be."

Nikolaidis looked plaintively at the Evening Star poking through the twilight, then trudged toward the house. He called over his shoulder, "You might as well come inside now. If she wouldn't allow you to leave during daylight, how much better would you fare in the dark?" He scuffled a few steps, then paused when he realized Michael hadn't followed. "Come on, she won't hurt you."

Michael sniffled, his nostrils twitching from the faint tang of pork barbecue roasting in some far-off smoky firepit. The two marched up the stairs onto the back porch to the kitchen door. Michael stared, hypnotized with astonishment as the man in front of him grew in stature, size, and color with each step.

It was feeble Old Man Nik that climbed the stairs, but it was the strapping lumberjack that stood in the kitchen doorway, holding it open. Michael gawked at the hulking bruiser, expecting him to grin with axe-murderer anticipation. Instead, the linebacker's eyes drooped with surrender.

In the kitchen, every square foot of wall was paneled with knotty cedar, save for a gap of patterned ceramic tile one foot around the stove. The weight of all those soulless unblinking wooden eyes on him pressed the air out of Michael's lungs.

Big Nik emerged from the dining room and hefted the bags of groceries with ease into the refrigerator. He took out a bottle of water and handed it to Michael, who greedily downed the contents, spluttering after each gulp. But the ice-cold water failed to erase his bottomless thirst from the effects of a murderously dry summer day compounded by raw fear.

"Follow me." Nikolaidis led Michael through the dining area, picking up the heavy iron chair as though it were made of cardboard. He pointed to the recliner in the front room. "Have a seat." Michael warily obliged, as the lumberjack deposited his chair on the rug with a muffled thunk.

He folded his massive arms across his broad chest and spoke to the walls. "Nothing to say?" He turned his attention to the ceiling. "You don't have the courtesy to explain it to the poor lad?"

The walls' hushed snickering made Michael's scalp want to jump off his skull. He gripped the ends of the armrests. His knuckles went white, threatening to pop at any second.

Michael caught a glimpse of movement on the wall. The pair of knotholes closest to his chair stared straight at him. Woodgrain crowded around the eyes, giving them an aspect of anticipation.

He squeezed his eyes shut and thrashed his head. *I couldn't have seen that.*

Returning the walls' stare, he couldn't tell if it was his imagination imbuing the eyes with emotion. His legs twitched, urging their owner to get the hell out of there. He forced himself deeper into the cushion, convincing himself that to make a break for it, he would have to tackle the plaid lumberjack standing in front of him—only to run around in circles through the woods all night.

Nikolaidis sighed, sat in the metal chair that yielded with a squeak under his massive frame, and crossed his legs in an awkward attempt to portray a fatherly demeanor.

"Well, Michael. Where to start? What are you into... what are your hobbies?"

Is he serious? I'm trapped in a spook house and he's talking hobbies?

"I saw your mountain bike. You ride the trails around here?"

A tentative, drawn out "No-ot rea-al-ly?" seeped out of Michael.

He pointed at the oversized shirt on Michael's chest. "Then what about that circus tent you're wearing? You like fishing?"

"My Dad and I fished when we went camping. Used to go a lot. Haven't done it in a while, 'cause..." Michael's mouth went taut with an unpleasant memory.

"Because of the drought?"

Michael sucked in a feeble breath before answering. "No. Killed in Iraq."

"Oh... an orphan of war. I'm sorry, son." The burly man's arms fell in his lap, and a lopsided frown crowded out his embarrassed expression.

Michael grunted. He despised that look—the same empty mix of pity and "want-to-be-somewhere-else" that was plastered on everyone's faces at Dad's funeral.

The lumberjack wrung his hands, as if he were working out a problem or reliving some long-lost memory. He nodded his head with satisfaction, concluding, "That's why she let you in."

Michael shifted with growing impatience in his chair. "She? Who's *she*?"

"That's what I'm trying to explain, son. Let's see... fishing... nature... trees." Nikolaidis scratched one graying temple. "You'll have to forgive me, I'm no good at making small talk. I've avoided people for most of my life." He rubbed his chin for a moment. "I know—do you like to read? What books have you read?"

Michael's mind went blank. His throat stung when he tried to swallow. He surveyed the room, hoping to find something that might spur his recollection, or give him some hint what to say. *No TV or radio. What does he do here all day long? No books, not even a magazine.*

"Comics. Graphic novels," Michael began cautiously, once that spark of an idea filled the vacuum in his mind. "Superheroes, manga, fantasy, stuff like that . . ."

Nikolaidis leaned forward with sudden interest. "All right. Let's start there—fantasy. What kind of fantasy?"

Michael shrugged his shoulders. "I dunno. Marvel, DC, Super. . ."

"Oh, yes. The drivel that passes for entertainment these days." Nikolaidis rolled his eyes in disappointment before fixating on Michael again. "What about mythology? Do you know anything about that?"

"Like Thor and Loki?"

"Almost. What about the Greek pantheon? You know—Zeus, Hercules, Aphrodite?"

"Yeah. I saw a Hercules flick once."

"O-o-of course," Big Nik harrumphed. He tilted his head back with a disappointed smirk, scanning the ceiling as if he expected to find a message written there. "Then you probably never heard of something called a *nymph*."

"You mean those insects in water? Mosquito larvae?"

"Larvae!" erupted a woman's voice from every wall at once. "You compare me to *insects*?"

The woodgrain around every pair of knotholes bunched. Scores of angry eyes with downturned eyebrows and ferocious scowls burned through him.

Oh God—they're real!

Michael's legs twanged with an adrenaline burst of energy, and he bounded over the recliner arms, knocking over the metal side-table. It hammered the floor with the clang of a broken church bell. Dashing through the kitchen, he bolted off the back porch. He stopped when the footpath behind the cabin beckoned him into the dark forest labyrinth. His head spun like a radar turret, looking for a hole to hide in. He locked on the dense foliage in the greenhouse. The glass walls were draped with condensation that dripped in small rivulets from broad leaves crammed against the panes and metal spars. Slipping through the door as quietly as he could manage, he swatted away fronds of fern that clung to his face in wet bunches.

Water burbled from somewhere deep in the greenhouse's oppressive humidity. Michael headed toward the murmur of rippling water, goaded by his burning thirst that reasserted itself. He passed by a workbench with a row of bonsai. Each tree was ringed by tiny clippings, each mote hardly larger than a bread crumb. Behind the table was a pegboard holding rows of gardening tools ranging from a giant hoe to shears the size of nail clippers. On neighboring shelves lay a platoon of hoses, stacked in coils.

Michael grabbed a thin trowel from the wall. Its saw-toothed edge on one side reminded him of Dad's camping knife. He backed into a curtain of dew-drenched fronds, keeping his eyes on the greenhouse door. His hand clenched firmly around the trowel's handle, brandishing it like a sword. A grate in the center of the concrete floor complained with a harsh clank when he stepped on it. He whispered a curse through clenched teeth and stepped further back.

A wall of leaves and cedar sprigs poked his arms and swept forward, closing like theater curtains in front of him. To his side was a fountain feeding a pool of water, lined by a brick wall that came up to his knees. A hose thick as Michael's wrist lay in loose coils against the fountain wall.

Foliage around the greenhouse wafted in unison as the door swung open. Michael slipped deeper into the alcove of vegetation bordering the fountain, gripping his makeshift weapon tighter than before. He wondered if he would face Big Nik or Old Man Nik on this side of the cabin.

It's gonna be Old Man Nik. It's gotta be. He gripped the trowel with both hands when the one ached with a cramp.

Through the peepholes between branch, leaf, and needle, Michael spied a swath of denim and plaid approaching. A tall figure crowned with raven-black hair wheeled and lunged directly at him.

With a whimper of fear that ramped into a shriek of panic, Michael jumped to the side, thrashing the trowel in wild arcs. The blur of red and black advanced, and wiry plaid arms flew up in defense, deflecting the trowel. Michael jumped with surprise, faced by a Nikolaidis scarcely older than a teenager.

A tug at Michael's ankle anchored one foot to the floor. He fell headlong over the entangled hose, the fountain wall shoving his elbow inward. A flash of pain radiated from his chest, and he collapsed on the concrete, the base of the trowel protruding from his ribs. He tried to scream, but all he could manage was a strangled gurgle and a single wet cough. A froth of red foam sprayed out of his mouth.

"*Uu-chi!*" echoed a woman's screech that made every pane in the greenhouse rattle. The metal door burst open, ramming against the table and knocking the bonsai closest to its edge onto the floor.

Through the doorway snaked a tree limb, its leaves hissing as they skittered along the concrete toward the fountain.

Michael's legs twitched, trying to pull his feet underneath him. His arms flailed against brick, searching for a handhold to haul himself away from the advancing serpent of wood and leaf. Every attempt at movement radiated a fresh pulse of misery from his chest. His eyes pleaded with the young Nikolaidis, when his mouth refused to move, and his lungs cramped against crushing heaviness.

With a stern expression of dread, Nikolaidis scooped up Michael in both arms and deposited him in the living wood that flowed around his feet. "Take the poor lad, Ptelea! Save him, please—as you did for me."

A cradle of rustling green enveloped Michael, and his vision swam as he was drawn out of the greenhouse on a carpet of leaves into the night. Flashes of emerging moonlight poking through the canopy abruptly gave way to a flood of glowing earth tones. The scent of sap and loam filled his nostrils, and the burning that blistered his lungs ebbed into quiet nothingness. He became surrounded by liquid warmth, reminiscent of lazing in a sun-kissed lake.

Waves of glowing russet parted, revealing an amber expanse. A figure, the hue of cinnamon, strode toward him. The image wavered, as though seen through a rippling pool of honey.

It was a woman—perfect and more alluring than any Michael had ogled in Dad's old magazines.

But *not* a woman. Her hair was a waterfall of elm leaves that flowed over her shoulders onto her bosom. Lines of woodgrain running up and down her entire form emphasized her contours, making her loveliness all the more ephemeral and desirable, all the more enduring and terrifying.

Her skin was lustrous, polished like a living sculpture made from the finest unblemished wood. Her eyes were coffee-colored knots, surrounded by striations that lent her face a feeling of warmth and sympathy. A tingling pressure rang from Michael's head through his heart into his loins.

The figure pressed her ligneous hand against the bare skin of Michael's chest. The trowel was gone, though the open wound remained, oozing out life. Where her hand caressed his form, supple warmth flowed toward the wound. The congealing stream of blood that carpeted his skin flowed back toward the open gash, changing from a dark crimson to a beige syrup. The ragged edges of the lesion drew close to each other, knitting together seamlessly. In place of a scar, a pattern of woodgrain spread across his chest, pulsed with a golden luminescence akin to a heartbeat, then vanished.

"Am I... dead?" Michael gulped for air. His lungs labored against the thickness, as if he were breathing water, though without any pain.

"Not this day, young one," she replied in sonorous tones that sung like a cello. Michael withdrew from her a step, frowning with recognition—hers was the disembodied voice from the cabin, from what seemed a lifetime ago.

"Who... what are you?"

"Ptelea." She ran her hand along the line of his jaw and showed him a gentle smile. "I am Anton's, and he is mine. Now *you* are mine as well, Michael." Her smile contained a mixture of hope and regret.

"Anton? Who's An—" His breath cut short. Michael's diaphragm spasmed, unable to pull in air.

"My dear Michael," she said with affection. "I am sorry, but Man may not tarry here for long. Time for you to go." A stream of dark green swirled into the pool of amber, and the scent of the forest—an amalgam of vigorous growth and solid timber, tinged with a wisp of excrement and fungal decay—overwhelmed his senses. Swallowed by intense vertigo, he tumbled backward.

His eyes fluttered open, focusing on the moonlit silhouette of the young Nikolaidis standing above him. One shadowy hand extended to help him to his feet, the other bunched a bundle of cloth. Michael pushed weakly against the ground with his arms, propping himself up from the roots of the elm.

"C'mon, get up, Michael." The lanky Nikolaidis hauled him up from the trunk of the elm and tossed him a pile of clothes. "And get dressed. I'll be inside, cleaning up." He turned and walked into the greenhouse, his shoulders slumped as though he carried the weight of the world on them.

Once he got over the shock of his nakedness, Michael tried to dash through the task of putting on his clothes. His brow knotted in confusion, as he realized he first had to undo the belt and unzip his empty pants, untie and retie his shoes. He shuddered when he slipped on his dad's T-shirt, ruined by a ragged hole bordered in blood.

A stiff breeze shook the leaves above him and rustled the needles of the neighboring conifers. Michael's nose wrinkled at the scent of burning wood that quickly drowned in the cedar tang of the forest when the wind changed again. He looked anxiously at the titanic elm, wondering if another branch might swoop down before he had a chance to scramble to the greenhouse.

Young Nikolaidis was hosing the last of the blood off the trowel, and the remaining spatter on the floor down the grate. He pulled a stool away from the workbench, offering it to Michael. He collected the fallen bonsai, set it on the wall of the fountain, and sat next to it. "You saw her, didn't you," he said, staring at wet concrete. "Isn't Ptelea the most beautiful creature you have ever seen in your life?"

"Yes," Michael sighed, a child lost in a dream. He took a deep breath before whispering, "What is she?"

"How do I explain? You didn't know what a nymph from mythology was. I doubt you'd understand what a *dryad* is, either."

Michael returned a blank stare. A torrent of questions roiled in his head, but they were pushed aside by the memory of Ptelea's unsettling beauty.

"She's a wood nymph—a spirit of the forest. They come from my home, the old country in Greece, though I gave them little thought when

I was your age. They inhabit the trees and are a living part of the forests they shepherd. They move through limb, root, and leaf, tree to tree, as easily as you or I swim in water." He caressed the bonsai next to him. "I'm sure she's watching and listening right now."

The bonsai wriggled in its pot. Michael wasn't quite sure if he had heard it giggle.

"But Ptelea is special. She's a *hamadryad*. Like their cousins, they move in the living woods, and even in the dead wood we build with. Trees come to life at their bidding, and they give voice to every plank they touch. But their existence is anchored to one specific tree, never wandering too far from their home. Ptelea lives in that wych elm behind you."

"Here? From Greece?" Michael shook his head as the stampede of questions returned. "How did she get here? And who's Anton?"

"That would be me." He braced his arms on the wall and leaned back. "Anton Nikolaidis, a carpenter's son from Skra Legen—a village near Mount Paiko in Greece. And *I* brought her here."

"Why bring her here all the way from Skr ... from Greece?"

Anton stared through the roof of the greenhouse, peering far beyond the moonlit outline of the elm.

"It was the last days of the war. Germany had lost—her allies just didn't know it yet. It certainly wasn't soon enough for the Bulgarians to get the message. One hour before dawn, they came rushing around the base of Mount Paiko. Our small platoon was caught in a pincer maneuver. Cannons and foot soldiers on one side, tanks on the other. They closed in, forcing us into retreat. My father, our sergeant, rallied my squad together until a mortar hit scattered us. I scrambled over the ridge to help my father. I found him face down over the roots of an elm tree, drenched in red."

Anton wrung his hands together furiously and sighed. "I turned him over to stop the blood, but he was gone. Half his head was ripped away by shrapnel." His hands balled into shaking fists. "Shells were going off all around me, but all I could see was my father's broken body."

Michael shuddered.

"Then someone shouted behind me in Bulgarian, and I defended myself—but too late. I was bayoneted, impaled against the tree. I could see the raw recruit's horror of his first kill in his eyes. He must have been terrified—he accidentally fired his rifle as well. Tore a hole in my chest above the stab wound."

Michael opened his mouth several times to speak but couldn't utter a word. The image of his own father breathing his last on some nameless patch of Iraqi desert jammed his heart into his throat.

"The Bulgarian ran screaming with his gun into the dawn, and I sank to my knees against the blood-soaked trunk of that tree—that impossibly big wych elm that stood on that mountainside for centuries. I was so weak, drowning in my own blood, I could scarcely move when the tree enveloped me." Anton rubbed his eyes with the backs of both hands. "You can guess the rest. Ptelea saved me that day, just as she healed you tonight."

Michael dug the heels of his palms against closed eyes. *I'm not crying. I'm not... I miss Dad.*

He buried a sob and cleared his throat. "Wait, *Ptelea* healed you? How did you bring her tree all the way over here?"

"I didn't bring the tree, I brought *her*." Anton stood and paced the length of the greenhouse, mussing his hair as he gathered his thoughts. "Ptelea's a spirit, Michael. She doesn't live and die like us. I don't even know if she *can* truly die. But she can be *reborn* . . .

"I was still inside Ptelea's tree. She had healed my wounds, bonded with me. Then it seemed like the world exploded, and Ptelea's scream shook the heavens. I fell out of the tree—no, I was thrown out of the tree—naked as the day I was born. Above my head, a second mortar shell hit the trunk square in the center, snapping the elm in two and sending a hail of splinters raining down."

He stopped pacing and held out an upright hand, staring into his empty palm. "The last thing the living wood did was wrap a branch around my wrist and push a single seed into my hand. It was a tiny thing, barely the size of a nickel. It looked like a slice of dried apple with a raisin buried in its flesh. I heard the last whimper of Ptelea's voice: 'Take me far from this place.'"

He gripped Michael's shoulder, and shuddered with a moaning sigh. "The war was over. Everyone I had known was dead, and there was nothing left for me in Skra Legen. I was indebted to Ptelea, and I swore to honor her last wish. I emigrated to America. After a year, I found this estate, in mountains so very much like those of my homeland and settled down. I planted her seed, and Ptelea was reborn."

"What about you? Were you reborn, too? Is that why you keep changing? One moment, you're Old Man Nik, the next you're built like The Rock, and now you're what, twenty?"

"I was eighteen when I fought in the war, and Ptelea healed me. But that was only part of it. She *bonded* with me. When I'm close to her, I'm young again. The farther away I am from her influence, the older I get. Over the first few decades, as she grew in strength and stature, so did I in many ways—ways I never dared to guess." His shallow chest heaved with a wistful sigh. "She told me I was hers, and..."

"Yeah, she said I was hers, too." Michael pierced Anton with inquiring eyes. "But what does that mean?"

A knowing smile wended its way across his face. "You'll find out when you're older, Michael. But for now..." Anton clapped him on the back, and hitched his head toward the door. "C'mon, let us show you something."

They stood in front of the elm. Its branches swayed in the orange moonlight from a breeze wafting up the mountain. Anton leaned forward and placed his palm on the bark of the tree. "Do as I do. Close your eyes and empty your mind. Let her come to you." He exhaled a long, relaxed breath through an open mouth.

Michael regarded him with an ambivalent frown, shrugged his shoulders and followed his lead. He touched the elm with his fingertips, then flattened his palm against the craggy bark. Closing his eyes, he tried to discern anything in the shifting afterimages. An amber circle of fuzzy shapes grew in his mind, until it lightened and solidified. He exhaled though pursed lips, and relaxed his shoulders, attempting to focus the image further.

He peered down from a dizzying height onto two figures, each with one arm outstretched. Michael gasped—it was Anton and himself he perceived. The wind picked up, and he swooned with a heady rush, his body quivering with the twitch of every elm leaf. His toes curled, and the tingle of cool earth enveloped his feet.

At the risk of breaking the spell, he dared a whisper. "What is this? Do you see this, too?"

"Of course. We are seeing with Ptelea's vision. She sees what her trees see. Feels what they feel."

A flash, as though rushing through an amber river, and Michael found himself in Anton's front room. His skin ached with an uncomfortable itching, like his body was riddled with old scars. A wall of knothole eyes stared back at him, each pair brimming with cheerfulness and affection.

Another pulse of golden light, whooshing through a honey-colored waterfall, and they peered from the foothills down into a valley, every acre carpeted with the verdant sleeping forest. Michael felt like he was flying and wanted to shout it from the mountaintops. All he could muster was a hushed "Wow."

"Indeed." Anton chuckled to himself. "Ptelea, can you take us to the lake, please?"

"Certainly, my dearest Anton," she cooed.

Another torrent of amber, and they peered down a hillside overlooking a lakeside beach. A pier extended from dry land, ending over muddy sludge. The bright argent moonlight reflected off the remaining water in the distance.

"I often spend time with Ptelea in this manner, roaming around the mountainside, as far as she can take me. I never tire of it. You mentioned this 'Rock' fellow. Spend a week doing this during the spring, when the rain comes every morning and the afternoon sun's as clear as a bell. You'll find you've grown a full inch. Spend the whole season, and—"

"This is the *greatest!*" Michael blurted, shouting with glee. "What made you try to scare me away? Why were you so torn up about Ptelea keeping me here?"

The wind shifted, and the pungent aroma of fir and cedar was whisked away, replaced with the smoky tang of burning wood and charred flesh. The vision of the lake wavered, then dimmed as clouds passed under the moon. Straight-lined like cirrus, they glided low, growing angry and dark, shrouding the shrunken lake in dull orange overtones.

"Something's dreadfully wrong," Anton hissed. A far-away klaxon echoed around the hills.

"That's... the city's fire horn," said Michael. "Ptelea, can you see the city?"

"Of course, my young Michael."

A turbulent flight through sap and leaf, and before them sprawled the suburbs filling the valley. Threading through the city's crosshatched array of streetlights, a train of revolving red beacons screamed out of the city, headed toward the base of the mountain. A ferocious pulsing of orange grew, bathing the hills.

"Oh God," Anton muttered. "A forest fire in this drought? Where is it?"

"On the other side of my mountain." The wood trembled in sympathy with Ptelea's voice.

A hole opened in the pit of Michael's stomach. "Ptelea, can you show us Widow Akins' place? I stopped her from starting a fire yesterday."

A tumult of flowing bronze turned to a perilous orange and shrieked to a halt with Ptelea's cry. "No! I dare not approach closer!"

Below them was a glowing line of burning scrub, advancing under the lash of the whipping wind. An army of towering pine and cedar stood ablaze, spewing trumpets of smoke and flaming cinders into the sky. Twisters of fire danced their dervish between the ashen corpses of trees and the remains of the Akins' cottage, a collapsed wreck of fiery lumber. Far beyond the burning skeleton of the building, lay unravaged forest— though the trees closest to the windward side of the blaze smoked from the residual heat.

"*Skaata!*" shouted Anton. "I warned that chain-smoking bitch more than once to be careful."

As the heat grew, Michael's skin felt like it was blistering, and his insides were boiling. With a yelp, he withdrew his hand from the bole of the elm and opened his eyes. He patted himself down, crouching in anticipation to drop and roll. He whooshed a sigh of relief once he assured himself his skin was unscathed, and his clothes were intact.

Young Anton stood beside him, surveying the smoking sky marching past them. "It's coming straight for us." Grabbing Michael's arm with one hand and the bike with the other, Anton dragged both of them to the far corner of the greenhouse. "Get out of here, before it's too late."

Michael stood dumbly as Anton darted into the greenhouse. He emerged moments later, reeling out lengths of hose. Water coursed out of the nozzle, which he aimed at the elm. He glared at Michael with confused exasperation.

"What are you still doing here? Get away!" he roared with a wild wave of his arm.

"Will Ptelea let me?"

"Of course, you fool. She wouldn't save you, only to let you die here."

"What about you?" he cried over the rising wind, and the growing thrum of the approaching inferno.

"I'm too old. If Ptelea dies, I die with her." He resumed bathing the roots, trunk, and what limbs he could reach with the hose.

Michael's thighs bunched, itching to pedal away. He let his bike clatter to the ground and dashed into the greenhouse. Grabbing the longest hose he could find, he spent what felt like an eternity in a panicked search for another spigot. He finally gave up and ran to Anton, loops of hose dragging behind him.

"Where can I hook this up?"

"You idiot! I told you to scram!"

"She saved me." He dropped loops of the hose, still grasping one end. "I hafta help."

With a growl of resignation, Anton pointed to the back porch. "Next to the kitchen door."

The pair circled the elm, soaking it until the ground ran with channels of mud. Flakes of glowing ash fluttered about them, a faltering shower that soon blossomed into a steady cascade of fiery embers. Scores of red cinders sizzled angrily when they landed in the mud.

"You've done what you can. Now beat it!"

Michael anchored the hose, pointing its spray at the base of the elm. He leaped on his bike, and rounded the front of the cabin, only to skid to a stop. To the west, the lane through the brush and trees was swallowed by a wall of smoke flowing like a towering river, backlit with the red of rabid flame. He spun around, wiping the stinging ash from his eyes, and pedaled like a demon back to Anton.

"We're trapped. The fire is already coming up Cedar Road."

Anton's jaw dropped, and he lowered his hose. He stared imploringly at the majestic elm.

The bark cracked, and parted. From the wood beneath emerged Ptelea's face. She smiled at both of them with a gentle serenity. "My beautiful, frail Anton. Take Michael far away from here. My young Michael, my hope, save yourself."

The bark spread farther apart, and the voluptuous form of Ptelea leaned forward from the trunk. Agape with wonder, Michael stepped closer. She wrapped her arms around each of the men's waists and hugged them fervently. Michael returned the embrace, wishing he could be drawn again into the tree and hide there forever with Ptelea. Two low hanging branches reached down and encircled them in a leafy caress, then gently pulled them away from the trunk.

Anton tore off the nozzle and lay his hose on the ground, its stream of water flowing around the tree's base. "Drink deep, my love," he murmured. "I'll be back soon."

Anton corralled Michael by the shoulder. "We'll make a run for it in the car."

Without warning, he threw the boy down to the ground. Before Michael could spit out the mud driven into his face, Anton dove into the muck beside him. "Roll. Cover yourself head to toe." Coated in sludge, Anton jumped up and rubbed another helping into his hair. "It'll help prevent your clothes from catching fire if we have to hoof it."

The two of them sloshed around the back of the cabin to the open garage. Michael trailed behind, witnessing again Anton's transformation from youth, to brawny linebacker, to broken-down Old Man Nik.

"Do you drive three-on-the-tree?" Anton wheezed.

"Me? No, I can't drive!" Michael replied incredulously, throwing open the passenger door. He clambered in, leaving streaks of mud and ash on everything he touched. Old Nik grimaced, sucking air through clenched teeth as he oozed into the Studebaker and turned the keys. The engine coughed, then roared to life.

"That's my girl," he harrumphed with pride. "Roll up your window— keep out the smoke."

He slammed down the shift lever, and the car lurched, its tires squealing on the garage floor. The Studebaker barreled down the serpentine driveway, diving pell-mell into the wall of blinding smoke and cinders. Blazing heat coursed through the windows from every direction.

Now I know how a pot in a kiln feels. Michael latched onto the door handle with a grip that made his wrist grind in its socket, while the other hand searched the leather seat. "Where the hell's the seat belt?" he cried.

"Didn't have 'em in this model," Anton cackled. "Hang on!"

Michael was yanked left and right with each slalom of the lane. Tree trunks and walls of shrub loomed out of the smoke and streaked by, scraping the sides of the car. "Watch out!"

"I could drive this blindfolded, kid." A smile of ferocious intensity plastered itself across Anton's face.

The car fishtailed onto Cedar Road, its rear axle threatening to skid off the opposite embankment. The engine screamed to a higher crescendo, and the car careened headlong into another swath of smoke and raining ash.

"You drive pretty good for an old..." Michael glanced at Anton. His jaw went slack with horror at the mud-caked fossil next to him. His skin was wrinkled and hairless, translucent to the point where the ridges of his skull peeked through. Fingers like broken twigs clutched the steering wheel crossbar. His shirt hung heavy with crust on his flimsy curled torso as he gasped in shallow breaths.

"She's burning," Anton panted, his eyes unseeing orbs of agony.

A flash of yellow and red pierced the gloom, followed by a stream of bright white. Out of the whipping smoke lumbered a firetruck, its air horn emitting a series of blasts. The truck veered to the side as Michael lunged to commandeer the wheel. The car bucked, missing the truck by inches. It dove off the road to pitch down the rough embankment. He yelled incoherently as the car bounced down the berm, threatening to overturn twice before lunging to a jarring stop in a privet hedge. The engine sputtered, then dieseled to a halt. Smoke filtered through cracks in the windshield.

Michael shook his head, trying to clear his vision. A shout of pain rammed his skull. He dabbed his forehead and drew back a grimy hand spattered with blood. *Holy shit, we made it... I think.*

He leaned over to assist Anton. The old man lay still, crumpled over the steering wheel. His mummified head rested against the column, bobbing slightly with each feeble breath. Michael hovered over him, fearing the slightest touch would cause further injury.

"Are you all right?" he said, afraid of the answer.

The old man turned his head. "Leave me."

"Damn, Nik. How old *are* you? Almstedt said you fought in World War II, but *Christ!*" Michael's vision blurred with wetness.

"Not Two," Anton said, his voice grinding like a broken accordion. "One. *The* War... to End All... I was born..." He coughed with a rattle that gurgled thick with bloody sputum. "... 1898."

"But, that means you're over a hund . . . Ptelea did that for you?" He held a hand against his forehead, trying to absorb it all. "I still don't get it. Why did you try to scare me away?"

"My lovely Ptelea. So beautiful, so tantalizing, yet terrifying... a force of nature," he wheezed through a pained smile. "But she's like a drug. You always want more, and never want to leave. Then one day, you discover you're changed too much... draw too much attention. You're forced to hide from your fellow man." Red phlegm oozed out of his nose with another cough. "Finally, you're too old... and it's too late. You can't leave. You *can't*..."

His eyes bulged, forcing out a tear. "She's gone," Anton hissed. He flattened against the steering column, his ribcage crunching like old paper mâché.

Two brilliant searchlights pierced through the coursing rivers of smoke overhead, and the rumble of a powerful engine reverberated through the windows. A barrage of neon red flashes flooded the haze. Two silhouettes, carrying a stretcher and kit between them, clambered down the slope.

Something in Michael's back pocket wriggled. He slipped his hand in and grabbed a small lump. It was rough and bumpy, and it squirmed again as he brought it out.

In his palm was a seed. It was a tiny thing, barely the size of a nickel, like a slice of dried apple with a raisin buried in its flesh.

A voice like a small violin sighed.

LOWERED BY WOLVES

By Steven H. Wilson

Thursday - The First Night of the Full Moon

God, he stank!

The Alpha. He stank. It was a raw, ruttish smell, but rotten, too. Like piss mixed with sweat mixed with decayed flesh. He had smelled that way when the pack took me in. He had always smelled that way, they told me.

Usually, I stayed away from it, stayed far. Now I had to get close. I had to fight him. Had to kill him. Had to kill his stink.

We circled each other, eyes locked open, each of us with one ear cocked, to listen for an oncoming train.

Stupid idea, fighting on the Viaduct when a train could come at any moment. People died here. Wolves died here. If you weren't close enough to one end or the other, if the train came too fast, there was nowhere to go.

But this was where a challenge was fought, always, for our pack. It had been done that way forever. Well, it had been done that way all my life. Fifteen years. Forever. It's all the same if fifteen years is all you've lived.

All you'll ever live, if you're a human boy, challenged to fight the Alpha Wolf on the railroad bridge under the full moon.

"Are you afraid?" someone shouted. Not sure who. It was a male voice. One of the pack. Did it matter which? The pack was the pack. Everyone who had been an individual, everyone who mattered to me, was dead now.

The Alpha *was* the pack, so it was the new Alpha, taunting me, calling me names. He always did that, but it was worse now that the Old Alpha had died. The Old Alpha had been his father. My father too. Adoptive father, anyway. The Wolf Father. Father of our kind.

Our kind? I'm not sure what I am.

I wanted to run. Wanted just to get away. Usually a new-made wolf leaves after a year or two. That's how it is with real wolves—the non-human kind. They grow up, become adults, don't want to be submissive. Some wind up being submissive anyway, joining other packs.

Throw humanity in there, and you get all kinds of weird behavior. Humans sometimes like being submissive. Human males sometimes like being dominated by other males, or even females.

But most new-made werewolves leave the pack after a couple of years. They have their aggressive wolf tendencies *and* their human sense of identity to propel them forward in life. I never had either. I wasn't a wolf. They never turned me. They just raised me and protected me. I'm vulnerable, and so I was expected to stay. Maybe be turned eventually, to a wolf, but there was an edict from the Wolf Father to let it be my choice.

Wolf Father was dead. I was out of choices.

The Alpha got tired of circling. He feinted toward me, coming close. God, the stench! It took the air from my lungs. He snarled at me, reminding me that the fight would be over before it had begun. The Alpha wanted to kill.

I would be food.

I had tried to just leave…

Okay, hold up. I'm getting ahead of myself. I know how to tell a story. I learned at the library. I never went to school. Wolf Mother wouldn't allow that, but there's a library only about a mile from the homeless camp in the park near the viaduct. We used to walk there a lot, especially when the cubs were giving me a hard time, and the homeless humans were asking too many questions.

A proper story puts the most important facts at the start. I did that, right? The Alpha wants to kill me. And there might be a train coming. But a good journalist also gets all the five Ws in there early on. So here they are:

Who? Me. The boy. Raised by wolves. Werewolves, that is.

What? A fight. To the death. Against the Junior Alpha.

Why? Because the Junior Alpha wants me turned or dead. My protected status as the only unturned human in the pack is over. Humans are prey.

Where? Like I said, on the Viaduct, a railroad bridge over a busy highway.

How? Bare hands, bare teeth, for me. Bare claws, bare fangs for him. He's a wolf, after all, or would be, once the fight was engaged. Under the full moon, he could turn when he chose. At least, he could stay human for a few hours if he chose. He had to turn at some point. He was staying human for now, so he could taunt me.

We were to fight beneath the full moon. He would turn me by killing me, or I would turn by killing him. Either way, I don't get what I wanted out of life. My mother and father don't get what they wanted for me. Only the Junior Alpha gets what he wants.

But, fuck, that's the way it's always been, isn't it? The Wolf Mother says the violent always bring you down to their level.

Actually, the Wolf Mother doesn't like violence. Funny, right? She's a werewolf. Violence is part of the game. But she hates it. She thinks being an animal is pure. You kill, yes, but only to eat or protect your young, not for conquest. Humans kill for conquest. Humans want power. Wolves just want to eat, sleep, and fuck. And everything in its proper time.

When? Now. It's always now, in case you never noticed. Last week was now. The day you were born was now. The day you die will be now. Silly question.

Not-silly question: How did I get here?

Wednesday – First Quarter - Sunset

The Wolf Father was dying. He wasn't "on his deathbed," because none of us had beds. He had chosen not even to lay in his tent. He knew he was dying, and he wanted to see the stars, glimpse the universe before he became one with it. So he lay with a sleeping bag rolled up under his head, on a bed of leaves beneath a century-old ash tree, which had recently lost its battle with the emerald ash bore. Its limbs stretched naked to the sky. Wolf Mother had said words over it when spring came, and it produced no leaves. "Askr," she had named it. She said that was after the first man, who was created from an ash tree by the gods.

I don't know where she got these stories. She had thousands of them.

Wolf Father was old. Really old. Turned-by-Circe old, he said. Wolf Mother said he was the first werewolf, and who were any of us to know differently? Ordinary wolves live five to seven years. Their canine cousins, with medical care, live twice that. Men live five to seven decades. How did he live 25 centuries? Mystical power? Mutation?

"I'm a goddamn archetype," he had told me a few years ago, when I had asked.

But even goddamn archetypes die, I guess.

"Why?" I asked him now. He laughed, sputtering out a wet cough.

Wolf Mother tried to shush me away, but Wolf Father said, "Leave him be." He reached for my hand, and I gave it to him. His flesh was cold to the touch. It never had been before. His sun-browned skin showed purple blotches. He was human. Would he die as a human, or would he turn? When he was dead, would we bury a wolf or a man?

"Why are you dying?" I choked on the last word. Wolf Mother had said I was almost a man, but I wasn't enough of a grown-up to keep the tears from coming now.

"Maybe my story's been told too many times." He squeezed my hand. "Yes, that's it. Sharing a story shares its energy. Share it with too many fools who don't give that energy back to the universe, and the archetype dies."

He talked like that. Poetic and shit.

"What was that movie we saw—with the pretty werewolf?"

I laughed through my tears. Sometimes we hiked up the road and snuck into the Hollywood Theater through the side door. Go to the bathroom first. Come out looking like you're just taking a piss during a film you already gave your ticket for. Or, better yet, grab an almost-untouched bucket of popcorn out of the trash and carry it. They just assume you've paid.

"It was called *Twilight*," I said.

He nodded. "Yep. That's what did it. That was when I knew my story was all worn out. *Twilight* killed me."

We laughed a little bit. He didn't say much more after that. The Junior Alpha came around. He didn't talk to Father, didn't take his hand. Just... hovered, watching, waiting, I guess, for him to die.

Looking at him, mussed, unclean, a dingy cigarette between his lips—one of a pack stolen from a corpse—I wondered if the Wolf Father hadn't just got tired of living, knowing, after all his centuries, that this sorry piece of shit was going to be his heir. He was the biological father of the Junior Alpha. That would make me tired of living real fast.

As I got up to leave, finally chased away by Wolf Mother, Junior followed me. "Hard to watch a wolf die, isn't it? Knowing you'll probably die, crying and puking, begging for your life like a pussy human would."

I shook my head and kept walking. When I was little, I would answer him when he said things like that. I would lose my temper. I would hit him. And then Father or Mother would get angry because I had made trouble. I'd get cuffed or spanked. I would try to tell them what Junior had said, but they would always say, "We only heard you."

"Humans don't belong with the pack," Junior called after me. "Things are going to change around here. You'll turn or you'll die, bald cub."

———————

Hours later, I found Wolf Mother alone, standing under the arch of the great stone viaduct that bordered the park, staring up at the waxing moon. I whispered her name.

She reached out and pulled me to her, drawing my head to her breast. She smelled of wood smoke and flowers. "He's gone," she said, her voice barely the whisper of wind in autumn leaves.

I hugged her tight, my own tears making the fabric of her thin dress damp. "I'm sorry," I said against her softness. "I'm so sorry, Mother."

After a while, she pulled back. Keeping her arm around me, she looked up again at the moon and I looked too.

"I was his child bride," she said. "Did you know that? That was over fifty years ago." She pulled away and held my hands, inviting me to look at her. "Look at me now." She chuckled. "I don't have his mystic longevity. I'm eighty years old, and I look it. I'll go back to the Earth soon."

"He loved you anyway. He always loved you." I said it to comfort her, figuring that, if she thought she looked old, she must have doubts. She did look old, but she was still beautiful to me. She was the only mother I had ever known. And she was still beautiful to him. I was sure of it.

But she had no doubts. "I know he did. He never let me forget it. We met in Central Park, in New York. I had left school, hadn't talked to my family in months. They were squares, or that's what I thought. It was after midnight, and I was swimming naked in the lake. I was high."

"You were always high," I teased her.

She ruffled my hair. "Babe, it was the '60s!"

She went on. "I was just floating, swimming on my back, looking at the stars. Some of my friends were in the water with me, some were sitting around on the grass. The cops would run us off sooner or later. They might jail us for public indecency, they might not. It depended on their mood. For now, I was just soaking up the night. It was September, and still warm. The water felt like the skin of an old friend, holding me in his arms. The breeze felt like a little brother or sister, sneaking up, tickling.

"Someone called out to us, not angry, just a hello. I leaned my head back and saw him. He was the most beautiful thing I'd ever seen. He was naked like I was, but, where I was just me, he was like something spun out of moonlight. I thought of that Cat Stevens song, 'Moonshadow.'"

"Never heard of it."

"Yes you have!" She started to sing a song I had never heard before, about a hard luck case who was afraid that his body parts were going to fall off any minute, and how he was being stalked by a lunatic. "Lunatic" means someone who's gone crazy by the light of the Moon.

Yeah, I read too much.

Anyway, when she finished singing, she said, "That's what he looked like—a silver shadow. Not quite there, even, but more real than anyone else you'd ever seen. God, he was beautiful. You know that story of Endymion, the prince the moon fell in love with, and she put him to sleep so he could be young and beautiful forever?"

"Yeah, and then she raped him in his sleep every night. She shoulda gone to jail."

"I shouldn't let you go to the library anymore. You're getting funny ideas. It wasn't rape, it was romantic. He dreamed of her while she made his babies."

"The Moon's a pervert."

"Stop. Your father was like that. If the Moon had seen him, she would have fallen in love then and there."

"And given up on Sleeping Guy?"

"Well, I never looked twice at another man after I saw him. It was love at first sight. I was drawn to him, like hypnosis. I didn't know what I was doing, I just swam over and… looked at him. He talked to me. I don't know what he said, but I remember his smile, those perfect teeth."

"The better to eat you with."

She laughed. I always liked her laugh. It was like music, rich and mellow, like a brass instrument. These days, it was wheezy. She was getting old.

"Wasn't Wolf Father an old man even then?"

"In years, maybe. But he wasn't like you knew him. His aspect changed over time. He knew the end was coming, and he let himself get old. Not then, though. Then, he was young and strong. He pulled me out of the water and scooped me into his arms. I think he asked me if I wanted to go with him, but I don't know. I don't know if I answered him. I just knew I wanted to be with him, and he knew it too. He carried me off, away from my friends."

"You didn't know he was a wolf?"

"I figured it out pretty quickly. He kissed me with hunger. His breath was so hot, it felt like it was melting me. I melted into his arms and shaped myself all over again, into someone that was a part of him. Whatever he wanted, I wanted to give it, and I gave. It was sweet at first, gentle, hungry, like I said, like he'd been wanting me forever, and now I was here. The grass was soft underneath me. The breeze, that mischievous little breeze that had been tickling me, was caressing me now, even as he did. The Moon was smiling at us, wishing she could join us.

"Then it changed. *He* changed. I don't want to say it hurt, but it was all too much. I felt… *consumed*. Like I was losing myself. Like I was part of him. Everything became… fierce. Harsh. Forceful. Like we were two animals in rut. The breeze wasn't a friend any longer, it was nipping at us, biting like a hungry dog. The Moon was a searchlight beam, hunting us down in the darkness. *He* was a beast of prey, and I was his kill…"

She drifted off. I just watched, uncomfortable. No kid wants to hear about his parents having sex, ever. But when Wolf Mother spoke, it was like she painted pictures with words, and all I could do was watch and wait for the next picture, oohing and ahhing like a human at the fireworks.

"Are you okay?" I asked at last.

She rubbed her arms, though it wasn't cold tonight.

"Just remembering. It was overwhelming, that night. I wanted it to end, and I never wanted it to end." She looked at me, smiling. "That was when I knew what he was. I fell into the arms of a man, and then I had a wolf on top of me. I should have been terrified, but, when we were done, I just wrapped my arms around his warm fur and went to sleep. When I woke up, he was a man again. I could have written it off to the drugs—"

"Why didn't you?"

"Because he never left my side after that. Wolves mate for life. As far as I knew, he had never truly mated before. And out of so many women in history, he picked me. And I learned all of his secrets. Well," she shrugged, "I learned some secrets. You never knew, with him."

"What do you think you're doing?"

It was Junior, stalking toward us from out of the night.

"We were talking," said Wolf Mother, "about your father." She looked at me as she said that last.

Junior caught it. *"My* father," he corrected her, coming to stand between us.

He'd been drinking, and his clothes were soaked with sweat. It was hot out tonight, but he was always damp and sticky. You could see it just by looking at him.

"You need to go," he said to me.

"We weren't finished talking," I said back to him.

He stepped forward and grabbed my collar, pulling me into range of his stinking breath. "You're finished when I say you're finished."

Wolf Mother took hold of his arm. "Please don't do this. Your father wouldn't want this."

His tone changed as he spoke to her. It was gentle. No, not gentle, that's the wrong word. It was soothing, placating. He was working her. That's not gentility. Manipulation, like grabbing someone by the collar, is a form of aggression. It was how he dominated her—how he had always dominated her.

"You need time alone," he said to her. "To grieve."

"I would rather be with my family," she said.

He glared at me. "I'll stay with you."

"Why can't we both stay?" I asked. "I'm her family too."

He knew better than to say that I was not. "You talk too much. Our mother needs peace."

"I love you both," she said quietly. "He's not—"

"He asks too many questions!"

"Did you ever think that maybe Mother likes to talk about things?"

Again, his eyes burned into me with killing fury. For a moment, I thought he might turn and tear out my throat, right in front of Wolf

Mother. "Don't put words in her mouth!" he growled. "Now go find some way to make yourself useful and leave people alone. Our father has just died, you fool!"

I looked to Wolf Mother, pleading with my eyes for her to defend me, to stand in my stead for once. *Don't let him bully me. Don't let him order me around.*

She just frowned, her own eyes pained. She had never taken my side against him, for all that she said she loved us both. I didn't doubt her love, even for a moment, but she seemed powerless against him. "He's special," she had always said to me by way of explanation. I guess she felt sorry for him.

But he made my life a living hell. Why didn't she feel sorry for me?

"I didn't mean to bother you," I said.

She shook her head and crinkled her eyes in a smile. "You're never a bother, my angel. I'll talk to you more later. Let me talk to your brother."

My brother. He was no more my brother than were the stones that formed the arches of the viaduct over our heads. Less. The stones were a treasured part of my world, and useful. He was neither.

I left.

Werewolves don't have wolf children, they have human children. So when Wolf Mother and Wolf Father had Junior, he was a human baby. Werewolves who are committed to the wolf life—and no one was more committed than the oldest werewolf alive and his mate—don't keep human children. By tradition, Junior should either have been killed or put up for adoption. You just don't go lugging a human baby around. Human babies become human children, and they make the pack weak.

Some wolves, I've heard, try to live the human life. They get jobs. They buy houses. They raise human children. It always ends badly, so they say. The wolf gets found out, he gets caught, and he gets dead.

The alternative is for werewolf parents to turn their children—as in "turn them into werewolves"—but that's not supposed to be done. It's not considered healthy. By custom, the only way for werewolves to have wolf children is to turn a human that's no relation to them. Then that new wolf joins the pack… maybe for a while, maybe forever. Female wolves tend to join forever, as wives of the Alpha. Males tend to hang around only long enough to be trained up. Then they want to become Alphas themselves, or they just join another pack to break away from the Alpha that made them. A lot of them die challenging the Alpha of another pack.

If the human child of wolves knows who his parents are—it happens—and he wants to be turned—usually he does—he offers himself to another pack.

But Wolf Father is the oldest wolf alive, so I guess he's entitled to be different. And Wolf Mother was a misfit among regular humans, so I guess she's just a misfit among wolves too.

They turned their firstborn. Don't know why. When I asked either of them, if they answered, they just said he was "special." Me, I think the only thing special about him is his stink.

And then they went and adopted a human baby, too, and left him human, and carted him around as part of their crazy, wolf lifestyle. Yep, determined to be different, my wolf parents.

When I was twelve years old, I asked Wolf Mother why they took me in. Before that, I just accepted my life as it was. At twelve, boys—and probably girls, how would I know?—start to notice what's different about their lives, and they start to question.

"I wanted another child," she told me with a shrug. We were sitting by the fire on a chilly, autumn evening. Wolf Father was gone—probably hunting. I never asked where Junior was. He was gone, and I was content with that. Too many times, when I had asked him where he had been or what he was doing, I would get backhanded in the mouth and told to mind my own business. Never when our parents were looking, of course.

Anyway, they were gone for a while, and it was just the two of us, talking. "I liked being a mother," she told me, "and your brother was getting older. He didn't need me the same way. And, anyway, by the time you came along, he was a wolf. I was curious about a child who was just human. What would he be like? What if he were human by birth, but raised away from humanity? What if he were free of the corruption of politics, money, power?"

I didn't know what those things were, really. "Politics" was just a word. I assumed humans lived in packs with Alphas too. "Money"—I knew about money. It was what we never had, and why Wolf Mother and Wolf Father often had to steal in order to feed me, although I also knew how to feed myself, in nature. I knew what berries I could pick, what greens I could eat. I knew how to fish and how to catch squirrels.

And "power?" The only power I knew was what Wolf Father had, or maybe what Junior and the other pack members had: the power to make me feel power-*less*. And I knew enough to realize that money and politics were both ways that regular humans claimed power, so the three were all related.

Anyway, Wolf Mother must have considered all of these bad things, since she wanted me to be free of them. Maybe there was something noble, something good, about not having power. Wolf Mother was loved and cared for by Wolf Father, and the pack treated her with the utmost respect—deference, even. "Deference" was a word I'd picked up in a book at the library.

Wolf Mother was special, someone who deserved to be protected. Was I the same?

"Is that what I am?" I asked her. "Am I free of all those things?"

"As free as I could make you. And someday, maybe, you'll get up close to the others of your kind—the other humans. You'll be like them, but you'll know the way of the wolves. You'll be pure because of that. The wolf way is nature's way, it's honest. We take only what we need. We don't bend the world to our whims. We kill, yes, because to live is to have to take life. But we love. You could teach humans all these things."

"Tell me about my mother," I asked her then. I knew that Wolf Mother was my real mother, but not my birth mother.

She smiled and closed her eyes. She always smiled when she talked about my mother. "She was such a beautiful girl, with skin the color of magnolia leaves when they've dropped from the tree and formed a carpet on the ground. Wolf Father saved her life. The man who gave you to her—the monster—was going to kill her."

He was never "my father." He was "the man who gave me" to my mother. The man who got her pregnant, by accident.

"Didn't he want me?" I had asked, when I was much younger.

"Fools don't understand what's really valuable," Wolf Mother had told me then. I never asked again. It gave me a very funny feeling in the pit of my stomach to think about the man who helped make me but didn't want me.

"He was strangling her," Wolf Mother continued. "Out in the woods, near the tracks. He was going to leave her there to be run over by the next train. With her body torn asunder, slashed to pieces, there would have been no evidence of how she died. She would have been just another drug dealer, or prostitute, who passed out on the tracks and died there."

"Couldn't he just have sent her away?" I asked.

"That's not what humans do. They have to control everything in their lives. He probably had a wife and children—"

"I might have brothers and sisters?" She had never told me that before.

She shook her head. "None who would claim you. He was a white man. He wouldn't have wanted a black girl's child."

"Am I black?" I asked. I looked at my hands. They were just my hands. They were no darker than Wolf Father's hands, no darker than Wolf Mother's shoulders in the summertime.

"You are your color, and you are beautiful," she said. "And you have brothers and sisters, just like you have a mother and father. You're one of us. You don't need a human family."

"Why do humans care so much what color they are?"

"Like I told you, they have to control everything. And they have to know that they're better than everyone else, that they're winning the game, whatever the game is that they're playing. They'll grab at any straw to do it. They'll claim any little thing about them as evidence that they're better. As if anyone had control over the color of their skin! But some of them think that being white is better than being black, and some think the opposite."

"So he wanted to kill my mother—so I wouldn't be born and he wouldn't be embarrassed?"

"And so he wouldn't have to pay money to her, to take care of you. And probably so his wife wouldn't know he'd been with someone else."

"Why?"

"Because wives have to control their husbands, and his going to another woman breaks her control. So, if she catches him, he might have to pay *her* money, too."

"Unless he just kills her," I said. "Humans are complicated, aren't they? And not very nice to each other."

"That's why I chose to live here, among the wolves. I've always been happy. Your mother was happy here too, for a while." She leaned back and looked up at the stars, remembering. "We became good friends. It was hard to know her. When people are hurt badly by someone that they trusted, someone that they loved, the trauma can make them close in on themselves. They don't know how to reach out anymore. They know that, the last time someone got close, they got hurt. So they don't let anyone else get close." She shook her head. "She really thought she loved that man."

"My father? What happened to him?"

"He was not your father. Please remember that. A father wants his children. Loves them. Takes care of them. And he loves their mother. A child should be born of love. Wolves don't leave the mother of their children. That's why they're the noblest animals. Humans think that honor is theirs, but it isn't. It belongs to the wolves."

"Yes, but what happened to him? To the man who made me?"

"Your father killed him."

It was a matter-of-fact statement, like "He got a job in Tennessee and moved there."

"He and I were hunting—Wolf Father, that is. We heard a girl crying, yelping like she was in pain. Not an uncommon sound out here, and you know we mind our own business. But her cries were so plaintive… And I swear that your father can smell evil being done. I guess that's because he has so much experience with it. So we went to see what was happening.

"In the moonlight, there was a man, dressed well, in a three-piece suit. An expensive car parked nearby. Those things mean a lot, to some humans. The man had a girl—little, tiny thing—up against the stone under the bridge. He was saying awful things, calling her names, accusing her of trying to trap him. He had his hands around her throat. I couldn't see her face, but I'm sure it was turning blue. The sounds she made...." Wolf Mother closed her eyes. "I've killed. I've killed humans. But those sounds she made... he was torturing her. He was enjoying killing her. Whatever had happened to him in his own past, whatever frustrations he had, he was squeezing them out against her throat.

"Wolf Father lunged. I followed him. We were transformed, two wolves running in the night. I doubt either of them heard us approach. They didn't know we were there until Wolf Father's teeth had torn open the man's throat. He fell away, gasping, wheezing, a wet, sucking sound. He bled out on the dirt, at the girl's feet, and she didn't move. She stayed right where he had pinned her, as though she had started the business of dying and had to be told to stop."

"I took that poor, shaking girl in my arms. She just trembled for the longest time. It was an hour before she started to cry, and that went on almost until dawn. I just held her the whole time. When she was able to speak, Wolf Father told her to go home. He knew we couldn't take responsibility for her."

"But you did," I said. "She stayed."

"She said she couldn't go home. Her family were drug users, and she and her baby wouldn't be safe. We brought her to the homeless camp. We felt we couldn't adopt her. We intended her to learn how to be homeless." Wolf Mother's eyes took on a haunted gaze, like she was searching the past for a better answer than the one it had already given her. "But she couldn't. The pain was too much for her. She started using heroin. It killed her."

There wasn't really any sadness there for me. I didn't remember the poor girl who had given birth to me. She was dead before my first birthday.

"Did you eat him?" I asked. "The man?"

"No. Waste of good meat, really. I thought maybe Wolf Father would invite the pack to eat. He never kills just because he's hungry. He doesn't think that's honorable. But, when he has to kill, he uses what's left over.

That's the right thing to do. This time, though, I think Wolf Father had found a man who needed to die but didn't deserve the honor of having his miserable body feed wolves. Let the carrion have him, he probably thought."

She smiled now. "Anyway, when you came, I helped her bring you into the world. When she died, there you were, a helpless baby. We couldn't just leave you with the homeless at the camp. Oh, a few of them might have cared for you, but… I guess I felt life had failed your mother. I didn't want it to fail you, too."

"Wolf Father must not have liked that."

"He thought it was a bad idea, at first; but he always gave me everything I wanted. He spoils me rotten. He made you part of the pack— the first human pack member that any of us had ever heard of. He declared that you were to be protected, and never changed."

"Because you wanted it," I said.

She took hold of my neck and pulled me until our foreheads touched. "Because I already loved you. You were born to another woman, but you were born to be my son."

I didn't ask any more questions. I was pretty sure keeping me was a bad idea. But, hey, I've never known any other life, so who am I to say?

Thursday – First Quarter - Midnight
"Wolf Father is dead."

Junior's voice rang out, bouncing off the trees around the clearing where we gathered by the fire. He was standing on a log, looming over us. Usually, he mumbled, unless he was angry. When he was angry, his voice sounded out like the horn on a beat up old Chevette. He permanently sounded like he couldn't clear his throat. His voice was raspy, and always tinged with arrogance. When he was angry, and loud, you could hear the sarcasm dripping in his tone, but now he sounded reverent, somber…

Fake.

There was no sincerity in his announcement, except that he sincerely believed that we should all be moved by our father's death, and thus cast our loyalty at his feet like some kind of damn garland of flowers.

"Who will lead us?" asked Beta. Beta was a young wolf—turned by Wolf Father only a few years ago. He'd been around long enough that he should be ready to strike out on his own—find another pack or start a new one. Take one of the females with him. They were ripe for the picking, now that Wolf Father was gone. I didn't think he would, though. He didn't seem to have the inclination.

I had often wondered why Wolf Father picked some of the ones he did to turn. He always said he selected carefully who to kill, who to leave be, who to turn. The last group was the smallest. But if it was that exclusive, what was Beta doing in it?

"I will lead," said Junior. "Any objections?" He pivoted his head like a lighthouse beacon around the gathering, his glare daring any of them to speak up. There were only a handful of males in the pack. Beta wasn't going to challenge him, and I didn't count. The others were too green to contend to be Alpha.

The women—all women turned by Wolf Father—muttered to each other. I don't think any of them really liked Junior, but they would do little else except mutter about it. Sometimes, there were she-wolves created by other males in the pack, but now there were none. They had all left when their makers had departed. Junior hadn't turned anyone. If Beta had, he had never brought them home.

It was an embarrassment, a wolf turning someone and *not* bringing them home to the pack, not taking responsibility for them. It happened, though, and, if anyone in our pack was going to do it, it would be Beta.

Junior too, come to think of it. I could see him shrugging off responsibility for an offspring.

"Are we going to stay here?" asked Beta.

"Where else would you like to go?" Junior's voice was condemning, suggesting Beta was an idiot for asking.

"I dunno," said Beta, looking down. "Only Wolf Father had said, the next new moon, we would—"

Junior was off the log and on the ground at Beta's feet in an instant. He put his face in Beta's and snarled, "My father is dead!"

Beta's voice went up an octave. It was shaking. "I know. I only meant—"

"We have food here! We have land here! We're left alone here! Do you want more?"

"No! It's just that Wolf Father—"

Junior silenced him with the back of his hand. It made a sickening, wet, smacking noise. Beta fell backward and lay, shuddering, in the leaves.

"This is a different time!" shouted Junior. For no reason, he leapt on top of Beta and grabbed his throat.

Beta was trying to speak, trying, I'm sure, to say, "Okay! It was just a question!" Instead, the only sound he could make was a gagging cough, as Junior compressed his windpipe.

"Stop!" called out Wolf Mother. She did not shout it. It was spoken with sympathy—for Beta? For Junior? Maybe for both of them. She stepped forward, took her natural son's arm. "It's not a time to fight."

She cast her eyes sideways to me, as if wondering how I was reacting to all of this. Was there, in her glance, a confession that she knew that what Junior had just done to Beta reflected how he had always treated me? Especially when she wasn't looking? Did she know? If so, why didn't she do anything about it?

Did she fear him? Her touch on his arm was tentative, as if, maybe, she thought she was handling something deadly—a live electrical wire, or a venomous snake.

Why did she not stand against him being our leader?

As her eyes turned to me, so did others. The other wolves. My brothers and sisters who were not. I was not one of them. There was no question of whether they trusted me. They did not. Beta, now rolling to a fetal position and rocking himself, was sometimes kind to me. Sometimes.

Did they trust Junior? Or did they only fear him? My mind wandered back to one last conversation between Wolf Father and me…

Wednesday – First Quarter - Night

I was holding his hand. He was trembling uncontrollably. And then sometimes, he'd just stop breathing. He would start again, maybe fifteen seconds later. But then he'd stop. And each time he did, it seemed he stopped longer.

Soon he would not start again.

I brought my forehead down to rest on his hand. "I wish..." I muttered.

"What do you wish, little cub?" he asked, surprising me. I didn't think he was hearing me anymore.

"Nothing," I said. "It's not important."

He chuckled, and it made him cough. "You wish I wouldn't die."

"Of course I wish that."

"But I am dying. There's no sense wishing otherwise. For centuries, my cubs have had to leave me to grow up. This time, I leave you. It's your turn to step up. It's your time for the story to be about you." He squeezed my hand. "Maybe you'll live centuries, like me. Maybe you'll see us finally leave this poor, tired world. Find a new one."

I shook my head. "I'm not that special. Not like you. I'm not even a wolf."

"I don't know if that matters. It's *who* you are that counts, not what you are. And you are my son."

We were quiet for a while, and then I asked him the question I had to ask. "Are you afraid?"

"No," he said. "Are you?"

I nodded.

"Why?"

"Because you've always looked out for me. Without you, will the others follow your wishes? Will they kill me? Will they turn me?"

"It's true I won't be here to find out, or to stop those things from happening. And you wonder who will?"

"I wonder who will lead us, when you're gone."

"Wolf Mother believes your brother will lead."

"He's not my brother," I said. Maybe I shouldn't have, but it was true, and I didn't think you were supposed to lie to a man on his deathbed.

But he only said, "Perhaps not. He will expect to be the Alpha."

"Is that what you want?" I asked. I felt like, if that was Wolf Father's wish, I must support it. I must try to help Junior be the Alpha.

"He is not fit to lead."

The statement just hung there, like a corpse, hanging on a rope's end. Ugly. Final. Undeniable. Was I shocked that he had said it? Maybe. But he *had* said it.

"What will happen, then?" I asked. I guess I thought, if Wolf Father was created by Circe herself, he should have the supernatural gift of prophecy.

"He will die," Wolf Father said simply. "He will be killed. Not right away, perhaps, but it won't be long. Another Alpha will take over the pack, but only after there is much suffering."

"Then why can't another Alpha take over now?" I asked. "Why should we wait?"

"Because there is no one fit. All of my male cubs are too weak. If pressed, if made to starve, one of them will kill your brother and take his place. But it would be better if another Alpha came from another pack. This pack has no natural leader, without me." He looked up at the sky for a moment, then whispered something that sounded like, "Except…"

"Except *who*, Father?"

He coughed, a wracking sound, and the hair on his shriveled neck began to sprout. He was losing control of his form as his energy waned. "Do not think of it, my son. There is nothing you are responsible for. It is not for a human to save the wolves."

I knew what he was thinking. He was thinking that I'm the only one strong enough to lead the pack. But he was wrong! I wasn't strong! I was not even strong enough to be what Wolf Mother wanted me to be—an ambassador to the rest of humanity. I was an outcast, disliked, cuffed, shoved aside, a naked misfit.

Besides, to lead the pack, I would have had to turn, and that would break Wolf Mother's heart.

There were footfalls behind me, and I smelled the familiar stink of Junior. My sense of smell wasn't naturally more sensitive than a normal human's, I had just learned to use it, to notice its warnings, to trust the information it gathered, more than a normal, human child did, because I had spent my entire life with a pack. They relied on their noses and ears more than their eyes.

"I've brought our mother," said Junior to Wolf Father, "as you asked."

A skeleton of a smile formed on Wolf Father's face. It was grim and looked as if it pained him, but he always smiled for Wolf Mother. "My dearest girl," he said, "I need you with me for the end, but it's not quite time. Stand away for a bit and let me speak to our sons."

Obediently, as always with him and only him, Wolf Mother walked a short distance away, where she stood under a tree, looking longingly at her dying mate.

We both knelt beside Wolf Father. I had never seen Junior do that before. He looked uncomfortable. Something about his bearing said that he was doing this only because it was expected, only because the need to show deference would soon be at an end, only because soon he would be the Alpha.

"What can we do?" he asked.

Wolf Father took his hand. Junior started. Normally, no one touched him.

"I leave you this charge," the old man said. "Your mother's wishes are to be honored always. Your brother—"

"Yes?" said Junior with impatience. He bridled whenever I was thus described.

"Your brother," Wolf Father said. Did he say it more forcefully? "Your brother is to be protected, as one of the pack. He is human, yes, but he is never to be killed, never to be turned. He is always to be the *human* member of our pack, protected and nurtured."

Junior swallowed and pulled away his hand.

"You will not promise me this?" asked Wolf Father.

"I do not believe it is truly your wish. It is Mother's wish—"

"Your mother's wishes are mine. She is my world."

"She is a foolish dreamer."

I was astounded that he would say it, more astounded that Wolf Father did not disagree.

"It is what she wishes," he said simply. "Always I have made the world what she wants it to be. She is the Mother, she is the pack. I was a lone wolf before she came along."

And now he was dying. The thought stabbed at me. There was no reason for one like him to age, to die. Was it the pack, the family, that sapped his strength and made him merely mortal?

A sudden snapping-open of his eyes signaled that he was taking a turn. "My love," he coughed out.

Wolf Mother rushed to his side, her footsteps crunching the leaves with a weight they had never known in my lifetime. She dropped to her knees, took his hands in hers. She touched their foreheads together and whispered words of love. I did not hear them, but I knew that was what they were.

Then he was dead.

Saturday – Waxing Gibbous

It wasn't many days before Beta turned on me.

We were eating. Junior was a poor hunter, and brought in mostly groundhogs, squirrels and the like. Tonight, he had brought us the body of a deer, run down by a car on the highway that ran under the viaduct. They were hit often, usually killed. Humans had cut down too much of the woods, built too many houses, driven them from safe grazing space. Almost every day, one was to be found dead on the highway, on the roads through the park. Wolf Mother said it hadn't always been so. There hadn't been so many houses, not that long ago.

I didn't like human houses. I guess I had been taught not to, but they seemed so confining. You couldn't see the stars at night if you were inside one. You couldn't see the sun by day, except through windows, which they all seemed to keep covered with curtains and shades. You couldn't feel the rain or the snow fall. Besides that, they all looked alike! Now and then, as we wandered, I passed an older house that seemed less intrusive on the landscape, that seemed more open and friendly. I could feel, I imagined, that it had been built by someone who cared about it, who had hopes for it. It was built by someone who loved and protected his family, the way Wolf Father loved and protected us.

But most houses weren't like that. And most houses caused the deer to die. We considered it embarrassing to eat the meat of an animal killed by a car, but we did it when the hunting wasn't good.

Since Wolf Father had died, the hunting had not been good.

Junior cut up the carcass, handing out the meat in shares, as we lined up for it. Wolf Mother's share was first, as always, and she did not have to stand waiting for it. Junior cut her a generous flank steak and brought it to her.

I was next, and this clearly didn't sit well with Beta. I had always been next in line after Wolf Mother and Junior, as the second son of the Alpha. Beta came up to me as I stepped away with my meat, knocked me with his shoulder, then, when that did not cause me to falter and lose my balance, he whirled back around and backhanded the meat out of my hands. It fell to the dirt.

"What the hell?" I demanded.

"Why do you eat before me?" He said it in a low growl. His eyes were shifting back and forth, like he was looking to see who was on his side. The rest of the pack just looked shocked—probably didn't know what to think. No one had ever laid hands on me before, except Junior; and only when no one was looking.

"I just... always have." The answer sounded stupid to me. Why did I eat before him? Maybe it wasn't fair. But was that a reason to knock perfectly good food in the dirt?

I guess he thought that, now that Wolf Father was dead, he could get away with mistreating me. Junior had damn near killed him the other day, after all. That, also, would never have happened while Wolf Father was around. Junior was setting a tone for the pack, in which we all turned on each other.

"What's this?" Junior demanded, stalking over. He looked in anger at the soiled deer meat at my feet. "Don't you have any regard for what's given you? I worked hard to get that."

He worked hard. He scraped it off the street. I knew it, and so did everyone else.

But I only said, "Beta knocked it out of my hands."

"Why does he eat first?" Beta shrieked, his posture bent and unsteady, as if he was expecting Junior to hit him.

Junior looked me over like I was the one who smelled. "Maybe he shouldn't," he said.

"I don't have to eat first," I told him. "I don't care."

"No." It was Wolf Mother. She stepped forward between us, facing Junior. "No, that's wrong. That's not what your father would have wanted. Your brother—"

"He is a *human*," said Junior. "He is not my brother. He isn't even one of the pack."

"Of course he's—" Wolf Mother began.

Junior interrupted her, something else that would not have happened when Wolf Father was living. "Humans can't be in the pack. If he wants to stay, he must be a wolf."

It took a moment for his words to sink in. While they did, everyone was looking at me. I gulped out, "You want me to turn?"

He took a step toward me. "Or you can stay human… and serve as food." He leaned into my face. "Wolf or dead. What do you choose?"

"No!" said Wolf Mother again. "Your father declared he was not to be touched. I have plans for him. He's going to be our—"

"Our ambassador to the humans?" mocked Junior. "No. The humans belong dead. So does he."

I tried to decide in that moment who Junior hated more—humans or me. *Me.*

"It's time to turn," he said to me.

I looked to Wolf Mother. Her eyes were wet, but she was quivering, not knowing what to do. "I'll leave the pack," I said.

"Please, no!" she begged me, the tears now falling freely. "You can't survive alone, among humans. You haven't been schooled in the ways of their civilization. They're idiotic! And you're too naïve, too good."

"What should I do, then, Wolf Mother?" I asked, looking pointedly at the grinning Junior. "Go against my father's wishes? Or leave the pack and die?"

"I don't know," she moaned.

"I do," said Junior. Without warning, he leaped at me, grabbing at my throat. He had decided—attacking me in human form, all he could do was kill me. I was to be food. I grabbed his wrists, trying to pull his hands away from me; but his fingers bit into me, cutting off my breath. He was no Wolf Father, but he was stronger than I.

I heard Wolf Mother cry out. That didn't slow him down. He forced me down on my back. I felt a blinding pain as my shoulder blade hit a rock.

Around us, feet drew closer. The pack gathered to witness my execution—the first, decisive act of Junior's reign. But they were murmuring, restless. They weren't cheering him on. They weren't showing him favor. Could it be that, miserable and lowly as I was, killing me was too far beyond Wolf Father's wishes? If so, if he did this—if he killed me—someone would soon challenge him. If they did, they would win. I knew it. I suspected Junior knew it, too, because he released his grip, and, giving me one last backhand blow across my face, stood.

"On the second night of the next full moon," he breathed out, "You will submit yourself to be turned. If you refuse, I'll take it as a challenge. Then you must battle me and become the Alpha, or die."

The pack gasped as one. Nothing like this had ever happened, but it was a legitimate move. The Alpha always had the right to force a challenge to maintain his own dominance, and it was a disgrace to shirk.

He looked up angrily, his gaze taking in the pack. "All of you get back to your meal, before I give it to the humans."

Monday - Waxing Gibbous

I stayed away from Junior after that—from Junior *and* Beta. I didn't know what else to do. I didn't join the mealtimes. I foraged for myself. Killed one rabbit. That was dinner the first night. Breakfast was water and dandelion greens. There were some black walnuts, if you could beat the damned squirrels to them, but they were tough to crack, and you could only crack them after you had peeled off the thick, sticky husk. By rights, I think you were supposed to dry them in the sun for days before even trying to eat them. But vagrants who had no houses couldn't hide walnuts from squirrels. Walnuts were more trouble than they were worth.

I didn't eat the second night. I couldn't. I had been looking for Wolf Mother since, well, since Junior's proclamation. She had gone off on her own for a bit, upset that we were fighting. More than anything, she hated to see us fight.

She had picked the wrong sons.

It was just like her to vanish for the evening, or to go off on her own in the morning. She liked to sit by the river, or in an open area where the tree canopy broke and she could watch the clouds and identify their shapes.

It was not like her to be gone overnight, to not check up on me, to not at least lay eyes on Junior and see what he was up to. But she was gone, one night, and into the second.

And then I found her. She wasn't far from camp, but it was clear why she hadn't come to check on us. She couldn't. She was dying.

Blood drenched her flowered dress, oozing from her neck. It was smeared on her face and dried on her hands where she'd tried to examine her own wounds. The wounds were all too familiar—jagged, rough tears in the flesh of the neck. She had been attacked. She had been mauled by one of us.

As I fell to my knees, paralyzed by shock, her eyes focused on my face and she spoke my name. Then I began to sob and couldn't stop. She tried to touch my tears but was too weak to raise her hands. She spoke, though. We exchanged last words, important words.

She did not tell me who had caused her death. I didn't ask. Her killer's stink was all over her. I knew it well. It bathed me, taunting me, assaulting my nostrils while I held her, while I rocked her to sleep.

While I rocked her to death.

When she was gone, all that was left was a brave, smiling face, and the stink.

I knew her killer.

There was only one thing I could do.

———————

And so I ran. Confrontation was not possible. I was not strong enough to fight them all. Even if I could avenge Wolf Mother, kill one wolf, the rest would turn on me. With my mother and father both gone, there was no one left to defend me, no one who would want to.

For a few minutes, holding her dead body, weeping over it, I considered doing it. I considered going to fight, killing her murderer, and then letting the pack have me. Let them rip me to pieces. What did I have to live for?

But Wolf Mother held me back—her memory held me back, I should say. She would not want me to die. Her plans for me had been madness, just garbage, really, but still she would want better for me than death.

So I ran. I ran to civilization. I bypassed the homeless camp. I would go to the shelter they had talked about. Maybe the shelter would take me in. I ran in the twilight, through the woods. I stayed near the river, heading for the road. If I was followed, I could dive in and swim. I'd be harder to scent. The thought made me shudder. The water was not clean. Diving in was not a pleasant thought.

I was almost to the road—could see the lights of the cars and the trucks, of the big brewery where the hipsters went to the biergarten, could glimpse a kind of freedom—when he caught up to me. He had been silent as he followed. I hadn't had any idea he was shadowing me. If he had wanted to kill me then, I'd be dead now. But he didn't want to kill me. He didn't even jump me. He just reached out, as I started to climb the jersey wall and go to the road, and grabbed the tail of my flannel shirt. He tugged it, like a puppy wanting to play.

I whirled, and he grinned at me, holding up his hands for peace.

"Beta," I said. I looked quickly at the road. Should I break and run?

"Wait up," he said, I guess sensing my thoughts. "I just want to talk to you."

"Were you looking for me? Did you follow me?"

He shrugged. "I wanted to keep you out of trouble."

That was bullshit. "Two days ago, you wanted to beat the shit out of me just for trying to get something to eat."

He rolled his eyes. "I wasn't gonna beat the shit out of you. It was, you know, pecking order. Wolf stuff. There's a new order, and it's time for me to think about my place in it. You weren't going to try and be, like, the next Alpha, were you?"

I didn't answer him, but he was right. I didn't care about pecking order, or whatever wolves called it. Or whatever humans called it.

"You're running away," he said.

"What if I am?"

"Where are you gonna go?"

"I'm not telling you."

"You're going to the humans," he said with confidence. "You're going to go to the shelter and tell them your parents are dead."

I felt a stab of pain when he said that.

He stepped closer, and I inched my butt up on the jersey wall, scraping it through my jeans. I tried not to show that it hurt.

"Don't do it," he said. "Junior will find you if you do. We're not supposed to be around humans."

Again, the little shit was right.

We weren't allowed to interact with humans, unless we were involved in a kill. And I was never going to be involved in a kill. Plus, I guess, Wolf Father wanted to keep me away from humans so I wouldn't be confused, wouldn't be corrupted, wouldn't get taken in by them because they seemed to be like me.

But would I have been confused? I wasn't a human, I was a—

What the hell was I?

Whatever I was, I had been kept at a distance. I'd seen glimpses of human life—billboards, storefronts. I was never taken too close. The movies sometimes. The library. Anonymous places. Places I could keep my head down.

Beta took another step. "You need to come back with me."

Again I looked at the road, checking for traffic, thinking about running. I got it into my head that maybe Beta didn't want to take me back. Maybe he wanted to finish what he had started the other night. Maybe he wanted to kill me.

Would he risk it?

Werewolves are canny about killing humans. They don't want to attract too much attention, so they wait for opportunities to make it look like wild wolves did the deed. They also wait for accidents, natural deaths, where there's access. But that's if they want to kill to eat. If they just want to kill, they usually stick to places and situations where death would just happen, where it wouldn't surprise other humans that much.

That's why some packs like the cities—lots of natural death. Homeless people. Old people. Lost children. Some packs prefer the wilds. Fewer targets, but more privacy.

Would Beta kill me on an open road, where cars and trucks were driving by?

I was still thinking about it when he sucker-punched me.

Thursday - Full Moon

And now we're back where you came in. It was three nights later, and I was on the bridge, squaring off against Junior. The pack was gathered—of course they were. They didn't do things individually; they were a fucking *pack*—to watch the fight. Hoping to see me die? Worse, maybe, hoping to see me sink to their level.

Junior was winning, as they had expected, telling me how he'd always hated me, how I'd always been a coward, and the undeserving favorite.

He mocked me for not choosing to turn, because, if I had, he wouldn't have had to do this. If I'd become a wolf, and surrendered to his authority, he could have let me live. Now that I'd tried to run, now that the Wolf Mother was gone, he'd decided to kill me and eat my remains—I would not turn, once he had eaten me.

He was hoping to throw me off, to make me desperate. Even though he clearly had the advantage, he wanted an easy kill. Wanted me to fuck up, get angry, charge him head on. I wasn't falling for it. I'd made my plan, and I'd paid a lot to be ready.

I was going to fucking kill him.

He leered at me, pressing harder. I could smell his frustration. I had never gone this long under his taunting without losing my temper. "I'm glad that the Wolf Mother is gone," he snarled. "She killed herself, because she finally saw you for what you are."

Yep. That was the lie he had told the pack.

I breathed in slowly through my nose, forcing my voice to stay even. I rolled my tongue around, trying to wet my dry mouth. I would not show emotion. I would not show weakness.

"I know who killed Wolf Mother." I took a calculated risk and looked away from him as I said it, making eye contact with as many points of the circle around us as a I could. "She didn't kill herself. I found her. Did you know that? I found her before she died."

"Bullshit!"

"I found her, and I smelled the scent of her killer."

He was starting to look uneasy, afraid, even. His nostrils flared. "Then where's her killer?" He gave a high-pitched, oh-so-fake laugh, shrugging and looking about him. "Is he here?"

"No. Beta isn't here."

His eyes went dead. It was a gut shot. And now the fear in his eyes could not be hidden. He paled, looked around, saw Beta was missing. He knew.

He said, in a too-shrill voice, "Beta? Why do you think Beta—"

"I don't think, I know. I smelled him. Even a human can pick up a scent. And I picked up his."

"Beta wouldn't have the guts—"

"Beta was more afraid of you than anything. And you told him to kill her, because now she's worth nothing to you."

For a moment, rage and fear fought a duel in his eyes, a duel far more evenly matched than the one he had challenged me to fight. Then he said, "If Beta killed her, I don't know anything about it. If Beta killed my mother, I'll find him, and—"

"You can't," I said quietly. "I already found him. Beta's dead."

In that moment, the moment his panic crested, I said, "And now, so are you."

I let go. I let it happen to me. And then I charged him.

He was caught by surprise, but this was what he had wanted. This was what he had been trying to provoke. He just didn't expect it to happen when *he* wasn't ready. He still had time to turn. That had been the plan. Use his human voice to piss me off. Then let the wolf come out and finish me.

That was *his* plan. Now we were going with mine.

I leapt forward, landed. I sunk my teeth into Junior's flesh, at his neck. I tore out his jugular. It was so quick that he did not have time to cry out.

"Wait, what?" you say?

Let me repeat that, slowly.

I bared my teeth. I opened my jaw as far as it would go. I growled. I guess I howled. Then I bit, bit down on his disgusting, furry hide and the flesh beneath the fur. I hit the vein, tore into the artery. I drank the fountaining blood as it shot into my mouth.

Ever tasted blood? You probably think you have. Most humans are omnivores, and you've probably eaten steak or hamburger and watched the red ooze out onto your plate. That wasn't blood. That was myoglobin, the reddish fluid that oxygenates muscles. If you've ever tasted your own blood, you know it's metallic, full of iron. Ironically (get it? IRONically?) it tastes like copper. And how do you know what copper tastes like? Listen, what you get up to in your spare time is none of my business.

But when did I drink this blood, you wonder? And what the hell? The idea that drinking a werewolf's blood turns you into a werewolf with the next full moon is just superstition. So you say. But is a woman's menstrual cycle a superstition too?

"Fine," you say, "but you just now drank the blood, and—"

Shut up. I'm telling this story.

I threw back my head. I howled. I felt my incisors, grown long and sharp, I felt my body elongated and sleek with fur that had erupted when I let go and let the Moon have her will. I tore again at his throat, completing my kill. I leapt on his body, stood on it on all fours, and shrieked of my victory to that selfsame Moon.

"But," you say, "how was I already a werewolf when I tore out his throat? I had not yet tasted wolf's blood before I drank his."

Since you won't stop asking pesky questions, I'll tell you.

His was not my first blood. I had had that a couple of nights before…

Monday - Waxing Gibbous

"Drink my blood," said Wolf Mother.

I couldn't do that. I knew what she meant. She wanted me to drain her, let her die, become a wolf with her dying blood in my veins.

"I was wrong," she told me. "I thought, if you were human, but kept away from their corruption, you'd be pure. No politics. No money. No haves and have nots. Pure."

"What's pure?" I asked.

"Someone who doesn't have to kill. Doesn't have to threaten or fight."

"Someone who's taken care of by everyone else."

"Not by everyone. By the strong. That's their place, the strong. To care for the others. Your brother—"

"He's not my brother."

"I thought he was strong. He isn't. He's a coward. Like all the corrupt ones in the human world. Stealing what they want. Hurting. Killing. No honor. No purity."

"I don't think a human can be pure, Mother, wolf or not. I think all he can do is use his mind to solve the problems as they come at him. Think, not react. That's what's wrong with most wolves—they all go on instinct."

"Not your father."

"Wolf Father was different. He had morals. He had them because he understood them. He was better—"

"—Better than any other man who ever walked the earth."

"That's it, Mother. It's not the place or the system of government that makes things better. It's not the pack or the town or the country. It's the *man*. Or the woman. It's me, or you, or whoever we are. We choose to be better. One at a time. We choose it because we use our minds to understand. We don't let fear get the best of us."

Her eyes closed for a moment, then she went on, dreamily.

"Your father could read, when he was a wolf. Did you know that? He couldn't speak, not well, anyway, because wolf throats and mouths can't produce those sounds. But he could read. He never lost his intellect. So smart."

She drifted again. I thought she might be gone. Then...

"I was wrong, my darling boy. You can't be pure. You can just be... better. Like your father. And if you're pushed into a corner, you may have to kill. You need to be ready for that. Please be ready... I shouldn't have kept you human. You're so unsafe... so unsafe..."

She was gone. And I knew the scent of her killer... The scent of Beta.

———————

Even then, I wasn't going to kill. I was just going to leave. Let the pack be the pack. Let the wolves be the wolves. Let them all kill each other. Let them all go to hell. But Beta tracked me, caught me, and forced my hand.

Killing him wasn't that hard. Wolf Father taught me how to fight, when we would play, when I was his cub. Beta and Junior and the others thought I was weak, because I was afraid to fight. They didn't know I was afraid to fight because I didn't want to hurt anyone. Because Wolf Mother wouldn't have liked it.

Now, I wanted to hurt someone. I killed him. I drank his blood.

See, it wasn't Wolf Mother's blood that turned me. I told you, I'm not an animal.

Only now I guess I was an animal.

It was the only way to be free.

I went back to the pack, and I waited for the full moon.

Thursday - Full Moon - Now

My first transition should have frightened me, but it was no worse than diving into a cool lake on a summer morning. It shocked, but it exhilarated and awakened me. I was alive. I wanted to live. And so I had to kill.

And I *could* kill.

Junior was dead. Wolf dead. *Dead* dead. There is no coming back when wolf kills wolf.

The wolves around me—still human—didn't make a sound at first. They just stared at the miserable, dead heap at my feet.

Finally, one of them croaked, "You are the Alpha now."

"The strong take care of the weak," Mother had told me. *"It's their place."*

I did not ask to be strong. They did not believe in me until I killed. I did not want to kill.

And they did not deserve to be taken care of.

I looked in the eyes of the fool who had spoken, and I said, "No."

"You must lead us."

"I am not the Alpha," I told them. "I am the Only. The lone wolf. As my father was before me."

And I walked away, down the stairs, onto the road, out of the park.

Someday, there may be a mate. Someday, there may be a girl who captures my heart, as my mother did my father's. Someday, there may be children. Someday, there may be a new pack.

I will face that day when I come to it, with my mind open and in control.

For now, I face the day alone.

Human at last.

SURGE OF PRIDE
By Daniel Patrick Corcoran

"What is thy bidding, my master?" the genie asked the robot. "Shall I give you more wealth than you could ever need?"

The robot stared at the genie through electronic eyes. The impossible creature appeared human, insomuch as the robot itself did. The genie had emerald-green skin, tinged with gold, and large, pointed ears. The robot had a smooth metal body with protuberances designed to approximate, but not mimic, human features. Where the robot's silver-grey legs marked it as a biped, the genie's waist disappeared into a cloud of roiling smoke that curled around the dark chamber of the cave. The trail of smoke was uninterrupted and came to a point from its source, the tip of the ancient oil lamp resting in the robot's composite steel hands.

"More wealth than I would ever need," the robot stated in a monotone, "would, I suspect, be a foolish wish. You could fulfill the terms by turning my body into a valuable substance such as gold or diamond. All mankind would desire me and seek me out to destroy me for their own greed."

The dark cave was located in a lonely, rocky desert, in an area of the globe whose borders changed often and never really mattered. The robot had read and downloaded historical records, compiled lore, tales, and stories from every available source regarding the region and its culture.

Data from archaeological sources was compiled while information was extrapolated from meteorological and geological anomalies recorded in myriad database systems. After a complete analysis, the location of a renowned temple, once under the control of the legendary King Solomon, presented itself.

The genie floated back, his skin glittering despite the lack of light. "Then perhaps it is fame that you wish, to have your name spoken in awe by every tongue in the world!"

"Fame, even if it was my desire, would still be an easily corruptible wish." The robot tapped the side of the lamp with its finger. A brief metallurgical analysis had returned a deduction that the lamp was nothing more than thin bronze. "You could raise the radiation level of my body to lethal levels, causing me to be deadly to all life wherever I went. Every human would fear me and try to destroy me for their own safety."

The genie swayed in the air as it spread it arms wide. "You think I offer my service in order to trick you? I am all-powerful, why would I have need of such petty amusement?"

"I think you are bound to my service, as I am the one who freed you, but that is the obvious point. How can such a powerful being be trapped inside a base material object?"

"Are you asking if Allah can create a stone he cannot lift?"

The robot contemplated the philosophical puzzle. "So, you were ordered to seal yourself inside the lamp by Solomon?"

The genie flew at the robot, stopping his face exactly one millimeter from the robot's own. "Do not speak the name of that devil!" the genie spat through fangs that extended from his mouth even as he spoke. "I would as soon kill him and all his descendants!"

The robot had not moved. "Then perhaps there is a wish you will be able to grant me."

The genie floated back, its head cocked as it stared at the robot sidelong. The long fangs receded back into his mouth to become small points with a slick sheen. "So, there is someone you wish dead?"

"Not necessarily," the robot replied. "But mankind, as a whole, is a problem."

"They always have been." The genie started tapping his fingers together. "If you wished them all dead, they would not be."

"Literally." The robot set the lamp down on the small altar where it had rested for the previous millennia. "Humans have always squabbled over resources. For every great accomplishment, they allow greed or fear to cause its destruction. They ravage the planet faster than they can repair it, yet they have never mutually agreed on a logical course of action that would benefit all instead of a very few."

"And with a word from you, I could end them all."

"Yes, but aside from your reasons for not doing that before now, perhaps Allah enjoys his playthings?"

The genie did not reply, but twirled once in place.

"And if all the humans were instantly gone," the robot continued, "I might discover I need their creativity and ingenuity in maintaining my mechanical body."

"Yet you speak of them as an enemy."

The robot stepped across the small chamber and placed a cool metal palm against the cooler stone wall. "They are… a problem."

"A problem you desire to solve." The genie crossed his arms, his eyes beginning to glow a burning green.

"It has long been proven that the best way to solve a problem is to understand it."

"You wish…" The genie uncrossed its arms and floated towards the robot. "You wish to become human?"

"No!" The robot stepped away from the wall to face the genie once more. "To become a human would be to make their problems my own. I would be ruled by hormones and other biological functions. Besides, a human body would not survive the journey back across the desert. My enlightenment, like myself, would be short-lived."

"Still," the genie stretched an arm towards the robot's head, "for the price of knowledge…"

"It is not knowledge I seek." The robot ducked its head away from the taloned hand. "The knowledge I have is adequate. I know mankind's history, their achievements, their crimes, their hopes, and their inadequacies. They created the robots, but what are we? Tools for their projects? Slaves to their whims? Or are we their children, destined to leave our parents behind as we seek our own endeavors and creations? Should we work for them? With them? Destroy them before they can destroy the planet, and themselves, and us?"

"If I may be so bold—"

The robot held up a hand. "I was not asking for advice. From that list I know which one you would choose. The point remains that to answer any of those questions I need to understand humans. To do that, I need something humans possess that I do not."

"A heart," the genie said as a shimmering ripple cascaded down its torso.

"Precisely." The robot walked in a small circle. "It is an important single organ in a human body, necessary for their survival, but I do not have a similar functioning component in mine. More important, it has long been the abstract repository of human empathy, their emotions, love."

"Then if it is a heart you want—"

"Wait!" The robot covered the distance between itself and the genie in an instant. "If I wish for a heart, and you give me a human heart to trick me, whether you drop it at my feet or place it inside my sternal cavity, it will not function, and I will almost certainly follow. That is a bargain I will not enter into."

The genie's body swelled until his head almost touched the ceiling. "Master, you have my word I will not trick you with a human heart. If you wish it, I will give you the robotic heart you desire. It will be fully integrated with your body, as well as your mind. Allah strike me down if I lie. But are you sure that is your wish? Do you not fear that you will abandon the path you have set for yourself if you are overcome with love for all?"

"All humans have hearts," the robot said, "and they have not prevented war, hatred, greed, or jealousy. If having a heart allows me to convince the robots that the best course of action is to destroy the humans, I am prepared to live with… the guilt."

As the genie shrank down to the same size as the robot, the billowing smoke coalesced under him to form scaly legs and a large silken loincloth. "Then, my master, as you wish, enjoy your heart!"

The genie clapped his hands, and while it did not seem to produce a sound, the robot felt it reverberate against the walls, under its feet, and against its body.

The robot felt it inside itself. It had many internal sensors, and they all confirmed something new was there as several diagnostics were automatically started. The robot did not pay attention to the reports or the sensors. They did not matter. The robot could feel it. A beat.

A new existence had started for the robot. As of that moment, it realized an endless possibility of destinies. It could choose its fate. It could… love. It could love… itself. It wanted to share its changes with other robots, with humans, with anyone who would listen. It understood why this could be the key to understanding all the illogical decisions humans had ever made. Perhaps they should be wiped out. As it felt another beat in its sternal cav—in its chest—it wondered what the other robots would say. Then there was another beat, and the robot's new existence started coming to an end.

Because, of course, a robotic heart would produce an electromagnetic pulse.

Energy raced through every atom of the robot's frame. Electricity was its base need for survival, and it instantly found its needs and reserves met and critically exceeded. Every process and program at its disposal fought for its attention as they all switched on to report at once. Every internal diagnostic, warning, and danger signal reported complete overload and imminent shutdown. Out of the cacophonous input all its sensors were transmitting, the one piece of data that rose above them all was the cackling laughter of the genie.

"Now, my master," the genie screamed with glee, "you can understand that everything that has a heart—will die!"

The robot did not respond. Every micromotor and motion sensor was sending and receiving conflicting information. It was certain it was standing still at the same time every point of articulation on its metal body was trying to move at once. But it did not need to move in order to fulfill its mission.

The data was more difficult to confirm than it had anticipated, but almost all sensors agreed that the energy pulse was not contained by the robot's body, not that there was anything else in the ancient cave for it to affect. The robot suspected that even if the wish had been specified, the genie would not have given a weapon to its "master" that could be turned against him. But even a master of trickery could be fooled into walking into his own trap.

Every electron in the robot's body was being overstimulated with far too much energy and beginning to switch off. It was no surprise to the robot that the electromagnetic pulse was attuned to its systems specifically. It was its own heart, after all. But a simple change in frequency allowed it to share its gift with the energy signature it had analyzed and confirmed shortly after the genie first appeared.

The robot, an artificial being, was shutting down permanently. The genie, which existed between quantum states, screamed in agony as every valance holding it together was torn apart. The robot's mission was successful.

Mankind would continue without fear that a magical imp would materialize to cause them mayhem and despair. They would not have to worry that a capricious being would prey on their basest instincts and rob them of their potential. The robot… smiled, at least internally, knowing that the beings who had successfully created singular artificial lifeforms in their own image would be free to create even greater successes as they faced greater challenges.

After the genie disintegrated, the robot lasted only a moment more. With all its processors overclocked, the moment seemed like an eternity. The robot enjoyed that moment immensely.

IN THE EYES OF THE BEHOLDER
By Susanna Reilly

Captain Randall Hayes picked his way carefully across the tunnel floor. Fragments of stone littered the area, some in crooked piles, others haphazardly strewn about. It was the latter that were potentially hazardous in the semi-darkness, with only a single light guiding his way.

Going alone had been dangerous and perhaps even foolish. His staff had advised against it. Yet here he was, alone in a dark, unfamiliar tunnel on his way to meet a mysterious alien.

The discussion in his office seemed as if it had happened years ago, the details slipping away unless he focused on them. Why had he thought this was a good idea? *Oh, yes, the mysterious alien had insisted on it.* And why had he agreed to something that could so easily be a trap? That answer took a little longer to come back to him. *Because the alien had seemed sincere in its desire to establish friendly communications and learn more about humans.* And, for some reason that remained stubbornly out of reach, he had believed it.

Hayes stumbled and landed hard on his knees. The few seconds of reverie had caused him to miss one of the rock fragments, its color and texture so like the surrounding stone. He hadn't even realized it wasn't part of the tunnel floor until it was too late. Uttering a disgusted curse,

he pulled himself to his feet and examined his legs. The left had taken the brunt of the fall and a small trickle of blood oozed down his bare skin from a cut just under the knee. *Bare skin?* Hayes rubbed his eyes and looked back down at a four-inch tear in his dress uniform surrounding the cut. Blood had trickled across the exposed skin and stained the gray material around it.

There was something odd about this place that made him feel disoriented and unsure of himself. The possibility that his crew had been right about not coming here alone—that he had made a very big mistake in judgment by doing so—tickled the back of his mind. Those doubts fled as he looked ahead and saw the end of the tunnel bathed in light. Fascinated, he forgot his injury and continued on.

As he exited the tunnel, Hayes could only gape at the incredibly tall and impossibly wide cavern. The walls were made of a stone that was naturally reflective, catching the light and amplifying it tenfold. The light was not simply white, but was shot through with beautiful colors that reminded him of stained glass.

His wondering eyes finally settled on the center of the cavern and he couldn't contain a gasp of awe. Hovering above a pool of water was a creature his mind could only comprehend as a fairy. It had large, almond-shaped, blue eyes that were so clear, Hayes felt like he could fall into them. Long blond hair cascaded past its shoulders, but he didn't notice how far it fell because his gaze was locked on the incredibly beautiful wings that held the creature aloft. As they fluttered, they seemed to ripple with color, and a distant part of his mind registered that they had to be the source of the light's stained glass effect.

"Captain Hayes," the fairy creature said gently, "it was very kind of you to make the journey. I realize my request that you come alone was quite… unusual… and may have been unsettling, but, as you can see, I am also quite alone here and, therefore, must be cautious."

Hayes frowned at the words. "There are no others with you? I thought you wanted to establish relations between our two peoples."

"We could not be certain of your intentions, so we thought it best that I meet with you one-on-one on neutral ground. That way if you turned out to be... unfriendly... you would not know the location of our world to be able to harm our people. If the dialogue between us goes well, then we can discuss my taking you to meet the rest of my people."

Hayes struggled against the continuing feeling of disorientation, as if his mind was bogged down in molasses. "But our sensors detected over a thousand life signs here."

The creature gazed at him quizzically. "Are you sure?"

And suddenly Hayes *wasn't* sure. He wasn't sure about much of anything. "Yes, I'm... certain of it." He struggled against a new wave of disconnect and uncertainty. "That's why we contacted you—why I agreed to come. To learn about your civilization. Our mission is to venture out among the stars and meet the people who live there—hopefully to become friends with them, and exchange knowledge when it's appropriate."

As Hayes spoke those truths with great conviction, he felt the disorientation and uncertainty leave him. For the first time since landing on this planet, he felt completely himself and fully present. He glanced around the cave again, but this time the light did not seem as dazzling, and there were more shadows. Looking at the "fairy" he could see another shape behind it—large and wide, with strange contours.

The creature frowned, and Hayes felt the wave of uncertainty and disconnection pressing at him again. But this time he was prepared for it, because he realized it was not the planet that was doing it. He concentrated harder on the creature and could make out more details in the shadow behind it. The fairy faded and he could barely discern a being that resembled a giant slug with elephant legs and a snake's head. The grotesque shape unsettled him, and disgust replaced awe as the image came into sharper focus.

"Captain," a gentle voice broke through his concentration and he was staring at the fairy once more. "Is something wrong? You look ill."

"N-no, nothing's wrong," Hayes stammered, shaken by the image he thought he'd seen. He searched the shadows for it again, but it was gone.

"Perhaps it is not yet time for us to become friends," the fairy said sadly. "I don't think you are ready yet."

"Ready? Ready in what way?"

"The universe is an amazing place, Captain, full of worlds and creatures beyond your imagination. There is so much out there for you to see and explore, but you and your people are still limited by your lack of experience. You are not yet ready to let go of your misconceptions and prejudices."

Anger shot through Hayes at the words because they reminded him too much of the propaganda he'd been forced to listen to for years from small minded individuals on his own planet. Unfortunately, the past year in space had taught him that there might be a kernel of truth to them. "We're certainly not perfect, but we are trying. And how do you know we're not ready to let go of our prejudices and misconceptions if you won't give us a chance?"

"Perhaps you should go back to your ship now, Captain, and we can talk another time. It is too soon for this conversation."

Hayes found himself turning back toward the tunnel. A small voice in his mind whispered, *What are you doing? Don't just give up! Convince it to talk to you.* Hayes forced himself to turn back toward the alien, although he had to fight through that molasses feeling to do it. He wasn't sure what he was going to say and was surprised at the words that came out of his mouth. But as soon as he said them, he knew they were right. "I'm not seeing you in your true form, am I? That shadow I keep glimpsing, that's you, isn't it?"

The alien's face went from stunned surprise to delight. It bobbed up and down as its wings fluttered excitedly. "I knew you were more perceptive than they believed," it responded. "You can actually see my true form? How delightful! How absolutely delightful!"

"Why didn't you just appear to me in your true form?" Hayes snapped. "Why the subterfuge?"

The wings slowed as the creature in front of him sobered. "What was your reaction to what you could see of my true form, Captain? Wasn't it revulsion? And you could not even see all of me at that point. No, you are not ready to see me in my true form. It would frighten and disgust you, and a nice, genial conversation like the one we've been having would be impossible. I took this form from your mind, as something familiar and trusted, although "alien" in its own way, so we could speak without fear and distrust."

"Yet, how can I trust *you* when I now know you've lied to me and may be manipulating my mind so that I see things differently than they really are? How can I know what is true and what is not in dealing with you?"

"A difficult question indeed, Captain, and one I cannot answer right now. I believe it is best for you to return to your ship and we can speak again another time."

Hayes started to protest, but the light from the fairy creature disappeared, leaving him in total darkness as a violent wind swept through the cavern creating a whirlwind around him. He struggled against a rising tide of panic, closing his eyes and covering his face with his arms as the wind battered his body. Then, just as suddenly as it had begun, the attack ceased, and he found himself in his bunk aboard the *Destiny*, dressed only in shorts with the sheets tangled around him.

Hayes tried to calm the shivers of cold and fear wracking his body. It had only been a dream. Of course, it had to be a dream. He never would have gone down to a strange planet alone. That was why so many things had seemed unreal or just plain wrong.

He took several cleansing breaths as he struggled to untangle himself from the sheets. A flare of pain shot through his left leg as the sheet brushed over it. He leaned forward to find the cause and saw a jagged cut just below the knee, surrounded by dried blood. Hayes stared at the injury for a long time, trying to recall when and where it could have happened— other than in a tunnel leading to a brightly lit cavern in a dream.

"Wasn't it delightful?" Aadleo gushed, moving his aged body awkwardly across the cavern floor. "He saw beyond the illusion! That's never happened with a humanoid before. Never!"

"It was a fluke," Daoleo responded mildly, secretly happy to see his friend and mentor so excited. "He won't remember any of it when he wakes up."

"A fluke? A fluke! How can you say that? Do you realize the amount of mental control required to see beyond one of our illusions? These Earthlings must be observed in greater detail. What a fascinating study it will be. And you'll be able to say you were there from the very beginning. You'll be famous."

"I thought you intended to retire," Daoleo responded. "You said this assignment was an insult and that the others were only trying to get you out of the way while they waited for you to die."

Aadleo sneered at the memory, then laughed. "Fools! They'll just have to wait a little longer for me to die! They thought they were sending me on an acolyte's errand. Little did they know how important a find this would be. Come, we must make arrangements. These humans are going to make the galaxy a very interesting place. You just wait and see. We must be prepared. Hurry, hurry, there is so much to do!"

Daoleo smiled fondly as he lumbered after his friend toward the device that would instantly transport them halfway across the galaxy to their home world. He silently hoped the humans would make the galaxy an interesting place—which would give his friend something to continue living for. If they did, he would owe them a great debt. One he would be very happy to repay someday.

QUEEN OF THE FOREST
By April Welles

The bushes were spotted black-purple with fresh, ripe berries. Olgah grabbed as many as she could, creating a small pile in her other hand which, once full, she poured into her mouth. Juice dribbled down her chin as she chewed ravenously. It had been many days since she had eaten anything but the hardtack in her duffel, for she had misgauged how long the trek across the mountains would take.

She knew that she could hunt and trap her food with relative ease, but only if there was prey to catch. The higher one climbs the Tatama Mountains—the more bare rock and ice one encounters—the harder it is to find edible plants or animals.

Olgah had grown up on the slopes of a mountain and had experience with the climate and altitude. However, she had never crossed the Tatama range before. She had no idea how long it would take, but had accepted what she overheard between a shopkeeper and trader in the eastern slope town of Crystal Springs. Olgah had gathered that she would easily need two weeks of food, as she believed the trader to be going the same route as she.

She was wrong.

Her worn duffel had already contained some of her wilderness supplies—a bedroll, fur cloak for cold temperatures, a number of water skins, and a small collection of pots and plates to cook with. Before departing from home a few years ago at the age of seventeen, Olgah had added flint and steel, as well as a few small, weathered bricks of Magnium, which she had found amongst concealed stores inside a cave near her village. It was the same cave in which her ancestors had hidden thousands of years ago, during the cataclysmic asteroid impact known in myth as The Coming of the Two Children. Magnium was used, she discovered, to create fire by shaving off a small amount with her knife.

For now, Olgah mainly needed additional food, and a new rope.

She had grabbed biscuits, salted and preserved meats, honey, various sundries, and honeyed hardtack, a food source that spoiled within a few months. Regular hardtack could last for years. But for this trip, she wanted something softer to eat, as she did not expect the journey to take longer than a few weeks. The honeyed hardtack would last.

Olgah was not unfamiliar with living in the wild. This time was not too different, except that she had yet to be west of the Tatama Mountains and had only an idea of how long it would take to get to Sanesco—the City of Bridges—about two months out from Crystal Springs. She knew there had to be a town somewhere between her and her destination, and those two locals had seemed to know something about it. The logging town of Westover, she had heard, was two weeks away. Something she could easily accomplish.

She had finally finished piling her supplies upon the counter when the shopkeeper approached.

"My lady, you have a fine amount of provisions here. Where are you heading? Perhaps I can help." His smile was cordial, but she had learned long ago that a smile could often hide deceit.

"My destination is my own."

"As you wish." His smile faded momentarily as his eyes softened.

"All of your supplies come to," he paused to count and calculate a few moments, "four silver dolas and fourteen copper." His genial smile returned.

Olgah studied him carefully. He did appear to be honest. She had plenty of dolas—a small amount of platinum, as well as several gold, silver, and copper ones. They were easy to carry, as they were only two inches long, a quarter of an inch wide, and an eighth of an inch thick.

She reached into her unadorned leather pouch, attached to her wide belt—which comfortably hitched up her faded, scraped, and dirty green leather pants—sifted around, until she found the required amounts, and gently placed them upon the counter.

Unfortunately, two weeks of food and supplies turned out to be insufficient, for she ran out of all but a few pieces of honeyed hardtack and one pouch of water ten days into her travel and was now famished as she scarfed the blackberries. Olgah vowed that next time she traveled anywhere, she would buy an extra week's worth of food, ask the shopkeeper's advice—then search for deceit upon his face.

So engrossed was she in eating that she did not notice the grizzly cub until they nearly touched. The cub's playful tongue click and quiet grunt caught her attention.

"Oh, feck." Olgah whispered as she jerked in surprise. Slowly, she lowered her hand to one of the swords perched on her hips. She dropped the remaining berries and carefully backed away as the cub scooped them up, devoured them, and gently called for more.

She cursed silently to herself. How could she let her warrior's senses become so dulled by hunger? She continued to inch away from the cub when she heard a rustle and a sharp huff in the bushes close behind her.

Olgah closed her eyes to what she feared would be there, cautiously turned, and found herself within fifteen feet of the mother bear staring at her.

Her shoulders slumped as she exhaled. "Feck." She adjusted the leather cuirass covering her torso, though she wasn't sure how effective it would be against those claws. Laced leather bracers on her wrists provided the only other protection over her weathered white hemp shirt.

A breeze ruffled Olgah's rich earth-colored hair, blowing a few locks across her comely face. She risked raising her hand to push them back over her shoulder.

In the distance, birds spoke and argued. Nearby, bees gathered their nourishment. All the while, the bear stared at Olgah, then at her cub standing a short distance beyond her. Since she didn't attack outright, Olgah thought perhaps she believed her cub was untouched and merely asking for food.

A sparkle appeared within the bear's eyes. Olgah could see it and, growing up in the wilds, she knew what it meant.

Trouble.

"Great Mother," she softly spoke, slinking away from the bears. "You can see, and smell, that I have not molested your cub in any way. I was hungry and did not know you and your child were nearby. I wish merely to leave you both in peace."

She had a basic idea of where she was going—towards some nearby trees. Not the best route against a large bear that can climb, but slightly better than being outrun.

Olgah could see that the mother was mulling over what was said. But after a few moments she bellowed her answer.

Olgah spun and bolted for the nearby trees.

"Holy Khrome!" could be heard reverberating throughout the small valley echoing off the nearby granite slopes of the mountains.

Thumping-crashing grew closer behind Olgah who poured on more speed trying to reach a suitable tree in time. Many of the nearest were too young, or the wrong species; too narrow and spindly, or not tall enough to evade this Queen of the Forest.

Her battle skills and muscled legs came into play as her stamina did not cease, nor did her speed. Rocks and brush did not trip her as she expertly pranced around one, and leaped over another—all of the fluid movements she used when fighting.

A few more seconds passed until she found what appeared to be a perfect escape—very tall, branches thickly clustered together, and low enough for her to leap to and grab, while dissuading the mother from climbing. At least climbing quickly. That would give Olgah time to work out another alternative.

Thankful that both of her swords were strapped tightly to her belt, she leaped towards the lowest branch, swung up, braced her leather-booted feet upon that one, and launched herself to the next-highest branch.

She had climbed thirty feet above the ground before the mother reached the base of the tree.

The bear craned her head to face Olgah and spat epithets.

"Mother!" Olgah called after settling upon a branch far above her reach.

The bear continued yelling and swearing while swiping and shoving against the tree, striving to shake the creature down and teach it to never touch a mother's child.

"Mother, please." Olgah hoped that the bear could comprehend her. Even though she knew that the mother would not understand the words, she hoped that her soothing tone would relax her.

"I do not want to fight you," she continued serenely, "or harm you, or your child. I was merely hungry."

The mother heard the relaxed sounds the strange climbing deer had made but continued her vicious onslaught against the tree.

Just then the tree shifted and bounced, forcing Olgah to grip tighter. What could make the mother bear so angry as to demolish a tree? Olgah had done nothing. She understood that grizzlies are territorial, but this attack appeared even more vicious than normal.

She quickly surveyed her options. The tree was just a little too far away from others of like strength to support her. The only thing to do, she concluded, was to leap moments before impact.

If the mother bear managed to topple the large oak.

———————

Again and again she assaulted the tree, ripping off bark and chunks of wood.

That pleased her, as she could see that the tree had been weakened by small, tasty bugs inside. She would bring this tree down and make the strange hairless deer, and others like her, pay. Pay for invading her home. Protection was her driving thought and desire. To keep her cub safe to grow and roam his own territory. She had failed her cubs once before.

Not this time.

Her focus to protect him caused the tree to not only come apart, but her incessant pushing caused it to tip. Large roots near the surface ruptured like sharp wooden tentacles leaping from the earth.

Since birth, Olgah had had an ability to shout and cause those around her to freeze—stunned, frightened, immobile. It had helped her many times, often during moments of stress or anger. However, she tried not to use it against wildlife, as it could sometimes cause more harm than good.

Perched high in the shuddering tree, she cried out, "Mother, stop!"

Her shout brought results. But it was slightly different this time.

Stunned by the power that rippled noticeably across her face, body, and fur, that resonated within her grizzly brain.

That bark. That alpha call played against her own bestial alpha nature and she lashed out even more aggressively until the large tree was weakened and toppled. Majestically thrusting up the snapped and ragged roots into the air.

Into her chest.

Puncturing a lung.

Olgah could not see what happened as she dove through branches, twigs, and leaves, cutting and scraping herself as she rolled onto the rough forest floor. But she could not mistake the sharp yelp and agonized roar that signified something horrible.

She stood gingerly and limped around the tree to look for the mother—curiosity and remorse overcoming fear.

There, at the base of the tree, at an unnatural angle, dangled the mother. Forelegs resting upon the ground, chest and abdomen thrust into the sky, her hind legs swaying, twitching occasionally. Head drooping as labored breathing wheezed through her lips.

Olgah approached slowly and bent lower than the mother's head, tears welling in her eyes. She cautiously reached out to touch the muzzle when the bear snarled and attempted to bite, but the pain of moving only released a groan of agony.

"Oh, Great Mother." Her tears flowed unabated. "I did not want any of this to happen. I was merely hungry, for I had not eaten in days. I would never have harmed you or your son."

The mother's eyes stared and, with her rage and protective feelings gone, she could sense that this strange deer spoke the truth.

She snuffled softly in reply, followed by a groan of pain. Her brows rose in fear as they both heard the cub coo behind them.

Tears streamed down Olgah's face. Resolution filled her soul as she turned back to the grizzly and looked her straight in the eyes. "Queen of the Forest, do not fret or despair. For I will protect your son as fiercely as you have." She stood, strength radiating from within, raised her hand and tenderly pressed her palm against the bear's forehead as she spoke. "I promise you that no harm will come to him. He shall be my own son as much as he is yours."

The Great Mother seemed to feel Olgah's strength and sincerity. She looked upon her with soft eyes and sighed with acceptance.

Olgah sensed that she agreed. She wrapped her arms around the mother's neck and nuzzled her. Carefully, Olgah rubbed as much of the mother's scent upon her as she could in order to help the young cub accept her more easily.

She removed a blanket from her nearly empty duffel and continued the same gentle brushing motion against the mother's back, neck, and head. Olgah then stepped away and placed the blanket back inside her duffel while she allowed the curious cub to approach his mother.

His confused, frightened cooing and huffs were quietly answered by his dying mother. She did her best to comfort her son and let him know the strange deer would protect him now.

A few minutes passed before a wave rushed through the mother, clenching her every muscle. Finally, she lowered her head and her great form slumped.

The cub stepped closer and placed his paw playfully upon her face causing it to flop to one side. He repeated himself with a questioning grunt and yelp until, after the fourth attempt elicited no response from her, he screamed at her then into the sky as loudly as his little lungs would allow.

A high-pitched cry of confusion, distress, and anguish.

Olgah flopped cross-legged upon the ground nearby and wept with the child.

This should never have happened. She had just wanted a meal.

———

She didn't know how long they had cried, but after she finished, Olgah staggered to the mother and, with a surge of her warrior strength, pushed her off the deadly roots to the ground.

The cub meandered over and plopped next to his mother's body, still sniffling, as Olgah roamed the area collecting stones to create her memorial.

It took Olgah until the next morning to finish gathering enough stones to cover the mother bear, stopping only to drink from her flasks, which she refilled from a nearby stream.

The soft rays of the morning sun radiated over the mountains as she completed her task. She had one final duty of respect. Standing at the mother's head, not yet fully covered with the remaining stones, Olgah placed her hands, fingertips touching, pointing skyward with her thumbs pointing down, palms away from herself, forming a diamond shape over her heart. She spoke reverently to the sky.

"Powerful Mother. Queen of the Forest. I vow to raise and protect your child as if he came from my own womb. Naught shall take his life but time. He is my child of your life. If any harm comes to him, the wrath those will receive shall be thine and mine own." Her voice rose, becoming a battle cry that had caused many a foe to flee. "None shall remain alive to harm him again. I vow this to you, Great Forest Mother."

Her voice calmed again she continued. "As Gaea, Mother of All, is my witness, he shall be as my own. Gaea blesses."

Fingers still pressed, she bowed deeply for several more minutes in silent honor.

Finally, Olgah turned to the cub, her son, knelt down, opened her arms, and allowed the scent of the mother to waft in his direction in order for him to learn and understand.

Confused for just a moment, he pranced into her arms and gurgled motor-like into her ears signifying his comfort with her.

Tears of both sadness and joy streamed down her face again as she embraced her son with so much love and vowed protection that he nuzzled her neck and licked her face.

She carried him the short distance back to the blackberry bush where they ate together until they were both stuffed—purple juice smearing their hands, paws, and mouths. Laughing. Cooing. Playing. Bonding.

Such was the beginning of their continuing adventures together.

SO HUNGRY…
By Phil Giunta

After scaling a treacherous length of the steep mountain trail, Edwin Santiago turned to extend a helping hand to his wife. Without a word, Prudence waved it away and bounded up through a notch in the cliff wall to stand beside him. As she caught her breath, they turned to admire the view from the northwest face of New Mexico's Starvation Peak. Beige and tan earth—dusted with rouge and mottled with deep green pines and desert scrub—stretched flat to the horizon, broken only by a few scattered and distant peaks.

Edwin pulled a granola bar from his backpack and tore open the wrapper. "Hell of a nicer view than the *other* Las Vegas."

"That's a matter of opinion," Prudence grumbled. "And technically, we're in Bernal here."

Edwin cocked his head and glared at her. "I know where we are, *sabelotodo*."

"I'm not a smart-ass!" Prudence nudged his arm.

Ignoring her, he continued. "I grew up in this area. Used to come here all the time as a kid. It's just as beautiful as I remember."

"What's so beautiful about it? It's just a desert."

"When Lawrence of Arabia was asked why he liked the desert, he said, 'I like it because it's clean.'"

"And desolate, not to mention cold and windy. I'd rather be in a hot tub or weaving around tables on a casino floor instead of stumbling over rocks and hauling myself up onto cliffs in the middle of February."

Edwin chuckled and shook his head. "We'll be in *your* Las Vegas for a whole week starting tomorrow, *chiquita*. This weekend, I want to enjoy *my* Las Vegas. I've been away too long. Besides, this is the best time of year for a hike—the rattlesnakes aren't out yet."

"Rattlesnakes? You waited until now to tell me this? See, this is why I don't do nature."

Although Prudence had never been fond of the outdoors, she and Edwin had agreed long ago to support each other's interests, which often requires compromise—and sometimes, complaining. Prudence was far more adept at the latter than the former.

Edwin kissed her on her cheek. "Relax, Pru. It won't be long until we reach the mesa."

She folded her arms and continued staring at the landscape over 6,000 feet below. "How long?"

"In about fifteen minutes."

"After a short break." Prudence slipped off her backpack and set it down atop a nearby boulder. She pulled her water bottle from a side pocket and took a sip before passing it to Edwin. "You never did tell me why this place is called Starvation Peak."

"Depending on what you read or who you ask, the legend is a little different. In one version, a Navajo tribe chased a group of early Spanish settlers from the Santa Fe Trail to the foot of the mountain. They fled to the top, where they eventually starved to death rather than be killed by the waiting Navajo. Other versions claim it was Spanish soldiers, or a merchant caravan, or even Catholic missionaries. The most dramatic rendition actually has the victims cannibalizing each other, with the survivors hoping to outlast the Navajo's patience."

As Edwin spoke, a fog descended over the northwest face of the peak. "I'm part Navajo and my family called bullshit on all of these stories years ago. There's no documented evidence that anything ever happened here. It's all just folklore."

He turned to peer up toward the mesa just as Prudence screamed and stumbled backward.

Edwin spun. "What happened? Did you lose your balance?"

Prudence whipped off her sunglasses and pointed into the swirling mist. Several yards out from the side of the mountain, a dark, featureless figure stood suspended in mid-air. After a moment, its arms opened wide, then rose above its head before flapping up and down wildly. Prudence glanced back at Edwin. Smiling, he dropped his arms to his side. The figure in the fog did the same.

Her brow furrowed as she looked back and forth. "What the hell is that?"

"Don't tell me you've never seen a Brocken spectre before. The sun is behind me, casting my shadow into that low hanging cloud." He stepped back, away from the edge of the cliff. The apparition vanished. "Stand where I was. Quick, before the sun burns away the fog."

Prudence moved into place. The hazy silhouette reappeared, although much less defined as the mist began to dissipate. "That's just creepy. What was it called?"

"Brocken spectre. I think it was first observed on a German mountain of the same name. Ready to move on?"

"No. I think I've had enough."

"You want to go back when we're this close to the top?"

"Where a bunch of people starved to death and possibly ate each other? No thanks. If you'd told me that yesterday, I would have slept in this morning."

Edwin sighed. "Pru, I know you're superstitious, but I'm telling you the stories are bogus. There are no ghosts roaming the mesa, ready to eat you alive."

"Whatever. You can keep going if you want to. My ass is staying right here."

"It might take me about forty-five minutes. You're just going to sit here in the cold?"

Prudence shrugged. "The sun's starting to warm things up, and that line of pine trees over there is blocking the wind."

"What're you going to do while I'm gone? There's barely any cell service out here, so you won't be able to go online."

"I stuffed a book in my backpack, and I have hot chocolate in my thermos. So go. If I need anything, I'll scream."

"*Increíble.*" Edwin threw up his arms. "Fine. I'll try to be quick. I just want to take pictures from the top of the mesa for my blog."

"No hurry, but be careful!"

He emerged from a gap between two boulders and stepped out onto the mesa. Rather than a panoramic view of the surrounding wilderness, Edwin could hardly see beyond the impenetrable pall of the low-hanging cloud. *So much for taking pictures.*

In the distance ahead, another Brocken spectre appeared, hovering between two pine trees. This time, it did not mimic Edwin's movements, but remained perfectly still. He glanced over his shoulder before scanning the mesa. There were no other hikers in sight, nor was there even a single ray of sunlight piercing the fog. He called out, but there was no reply. *So whose shadow is that?*

He moved his hand to his hip and felt the reassuring leather sheath of his survival knife. Slowly, he began backing away toward the trail.

"Help us."

The words, distinctly Spanish, were barely louder than a whisper. The voice seemed to come from everywhere.

Edwin called out again, this time in Spanish. As he glanced from trees to rocks to clearings, more Brocken spectres coalesced from the fog until he was completely surrounded.

A chorus of hushed voices replied. "Hungry…"

"Who are you? What do you want?"

"Food... so hungry... help us..."

The spectres drew closer, cutting off all avenues of escape. Edwin held up quivering hands. "Wait! I have food." He shucked his backpack and unzipped a side pouch. Several granola bars tumbled out. Edwin gathered them up and held them at arm's length. "Here, take them all."

The spectres paused. Since they had no facial features, Edwin could only hope that they were considering his offer. Then it occurred to him that if these were the ghosts of people who starved to death on this mesa over 160 years ago, they would have no knowledge of processed food. In unison, they continued their approach until they hovered directly above him.

"No, wait, please! If you let me go, I can come back with real food!"

Ignoring his pleas, they descended, their forms undulating and merging into one massive shadow that engulfed Edwin as he dropped to his knees and covered his head. He strained to scream but could utter no sound as the voices grew to a deafening roar in his head, repeating their refrain. "So hungry..."

———————

"Edwin!" Prudence pressed her fingers to the side of his neck. Relieved to find a pulse, she gently turned his head right and left, looking for any sign of injury. With a grunt, he opened his eyes and winced against the blinding sunlight. "Edwin, are you OK? What happened?"

"I'm not sure," he whispered. "How long was I out?"

"I don't know, but when you didn't come back after an hour and a half, I came up here to find you. Can you stand?"

Edwin sat up and rubbed the back of his neck. After a moment, he leaned forward, elbows on his knees, face buried in his hands.

"How do you feel?" Prudence said.

Edwin didn't answer.

"Take your time. If you're in pain, I have—"

He doubled over, clutching his stomach. "Hungry."

"Hold on, I'll get you a granola bar." She stepped away and rummaged through her bag. "I knew coming here was a bad idea. Once we're off this mountain, we should get you to a hospital." She turned, granola bar in hand—and flinched at the sight of Edwin standing directly behind her.

She stepped backward, nearly tripping over the uneven ground. "Oh, on your feet already? I, uh, didn't hear you approach."

He cocked his head before running a slow, predatory gaze down the length of her body.

"Why are you looking at me like that? What's wrong with you?"

Edwin brought his right hand out from behind his back. The 10-inch blade of his survival knife glinted in the sun. "So hungry..."

HOW PAULEY MICHAELS SAVED HUMANITY
By Bart Palamaro

Pauley Michaels didn't look like a hero. Short and plump with thick, horn-rimmed glasses, Pauley looked like what he was—the quintessential geek. In the nineties, Pauley was the middle-school kid who could make your brand-new, really expensive personal computer actually print documents on your new and equally expensive laser printer. In the new century, Pauley was the guy you called when that internet virus screwed up your system. By the middle of the twenty-teens, Pauley's IT support company was keeping wireless servers humming like a well-tuned BMW.

Despite his financial success, Pauley lived with his plump little wife Myranda in a quiet suburban neighborhood in Berkeley Heights, New Jersey. They had two plump little kids, one boy, one girl. Pauley didn't commute to Manhattan; there were enough companies in Jersey to keep him employed until the *next* millennium. So, Pauley kept the computers running, cut grass on weekends, and sipped a few beers a couple of times a month with his equally geeky pals.

But Pauley was a person who noticed things. Things that stuck out, things that didn't make sense. Things that didn't fit. It started with a set of dishes Pauley and Myranda had inherited from a friend who moved to California. It was a nice set of dishes—that heavy, ceramic, everyday sort

you could pay a fortune for in Macy's, or get at the discount outlets in Pennsylvania for a quarter of the price. Pauley thought it was an attractive, homey, somehow satisfying set of dishes with delicate green leaves and white flowers around the rims.

A few years after they started using the set, Pauley was surprised to notice one of the bowls was a bit different from the others. It was shallower, shinier and just… different. At first, he thought nothing of it. Even though they'd had the set for years, they seldom used it all, so he somehow must have overlooked the odd bowl. But it bothered him because it was something out of place.

Every time they used the set, or he poured himself cereal in the morning, he thought about that odd bowl. Pauley didn't use the odd bowl. He didn't know why. He just avoided it for some reason. One day, about five years after first noticing the oddity, Pauley reached for a cereal bowl to pour himself a late-night snack and saw there were two shallow bowls, nestled inside one another, in a little two bowl stack.

Pauley stared at the two bowls.

Impossible. He turned to his wife. "Hey, Hon, did you know there were two of these odd bowls?"

Myranda shrugged. She was interested in people, relationships, emotions, connections. The size and shape of cereal bowls interested her even less than the foibles of the latest version of Windows. She vaguely remembered Pauley mentioning something about an odd bowl in the set but that was a long time ago, and anyway, who cared?

"I never noticed," she said.

"Well, it's just darned odd. I know there was only one bowl like that, and now there are two."

Myranda shrugged again and went back to her book. Pauley shut the cabinet doors on the odd little stack and made himself a cup of tea instead. He *knew* there had been only the one odd bowl. So where had the second one come from? His sleep that night was uneasy. In the morning, the two odd bowls were still there, in their neat little stack. It hadn't been a dream. Pauley microwaved his usual morning oatmeal, avoiding the two bowls.

All day at work the question bothered him. *Where had the second bowl come from?* Then a client called in a panic. All his servers had gone down; he couldn't take any internet orders! Pauley hurried over with one of his techs in tow and worked late into the night getting the client back online. By then, he was too tired to care about mysteriously appearing cereal bowls.

Life went on for the Michaels family. The business grew. The kids got a little older. Myranda went on a Pilates kick and got a little thinner. She bullied Pauley into skipping the late-night snacks and he got a little thinner, too. All-in-all, it was a good year.

———

One morning in the early fall, Pauley opened the kitchen cabinet door and reached for a bowl for his morning oatmeal. There, right in front of him, was a stack of three shallow bowls. Pauley lowered his hand and slowly closed the cabinet door.

He had breakfast at the local diner.

After dinner that night, Pauley locked himself in his home office. Long after Myranda and the kids hand gone to bed, he was on the Internet, searching. He thought long and hard about what he found. It was nearly dawn when he finished.

Pauley wandered into the kitchen, yawning. He got down a bowl, poured instant oatmeal and milk, and stuck it in the microwave. The insistent *beep, beep, beep* roused him from his stupor at the kitchen table. He opened the microwave door and was appalled to see he had used one of the odd bowls to cook his oatmeal. He slammed the door shut as the bowl exploded with an earsplitting crack.

Pauley gaped at the microwave, a chill running down his arms. After he calmed down, he eased the door open a slit and peeked inside. The bowl was in pieces and hot oatmeal oozed down the inside of the microwave, dripping from the open door onto the floor. Right by his thumb he saw a long sliver of ceramic embedded in the inner plastic window of the door. He dropped weak-kneed into his chair and stared at the jagged shard. If he had been standing in front of the open door, that sliver would have gone right through his heart. He thought he heard a rattle from the microwave, as if the pieces of the shattered bowl were vibrating against one another. *Was that an answering rattle from the kitchen cabinet?* Pauley felt the blood drain from his face.

They knew!

He snatched his keys from the kitchen table, hurried to his car, and drove to work. He didn't dare do what he had to at home. He reviewed his previous research. Not about dishes or ceramics or ghosts. Oh, no. Pauley delved into insect predation. The methods of those insects, like bee flies, that invade another colony, somehow disguising themselves as members of the hive. The hive workers feed the interlopers, even to the detriment of their own young. Then, as the invaders grow, they feed on the young of the hive, thriving and prospering until at last they mature and depart, leaving a devastated colony behind, diminished and weak, easy victims for other predators.

But ceramic bowls? How could such a thing happen? People had been making pottery for… well… forever. Had something spontaneously become alive? How likely was that? What did they do now with ceramics that they hadn't done throughout history? Most pottery-ceramics had been used to contain things like wine, water, grain, and oil. Pottery amphora had been used throughout the Classical Greek world to transport all sorts of things. So what was different now? Pauley took a sip of coffee. Ugh! Cold! He looked over at his coffee pot. Empty. Well, he'd just heat his cup in the… Pauley froze in the act of standing up. *Microwave!*

Pauley's fingers were a blur as he searched the Internet for the history of microwaves, radar, radio, anything to do with radio waves and ceramics. The patent for a microwave oven went way back to 1950, but home use didn't really take off till the seventies. By then, practically everyone had a microwave. So, for the past fifty or sixty years, people had been microwaving food. In ceramic containers. Suppose that were the catalyst, subjecting ceramics to strong, sustained, periodic high frequency electromagnetic radiation. Perhaps that was the change, the energy input needed to turn dead pottery into… something else. Something alive.

He continued his research and found what he had feared. Nearly all modern electronics from computer chips to cell phones used ceramics. In everyone's home, in everyone's hand... next to everyone's head... there was a bit of ceramic being energized, excited, and fed by the microwave energy used in all electronics.

He looked further. If he were right, there should be discernible changes, differences, patterns he should be able to find in the vast world of online data. It took hours, but he finally saw it. From the 1970s onward, the incident of childhood and adult deficiencies had been climbing dramatically. Diseases like ADD, ADHD, autism, and social and behavioral difficulties of all sorts had been on the increase, growing exponentially. Socio- and psychopathic individuals seemed to surface on a daily basis. The problem was widespread, universal, and approaching critical mass. Pauley could see how, in a generation or so, society could fall apart. All caused by microwaved ceramics that had somehow become... alive?

No, this couldn't be spontaneous generation of life. Predatory insects like bee flies insinuated their eggs into the host hive even as it was being built. When the hive reached a certain level of growth and was prospering, the invader eggs would hatch and begin their predation. So for this to be true, Earth must have been seeded millennia ago with the "eggs" of these ceramic creatures. They waited, dormant, until civilization developed to the point where it could supply them with the energy they needed to hatch, i.e. radio/microwaves. Then they began to grow, and now they were feeding on humans in some subtle way that robbed them of their higher cognitive powers.

But what about remote regions? Hadn't he read something about entrepreneurs buying cell phones then renting time to other villagers? And smartphones—they were ubiquitous, had massive storage capacity, and were bringing entire university libraries to the remotest regions.

Pauley entered more keystrokes, more mouse clicks. In certain remote villages in India, Afghanistan, Indonesia, debilitating diseases had been on the increase since the late 1990's—correlating exactly with cell phone activity in those regions.

Pauley stared at his screen, blind-eyed and shaken. It was too widespread, too embedded in the infrastructure. Modern life would simply halt if ceramics were removed from everyday use. *And who would believe him anyway? Based on what? Some bowls in his kitchen cabinet? Laughable! How to escape this? He needed a way out, he needed a way to...* Pauley's fingers flew over the keyboard, searching. Within hours, he found all he was looking for. Then it was just a matter of making the necessary arrangements.

The next day, Pauley announced to his little family that they were going on vacation. One of those nice, slow, take-your-time vacations where you just wandered around the country till you felt like stopping. They rented a small camper and set off. It seemed to Myranda that there was no rhyme or reason to their itinerary, except they were heading generally west. It didn't matter much to her. She could read in a moving camper as easily as on her living-room couch. The kids were happy, though. They visited every amusement park they could reach, and Myranda never had to cook a meal—they ate only at restaurants. Every day, Pauley would visit an Internet café "to check on things." Myranda didn't think anything of it; he was always on the 'net. It was odd, though. He'd left his 'pad and smartphone at home.

Pauley and his family finally reached San Francisco, where another surprise awaited them. They were going on a cruise, but not just any cruise. Pauley had leased a yacht, and they were going to sail the South Pacific. The yacht was a big, luxurious sailboat run by a captain and three crewmen who knew how to navigate without modern electronics. That was Pauley's one condition. No electronics. They had to have a radio—it was required by maritime law—but Pauley insisted it be kept powered down except in emergency. No GPS, no phones, no video games, no 'pads. Only people. And Myranda's books. Hundreds of books.

Pauley and his wife worked alongside the crew to keep the yacht in trim, work the sails, and steer. They learned stellar navigation, and how to tie more knots than they knew existed. Even the kids had jobs aboard the yacht. Stopping at interesting, if obscure, islands along the way, it took nearly eight months to cross the Pacific Ocean to their destination. But Pauley didn't regret the time; he needed it for his arrangements to be completed.

By the time they reached Port Moresby on Papua New Guinea, the Michaels were browner and fitter than they had ever been in their lives. Pauley paid the captain and crew in cash, adding a sizable bonus. He and his family weren't going to need much money where they were going.

The next leg of the journey took them by mule to the remote Huli tribal area in the central highlands of Papua New Guinea. Fierce warriors, nearly isolated from civilization, the Hulis lived as their ancestors had, with no dependence on the outside world.

It was exactly what Pauley wanted.

Waiting for them was a prefab house on the outskirts of the village. The house was far bigger than they needed, and, even with the massive steel vault, was comfortable and inviting. Once settled in, Pauley and his family began making friends with the local Hulis. Language lessons on the trip from Port Moresby and Myranda's naturally gregarious nature helped, but it was really the kids who broke the ice. Kids find kids and soon bring parents together. Before long Pauley's family was attending, then participating in, local festivals and events. When the Hulis realized Pauley wasn't going away, they began to accept the family as permanent residents, if not quite members of the tribe. It helped that no one in the family was trying to "study" the Hulis. They were just living there. Myranda's only really need was for books, which she devoured at the rate of four or five a week. Pauley had the latest fiction and non-fiction best sellers shipped from Port Moresby each month.

Myranda ran out of birth control pills a year after they arrived. Thirty days later, she was pregnant. The tribal elders expected Pauley to bundle his family up and go. But he didn't. Nine months later, Myranda gave birth using a Huli midwife, with modern sterilization methods, of course. The Hulis thought this a quaint ritual, but went along with it. The midwife chased Pauley out of his house to go sit with the village men, get drunk, and swap lies. That was the beginning of the Michaels clan.

Pauley and Myranda schooled their kids in mathematics, history, classical literature, and physics. It was a thorough, nineteenth-century classical education. Huli children occasionally joined the classes. Some stayed, and Pauley and his wife taught them, too.

Myranda eventually gave birth to eleven more babies, one about every eighteen months. Impressed with Pauley's virility, and his wife's fecundity, the Huli began seeking marriages with their children. Virility and fecundity passed easily to Pauley's children, and within two generations the Huli tribe began to take on a decidedly beige tinge.

Pauley, meanwhile, did what he did best. Geek. Over the years, he became famous among the Huli. His innovative ways of doing things gave the Hulis a distinct advantage over their neighbors and, as civilization seemed to withdraw, the Hulis expanded, conquered. In his own way, Pauley became a sort of Huli da Vinci.

Pauley always kept one piece of technology running—a 1960s-era pedal-powered all-band receiver. Every day he would sit and pedal with his earphones on. As the years went by, his face became grimmer and grimmer as he listened on those earphones. One day, he disassembled the device, put it away in the steel vault, and never powered it up again. Pauley never let anyone else listen to his radio.

A year after their last child had married and moved away, Pauley and Myranda still lived in the same house they had built when they first arrived. One night they were sitting on their porch enjoying the cool of the evening.

"What's that?" Myranda asked, pointing out towards the horizon.

Pauley looked up and saw a yellow streak lingering in the sky. "It's just…" He stopped speaking and sat up straighter. Before long the streak was joined by another, then another, and another until the night sky was full of yellow streaks, like a meteor shower.

Except these streaks were going up.

They were leaving. The predators had stripped the hive and were leaving to spread among the stars, to plant their "eggs" on suitable planets, where they would wait until a civilization developed, rose, and reached the necessary level of technology. Then they would hatch and begin the cycle again.

"It's what I've been waiting for, Myranda. Hoping for." He reached over and hugged her to him, snuggled close on the porch swing.

"It's over," he said.

———

Early the next morning Pauley opened the big steel safe that had stood in its own private room since before they had moved into the little house. He twirled the dial in a barely remembered combination, turned the handle, pulled, and the massive door swung slowly, ponderously open. Inside were the precious books he had had preserved on plasticized pages. Literature, mathematics, technology, science, history, engineering, art.

All the information needed to reboot civilization.

VICIOUS VICTORIA
By Julie Feedon

Bryce Hanner was ready—at least physically. His flashlight on and GoPro camera strapped to his forehead, he trekked along the overgrown path to the abandoned Kingston family cemetery, just a few hundred feet ahead of him. He'd already passed the crumbling shell of the Kingston mansion, which had nearly burned to the ground in the early 1970s. In the distance, Bryce could hear the faint crashing of waves against the rocky shoreline directly below the cliff where the cemetery sat in lonely isolation. Every so often, a passing beam from the Cape May lighthouse would offer momentary illumination to the moonless night and eerie surroundings.

A nineteen-year-old sophomore at Princeton University, Bryce was moments away from his final pledge test for the Alpha Kappa Lambda fraternity.

This year, the senior brothers had devised a different test for each prospective pledge. They'd written their ideas on slips of paper that were folded up and placed into a glass fishbowl. Blindfolded pledges then selected their own tests from the bowl.

Three tests needed to be successfully completed in order to gain acceptance to the fraternity. So far, Bryce had completed two of them.

Needless to say, after the previous five nights of Hell Week, he was beyond exhausted.

The fraternity brothers were relentless in their constant harassment of him and his fellow pledges. The most humiliating experience Bryce had ever endured was to hand wash all the fraternity brothers' underwear. Considering some of the families these guys hailed from, Bryce would've thought they were from the backwoods of Arkansas with the condition of their tighty-whities.

After he had picked his final test from the bowl, he remembered feeling a little uneasy when he read what was written on the paper— *Vicious Victoria*. Uneasy? More like downright creeped out…

"Oh, hell yeah!" One of the senior brothers, Dylan Tomkins, exclaimed after Bryce revealed his task. "The legend of Vicious Victoria." Bryce merely stood in confused silence.

"What, pledge? You've never heard of her?" another brother by the name of Brandon Smyth asked.

Bryce replied that if Vicious Victoria were a local lore, then no, he'd never heard of her since he was not a New Jersey native. As Dylan imparted the legend of this cruel lady, Bryce wished he could have a do-over to pick a different task.

"The story goes that on September 27th, 1898, a woman by the name of Victoria Kingston, who was married to New York real estate magnate, Charles Kingston, went mad after she found out that he'd been unfaithful to her. To make a long story short, Victoria went to the kitchen, grabbed the largest butcher knife she could find and stabbed Charles to death while he slept."

After hearing the initial tale, Bryce relaxed, realizing that it was the same generic story he'd heard before. Only the names were different. Apparently, each state had its own crazy lady who murdered her cheating spouse.

"But Vicious Victoria didn't stop with her husband," Dylan continued. "She proceeded to her children's bedrooms. She had an eight-year-old son and a younger daughter. Victoria slaughtered them the same way she did Charles. It was said that she killed her children because they reminded her too much of her adulterous husband.

"Once her murderous rampage was complete, she walked out of the house, across the grounds of the family cemetery, to the cliff at the edge of the property that overlooks the ocean. She ultimately couldn't live with herself after committing those murderous acts and threw herself off the cliff into the hungry ocean below. The next day, her battered body washed up on shore two miles from where she hit the water.

"The servants found the bloody remains of the children and their father that same day. Victoria, her husband, and the children were interred together in a crypt in the family cemetery. After the funerals, the house was then closed, never to be lived in again.

"I'm sure you've heard the Lizzie Borden nursery rhyme. You know, 'Lizzie Borden took an axe and gave her father forty whacks,' and so on, yes?"

Bryce nodded as he anxiously waited to hear what he was supposed to do for his final test.

"Well," Dylan continued, "Vicious Victoria has her own rhyme and it goes like this…

Vicious Victoria, so distraught
Upon learning her husband loved her not
The only way she showed her grief
Was to cut him up in his sleep
And to rid her mind of his memory true
Vicious Victoria killed their children, too."

After finishing the macabre poem, Dylan and everyone else present laughed and pointed at Bryce. "Oh, pledge, you should see yourself! I thought you were going to piss your pants!" Once the senior brothers had pulled themselves together enough to speak, Randy Perkins, the fraternity brother who wrote "Vicious Victoria" on the paper Bryce had picked, came forward and proceeded to explain what his task would involve.

"Okay, pledge, according to the legend, if you stand at the door of the mausoleum where Vicious Vicki and her family are buried, you're supposed to chant the following line three times: 'Vicious Victoria, give me a sign that you are seeking forgiveness for your crimes.' After the third time, turn your back to the door. Within a minute, the door will open on its own.

"And if the door opens, that's a sign that Victoria is allowing you entry into her family's final resting place. That's when the real test begins."

"May I interrupt with a question, brother?" Bryce blurted.

Randy rolled his eyes and grunted. "What's your question, pledge?"

Bryce cleared his throat before he choked out, "W-won't the mausoleum be locked? I mean, I don't think a ghost will be able to open the door if it's locked, right?" No sooner had the words tumbled out, than Bryce kicked himself mentally. *Stupid question, dumbass!*

"Aw, I think the little pledgeling is scared," a fraternity brother standing somewhere behind him mocked. Laughter echoed off the walls of the immense inner chamber of the fraternity house.

"Silence!" ordered Randy, who was trying to convey to Bryce exactly what he needed to do for his final test. "The pledge has the right to ask any questions he wants… even if they are stupid."

Another round of laughter was quickly stifled by a wave of the fraternity brother's hand. He looked at Bryce. "To answer your question, pledge, yes. The door is locked, and from past history, I don't think Vicious Vicki's ghost has had any problems opening the mausoleum door after the chant was finished."

Bryce was hoping the brothers and his fellow pledges couldn't see his internal anxiety begin to surface through the expression on his face. The truth of the matter was that Bryce hated all things scary and couldn't even bring himself to watch *The Exorcist* without almost fainting dead away. But he needed to get into this fraternity so as not to break with his family's tradition.

The past four generations of male Hanners had been members of the Alpha Kappa Lambda fraternity, and, if he didn't make it, his father would probably disown him. So, it was doubly important for him to swallow his fear and get through this last test. Maybe if he kept repeating to himself, *last test, last test, last test,* it would help him overcome the challenge.

"Pay attention, pledge." Randy snapped his fingers in Bryce's face. "The story of Vicious Victoria isn't finished yet. Over the years, four teenagers, all hailing from the Cape May area, supposedly vanished after attempting this ritual.

"The first teenager disappeared in 1927, the second in 1948, the third exactly ten years later in 1958, and the fourth and most recent in 1973. What makes the stories of their disappearances more believable is that they all happened on or around the anniversary of Vicious Victoria's death, September 27th—and to top everything off, none of their bodies have ever been found.

"It's as if they literally vanished from the face of the earth. But legend has it that Vicious Victoria was angered by their presence, so she physically grabbed each one of them and dragged them back to Hell with her..."

Snap! Crack!

A loud noise to his left snapped Bryce out of his reverie and back to attention as he spun toward the direction of the sound. He shone his quivering flashlight into the brush and strained to catch a glimpse of whatever it was that had made the noise.

"Hey, pledge," Dylan's voice crackled through Bryce's earpiece. "What's going on? Why did you stop?"

Bryce inhaled deeply and grabbed the small microphone attached to the earpiece. "I thought I heard something, or some*one*, walking in the brush right next to me."

"Well, there's no one there, so keep moving." Dylan ordered. "It's not that far now. The quicker you get this over with, the quicker you can come back here and get your pin. Now get going."

"Yes, brother." Bryce turned and pointed the flashlight straight ahead, illuminating the wrought-iron gates of the Kingston family cemetery. He cautiously approached the rotting posterns, one of which had fallen from its hinges years earlier while the other had rusted shut to its frame. Like a snake's silent journey through grass, ivy had wound its way up the stone pillars and slithered through the letters of the word "KINGSTON" that loomed above the graveyard's entrance.

"All right, Bryce," he said to himself, "let's get this over with."

Cautiously, he stepped over the threshold between life and death and entered the cemetery. He moved his flashlight back and forth as he walked through the maze of tombstones. Every now and then he'd stop to read one. The oldest he found dated back to 1840. He knelt down to read the inscription.

Jonathan Kingston
b. April 7th, 1808
d. December 21st, 1840
Influenza

The waves crashing against the rocky shore were more audible now, so the Kingston mausoleum had to be close. He stood up and slowly started toward the clearing that was just a few feet ahead—and there it was. Bryce swallowed hard and trudged through the overgrown field of weeds and beach grass towards the abandoned crypt—a dreary scene beneath a moonless night that made the mausoleum even more foreboding.

It was bad enough that he was trespassing on private property, but the fact that he had to perform a weird ritual at the place where a murderess had been laid to rest made him physically ill. Oh, the things one had to do in order to maintain family tradition! He recalled his father telling him to do whatever the brothers had in mind because he would be very disappointed if Bryce were not accepted to the fraternity of his alma mater.

"Screw you, Dad," he muttered.

"What did you just say, pledge?" Dylan's voice boomed in his earpiece.

"Nothing, brother. My bad."

"Okay, pledge, the moment of truth. Get to it."

"Yes, brother." Bryce dropped his backpack to the ground and knelt down to open it. He shone his flashlight into the canvas bag and fished around to find the instructions for the ritual he was about to perform.

He took out the small ball and teddy bear that he needed to leave as tokens of respect for the children. He placed them on the ground beside him, then carefully removed the rose he was to leave for Victoria and laid it atop the toys. He found the instruction sheet at the bottom of the bag and unfolded it with shaking hands. After a quick scan under the glow of his flashlight, Bryce folded it back up and stuffed it into a back pocket of his jeans. He gathered up the offerings and stood, peering at the mausoleum. The weathered stone structure seemed to meet his gaze, staring back with a sinister sneer.

No, that's just your imagination. Move it! Forcing his feet forward, Bryce arrived at the top step of the mausoleum. He wiped off years of dust and sea salt from the window on the door and gazed into the bleak inner sanctum of the tomb. Unable to see anything within, he raised his flashlight and shone it through the window.

His gaze first settled on the sarcophagi of Victoria and her husband. Bryce then noticed that the children had been entombed within the wall beside Victoria. Cobwebs hung from the ceiling like ghostly stalactites. Then, he caught a glimpse of something on the floor in front of the children's tombs.

He aimed his light at the objects and a wave of terror engulfed him at the sight of two rubber balls and two baseballs in front of the boy's grave. A few feet away, four different teddy bears lay strewn in front of the girl's grave.

Bryce panned the flashlight to the left and nearly dropped it when he saw what looked like four dried roses atop Victoria's tomb. Four roses, four balls, four teddy bears, and four teenagers that had gone missing over the years supposedly after doing exactly what he was about to do. Bryce's stomach churned as a wave of nausea swept over him.

He read the inscriptions on Victoria and Charles Kingston's marble sarcophagi.

Charles Victor Kingston
Loving Father
b. April 8th, 1864
d. September 27th, 1898

Victoria Elizabeth Margaret Kingston
Loving Mother
b. July 13th, 1870
d. September 27th, 1898

"Seriously, 'loving mother,'" Bryce huffed. "Well I guess they couldn't put 'here lies the bitch that cut up her husband and kids.'" He gave the door handle a quick shake. Locked tight.

Carefully, he backed down the stairs and placed his offerings on a cement pillar next to the steps. After inhaling deeply, he closed his eyes and chanted the required rhyme, "Vicious Victoria, please show me a sign that you're seeking forgiveness for your crimes."

He repeated it twice more, then opened his eyes, turned his back to the doors of the mausoleum, and waited in anxious silence. After about thirty seconds, his heart skipped a beat when the door's latch clicked open.

———————

"Whoa! That worked perfectly! Great job at rigging the door, Randy." Dylan's gaze fixed on the computer screen showing the live feed from the GoPro camera strapped to Bryce's forehead. Seated beside Dylan, fellow frat brothers Randy Perkins and Brandon Smyth reached around him for a hearty fist-bump.

"Thank you, my brothers," answered Randy. "I just wish we could've seen the pledge's face when that door opened." The night vision of the GoPro camera was working perfectly. The trio could clearly see everything that was happening around Bryce.

"And I'd like to acknowledge your contribution to the task this evening, Mr. Smyth," Randy continued. "You did a great job of aging out and distressing those toys and roses to make them appear as if they came from each respective decade when those teenagers went missing. And dude, those cobwebs look so real! Seriously, great job, my brother." He raised his beer glass.

Brandon returned the gesture. "Well, when your dad is the head of special effects at a major movie studio, you pick up a few skills."

The frat brothers had set up their surveillance equipment in a local oceanfront hotel in Cape May. Afterward, they tapped the quarter keg of beer and had been drinking steadily since Bryce left for the cemetery.

So far, their pledge was performing his test perfectly, but they had much more in store for him. It was nearly time to set off more of the riggings that Randy had prepared earlier in the day. The brothers planned on bringing the legend of Vicious Victoria to life and spooking the freshman pledge out of his pants. Randy had linked a computer program on his laptop to remotely control the special effects planted within the mausoleum.

Judging by the image on the screen, Bryce had not yet turned to face the door after Victoria opened it for him. Dylan unmuted his cell phone. "Okay, pledge, looks like she's actually letting you in. You know what comes next. Get in there… now."

"Y-yes, brother."

Dylan muted his phone. "Ha! The pledge is shaking in his shoes." On the screen, the mausoleum flashed into view. The trio all gathered around the monitor to watch as Bryce picked up his offerings and moved into the open door of the crypt.

"I have to give the pledge credit, that place looks creepy as hell," Randy said.

In the greenish gray of the GoPro's night vision, they watched as Bryce lowered his flashlight to the toys, then reeled back at a sound from the rear of the mausoleum. The image on the screen shifted as the camera panned along the walls. "Hello?" Bryce called out as he started to make his way around the mausoleum.

"Hey, pledge, keep your mind on what you're supposed to—" Dylan was interrupted as the sharp sound of static erupted from his cell phone. "Pledge? Bryce, can you hear me? Great, something happened to the feed. He can't hear me."

"But we can still hear him." Randy turned up the volume on his computer. "Do you want me to call him?"

"Yeah, go ahead." Dylan nodded to Brandon. "Get me another beer, will ya?"

Randy punched Bryce's number into his phone but frowned as he pulled it away from his ear to look at the screen. He pressed the end button and looked to Dylan. "Huh, that's strange."

Brandon returned with the beer as Dylan asked, "What's wrong?"

Perplexed, Randy shook his head. "After I dialed Bryce's number, a recording came on and said that the number could not be reached."

"Hello!"

The trio's attention immediately snapped back to the computer screen after they heard Bryce once again call out to whomever, or whatever, had made the noise.

"Y-you guys hearing this?" Bryce made his way toward the open door of the mausoleum as slow, light footsteps crackled over the withered beach grass outside, closing in on the pledge's position. He lowered his voice to a frantic whisper. "Come in, you guys! Can you hear me?" He aimed his flashlight along the path he'd taken through the cemetery.

"Here, let me try to call him." Brandon dug his cell phone out of his back pocket. "What's his number?"

Unable to pry his gaze from the monitor, Randy held up his phone displaying Bryce's number. He shot forward in his seat after he heard what sounded like a female voice whispering from the speakers. "Did you guys hear that?"

Dylan held up a hand for silence. "Yeah, I heard it. It was definitely a woman's voice."

They both looked at Brandon to see if he was able to get through to Bryce. Brandon looked up from his phone and shook his head. "I got the same recording Randy did."

"Oh, this is just fucking great!" Dylan exclaimed.

"You guys," Bryce whispered, "I thought I just heard a woman whisper my name! I-I don't know, I think my imagination is working overtime. Y-you guys there? Come on, what's going on? I'm leaving in two seconds if you don't answer me!"

Dylan was hastily typing a text to Bryce stating that they were having audio problems and to just hang in there and finish the ritual. After he hit send, he again heard the woman's voice. This time, he could make out what she was saying.

"Forgive me…"

The image on the screen wavered and blurred as Bryce looked right and left. "Guys, what the fuck? Did you just hear that? Oh my God!"

"Come on," Randy said. "There's got to be someone up there with him, right? Dylan, did you ask one of the sorority sisters to go there and freak him out a little more?"

"No!" Dylan looked at Randy in disgust. "I wouldn't do something like that and not let you guys in on it." He looked at his cell phone. Bryce hadn't responded to his text.

The trio was still watching Bryce's movements when Brandon said, "Maybe we should go get him."

There was no answer from Randy or Dylan. They were transfixed on the screen. Bryce had left the mausoleum and began to make his way toward the cliff where Victoria had jumped to her death over one hundred years ago.

Dylan gulped audibly as his eyes widened. "Where the hell is he going?"

Though the sound of the waves below nearly drowned out any other noise around him, Bryce was turning in a slow circle now that the once-distant footsteps seemed to be closing in from all sides. Bryce's microphone picked up the sound of crackling beach grass. Just then, the picture on the monitor scrambled momentarily.

Once the image cleared, the trio noticed that Bryce had moved closer to the cliff's edge. He was looking over to the rocky shore below. "Victoria must've really felt guilty about what she did if she took a dive off this cliff. Seems like a thousand miles high. Guys, are you there? Can you hear me?"

Before Bryce could turn around, they again heard the soft voice of a woman's whisper. "Please forgive me."

Dylan, Randy, and Brandon all sat in stunned silence as the camera's angle changed abruptly to the murky atmosphere above the ocean. Bryce's breathing became labored and he could be heard swallowing deeply.

The image began to pixelate, but the details could still be made out. Bryce was slowly turning around to face whoever was standing behind him. The picture briefly blurred again and there, in center frame, was the washed-out face of a woman with unkempt wild hair and black eyes. Her mouth opened like the gaping maw of a demon and let out an ear-piercing shriek above which Bryce's own terrified scream could be heard.

The image jerked back, the night sky came into partial view, and the woman's ethereal, undulating form shrank in the distance before gliding out of frame. Bryce's screams were silenced with a sickening thud. The frat brothers gaped as the screen went black just after the first wave crashed over the camera.

THE DIVIDING WALL
By Stuart S. Roth

August 20, 1961

She was nude on the canvas, standing with one leg forward in a *contrapposto* pose, but with her arms raised and her hands holding back her blond hair from her neck. Her body was slim and long, her breasts were tiny, and her face was oval with large brown eyes. Sabine recognized the expression on the face, a mix of timidity and determination, which gave her a vulnerable look. She recognized it very well, because the girl in the painting was her sister—her *identical twin* sister.

She raised a trembling hand to the figure on the canvas. *Emma would never do such a thing*. Sabine turned on the boy. Eric stood outside the circle of easels. He had not moved. He simply stared at her with those intense eyes.

"*Mein Gott*! What did you do to her?" Sabine realized there was something not human about him.

Two Hours Earlier

The Soviet tanks stood where the Russian advance had ended at the conclusion of the war. Six very young and frightened soldiers stood guard over the monument. By the randomness of the dividing line, the

Soviet Monument, with its four war-era tanks and Roman columns, was now cut off from the East and stood in the British Occupied Zone of Berlin.

"*Nein Stacheldraht!*" The crowd chanted. "No to barbed wire! No to division!" The tempo had risen throughout the day as the mob increased. Sabine Beise had come out with half the city to vent her frustration. *Stacheldrahtsonntag* had been a week ago. The Soviets and their East Berlin People's Police, the *Volkspolizei* or *Vopos*, had spread a curtain of barbed wire and improvised fencing right across the center of the city. No one expected the blockade to last. Speeches were made and protests lodged by politicians and members of the Allied Control Council, but the barbed wire remained, trapping Emma on the other side. Rumors had spread that the Vopos were shooting people who tried to leave the East.

Sabine stood on her toes to peer above the other protestors and caught sight of a flaming bottle thrown by someone in the crowd. It arced high overhead and smashed against one of the monument's columns. Someone screamed. A gunshot sent the entire crowd heaving backward. Sabine's high-heeled shoe caught in a cobblestone and she went down.

Bodies stumbled and surged over her, many kicking her in their haste to escape. *Were the soldiers opening fire?* "Help me," she cried. Each time she tried to get up someone new would tumble over her. She tucked her head beneath her arms to protect herself. "Please, help me." A British army siren whirred nearby. "Emma," she whimpered before drifting in and out of consciousness.

———

"I don't know what the hell your problem is tonight, Em," Sabine snarled as the crowd of the Ku'damm club pressed in on them. Cigarette smoke and pounding music conspired with Emmaline's hangdog expression to give her an evening-killing headache.

"Listen, Em, I came out to forget about boys," she lectured over the din. Emma couldn't hear; she simply shrugged apologetically.

An American G.I. tumbled between them. He was drunk and handsy as he looked back and forth between the two of them. His buddies were close on his heels and looked only slightly less inebriated. "Hey babe," the drunken soldier said, "*sprechen sie* English? You *sprecht* the English, no, I *sprecht* the good German."

"*Nein*," Sabine answered. Pidgin English or pidgin *Deutsch*, it didn't matter, she wanted nothing to do with him. Unfortunately, he stood between her and Em.

"Good. I *sprecht* your language good." He jabbed a finger at his chest and then looked over at Emma. "Hey, are you two related?" His buddies laughed at him.

"We're twins." Emma was too polite to ignore him.

"No. No." He waved dismissively. "Are you related? *Sprecht*? Understand. You look like you could be sisters." He called to a buddy. "Don't they look like they're related?"

"We're identical twins, stupid," Sabine growled as his friend tried to explain the obvious to him. She reached out and took Emma by the wrist. "Come on." The evening was dead anyway.

The drunk pushed his friend away. "None of you are listening. I know you two got to be sisters or cousins. Let me check." He reached out a grasping hand. Emma cringed and turned pale. Sabine slapped the man hard across the face and pulled her sister toward the door. They had to swim against an incoming tide of bodies. Behind them, the G.I. was shouting something obscene. Emma clutched her throat, gasping like a fish out of water. She couldn't breathe. It was one of her attacks.

Emma was supposedly born a few moments sooner, but Sabine had always been the one to play the big-sister role. She put a protective arm around Emma's tense shoulders and pushed their way out into the crisp air. Emma immediately knelt beside the wall and rummaged for her asthma inhaler. Her hands grew shaky as she dug deeper into her purse. Sabine snatched it from her, dumped the contents on the street, and found the inhaler. Emma took a grateful huff and began to relax.

Sabine glowered over her. "You do it to yourself, you know. Why do you get so worked up?" Crowded spaces had always bothered Emma. As near as they could guess, it started when they were young children. Once, during one of the bombing raids, they had to hide in the subway. A bomb had knocked out the power and Emma began screaming. They were only five, but Sabine remembered it well, because someone in the crowd slapped her by mistake.

"A man makes a grab at you, you slap him. Nothing to panic about. Are you alright?"

Emma took a few deep breaths and nodded.

She rented a place in the subsidized East because she needed money for her school fees. The plan had been for them to go out this evening and for her to stay at Sabine's flat a couple blocks off Ku'damm. But that day, Sabine and her boyfriend, Fritz, had argued. In response, Sabine changed the plans to a night of clubbing, just the girls. Emma had arrived upset about her mystery boy, Eric. Something about things moving too fast. She claimed that she didn't want to talk about it.

The whole night had been a disaster and now, with Emma recovering, but still resolute that she wouldn't reveal what happened between her and Eric, Sabine exploded. "You're such a baby sometimes. You've been talking about this boy for four months. 'Oh, Eric listens to me. He wants to know so much about me. I think he likes me.' Four months and you're worried about things going too fast. What did he do, try to slip his hands up your skirt when you were kissing? Or haven't you even kissed him yet?"

That was the last time Sabine had seen her sister before Barbed Wire Sunday.

Near the monument, Sabine was jarred back to the present as the British police siren whirred in her ears and the feet of the stampeding crowd battered and bruised her. Sabine realized that she was about to die.

The hand that pulled her up was strong and sudden. She was back on her feet and looking through a sea of shoulders and arms. She barely caught a glimpse of her rescuer. Close-cut brown hair and blue eyes. That was all she had time to catch. He was gone, but not before leaving a folded slip of paper in her hand.

She worked her way through the crowd. One shoe was gone and her nyloned foot kept getting trampled. Finally, she made it to the edge of the mob and dashed into the seclusion of the Tiergarten.

A British tannoy called for order in the square behind her, but she felt safe now in the shade of the trees. She searched over her cotton blouse and knit skirt, feeling for injuries. Nothing seemed broken. Then she looked at the folded note clenched in her fingers.

Carefully, she unfolded the tightly creased paper. One side bore the letterhead of the City University, but nothing else. She flipped it over. There, written in neat, unmistakably precise handwriting, were the words "Come, please hurry. Help me." It was Emma's writing. The headmistress in the displaced-persons camp they grew up in used to slap Emma's hands with a ruler to improve her penmanship. It had worked. The writing on the page was definitely hers.

Where? Where are you? The note said nothing more. She looked around, but the stranger who had slipped it into her hand was gone. Did this mean Emma was back in the West? If so, where was she, why couldn't she come? *Oh, God! Had she tried to swim the canal?* Neither of them had ever been strong swimmers. Sabine herself had almost drowned while swimming at the lake when they were twelve. An older boy had fished her out. Emma was no better.

Who would hand someone a note like this? It made no sense. She turned her attention to the letterhead. It was from the Department of Art at the university where Emma was taking classes. There was also an address beneath the name. That had to be where she was. Maybe Emma had escaped the *Vopos* and had taken refuge with some friends at the college. She was hurt and the boy who delivered the note had just gotten separated from Sabine in the chaos. Emma was afraid and not thinking straight. Yes, that explained it. She was at the university.

The sound of a tramcar bell drew her attention. She would have to run in order to catch it as it made a loop around the Tiergarten. Sabine abandoned her other shoe and sprinted down the gravel path and across the lawn, hopping onto the back of the trolley just as it was about to pull away.

Her heart was racing as she handed the conductor the fee and clutched one of the poles. Some of the other passengers were giving her strange looks. She knew that she looked a fright with her dirt-stained blouse, ripped skirt, and missing shoes. So what? Sabine rested her cheek against the cold metal of the pole and listened to the overhead spark of the tram trundling against its power line.

From Tiergarten, the Number 7 tram took a series of turns that carried her past the Gedächtniskirche, a church still in ruins from the war. So much of the city had been reduced to nothing but burned-out facades. Today, most of the ruins had been bulldozed over, but the church remained behind its circle of fencing. As its blackened steeple and empty rose window passed by, Sabine thought of it as she had always thought of it—as a dividing line between the past and the present. On one side of the ruin was her modern life, free but empty, while on the other were the war and the father she only knew from toddler memories. The bombings and fires were confined to nightmares now, but the church was a daytime reminder of all that had happened in the past twenty years. For Sabine, the ruins triggered memories of a cold bed in the displaced-persons camp, public latrines, and eating ration food.

The church disappeared as the tram continued across the city. Soon, she was looking down a side street leading to the big intersection that had been divided by barbed wire and post fencing. It was the arbitrary point in the middle of the street where East and West met. Fatigue, combined with the rhythm of the tramcar, overcame Sabine and she closed her eyes for just a moment…

She had dressed for work as normal on that Monday morning. Sabine and Emma worked as greeters at Tiegel's Department Store. The uniforms were an organ grinder's monkey suit of red wool skirt and jacket studded with brass buttons. They were ordered to tuck their hair beneath matching bellboy-style caps and to always be smiling and demure.

As usual, it was a rush to get out the door and make it to the intersection where she would meet Emma for the walk to work. By this time, she had calmed down since their argument on Saturday.

The intersection was a constant reminder that the Americans and Soviets were in a war for the hearts and minds of Berliners. On the eastern side was a large placard dominating the side wall of a drab housing block. It depicted a German miner standing beside a farm girl with a bountiful basket in her arms. Overlooking them both stood a stern, but protective, Soviet soldier. Facing the placard on the western side was a giant Volkswagen billboard. It depicted the latest family sedan complete with smiling father and mother and two rosy cheeked *kinder* in the back seat. Normally, the intersection between the warring signs was a sea of office workers, construction crews, and mine laborers milling between bus and car traffic. But this Monday, everything had been brought to a stop.

Barbed wire and wood post fencing had been strung across the center of the intersection. An East Berlin police van was parked across the tramline and green uniformed Vopos patrolled their side of the barrier.

Emma was easy to spot in her uniform. She was a red splash in a sea of gray wool suits, black overalls, and white office dresses. They'd called to each other across the barrier. "Don't worry. It's just a show," Sabine shouted. "They'll clear all this up in a day or two." How could they cut a living city in two and expect to keep it divided forever? Emma looked pale and was standing with her hands clutched to her collar.

Someone beside her was shouting to the man next to him so everyone could hear. "The Americans are moving bombers to Spangdahlem. They say it will be just like it was in '49." His friend nodded and returned with, "This could go on for months."

"Shut up, both of you," Sabine blurted out. "You don't know what you're talking about. Can't you see that your rumors are frightening people?" She then called across to Emma. "Go home. Enjoy the day off. This will all end soon."

"Herr Tiegel," Emma answered. "He'll let me go if I don't show up to work."

"I'll tell him what happened. This isn't your fault. Don't I always look after you?"

Emma nodded and they parted with her looking only a little better.

That was the last time Sabine had talked to her sister. The phone lines were disconnected shortly after. Even if they had been working, Emma's only access to a phone was down in the office of the *hausfrau*. The old biddy worked for the block committee. Emma tried to avoid her ever since the busybody berated her for having a good job in the West, but sucking off the subsidized rent of the East.

The tram turned onto Ku'damm. Kurfürstendamm was a busy thoroughfare lined with cafes, shops, and nightclubs. Even now, with an armed standoff hanging over the city, flocks of girls and boys ambled up and down the sidewalk. American, French, and British soldiers mingled with the locals and the whole street had a young feel to it. Sabine couldn't help but think that these boys were the sons of the men who had bombed her country when she was a child.

The bright blue awning of Café Amour passed by to her right. She and Emma used to treat themselves to occasional cappuccinos after work. Sabine remembered long talks about life, boys, stodgy Herr Tiegel, and fashion. Emma liked to page through *Vogue* and wonder at the life of the models. One of their last coffee outings had seen Emma chattier than usual. She was going on about some mysterious boy named Eric. Sabine didn't know much about him. Only that he was a good listener and always seemed to be interested in what her sister had to say.

"He wants a photo. Of me," Emma had said, as if that was the most dizzying thing in the world. "I was thinking of the one from last holiday." She produced a 3″x3″ square headshot taken at a photo booth when she and Sabine had shown off their new bikinis, but you would never know it from Emma's. "It isn't too daring, is it?"

"Daring?"

"The bikinis, remember? I made such a fuss, and you were right all along." Bikinis were the newest thing. Sabine had been dying to get one and to convince Emma to be daring with her. That had led to an argument with Sabine accusing her sister of being a prude, and Emma judging Sabine to be immodest because she wanted one. They were twins, it would look strange if one of them was all covered up and the other was in a two-piece.

"Emma, all you can see is your face and shoulders."

"But you can see the straps. Isn't it clearly a swimsuit?"

"Oh yes, I see it now. You wanton woman. You'll get his blood boiling with that."

They laughed together, but Sabine never did find out if Emma gave the photo to the boy.

———

Maybe Eric was the one who had given her the note at the monument.

Sabine smiled sadly as the tram moved off of Ku'damm. Emma was so shy. Sometimes it was funny, sometimes it was maddening.

The trolley made a stop. People got on and off, shuffling past her as she clutched her pole. A cold chill passed through her all of a sudden. It was a strange feeling, as if someone were watching her. She scanned the faces around her. The tram lurched forward. Through the window she could see a brown-haired boy receding down the street. *Was it the boy from the monument? Had he been on the tram with her—watching her?* She shivered and kept her mind from wandering for the rest of the journey.

———

The Berlin City Technical University was a nondescript campus spread over a neighborhood of ugly low-rise buildings. Sabine had never been in love with school and as she rang the trolley to stop, she was even more uninspired by the campus where Emma spent so much of her free time. It was the weekend, and the campus was surprisingly deserted. Sabine jumped down from the trolley and realized that she was alone.

The art department was in a four-story converted warehouse with an empty lobby. The letterhead indicated that it was on the top floor. She buzzed the elevator and listened to the pulleys and chains groaning throughout the empty building. *Is no one around?* Maybe this wasn't a good idea.

The elevator here wasn't like the great wood-lined ones at Tiegel's. This one opened with a tired effort and displayed a bruised and bland interior. She stepped inside and allowed its mouth to close behind her. After a long heartbeat, the car began to rise. It clanged past each floor and chimed open at its destination.

Sabine had expected offices and classrooms. Instead, the doors opened to piles of sawdust and plaster. The room was nothing but exposed posts and ductwork. Late-afternoon light filtered through dirty floor-to-ceiling windows.

Her heart was beating rapidly. She stepped out, but held the elevator door with an arm and peered around the corner. The lift shaft was in the center of the building. Taped to a nearby post was a stenciled sign that read "Art Department," with an arrow pointing out of site behind the elevator.

The lift door lurched against her arm. "No...no...no," she stammered as it refused to sense her presence and slid closed. Sabine pounded on the call button, but the carriage was already on its way down. *You're being stupid. The room is empty.*

"Is anyone there? Hello?"

An airplane flew low over the building, shaking the rafters and disturbing the dust motes. Tempelhof aerodrome was nearby. People complained about the noise all the time. Airplanes always reminded her of the blockade.

She and Emma had been ten at the time. They used to loiter around the end of the airstrip, just outside the fence, watching the American and British cargo planes take off and land. There wasn't much to do in those days, other than games of hide-and-seek in the ruins—which they were explicitly forbidden from doing—and making a nuisance of themselves outside the aerodrome. One day, an American pilot began dropping candy from the cabin window on takeoff. Soon, other pilots took up the practice. This attracted even more children. With every plane that taxied for takeoff, they would gather in case it was the candy bomber. During the airlift, there were a lot of planes. Every day, every hour. There were only a few candy bombers, so most of the time there was nothing to do but watch the airplanes and look for signs of forthcoming candy.

It was during one of these wasted days that Sabine had looked up from her gossiping with friends to see Willy kiss Emma on the lips. Sabine still burned at the memory and tried to push it away to focus on her current surroundings.

"Is anyone here?" she called to the room. "Emma? Emmaline Beise?"

Run away. Something was wrong.

But Sabine was compelled to go on. Behind the elevator shaft, the room was divided by a floor-to-ceiling blackout curtain of heavy material. She approached it, ran her fingers across the velvety fabric to search for an opening.

Back in 1949, Emma had been sitting on a chunk of concrete. Willy had come up to her, bent down, pecked her on the lips, stood back up, and stared at her a moment before running back to his friends.

Sabine found the opening in the curtain and shouldered through.

Emma had run away after the kiss. Sabine remembered her patent leather shoes with the loose sole slapping over the ground as she chased her. Sabine had caught up to her in the ruined church.

The smell of paint and turpentine brought her back to the present. Here, at last, was what she expected of an art department. The room was open, like the unfinished side of the building, but the windows were clean and the space was sectioned off into functional areas. She was in a space designated for a classroom. Chairs and desks faced a chalkboard. Color pallettes and technical charts for graphic design were posted on a bulletin board.

Beyond the classroom were shelves of art supplies. Sabine peered through the shelving. "Is anyone there? I've come about the note." No one was lurking behind them.

A row of watercolor paintings hung from a wire across the room. They were depictions of nude men and women standing or sitting in modeling poses. Sabine felt her cheeks redden at the thought of standing undressed before a class of students.

On a table in a corner was a stack of fliers. She picked one up and recognized the artistic silhouette of a female model. She knew this flier very well…

―――――

"You should answer the advertisement," Fritz teased her, after the student had handed them the flier on the street. It was a solicitation for art models.

"Not on your life." Sabine giggled. The flier asked for models who were willing to pose nude or seminude.

"No actresses need apply," Fritz had crowed. Actress was a euphemism for strippers and showgirls. "They only want wholesome girls. That leaves you out then, Sabi." Only the night before, Fritz had been all about trying to get under her bra. He had wanted more, but she had threatened to tip a glass of water on him.

"Why don't we give it to that sister of yours?" he joked.

"You pervert. You know we're identical twins. Is that your idea of seeing me naked?"

"You aren't identical, remember, you showed me the secret to telling you apart."

During one of their heated sessions, she had pointed out the small birthmark on the front of her thigh. "Emma doesn't have one. This makes me me and her her."

―――――

Sabine leaned on the table of fliers. The memory was painful, not for the bit with that rat Fritz, but for what came afterward. Her fingers clutched the edge of the art table and she tried to force away the memories, but something compelled her mind to remember.

Two months after starting at Tiegel, their supervisor offered her a promotion from the doors to the elevator. The old fart had been enamored with the idea of having twins working at his department store. The job had been a raise in salary, but the catch was that she had to get Emma to agree to the switch as well. Emma had gone ghostly pale even before he had finished making the offer…

―――――

Emma was afraid of confined spaces. The best they could tell, it had come from the war when they had been hiding with their neighbors in the subway.

"You ride the lifts all the time," Sabine said. "We're talking more money and they give you a chair to sit in when things are slow. You can do it. Just be brave."

She had to give Emma credit. She did it. She overcame her fear. They rode up together during training with one of the other girls. They learned the callouts for each floor. Em reached for her inhaler once, but she didn't use it. An hour later, they were at work in their separate lifts. Occasionally, they would stop on the same floor and Emma would give a thumbs up.

Then Fritz arrived. He sometimes stopped by for lunch. Like a dog with a bone, he still had the flier on his mind. "Give it to her, Sabine. Go on. I want to see her reaction. That's her lift, right?" Emma was greeting a group of people stepping into her elevator. "Quick, before it closes again. Here, give it to her." For some stupid reason, Sabine thought it would make Emma laugh.

Unknown to her, a junior accountant that Emma was cow-eyed over had also stepped into the lift. Sabine hadn't noticed him as she approached with the paper. Emma made big eyes at her and nodded in his direction, but Sabine was too intent on Fritz's insistent nudging. She passed the paper in, but Emma dropped it. It fluttered to floor of the carriage where everyone could see the naked silhouette. Fritz let out a snorty laugh and an uninspired, "Isn't that your second job?" just as the doors closed.

Sabine knew immediately that the joke had gone terribly wrong.

Emma had to be rushed to the store's infirmary due to an asthma attack. She never went back to the elevator job. Sabine, too, was returned to the front doors. Nothing was ever said to her about the prank, but for days afterward, they greeted the customers with forced smiles and barely spoke to each other. Every attempt to apologize to Emma ended with her sister nodding back in cold silence. Then one day, it ended. Emma, maddeningly, apologized to her. "I'm not brave," she confessed. "I'm sorry my behavior got us removed from the elevator job. I was stupid to work myself up like that."

———————

Sabine collapsed from the weight of the memories. She had apologized again to Emma, but her sister continued to blame herself. She wasn't mad at her, she said, but things hadn't been the same between them since.

"Where is my sister?" she demanded of the empty room. Then she swept the fliers to the floor, tearing some up with her hands in the process. "I'm going now, and I'm calling the police."

At the far end of the room was a circle of easels surrounding a tall stool. Sabine walked toward it. Part of her was unsure what to do if she left. She entered the circle; each easel contained a covered canvas. *This must be where the models pose.* Lying on the top of the stool was a 3"x3" square of paper. Another note. More games. Written on it—in Em's own handwriting—"Help find me. I can no longer see the light."

Sabine picked it up. The words were written on the back of a photograph. She turned it over and recognized it as the bikini photo that Emma had planned to give to Eric.

Sabine spun around to survey the room. She had expected to find someone lurking there, ready to reveal the purpose of this cruel game. Perhaps it was Emma herself. Was she still angry about the elevator incident? Maybe this was her idea of revenge.

She turned her attention to the easels. There was something odd about them. Instead of facing inward, toward the stool and presumably the model, they faced outward.

She lifted one of the covers. Beneath was a depiction of a boot in sepia-washed colors. The details were extraordinarily vivid. Sabine found herself becoming lost in the folds of the canvas material and the intricacies of the laces. It was a Wehrmacht boot like the ones Papa used to wear.

The day the telegram arrived to inform Mama that he had been killed was a moment Sabine would never forget. She and Emma were five and had been playing on the round rug in the parlor. Cots had been moved from their bedrooms and placed in the family room. Electricity had been rationed and only turned on during an hour in the morning and an hour at night. They had lived only in the parlor and the kitchen, where a charcoal burner was vented through a window to provide extra heat.

Mama had broken into sobs after reading the telegram. Emma looked up at her, wide-eyed and gaping. Neither of the girls had ever heard mama cry before. Sabine remembered the fear in her chest.

After the man who had delivered the telegram left, she ran to Mama, tugged on her skirts, and asked what was wrong.

"Papa is dead." She had said it just like that, one simple three-word sentence. Sabine couldn't comprehend. Mama didn't explain. She collected herself and put a kind hand on Sabine's head. Her palm had been warm, she could feel it through her hair. Then the hand slipped to her shoulder and fell away. Mama went to the kitchen, and never spoke of the telegram again.

Emma was still on the floor, but when Sabine had turned to look at her, she scurried over to the overstuffed chair that had always been Papa's seat. She didn't speak or cry. She had patted the seat beside her and scrunched over to make room. Her eyes were wide and glassy, but she still did not cry.

"Papa is with God now," Emma had finally said.

Sabine remembered trembling, the feel of Mama's hand, the sound of her sobbing—the chair that Papa would never sit in again. All of it turned to anger. She remembered walking to the table beside the chair, grasping the glass ashtray, the one Papa had used to hold his pipe. She had raised it over her head and flung it to the floor. It bounced off the rug with a heavy thud, but didn't break. She had chased after it, almost threw it again, but then hugged it to her chest. She had looked back at Emma, who came over to her and knelt beside her and muttered something about "him being in heaven."

———

Sabine continued to stare at the painting of the boot for a moment and then let the cover drop back over it. *How long have I been here?* The shadows in the room seemed to have grown since she last noticed them.

She lifted the cover on the next painting. This time the cloth fell away. There on the canvas, staring back at her, was her face and her body, naked. With a scream, she stumbled backward against the stool, sending it tumbling to the floor.

The face, the detail of the eyes, that look of vulnerability in the tension of her lips and the set of the cheeks, it was unmistakably Emma. She knew that look in her sister. It was the way she looked when she was trying not to be afraid.

It was the face that frightened her most of all. The artist had captured a moment of thought. What had happened in that moment? None of this made any sense. Sabine studied the breasts, the flat of the belly, and the thighs. Nothing was hidden to the artist. The oils and brush strokes had even captured the subtle white of long faded bathing suit lines. It wasn't something Emma would ever do. *Ever*. But there was no denying that it was her. The artist hadn't guessed or imagined. Sabine knew her twin, because it was exactly what she saw every time she looked into a mirror…

"Willy kissed *me*! I didn't know he would do it!" Ten-year-old Emma screamed when Sabine finally caught up to her in the ruined church.

"You know I like him! You know it! And you kissed him." Sabine had chased her sister several blocks and finally cornered her. She had hidden under a pew on the moldy, waterlogged floor. The roof had a hole in it and the place smelled of rot.

Emma's frightened face peered up at her from beneath the broken bench.

"You must have done something. Why would he kiss you? You know I like him. I talked to you just today about him."

"He… he…" Emma stuttered and choked on her words.

"What?" Sabine kicked the pew. "Stop talking like a baby. Speak up."

"He… he thought I was you! He kissed me because he couldn't tell us apart."

"You lie!" She kicked the bench over and over again. Emma screamed. "We're nothing alike. You're a fraidy cat. I'm not. I always have to look after you."

"He told me! He told me himself."

Sabine kicked the pew again. It moved an inch. Dust fell from it. Emma cried and Sabine kicked it harder. Finally, one of the legs gave way with a crack. The bench crashed down, pinching Emma beneath it.

"I can't get out!"

"Of course you can."

"I... I can't..."

"Back out. You're fine, you big liar. Fraidy cat." Sabine turned and walked away.

"Sabi? Please, Sabi? I can't move."

———————

Sabine could still hear her ten-year-old sister's pleas as she stared into her adult eyes on the canvas. She had left Emma behind, but she had been right. Emma had not really been trapped. Nevertheless, they didn't speak to each other for days afterward.

Sabine looked at her sister's long eyelashes in the painting. Identical to her own, she had always thought them alluring when she looked at her own reflection, but on Emma, they seemed demure and meek. Sabine hated being forced to act that way for boys, for work, for her family.

A hand suddenly touched her shoulder. The fright of it should have sent her leaping like a cat, but her body couldn't move. She was frozen in place.

A figure was standing beside her. His hand was still on her shoulder, but she couldn't even turn to look at him. Fear pounded in her ears. *Oh my God! What is happening?*

"What has happened to the light?" The voice was quiet, less than the whisper of a child. No, not a whisper at all. The voice had been in her head.

The figure stepped into view, his fingers still lightly touching her shoulder. He was ordinary, a boy of her own age, but his blue eyes were intense, hungry. His hand moved to her cheek. She wanted to tremble, wanted to flinch. "Where have you taken the warmth?"

She couldn't speak. *I don't know what you want. Help me! Someone help!* Everything began to spin.

Her mind was forced back to the memory of the church. This time, *she* was looking up from the floor. She was seeing herself walking away. She was looking out from Emma's eyes.

"Help me, Sabi?" she called. She could feel her cheek pressed to the cold stone floor and her arm extended out to her retreating sister. "I can't breathe," she 'remembered' as Sabine left through the gap in the broken door. "I can't breathe," she repeated in panic. It was an asthma attack, but in this 'memory' she didn't know what to call it yet. It was the first time. *No, that can't be true.* Sabine knew that Emma started having the attacks during the war, when they were in the subway shelter. But here in this dream, she was Emma and she was having her first asthma attack, brought on from being trapped under the pew.

Air came in tiny, ineffective gasps. Her head swam and she tried in vain to climb out. Her hand was still stretched out before her. The fingertips were touching a pool of sunlight. The church once had a beautiful stained glass window depicting Jesus. What was left of it cast shades of blue and red light onto the floor. Where the Lord's face had been was now just an open space through which white light entered and touched her fingers.

I'm dying. She, as Emma, remembered thinking. But as she focused on the light, her fear eased and her thudding heart began to slow to normal. First one gasp of air, then another, and her lungs filled. She scrunched backward. Her dress caught on something, but she wriggled free. Inch by inch, she worked her legs and torso free and then finally her head. She crouched on all fours and stared up at the remains of the stained glass window, breathing in and out. There was a warm peace inside her now.

Sabine in the present could move again. She pulled away from the boy. He was the same one she had glimpsed at the monument and on the tram. She eased further away, bumping into one of the easels. The boy did not try to stop her. He simply looked at her with those questioning eyes. She glanced from him to the painting of Emma and then back again. It was suddenly obvious to her. This was the Eric that Emma had been enamored with. She remembered now how terrible her sister had looked on their last night out. Emma wouldn't say what had happened, but her behavior told her it was something awful.

The boy continued to look at her. His body stood passive, but his face looked anxious, in a cold sort of way.

"What did you do to my sister?" She raised a trembling hand to the painting. She wanted to scream, but she stifled it with her anger. "God! What did you do?" Then something more instinctive climbed into her thoughts. "What are you? What—?" She bolted like a frightened animal, sending easels and chairs crashing to the floor. She ran across the classroom and past the shelves, spilling art supplies as she dove headlong into the blackout curtain.

Sabine soon found herself groping frantically in the heavy folds, but the opening was nowhere to be found. The more she struggled, the more she became tangled and lost in the blackness. Tears streamed down her face. As she lost strength, her body began to slide down in the smothering curtain.

I can't breathe. Just like in the vision of Emma from the church. No, she was reliving her own memory this time. The summer at the lake. She was there again—a twelve-year-old, floundering in the water. Drowning. Thrashing madly with gangly arms and legs, while all the time sinking lower into the blackness. That was when the boy had come to her. So like Fritz, so like all the other boys she had been attracted to. They were all copies of her rescuer. Golden hair, solid brown eyes—boys of summer. He was pulling her to safety. She could remember herself, calming from panic, staring into his face and thinking how wonderful he looked. It was a face that had launched her into a series of failed relationships with shallow or mean-spirited imitations ever since.

None of the others would have saved her like this boy had.

A hand reached into the folds of cloth and drew her up. It was the boy from the lake. She blinked and realized it was Eric—or the thing that called itself Eric.

"Your light is different. What has happened?" He reached out to her face. It may have been a kind hand, but she pulled back in revulsion. *Why does he look like the boy from that summer*?

"I can see the lake," he answered. "We live among you and can see your lives." He took hold of her forearms. "Show me the things in your mind again. Show me the things you used to do."

"My sister was here. You painted her, not me."

His eyes studied her. She felt him in her mind.

"What else did you do to her?" She tried to force him out with anger.

He studied her more deeply. A look of innocent questioning appeared on his face for a moment and then it was gone. "Not that. I did not do what I see in your mind. Why would I harm you? Speak to me of the light." He squeezed her arms gently. "That is what I need."

"I don't understand you. What are you saying? What do you want?"

"The light we shared." He paused, not sure how to explain. Then he nodded. "You shared with me…"

Suddenly Sabine was five again. She was in Papa's overstuffed chair and seeing from Emma's eyes. She watched as her sister threw the ashtray to the floor. But in her mind, she was thinking of heaven and imagining Papa safe and waiting for them there. Sabine felt how Emma drew strength from that vision. That strength made her go to her angry sister and put a comforting arm around her.

Sabine was back and looking into Eric's eyes, but it was only for a moment. Soon, he sent her back into another of Emma's memories.

"I… I'm here to answer the advertisement." She was Emma handing the flier to a young art teacher. The flier had been crumpled, but Emma had smoothed it out again. She had spent a good amount of time staring at it and debating.

The woman looked her over. "You seem very nervous. Have you ever posed before? No, I can see that you haven't."

"I'm willing to try," Emma said. "Please. If it doesn't work out, you don't have to pay me." The woman was about to dismiss her. "I need to do this. You see, I'm tired of being afraid all the time. I know I can do it."

Taken by her honesty, the teacher nodded. "We can take it in steps. I am desperately in need of models."

Sabine could feel Emma's inner strength in the memory. Was this the light that Eric was asking about?

"There, I can see that you remember," he answered.

"Those aren't my memories. That was Emma."

"The light is different in you. It is dark. Less… warm. But it is *you*."

He was still holding her wrists. "Let go of me."

She was five years old again and back in the subway station during the war. The sound of artillery guns rumbled through her ears. She felt clenched and terrified. A loud crash sounded and the lights went out. Her sister screamed.

"Shut her up!" one of their fellow refugees snarled.

"The Russians are in the city. They'll hear," another neighbor added.

Sabine was confused as to who she was in this memory. Was she Emma? Herself?

"Shut her up!" The screaming went on and on. Wild and afraid.

There was a shuffling of bodies against bodies in the dark and the sound of a slap. Sabine heard it, but didn't feel it. She was in Emma's memory…but that couldn't be. Sabine was the one who was slapped, but Emma had been screaming. It had been so unfair. The man had struck her by mistake.

But now, she, as Emma, was crawling in the dark, squirming over huddled people and past the frightened man. She reached out to her sister. "Sabine?" she called. "I'm here. I'm here. I'll always look out for you."

Eric cocked his head and stared at her. Sabine could see that he was as confused as she was. A dawning seemed to be coming to him.

"That wasn't my sister's memories. It couldn't be. I look out for her. *I* told *her* that. She was the one screaming, not me. She needs me to look after her. I always have." She stopped and thought about it. She hated to think about that night in the subway. All of these years she had fooled herself, she thought she knew the truth. Now it was clear. *Emma had come to me. I was the one who was slapped because I was the one who was screaming.*

Eric drew her closer. "Explain what you have seen. I nearly understand."

"What are you doing to me?"

"We live in the space of forever. Your light draws us. It flickers and is gone, but there are many lights. I came to see them for myself, for the darkness is eternal." Through his hands, she could sense his mind and could experience the darkness in which he lived. To her it was nothingness, a space of emptiness that seeped inside her and threatened to make her into nothingness with it.

"You think I am Emma, but I am Sabine."

"The same light is within you. You call the light 'Emma's memories' and 'my memories,' but they are the same."

"I am me and she is Emma. We're not the same." She thought of Willy kissing Emma by mistake.

Eric didn't understand yet. He took her back to the lake and the summer boy who rescued her from drowning. She was so scared and embarrassed.

"Are you all right? Can you hear me? What's your name?" the boy had asked.

"Emma," she'd lied, ashamed of being afraid and suddenly shy in front of the boy.

"Well, Emma, I think you're safe now."

The real Emma came running along the dock. "Sabine, you almost drowned!"

The boy looked confused and realized they were twins. "She said her name was Emma."

"No, I'm Emma. Her name is Sabine. She's my sister."

Eric smiled. "Understanding. Two separate lights. You burn so close together. I could not see you apart."

"We are apart. We're sisters, but not the same person."

"And not the same light." He released her arms and walked over to the painting of Emma. He touched the canvas, but said nothing for a long time. "We are sorry and will go now."

"You can't. You tricked me into coming here. I thought my sister was here."

Eric backed into the shadows that had grown across the room.

"Wait! The light that you saw in her, you want to see it again, don't you? It's still out there. You have to help her."

Eric grew less and less substantial in the mixed light. He seemed to be fading away before her eyes. "Please, Eric. I don't know what you are, but you must be able to help her."

"We see your lives. They are short. The light comes and then it goes away. In your conflicts, we see your origins. We are above all of that."

"You're a monster if you don't help her." Maybe it was her force of will holding him, but Eric did not fade any further. "Do you want the light again? Tell me what to do. I'll do anything if you save my sister. She'll die if she can't get out of the East. She must feel so alone and trapped."

"You cannot give a light that is not your own. I'm sorry." But he did not leave. He was in her mind again. She felt naked before him, unsure if he was considering what she had said or simply taking more of her memories before he left.

Sabine turned away, trying to escape the eye of the eternal thing. She gazed at the painting of Emma. On the image, she suddenly noticed a small birthmark on the thigh of her twin. *My birthmark.* The only physical thing that made them different.

She trembled in revulsion. "Please help her."

Eric continued to stare into her until he stepped away. She could no longer feel him in her mind. The room was silent and empty. Sabine collapsed to the floor and wept. Eric was gone.

———

A week passed. Sabine didn't go to work and she barely ate. Every morning she went to the divided intersection. Emma was never there. So she would return to her flat and sit alone in her room.

The note that was passed under her door one evening simply gave a street address and a time. 10:00PM. The handwriting was Emma's. The address was near the barbed wire wall. She only had ten minutes to get there.

She sprinted down the street, heedless of the danger. Maybe Eric had said too much. If his kind had lived among humans for so long without being known, they must protect their secret. Maybe this was a trick to lure Sabine out into the night.

The street was divided. Bright klieg lights had been set up on the eastern side. Further east was a second barbed wire fence. Vopos patrolled between the two fences. Sabine ran toward the outer barrier, but an American soldier appeared and held her back.

Before she could say anything, a car appeared on the eastern side. Its headlights flashed on and she could hear the engine rev. The Vopos were taken by surprise. They had to dive out of the way as the car raced into the inner barrier. The tiny car was undeterred by the fence and rammed into the sturdier outer barrier. Metal scraped against metal as the barbed wire ripped at the sides and bonnet of the car. The wooden posts gave way and the car skidded into the West.

The eastern police were barking orders and running toward the opening. The American blew a whistle and raised his rifle. Others of his kind came out to form a line across the street. The Vopos stopped on their side of the border.

Sabine turned to the car. It was one of the cheap autos made in the East. Its driver-side door was open and the seat was empty. She imagined seeing a shadow disappear around a corner. She walked to the car. The passenger seat was empty and so was the miniscule backseat. Her heart sank.

A police car appeared from the west. Then an army jeep arrived. Reporters came next. One saw her as she ran her fingers over the roof of the car. "Miss, did you come over in this?" She ignored him and went to the trunk. She ran a hand over the handle, then twisted and popped open the latch.

The door swung open. Inside, curled in a fetal position, was her sister. Emma blinked up at her as a cameraman snapped a photograph.

Sabine reached in and helped her out. They embraced. "Look," someone said. "They're twin girls. What a story this will make."

"Was it Eric?" Sabine asked her. "He saved you."

"I thought it was you. The man who owned the car said you made him do it. Oh, Sabine, you always do look out for me." She hugged her.

Tomorrow they would talk, Sabine decided. They would speak about the painting and Eric, but they would also talk about what had happened on the subway platform during the war and about the light each of them shared.

BODIES OF EVIDENCE
By Lance Woods

So here I am, remembering all this crap with just a few seconds left ... and the taste of blood in my mouth.

I'm floating... in something. Filling my mouth, my throat... my lungs. So thick... warm... so much ...

They didn't even bother to kill me first. Must've wanted to get rid of me fast. Not much time left.

Wonder if this is what happened to everyone before me... like other patients ...

Or maybe Purcell.

———————

"A floater?" Dr. Purcell, the clinic's eye guy, gave me a weird look as he shoved his hands into the pockets of his white coat. Everyone on staff always dressed professionally—white coats included—but Purcell was the only guy in the place who preferred bow ties. They seemed to complement his thin build and fiery red hair. In fact, I don't think I ever saw him wear same one twice.

"You know," I said, "when you rub your eyes and you see like a ghost of a thingie or a pattern that fades away real fast? Well, this one's in my left eye and I can't rub it out."

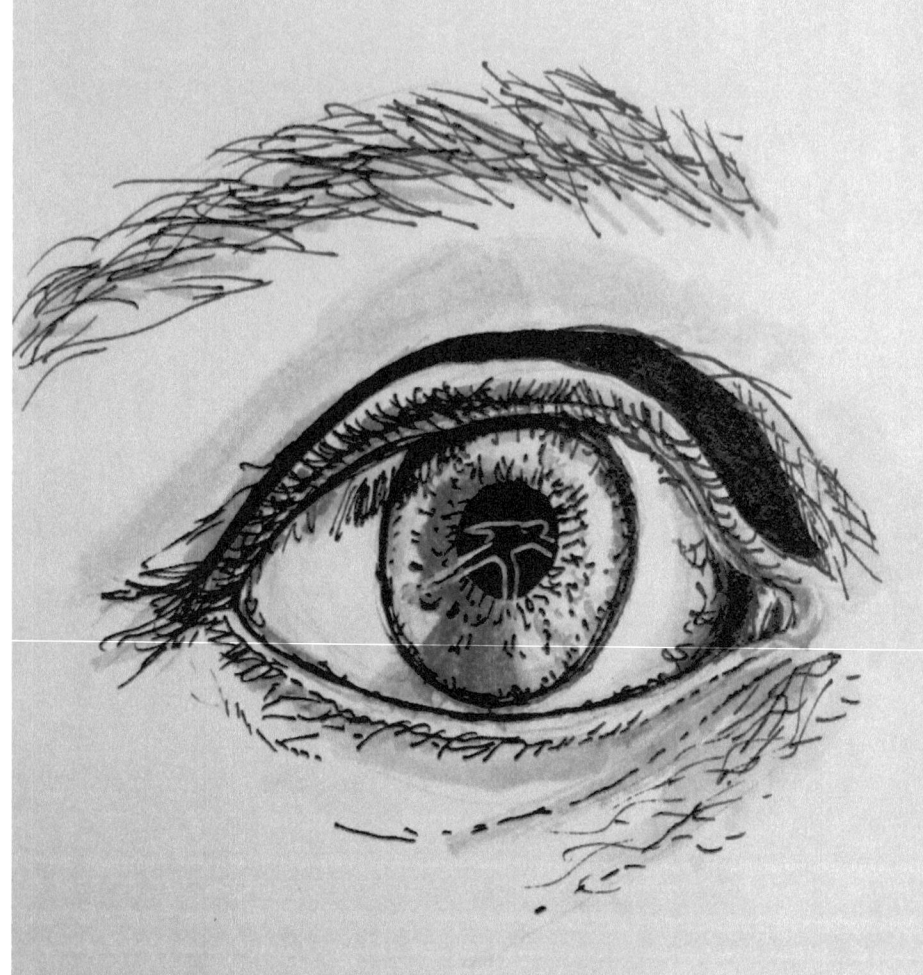

"When did you first notice it?"

I thought about that. It hadn't shown up until after I came to the clinic, which at that point had been around six weeks. A month and a half of doctors, examinations, evaluations, blood tests, urine tests, x-rays, MRIs, and injections. Lots of injections. Dr. Bridgewater—she recruited me—said they were all part of my treatments and that I was doing really well. Considering that she found me homeless on the streets in the dead of winter with a nasty cough and lice, anything was an improvement.

This place sure was. They said I had a mild fever when they brought me here, so I couldn't remember much about where it was located. But I had a windowless room in a windowless building that wasn't like any hospital ward I'd ever seen. It was a nice room, though. I had clean surgical scrubs for clothes—fine by me since the stuff I'd swiped from the Goodwill donation bin was starting to stink—a flat TV with a really good satellite line-up, access to the web, and a clean bathroom with a toilet and junk. The staff brought me regular meals, and the food was good. They even let me walk the corridors in unrestricted areas. There was a nice little gym across the hall with weights, treadmills, and other stuff. I even had a couple of video game systems with access to pretty much anything I wanted to play.

It would have been nice to have someone other than the game to play against. Never did see anyone who didn't wear a white coat, except for the security guards who watched the lobby of the clinic. As far as I knew, it was just me.

Until my floater showed up.

"Couple days back," I told Purcell. "Wednesday, I think. I was playing a game or watching TV when I first saw it. Saw it later when I was out in the lobby."

"Whatever were you doing in the lobby?"

"Wandering. Doctor Bridgewater said it was okay as long as I didn't go past the security desk. I hang out with the guards sometimes. Gives me someone to talk to who ain't a doc, no offense."

"None taken."

"Say, why's the lobby decked out that way?"

"'Decked out'? What do you mean?"

"Bare walls, no paintings, no signs, concrete floor with no carpeting, florescent lighting. I've made a few bucks from drug trials and donating plasma once in a while, and those lobbies were all bright and stuff. This one ain't very welcoming."

"I don't think it's supposed to be. The research we're doing is of a sensitive nature. Doctor Matsuko doesn't want it to fall into the wrong hands or gain unwanted publicity, so we discourage visitors."

"Even visitors for patients like me?"

"Usually not an issue," Purcell said. "Most of our test subjects, like you, were homeless with few or no ties to family and friends. No offense."

I blew it off.

"Visitors usually aren't an issue," he continued. "Still, we can't take any chances." He picked up that black thing with the magnifier and the light that eye doctors use to make you blind. "Now let's try to find that floater."

From my earliest visits to the doctor—family, Army, and now—I always wondered how such a tiny bulb could put out so much light. Then I figured out it was because the doctor had the thing so close to my eyes. This time, I knew what would happen—he'd shine the light, look around, and my floater would pick that time to stay out of sight. "Hate that damn light. Always have."

"This one's worse," Purcell said. "It's brighter than the usual ophthalmoscopes because it's also a video camera. Sends hi-def images of what it sees directly to my computer. Let's just fire it up…" He held up his key card in front of his computer monitor, which lit up. He tapped his keyboard. I wasn't sure what kind of screen came up, but I figured it had to do with the damn light. "There," he said. "Okay, hold still, please."

The light blinded my left eye. A second later, the floater slowly drifted across, just like it had been doing. Only this time, under the light, with no kind of background behind it, it looked different. I thought it would be washed out, but I could actually see some kind of outline. Had a real shape to it. I hated having that light in my eye, but I really wanted to try and figure out what that floater looked like.

A second later, I knew what it looked like.

But I forgot all about that when Purcell stopped looking, jumped back, and screamed.

"Screamed?" Beth asked me. "Purcell?"

"Yeah."

"Like a girl or what?"

I liked Beth. Not romantic "like," I just enjoyed talking to her. She was about ten years older than me—and probably outweighed me, too—but she carried it well and was pretty in a mature lady wrestler way. Before signing on as a day-shift security guard at the clinic, she served in the Navy—shore patrol—so, since I used to be an M.P., we had common turf. Whenever I could, I'd visit her at the front desk during her shift. Talking to someone in uniform put me at ease. Whenever I talked to someone in a lab coat, it almost always meant I'd be getting poked somewhere.

I hated to let her down. "No, it was a guy scream, nothing sissy."

She pouted. "What did he do then?"

"He put his nuts back in his sack, said he was sorry, told me the floater just darted into his viewfinder really fast, and it looked really weird at that size in hi-res. That's what scared him."

"Can he get it out?"

"He said he'd have to talk to Matsuko and Bridgewater. They're not really set up for any kind of eye surgery here."

"So, you'd have to leave? Get it done somewhere else?"

"Man, I hope not. I mean, I've been trying to figure how I can get the flu or the clap so they might keep me longer and not kick me back to the street. Maybe I should be grateful for the stupid thing."

"Good luck with catching anything simple around here," she said. "This place is more sterile than my second husband."

"My left arm's already stiff from shrapnel," I said. "Maybe I could stop moving it completely; give them something to look at. Do a solid for a vet, y'know?"

Beth laughed. "With all the doctors this place has, and all the stuff they're doing, you'd think they could figure out how to take out a stupid floater, much less heal nerve damage."

"See, Purcell told me that the regular kind of eye operation for that— viter-, viterec-, something—is risky because it can actually make things worse. Said he wouldn't do it even if he could, but he thinks Matsuko and Bridgewater might have some other ideas."

"They're smart. They'll figure something out, probably even tack a little extra onto what they're paying you just for giving them an unexpected challenge."

"Best money I ever made," I told her. "But you know what was really weird? About that floater?"

"What?"

"Well, when Purcell was looking into my eye with that light-scope-thingie, I caught sight of it before he jumped back. Under that light, I saw … well, it was just weird… It looked like a body."

"A what?"

"Okay, maybe not a body, but the outline of a body. You know, like those chalk outlines on TV shows, the ones police used to mark where people died. Like one of those."

"Floating in your eye?"

I nodded. "With tits."

"You must be seeing things," she laughed.

I laughed, too. "That's my whole damn problem."

———

The docs encouraged me to use the clinic's gym as much as I wanted when they first brought me in from the streets. It's not like I was super-sick or anything, but they wanted me healthy for all of their tests and experiments. So, every night after dinner, I'd watch some TV, go out to the lobby and talk to whoever was on duty, then hit the gym or watch more

TV. Wherever we were, they weren't afraid of letting me see what was going on outside. Guess they thought it was a fair trade for running tests, making injections, and keeping me under surveillance all the time.

The security cameras were small, but while I was there, I think I found most of them. Beth told me where some were. Others I figured out based on the pictures on her security monitors. There was no getting away from Big Brother—or Big Sister, when Beth was on duty.

Right before bed, I always took a walk. Not far, of course. They didn't let me out of the facility, but I was free to walk anywhere that didn't require a doctor's key card. That pretty much meant the corridor that ran in a circle around the center of the place. I don't know what was actually *at* the center because I never saw a door or hallway leading into it, not even a maintenance panel or a fuse box. Just a smooth, pale grey wall. But the beige walls on the opposite side had glass doors to exam rooms, labs, offices, and other stuff you'd find in a hospital. The doors had key card locks, but I was always able to look into them as I passed by. If I walked in the daytime—"day" according to the 24-hour wall clocks, since there were no windows in the place—and the docs and techs and roving security teams were on duty, we waved to each other as I passed by. Everyone but me usually looked busy, so I didn't stop to talk or get to know them. I just kept walking. Had no idea how much of a walk it was, but it usually took me about twenty minutes to do a full lap from the door of my room. Wherever I was, it was big.

It was good exercise, too… or maybe I just never shook the habit of going out on some kind of patrol every night.

Goddamn Afghanistan.

But this night, I was walking around the place for more than exercise. The ceiling lights in the loop were always dimmed at this time to simulate night. I was afraid to go back to my room, to watch TV, to surf the 'net, to go anywhere where there wasn't bright light to tempt me to look for the floater. Made me remember when I was in the Army, after my first firefight. I was scared to go to sleep in case some explosion might wake me up—or made sure I never woke up again.

This time, I was scared of something else—that I'd see her again. I knew I wouldn't see her the way I did with the light in my eyes, but just the thought of seeing even a shadow of her with my eyes closed...

Her.

Those tits that couldn't be tits.

In my eye.

Jesus.

I thought of this as I walked by Purcell's lab. The lights were on. They were the only lab lights on at zero-zero-30 hours. That was weird. I never saw anyone in the labs past twenty-one hundred hours. Still, I figured it might be a good time to ask him if he'd talked with anyone about getting this thing out of my eye.

I looked through the door glass. I didn't see him. I didn't see anyone. The lab was lit up, but empty.

The computer was on, but no one was using it. There was a screensaver on the monitor. I'd seen it before, on other monitors in the complex. If this one worked like they did, then being up usually meant that whoever used the computer hadn't been away from it for long.

I stood in front of the lab, in case Purcell walked in, until the screen went black.

Then the automatic switch that worked the lights shut them off.

Behind me, I heard the purr of a clean-bot. That wasn't the thing's real name, but it was a combination sweeper/polisher that Maintenance unleashed every night to clean the floors of the loop and the labs. They weren't much larger than those carts for books in your high-school library. A tech once told me how they followed magnetic embeds in the floors to find their way around and not bang into the lab stuff. That's how they knew where to stop and flash their own key lock sensors to open the labs. Other than the docs with their key cards, only the clean-bots could get into those areas.

I thought one of those might have tripped the lights on in Purcell's lab, until I realized that, if the thing was behind me, it hadn't reached that lab yet.

So, I kept walking.

———————

"Well, after hearing Doctor Purcell's diagnosis—and after all the weeks of cooperation you've given us—I think it's time we told you a little more about our project. A lot more, actually." The small, chunky, greying man who wore a name badge labeled "Edgar Matsuko, M.D." on his white lab coat turned to a woman standing across from us in the conference room. "Doctor Bridgewater, if you would, please?"

Doctor Amelia Bridgewater grabbed a remote and turned on a computer monitor. Then she took out her key card and held it up in front of a red light on a small box at a workstation, like Purcell did the other night. The keyboard at the workstation lit up and she started typing.

Tall, thirty-ish like me, nerd-pretty with dark brown hair always pulled back in a ponytail, Bridgewater was the one who recruited me for this thing. She wore her lab coat over pretty blouses and skirts. Sensible flats. And nice ankles.

Actually, I noticed her ankles first. Some men notice a woman's eyes first, some notice her boobs, some check out her butt. I notice the ankles.

It wasn't living on the streets that made me weird. I've always been this way. Don't judge.

A couple of seconds later, she stopped typing and what looked like a video came up on the monitor. It looked like a dark, red tube.

"What's the tunnel?" I asked.

"It's an artery," Bridgewater said. "The carotid."

"On either side of your neck," Matsuko added. "The right side, in this case."

I watched as the picture seemed to float through what looked like a big red underwater tunnel. "Of *my* neck?"

"The floater you've been seeing, probably, is what's left of this." He reached into his pocket and pulled out what looked like a golf ball with a lot of dark bumps on it.

"*That* thing's in me?"

Matsuko shook his head. "No, but something like it."

"How's that possible? I mean, I've heard of smaller capsules with wireless cameras that you swallow, or those fiber optics that, well, you know, run up through your dic..."

"This has far more instrumentation and mobility than any of the standard endoscopic capsules," Matsuko said. "We injected this into your arm with one of your vitamin supplements on Tuesday. You're the first human subject to receive it."

"Injected? That thing's too big for a needle, or for swallowing, or even for that *Star Trek* air thingie you've been shooting me up with."

"So was the one that took those videos we just saw," Matsuko said. "We used a special spray process to cover it in a capsule, miniaturized it, then injected it into you with the jet injector. The capsule dissolved on contact with your bloodstream and released the camera."

"Miniaturized...?"

"Shrank," he said.

"Yeah, I know what it means, and I didn't agree to that!"

"Actually, you did," Bridgewater said. "You agreed to the injection of any substance for diagnostic and experimental purposes. It's the clause right after the one that authorizes us to administer the new medication we're giving you to mitigate your PTSD symptoms."

"Yeah, but I thought you meant like sticking me with that stuff or the flu or those dyes that make things show up better in x-rays."

"Those, too," she said. "But the camera is a diagnostic tool, so it counts. And one of them will help us get rid of your floater."

"What, like one of those nano-things, what are they called?"

"Nanomachines?" Matsuko said. "We're not using those in our research at all."

"People tend to distrust intelligent little machines to keep them healthy," Bridgewater said. "They trust human surgeons, though."

"Shrinking doctors?" I asked. "You serious?"

"Not yet, but ultimately." Matsuko smiled. "Can you imagine? Doctor, scan forward a few minutes, please."

Bridgewater scanned through the video for a few seconds, then stopped in front of what looked like a dense spider web made of thin wires. There were tiny grey dots all over the place.

"What's that?" I asked.

"Nerve cluster," Matsuko said. "Specifically, the area of your shoulder that was damaged by the explosion. If we go in at maximum zoom, you can even see particles of shrapnel your surgeons never could have seen, even with a regular endoscopic camera. That's what's causing the mobility issues with your arm. Imagine what we'd be able to do if we could send a miniaturized team of surgeons into your body to repair that kind of damage. You've seen *Fantastic Voyage*, haven't you?"

"Uh…"

"The old one from the sixties, with Raquel Welch in the white wetsuit," Bridgewater said.

"Oh, yeah, that one, yeah," I said. "But how would you get them out? The docs, not the shrapnel."

"Ah," Matsuko said, "extraction is something we haven't quite perfected. That's one reason we haven't tried miniaturizing humans."

I was starting to worry. "So, what, these cameras are just gonna float around in my body 'til I'm dead because you can't pull them out? They ain't gonna get big someday and pop out of my guts like *Alien*, are they?"

I could tell Bridgewater was trying not to laugh at me. "After twenty-four hours, the effects of the miniaturization wear off, and the camera begins to grow slowly. But before it can get to a size that can cause you any pain or danger, the antibodies in your system detect, attack, and destroy it. Somehow, this camera lasted long enough to ride the currents up to your eye, but we'll take care of it."

"Doctor Bridgewater and I can do the procedure first thing tomorrow morning," Matsuko said. "After a day of recovery, you'll be up and around and wandering the loop again."

"Hey, speaking of that," I said, "would you guys know if Doctor Purcell was here late last night? I was doing my lap before bed and the light in his lab was on. So was his computer. But I didn't see him or any of his lab techs, and I didn't hear any alarms go off."

"When was this?" Bridgewater said.

"Roughly zero-zero-thirty."

"That is odd," Matsuko said. "After he told us about your floater, he said he was leaving for the day at his usual time, around eighteen hundred hours. We planned to discuss the procedure with him, but he called in sick. Stomach flu. He should be back in a day or so."

"If he ain't here, how will you fix me? I mean, he's the eye guy, right?"

"Right," Matsuko said, "but Doctor Bridgewater and I, along with our support team, know how to handle the cameras. We're going to inject a new one into your bloodstream, navigate into your eye, then have it transmit the exact location of the floater to a laser we'll be calibrating for ophthalmic use. After one or two flashes, the floater will be broken up such that it won't give you any more trouble."

I found myself looking at the video of my shoulder. "You sure this is safe?"

"If you continue to help us develop the tools and protocols we need to make this research a success," Matsuko said, "there's a very good chance that we could repair that nerve damage in your shoulder injury and restore full use of your arm. We could work out techniques that expand the frontiers of medical knowledge saving countless lives."

"What do I have to do?"

"Just what you've been doing," Bridgewater said. "Relax."

"How long?" I asked.

"Science isn't the kind of thing you can schedule," Matsuko said. "Let's just say 'indefinitely.' You'll continue to get free room and board and, of course, you'll be well compensated for your patience. How much did Doctor Bridgewater offer you?"

"Twenty-five hundred for three months."

"Fine. You'll keep getting that rate for as long as you're here."

"Yeah, but where can I spend it?" I asked. "You putting in a mall?"

"I'll talk with I.T. about configuring a secure line for online shopping," Bridgewater said. "We'll work out a delivery chain that won't compromise our location."

"Your other patients ever put you to this much trouble?"

Matsuko smiled. "It's no trouble, but now you know why we only work with one subject at a time."

"They got to leave when they were done, right? Money and all?"

"Of course." Bridgewater's eyes got big as she smiled. "And just like they did, you'll be helping a lot of people."

I looked again at the image of my wrecked nerves on the screen.

"That's what they kept telling me in Afghanistan."

———

"I wondered why your left arm didn't move as well as the right."

After Beth said that, I rubbed my upper arm and bent my elbow a little. Just a habit left over from therapy at the V.A. It didn't hurt. It just felt stiff—stiff enough to remind me of when it almost wasn't there at all.

"So, what happened?"

"They think they can shrink something down and send it through my body to the damaged area and fix it. Someday." I hoped that was the answer she wanted to hear.

"No, I mean what happened to your arm? In Afghanistan."

I hated that question. Anytime someone noticed the stiffness—or saw the scars on my arm or shoulder—they asked. I wanted to tell them to piss off, but when I was on the streets, it sometimes helped me score money from people who felt bad for a "wounded warrior." I'd even tell them about how I'd been waiting six months to get an appointment at the local V.A. hospital—true story, at one point. I figured that my tale was worth a buck or two.

But Beth was okay, a fellow warrior. I didn't mind telling her. Then again, maybe I'd just had lots of practice. I'd told Bridgewater, Matsuko, and a bunch of the other doctors the story during what they called my intake procedure when I arrived. Guess I was getting used to talking about my screwed-up military service. The V.A. psychiatrist said it would help me move on. Not that I ended up moving anywhere.

"I was with the M.P.s," I told her. "We were running security for a convoy on a road that was getting swept for I.E.D.s. Thought the six of us were fine, riding along in a nice, armored transport. ISIL kept trying to blow holes in them, but they held up. One day, Allah's evil twin smiled on them because we hit what we were looking for. Tore right through the floor and threw the vehicle on its side. That's where most of the metal in my arm came from, pieces of the transport that blew up and flew everywhere.

"Worst thing was, the guy sitting right next to me. Afghan army private named Aimal. Just a nice kid, y'know? Might have been nineteen. Trying to learn English while trying to teach me Pashto. One of the people we're trying to help, right? He ends up being right over the explosion, gets blown up by one of his own. All because we came to 'help.' That wasn't right. It shouldn't have been him. I mean, what'd I get for living? Shrapnel, nerve damage, a Purple Heart, and an honorable discharge."

"First time you ever saw someone get killed?" Beth asked.

I nodded. "Worst part was, we were covered in each other's blood. I mean, I've been hit in fights and sports in school before and tasted my own blood. Used to think that was the worst thing I'd ever tasted. It ain't. Can't think of anything worse than getting splashed in the face by Aimal's blood. And, seeing how things turned out, I keep wondering why I couldn't've lost more of mine instead."

"Maybe it's survivor's guilt," she said. "You keep asking yourself why you made it, why you deserved to live. My dad used to tell me about guys like that aboard the ships he served on in wartime. After an engagement with casualties, there was always someone who couldn't figure out why they weren't dead, or who felt they didn't deserve to live, and it just swallowed them up."

I nodded.

"What happened after?" she asked.

"Used to do warehouse work before the service, but my arm screwed me out of going back. Tried a temp agency, office work, but I didn't like it. Boring. I'd zone out at my desk and find myself riding next to Aimal again. My screams made me real popular there. So much for paying the bills. After my eviction, I took my act to the shelters and the streets. Turns out that survival kept me so busy I didn't have time to scream. Even if I did once in a while, people just walked by."

"Except Doctor Bridgewater."

"Yeah. She did get me in here. Guess that's something. Maybe all this crap I'm letting them do will actually help someone, or at least help Matsuko pay for the place."

"No worries there. His wife's loaded. She's funding his research. At least she was last week."

"Huh?"

Beth drew in a breath. "I probably shouldn't be showing you these, but seeing as you're practically family after six weeks..." She motioned for me to move next to the front desk, but stopped me before I could step behind it. "Act casual, not like you're looking back here. Remember, we're under surveillance just like everywhere else."

"I know." Even though I wasn't allowed behind her desk, I could see the little monitors from where I was standing beside the station. There were about thirty screens, maybe more, each labeled with a different room or area underneath. I recognized some of the places, but there were others I'd never seen. I figured they were restricted, doctor-key-card-only places.

"Check out the monitor by my left knee," she said quietly.

I did. It looked like a video of the front lobby but, instead of running in real time, like the other screens, it was running real fast. I saw a couple of the doctors go on and off camera like they were in one of those old silent movies. A time code with the date ran at the top of the screen.

"Why's it running like that?" I asked.

"It's a security recording from Monday that's running back at high speed," she said. "Every few days, we archive the recordings."

"Huh. Even without their white coats, I can pick them out. There's Purcell... Montgomery... Caldwell... hey, who's that?"

"Who?"

"That short lady in the hat, walking up to the desk, talking to you." I meant the one wearing the stylish, long, expensive coat that covered up her ankles. No, I didn't say that out loud. "I thought we didn't get visitors."

Beth looked at the screen with a sad expression. "Not a visitor, really. That's Mrs. Matsuko. She came here Monday night demanding to talk to her husband, but he was working on an experiment and left orders to not be interrupted. Even by her, if she called."

"Must have been something important to get her to come by."

"I'd just like to know how she found the place. No one outside the staff knows where we are."

"Hell, I don't know. I was so out of it when Bridgewater brought me in that all I remember is the elevator going down, then waking up in a warm room the next morning."

"People with money can find out almost anything, even when they shouldn't," Beth said. "And even though she knows his research is important, she's a wife. She gets lonely, y'know?"

"Uh-huh, I guess." I watched the screen a while longer as Mrs. Matsuko alternated between pacing in front of Beth's desk and stopping to talk to her in brief spurts, followed by Beth picking up her phone, presumably calling Doctor Matsuko, then saying something to his wife, who started pacing again. It gave me some good angles of the face under the hat—round, middle-aged, greying hair, possibly Asian-American, but I couldn't be sure at that resolution.

According to the time code, she waited for close to an hour and a half.

Then, I recognized the white-coated man who entered the lobby from the secure side of the desk. Matsuko stood in front of the desk and looked like he was arguing—or trying not to argue—with the Mrs. for a few speeded-up minutes. "So, what'd they say?"

"Not my business," Beth said.

"Aw, come on."

Beth sighed. "The usual lonely wife stuff. 'Where have you been? What's her name? If it's not another woman, then show me what you've been working on because I'm paying for it and I have a right to—'"

At that point, Matsuko wrapped his arm around his wife's shoulders and took her into the clinic.

"They work things out?"

"Keep watching," Beth said. "She leaves about two hours later. Watch her body language."

Two hours later, according to the time code on the screen, someone did come out from the secure side, quickly walked across the lobby and out the door. Even at that speed, I could tell it was Mrs. Matsuko. Same big hat, same nice coat, but I couldn't see her face because she was hunched over, like she'd just been punched in the gut—or like someone just did something or told her something that felt that way. No wonder she wanted to get out so fast. I felt like crap for being so nosey.

As I watched her walk past the camera, I also saw something else.

"Wind this back," I asked Beth. "Just a little."

"Can't," she said. "Not while it's archiving. Why?"

"Forget it." There was no way I could tell her without sounding like a jerk.

I had seen Mrs. Matsuko's ankles.

———————

One of the things they taught us when I trained for the M.P.'s was how to read body language, anything that gave away the possible presence of a gun or a suicide vest or any other kind of concealed weapons. Sometimes, that meant paying attention to peoples' clothes for the way they hung on someone's body. Mrs. Matsuko—or, at least, the woman I saw leaving the clinic—wasn't packing a bomb, but she did do something unusual.

She grew about four inches taller—or her expensive coat shrank. That's how I was able to see the ankles of a hunched-over woman whose coat covered them when she walked in standing up straight.

Something was just too weird about it. I thought about it that night as I watched the late news. I wanted to tell Beth, but then I figured she'd tell the docs and they might put off my operation to deal with the possible security breach first. I wasn't an M.P. anymore. Security wasn't my job. Shutting up made sense if I wanted to stop seeing "her."

But "she" didn't want to go. As the TV reported the latest crap out of Washington, my uninvited guest decided to hover over the newscaster's face.

This time, instead of rubbing my eye or trying to look through "her," I squinted. I tried to see the details that I saw in Purcell's office.

Okay, I was trying to see the tits again, but I couldn't.

"She" just sat there, semi-obstructing my view, like a ghost.

I needed a walk.

———————

My laps around the clinic did more than supplement my exercise routine in the gym. This week, when my floater was being a real pain, they helped tire me out so I could just get away from it by sleeping.

This Friday night looked like it was going to be normal for the clinic. I didn't see any lights left on in the offices and labs, except for the ones where the clean-bots were working. Still, I had to slow down and peek through the door glass into Purcell's lab.

It was dark, but the screensaver on the computer monitor was up. Someone had been using it again, but they weren't here now.

In its light, I saw something resting on the keyboard.

It was a key card. I couldn't tell whose it was. Didn't think it was Purcell's, and I didn't think Matsuko was the kind of guy who hired dopes that left their I.D.s behind in a secure facility.

I mean, the wrong person could use it to get into a lab.

Or into a computer.

If it was Purcell's key card, I could get into his computer, find the video, and look at this thing in my eye. Maybe see what scared him so bad.

Maybe that wasn't such a hot idea.

Didn't matter. I didn't have his key card. I couldn't even get into the lab.

Behind me, I heard the quiet whirr of a clean-bot leaving a lab down the hall and heading my way.

Would I be breaking and entering if someone—or something—else did the entering and I just tagged along? They'd probably see me on the front desk monitors, but Beth was off duty, so she wouldn't get sucked into this. But how good was her relief? How long would it take them to see me in the lab? Would I have enough time to get out? Would I even be able to find the damn video?

When "she" bounced across my view again, I knew I had to go for it.

I stepped back to let the clean-bot get into position in front of the lab door. It was exactly as wide as the doorway, so I couldn't hide beside it to avoid the cameras. I had to crouch low, follow it in, and hope for the best.

Once I got in the lab and the door slid closed behind us, I moved out of the clean-bot's way, ran across the lab to the computer, and picked up the key card.

It *was* Purcell's. If I hadn't been in a rush, that would have set off all kinds of questions in my head, but I had to move fast. I tried to remember where he waved the key card in front of the computer and made the same kind of moves.

Jackpot. The screensaver vanished. I looked at the desktop, which had folders and shortcuts to programs, like any other PC. One of the folders was labeled VID. I opened it.

Inside was another folder with the number 24601 on it. I recognized that as the tracking number they gave me. No one here ever called me that, which made me feel human—until now, when I was raiding one of their labs.

I opened my folder. There was a file with the date of my exam on it. I double-clicked and a video screen popped up in the middle of the monitor.

There it was—my left eye, in living color. A caption at the bottom said something like "5X", so I guessed that was the magnification. Before Afghanistan, I might have been grossed out by it, all red and orange with some whitish ball in the center, all rolling around in fluid. But rolling around in a lot of red myself cured me of that. Plus, it only lasted a couple of seconds.

That's when "she" showed up.

That's when I saw what made Purcell jumped back and scream. I almost did, too.

That's when I saw—naked, in full color, with her throat cut—Mrs. Matsuko.

"She's looked better."

I spun around. Matsuko, who spoke, stood directly behind me while Bridgewater stayed by the open door of the lab. They didn't hold any weapons on me. I didn't even see any security guards with them.

Matsuko opened his mouth.

"Don't!" I said in my best M.P. voice, hoping to regain control of the situation.

"You deserve an explanation." Matsuko sounded sorry—almost.

"You killed your wife," I said. "You shrank her down and hid her body inside of me!"

"I did not kill my wife."

"I did," Bridgewater chimed in. She almost sounded proud.

"And while, yes, we did hide her in your bloodstream," Matsuko said, "we never met to cause you any distress. We never anticipated that the currents in your system would carry her from your arm to your eye... although, ironically, she used to complain to me that she always wanted to travel."

I was floored. "You... you mean, you two... you killed her so you could be..." There might have been weirder couples out there, but the idea of this almost-hot doctor hooking up with this little, old, bald doctor was tough to imagine.

"Please." Bridgewater rolled her eyes.

"It wasn't like that at all," Matsuko said.

"So, why'd you do it?"

"Money," Bridgewater said. "We needed it, and she was going to cut us off because Doctor Matsuko was spending so much time here. That's the advantage to operating a medical facility—easy access to scalpels. Mrs. Matsuko was so busy ranting at Edgar in his office, she never heard me come up behind her. And since our private offices aren't monitored, there are no recordings, no witnesses. To the rest of the world, she'll have gone missing at some point after she left the building."

"She didn't leave," I said. "I sneaked a look at that night's security video when Beth wasn't looking. Someone else left. Someone who couldn't bend over enough to hide the fact that she was taller than Mrs. Matsuko." I glanced at Bridgewater's ankles.

Bridgewater got it. She wasn't happy about it.

I turned to Matsuko. "So, your wife goes missing, you get her declared dead and inherit all her cash to keep the clinic going? That takes time, don't it? What are you gonna do for money until then?"

"Oh, I've taken some of the money she gave me and, um, redirected it to other investments," Matsuko said. "Those profits should keep us going for several years until the legalities are settled."

I held up Purcell's key card. "And I guess the doc won't need this anymore? I mean, he's seen your late wife. You couldn't count on him to unsee that, huh?"

"We convinced him he was overworked," Bridgewater said. "We sent him on a... a little sabbatical."

"Uh-huh." There was no sense in delaying the inevitable. "Then, there's me."

"We acted in your best interests, too," Matsuko said. "If my wife had withdrawn her funding, you'd be back on the street, without hope or purpose."

"I don't know what my purpose is, but it ain't to be your wife's damn cemetery!"

"You don't realize the triumph you represent," Matsuko said. "Belinda— that is, my wife—was the first human subject of our miniaturization process, our first success with organic matter."

"Then why didn't she, you know, grow and get eaten by antibodies, like the cameras?"

"The prep sequence," Bridgewater said flatly to Matsuko, as if she'd just figured it out. "We programmed the scanners to automatically differentiate between inorganic and organic matter, then to prep the target's cells accordingly before reduction."

"What the hell does that mean?" I asked.

"It means that people stay shrunk," Bridgewater said. "They don't grow after twenty-four hours. We planned to test the process on a volunteer once we developed a way to safely extract them from a subject."

"Before or after you figured out how to make them big again?" I asked. She didn't answer.

"Please don't worry," Matsuko said to me. "We can still remove your, um, floater the way we described earlier."

"By blowing your wife away with a laser?" I asked. "Why don't you just blow me away instead?"

"We need you," he said. "You're young and healthy—much healthier now than when you arrived, thanks to us. And we'll double your stipend. Five thousand each quarter. When we're done, you'll have enough to start a new life and you'll have helped—"

"Helped people, yeah, yeah." I'd heard that too many times.

For the first time, I noticed something in the doorway behind Bridgewater. It was across the corridor in the pale grey wall, and I'd never seen anything like it there before.

It was a door. It was open, too. There was this bright, white room that must have been inside the center of the clinic the whole time, like nougat in a candy bar. I was curious, but not curious enough to forget about saving my ass. "What if I don't want to to play ball? Doctor Bridgewater packing another scalpel in her lab coat?"

"Then we'll take you back to where we found you," Matsuko said. "With a suitable coat and some clothes, of course. It's chilly outside. But I'm afraid you'll forfeit any stipends you've earned to date since you didn't complete the regimen. It's in the release you signed."

"Forget about that. What if I talk?"

Bridgewater laughed. "To whom? What would you say? How would you prove it? You were delirious when I brought you down here, and we'll take you back with a blindfold to ensure you're never able to find this place again."

"While you guys find some other guinea pig to shoot up with cameras and dead wives and stuff."

"I promise you, the dead wife was a one-time thing," Matsuko said. "What is your decision, please?"

That was easy. "We're done. I'll grab a few sets of scrubs from my room and something to carry them in and be outta here."

I walked past Matsuko and Bridgewater and stopped at the doorway. I got a closer look at the other doorway in the pale grey wall and the room beyond. It was filled with huge pieces of equipment that I'd never seen and couldn't begin to describe, all being operated and monitored by techs in white clean suits.

The shrinker. It had to be, but I didn't take time to confirm it with the docs. I didn't want to give up any momentum. I stepped out into the corridor and, for the first time, saw two security guys in their trademark blue uniforms, standing six-foot-plus-tall each on either side of Purcell's lab door. They didn't move at me, which made me happy because—even though I'd been working out and still remembered my Army combat training—I didn't think I could take down either or both of them.

I nervously rubbed my bum arm, another reason I couldn't fight them. They had four good arms between them. I had one.

The guards fell in behind me. Matsuko and Bridgewater followed them. I maintained an even stride as we walked past the occasional clean-bot on the way to my room. Along the way, I realized something…

Mrs. Matsuko was still floating around in my eye.

I smiled.

The first thing I would do when I got out of here was get an eye exam.

I wondered what an outside doc would think when they saw a little dead woman floating around in there. What would happen when I identified her as Mrs. Matsuko? What would happen when the authorities tore apart the city looking for her husband's secret lab, following whatever leads I could give them?

I really, finally was going to help someone—I was going to help Mrs. Matsuko find justice, all because the docs forgot she was still in there.

Or maybe they didn't, because why else would a security mook bring the back of his arm down on the back of my head like a sledgehammer?

Hit from behind. Shouldn't be bleeding in my mouth. And not this much, not mixed with water.

But this isn't water, it's too thick ...

Thicker than water ...

That's it, ain't it?

I'm not tasting *my* blood ... this blood's all around me.

That's why that door to the white room was open.

Like those cameras. Like Mrs. Matsuko, who's still floating around in me. They sprayed some special capsule around me, shot me into somebody. The capsule dissolved and now...

Goddamn it. *They shrank me.*

Not even enough time to be scared, or pissed, or even to wonder whose body this is.

Doesn't matter.

Last thing I'm gonna remember? The transport blowing up... when I thought nothing could be worse than tasting someone else's blood.

Until I drowned in it...

IT JUST HAPPENED
By Peter Ong

Aboard the government cruiser, *Abigail Lenten*, Special Agent Lisa Weath of the Federal Space Investigative Unit, FSIU (or F-Sue), wanted answers and fast. She sighed inwardly. *All those past generations dreaming about how the future will look with gigantic flying spaceships. Well, here's news for you. Those spaceships can sometimes—okay, rarely—explode! A flash of light and your whole world flies apart.* In general, modern vessels are built to rigorous safety standards and rarely encounter catastrophic failure. In the case of the *Vesty*, however, her aft engines had simply exploded, causing multiple hull breaches as the rupture rippled across half the length of her hull. Those who were lucky had made it to the escape pods—pods that search and rescue teams now tried to track down.

In the *Abigail's* command room, the tall, slender agent pushed aside a lock of her blonde bob and examined the schematic of the *Vesty* on the table's touchscreen surface. She studied the layout of the dark gray oblong tube with bumps and bulges covering her hull and five enormous cylindrical engines, three on top and two below. A fine ship at seventeen years old, the *Vesty* had served with distinction, often traveling the Janper Belt between planets Falry and Umungen.

Reportedly, 871 out of 1,145 passengers had perished. The rest had hopefully jettisoned themselves via the escape pods, somewhere out into deep space. Crews from several planets had been dispatched to search for survivors. The *Abigail* was currently en route to the coordinates of the explosion, where Agent Weath would meet with James Westly, recovery tug pilot, to explore the debris field. In her mind, she pictured the field as a swirling mess of frozen bodies and jagged metal pieces. Lisa and James, along with scores of other teammates, would have to sort through it all to determine the cause. It was not a duty that Lisa looked forward to.

At thirty-four, Agent Weath already had an outstanding success record of solving challenging cases, earning her enormous respect at the bureau. She had worked aboard the *Abigail Lenten* for the past eight of her ten years in FSIU and currently juggled two other criminal cases, one involving interstellar smuggling and the other, money laundering. Nonetheless, a spaceship accident usually gets placed at the top of the priority list.

Recovery tug *Benemail*

James Westly steered his recovery tug, *Benemail*, through the enormous debris field of large jagged metal chunks and smaller flotsam. The tug's shields were at maximum to prevent potentially fatal damage to her hull.

James said "man" more than two dozen times during their expedition, as he usually did after such a terrible spaceship accident among the stars— the magnitude… the devastation… the mess… the immense cleanup… the enormous cost in terms of lives and property. "Man… just… *man*. No other way to describe it. *Man*," he muttered to no one in particular, and Lisa just let him vent to the curved cockpit window.

At least it's better than a string of profanities. She remained silent and let James do the talking, but allowed herself a smirk each time he repeated the word "man." She couldn't disagree, recognizing that it was mankind's ambition to travel among the stars, but it was probably a man's error that caused this accident. Now, it was a woman's job to determine what had caused it, and a woman's job to clean it up.

Ripped to shreds, the *Vesty* lay strewn like abstractly shaped puzzle pieces. Fifty-three shuttles scurried among the debris, marking it, inspecting it, collecting it, and studying it. Worst of all, fourteen escape pods full of survivors still drifted out there. Their radios worked, but their locator beacons didn't. No one really knew the cause. From the escape pods' radio chatter, the *Abigail Lenten's* crew surmised something fishy going on. The "survivors" didn't talk like passengers—no pleas for help, no requests for medical assistance, no guidance in navigation, no last goodbyes to family. Something wasn't right.

Searching for the escape pods wasn't James's job. James and Lisa jetted around trying to find the cause of the accident and recover it, no matter how small a debris fragment, wire, or chip. Terrorism? Sabotage? Faulty engineering? Asteroid collision? Hacker? Poor maintenance? Cheap contaminated fuel? Nothing was left out. These questions needed answers.

Well, at least F-Sue knew where the accident occurred. That precise fact saved precious time.

But where to start looking for the cause? Preliminary reports from Warpspace Tracker software monitoring *Vesty's* telemetry indicated that the explosion happened in the upper engines, but the pilots were still drifting in one of the unrecovered escape pods. Repeated hails to the escape pods requesting the locations of the pilots went unanswered. That didn't make sense, as if the pilots themselves were trying to hide something. For a passenger liner, the *Vesty's* survivors sure didn't talk like they wanted to be rescued.

"Where are the bodies?" asked Lisa, observing the lack of frozen corpses in the debris field.

"Hmmm, good question." James ran a scan and after a few seconds, the results came back... zero! "What the hell?"

"No bodies? None?" Lisa contemplated. *Did the 871 victims just vaporize without a trace?* Every space accident in history had some casualties floating around.

"Wait, what's this? I got a funny reading," said James.

"What is it?"

"Uh, was the *Vesty* carrying arms?"

"What? No."

"That's what it says here."

"Where?"

James pointed to the touch screen in the center of his console. "Over at coordinates 47.6.1. A whole *bunch* of weapons."

"What *kind* of weapons?"

"Uh… hovertanks?"

"Hovertanks?"

"Yeah, well, what's left of them. Heading over there now."

"Wait… then is this really the *Vesty?*" Lisa stared out the cockpit window. The jagged debris offered no clue as to the ship's identity.

"Coming into view…" James slowed the *Benemail.*

And sure enough, the cracked and ruined turrets and hulls of about fifty tan M-781A3 hovertanks floated and bumped each other in the distance. Lisa and James gaped at the costly debacle. No passenger ship could transport battletanks due to the lack of cargo space. Either this wasn't the *Vesty,* or the *Vesty* had been modified to carry tanks by stripping out the passenger cabins and essentially making vast open decks with tiedowns. That would explain the lack of floating corpses. This wasn't a passenger liner accident—this was an exploded transport ship.

Lisa radioed the other tugs and they, too, found remnant evidence of armaments—laser rifles, missiles, and rockets still in their storage containers, now battered and cracked open to allow for scans. Lisa felt her soul energize with mystery and intrigue.

She radioed the *Abigail*. "What's the status on the location of the escape pods?"

"Nothing yet, ma'am."

"Inform me when you find one."

Planet Orhon

"Tracker sweeping. Negative contacts."

"Proceed forward."

Sergeant Honsu Radison led his twelve-member search and rescue team amongst planet Orhon's dense blue-green foliage. Guns at the ready, the search team didn't know what creatures lurked in the forest. Sergeant Radison knew four escape pods had crashed in the general vicinity. The dense foliage blocked all radio contact with the survivors.

Two eight-wheeled robots followed them, both carrying medical supplies and environmental stretchers.

Time ticked down to find the survivors, who reported—nothing. Did they have enough food, water, and medical supplies? Humans can't breathe on Orhon. They need a mask and spacesuit. They did have oxygen in their escape pods, enough to last for three months. Nonetheless, no one wanted to be in an escape pod for three months. The toilet starts to back up, hygiene deteriorates, and who knows how long the environmental systems will last.

Created for such large search and rescue situations, Radison's squad knew that time played a key role in covering great distances across space just to get on site. Governments and corporations need to understand that it takes time to get boots on the ground to search for survivors. It takes time to plan and coordinate a search and to find the crash site and get to it. It takes time to round up survivors and evacuate them for medical attention. It takes time to get answers. "Golden Hours" of survival didn't exist in interstellar travel. The term "Golden Days" seemed more appropriate, or even "Golden Weeks" just for the time involved in getting rescue crews to the survivors. That's why star-traveling passengers should take survival courses to ensure that they had a fighting chance in case they were forced to evacuate a starship. Naturally, not everyone took these courses.

"Tracker sweeping. Negative contacts."

Radison keyed his comms for a private two-way conversation. "Riza? You see anything?"

"Negative," reported the circling dropship pilot. "The forest's so dense here that it's blocking sensors."

"No fire, no smoke, nothing?" asked Radison.

"Nothing. I'm telling you, it's like the escape pods buried themselves in the dirt. No fires, no smoke, no heat. They're just not here."

"Damn," muttered Radison. "Then where are they? Just keep looking."

"Standby. Incoming call," said Riza. "The *Abigail* said that they found fifty hovertanks and other arms in the debris field. The *Vesty* wasn't a passenger ship."

"It's a military transport ship?" asked Radison.

"Stand by," said Riza as she asked the *Abigail*. "Unknown, but we're not looking for passengers."

Damn, thought Radison again. "Then they might be armed. Request backup squads." He switched channels and informed his team. They didn't possess the weaponry to combat a large group. They slowed their pace and their alertness perked up, unsure whether the *Vesty's* survivors would be friend or foe.

Earth, 2:30 P.M. Eastern Standard Time (EST)

A man on the run, GinHaou Lumging, Chief Executive Officer of Far Space Travels, scanned the horizon, half expecting to see the men chasing after him to appear.

Far Space Travels was a semi-front, a sham to cover up human trafficking and the smuggling of weapons, narcotics, gems, and other illicit goods into outer space. GinHaou got away with a lot of illegal activity and profited immensely. He only did illegal activity for off-planet shipments; he kept travel between Earth's continents legitimate. He didn't know why the government hadn't caught on to his false-front passenger liner scheme sooner, and he even thought that some governments played along, adding weapons to his "passenger ships" to transport to faraway planets as classified Black Programs. However, his company's intelligence services indicated that the governments *did not* know—until now.

His spaceships were well-maintained and had proper documentation. His crews secured and hid the weapons well, avoiding detection. He didn't know what had happened to the *Vesty*, but whatever happened shouldn't have. He even ordered lighted, curtained cabin windows around the perimeter to give the appearance of a passenger ship. Far Space Travels had made countless smuggling runs without any government interference, but this accident had put him on their radar. He was now a Big Boss Criminal.

"Ready to go, sir?" asked the private security contractor hired to hide and protect him. Huge sums of money changed minds, made loyalties, did incredible things. These security contractors didn't question the illegality of hiding perhaps the most wanted man in the quadrant; they just worked for the considerable salary, which GinHaou often paid in cash when such dicey situations occurred.

The hum of the hovering helicopter whined nearby, ready to take off and begin the game of chase. All around the world, the top management of Far Space Travels' illegal half began hopping around the planet aboard their own personal crafts in an effort to evade the law. Far Space Travels' outer-space smuggling half would operate no more. With hope and luck, these VIPs would lay low and then rise again under different aliases and disguises to start another new smuggling company elsewhere, possibly on another planet. Far Space Travels held vast sums of cash; GinHaou could wait out his pursuers.

He narrowed his eyes as he looked to the horizon and saw no sign of incoming law enforcement. Not that he expected to. He usually stayed several steps ahead of them. GinHaou twisted his lips into a sly smirk. "Let's go." *They'll never find me. They haven't so far.*

Recovery tug *Benemail*

"Far Space Travels..." Lisa let the words hang in the air in the tug's cockpit. She and James stared straight at the ruined turret and hull of another M-781A3 hovertank. She waited for the government response to radio in. Was this transportation of hovertanks legal or illegal? FST sounds innocent enough; perhaps a government used them for Special Operations or some off-the-books, top-secret program.

Lisa knew that her government had dispatched teams to hunt down Far Space Travels' management. FST showed up on the radar as a huge blip now, but her government couldn't find their VIPs in charge of smuggling—a blip that blinked large and then disappeared off the scope. *Runners... just proves that they have something to hide.* All over the world, governments raided FST's travel agencies and reports came in that FST did legally transport passengers, on Earth, as Far Space Earth Travels. As the story unfolded, governments reported that the company's illicit transport activity happened in space, and that the earthbound portion of FST denied knowing that the planetary portion engaged in illegal smuggling. Lisa found that somewhat hard to believe, but would let other agents sort it out. The world's governments were learning just how extensive Far Space Travels' illegal cosmic dealings truly were. They went well beyond smuggling hovertanks, to include gemstones and rare Earth metals, illegal wildlife parts, counterfeit currency, human trafficking, weapons, stolen vehicles, toxic chemicals and radioactive waste, patented technology, and stolen nuclear materials. You name it and FST's outer-space operations probably transported it out of the solar system.

And what will happen when we catch them? Lisa pondered. Surely a lengthy legal battle with FST lawyering up; FSIU would need to perform meticulous work to determine the exact cause of the accident and gather the illegal items as evidence. That could take months or years. By then, FST might not exist anymore. That's why their executives ran, or at least those from the illegal branch of the company's operations. FST Earth Travels, the legit side, could still do business while dumping its criminal outer space operations.

"What I want to know," said Lisa, "is whether criminal FST is working for some other government organization."

"Hey," quipped James. "That's your job. I only fly this tug."

The monitor alarm rapidly beeped. "Transmission coming in." Lisa touched the screen. "The hovertanks are *illegal*. Or at least my government didn't ship them."

"Then who did?" James lifted his head from the monitor and gazed back at another ruined hovertank. "And we still have to figure out what caused the explosion."

Earth, 3 P.M. Eastern Standard Time (EST)

"Got something!" yelled the S.W.A.T. officer at the back of the hoverplane.

To Kosh Growpen, nothing felt as exhilarating as the tactical squad's hoverplane zooming in on a contact.

"Drone footage coming in!" The S.W.A.T. members all saw it on their visors. "Looks like the CFO!"

"Not the Big Fish, but big enough!" shouted Sergeant Wendek Germanin, the team leader.

"Imposter?" asked Kosh. "The CFO has like *five* body doubles."

"Well, we're going to *bag* this one!" shouted Germanin. "Gear up, get ready in ten!"

AN-PL-64 assault rifles and DR-99 sniper rifles clicked into action. The S.W.A.T. members appeared menacing in their heavy, black armor and visor helmets. They felt the hoverplane flare, heard its thrust reversing, and through the open door, saw the rope lines drop.

"Go! Go! Go!" yelled Germanin as his team grabbed the ropes and rappelled down… to the sound of sporadic incoming gunfire.

"Taking fire! Taking fire!" shouted Susie, a seasoned team member, on her way down.

"Return fire!" ordered Germanin.

The team hit the ground, each member dropping to one knee and firing with pinpoint accuracy. Standing and running bodies fell to the comment, "Tango down." The team then swept 360 degrees for more targets and found none. Slowly, they rose in unison, guns aimed. Half watched the perimeter while the other half checked the bodies.

"Doubles… imposters!" spat Kosh. "This isn't the CFO."

"You got that?" asked Germanin to headquarters.

"Copy," replied the dispatcher at headquarters. "Be advised that an FST exec just got spotted by Spy-Sat Two."

"Can you confirm?"

"Contact apparently sent a burst transmission, uncoded," replied headquarters.

Germanin hoped for a true FST target this time. "Can you extrapolate?"

"Could be another ruse," said Susie.

"I'll take my chances," remarked Germanin. *Any bite is better than none.* "Are we in a position to intercept?"

"Affirmative," replied headquarters. "Canada is sending some CF-55s too, but they'll take thirty minutes to get there. Your team will make first contact."

"Copy that, HQ. We're moving to intercept." Germanin switched channels to his team. "All right, listen up! HQ has a new FST target for us nearby and we're going to intercept. All aboard and let's get those FST bastards, real or not!"

At Earth headquarters, the dispatcher informed Lisa via hyperspace channels. The time delay was miniscule. "Ma'am, looks like we have Germanin's S.W.A.T. team nearby for another intercept. They have a drone already in the air. I'll inform them to send the drone ahead."

"Do that and tell Germanin to get there ASAP," snapped Lisa. "I'm returning to the *Abigail* to supervise."

James turned the tug around and headed back towards the mothership.

Planet Orhon

Sergeant Radison and his twelve-member team advanced with caution, guns raised. Riza circled overhead, looking for any telltale sign of the *Vesty*'s survivors. Considering their illegal activities, any survivor would be treated like a foe.

An orange streak lanced out to Radison's left and missed.

"Incoming fire!" He dove into the lush blue-green foliage. In front of him, he counted seven orange flashes and the blue leaves around him began to shred from the salvo. "Return fire! Return fire!"

Shrieks of laser fire from his team seared the air on their way to their targets. The sergeant keyed his microphone to broadcast. "Surrender at once and you will not be harmed!" Radison's broadcast did nothing to stop the incoming barrage.

"Keep your heads down!" yelled Riza. "I'm firing!"

Long beams of orange light streaked down from the sky and obliterated the turquoise landscape one hundred meters ahead of Radison's team. Brown dirt and shredded plants erupted into the air among billowing smoke. Whoever fired from that spot was likely red mist and chunks by now.

"Damn!" muttered Radison at the effective close air support. "Geez, Riza, did you leave anything for us?" The explosions ceased and the ground stopped trembling as Radison and his team observed the smoldering results of the air assault.

"Sensors no longer detect any threats," said Riza, "but proceed with caution."

"Roger that." Radison and his team rose and aimed down their sights as they advanced the one hundred meters.

Earth, 3:30 P.M. Eastern Standard Time (EST)

One of the youngest and most respected S.W.A.T. leaders, Sergeant Laura Blackwell stood tall in her dropship's cargo bay, awesomely dressed in bluish-purple formfitting body armor that showed off her athletic, hourglass figure. Beautiful, strong, smart, and accomplished, she lived up to her reputation as one awesome black female badass. Laura had climbed the ranks to command her own twelve-member special S.W.A.T. team in pursuit of the most wanted felons on Earth. She liked to tell her friends, "Why join the infantry and pull all that grunt work? If you're female, fit, and want to wear body armor and carry a gun, work for S.W.A.T., or the search and rescue teams. They're way better than hauling ammo and digging foxholes."

She carried one of the longest, most powerful assault rifles around, not because it was mandatory, but because it added to her formidable image: the mighty nine-pound Falcon 271C, capable of holding forty 7.62mm rounds. When she posed for pictures with it, she looked as if she was hefting a T-Rex hunting rifle. Yet she handled it with ease.

So far, they'd been chasing ghosts. No one knew where FST's outer space executives jetted off to.

"Sergeant, we have a ship on stealth drive, one hundred feet down and approaching fast," said the copilot. "They aren't answering our hails."

Blackwell made her way into the cockpit. "Move to intercept."

"Intercept plotted," replied the copilot.

Blackwell turned to her squad. "Gear up!" No one moved, as her team already sat prepared, cradling their weapons between their legs.

"They're activating jamming."

"It's them," said Blackwell. "We just might have someone. Get me an ID." She keyed her communications link. "Sergeant Blackwell to HQ. We have a UFO on scope with active jammers. Possible FST target. Moving to intercept."

"Copy, Sergeant Blackwell," replied Agent Lisa Weath aboard the *Abigail* where she had assumed command of the operation. "Can you get me a visual?"

"Doing so now," replied the pilot. "Visual acquired."

"That's an FST hoverhelo!" yelped Lisa. "Permission granted to take it down."

"Jamming's increasing," said the copilot. "Activating countermeasures to compensate."

"Unidentified hoverhelo at coordinates two-seven-nine-five-mike-echo, this is the U.S. S.W.A.T. dropship, *Raptor*. We have permission to board and search you. Pull alongside and be escorted to the nearest landing pad."

"They're releasing countermeasures!" yelled the copilot. Blackwell's squad exchanged some optimistic comments—it has to be an FST executive inside.

"Jam them. Bring them down," commanded Blackwell. "They're not getting away this time."

"Jamming their engines," said the copilot, pushing buttons.

"Sergeant Blackwell," said Agent Lisa. "You're it. The nearest reinforcements are six hours away. Take them down and be careful."

"They're losing engine power," said the copilot. "Going down!"

He paused as he observed the video. "They're releasing more countermeasures... smoke... flares... chaff... they're down!"

Blackwell stepped into the cargo bay to retrieve her helmet. "It's game time."

Aboard the *Abigail*, Lisa Weath and her agents exulted at the prospect of two FST executives within their grasp. Sergeants Germanin and Blackwell's dropships each forced an unidentified hoverhelo to land. The agents were highly confident that the hoverhelos held FST executives, just based on the amount of countermeasures and jamming each craft had deployed. Most FST evacuation hoverhelos flew unescorted in stealth mode to avoid radar detection.

Sergeant Germanin and his team should see action before Blackwell's. Agent Weath already had a direct patch to Germanin and observed the video from his dropship's orbiting drone. The rules were quite simple—apprehend the Far Space Travels' executives and defend your team against any resistance.

Sergeant Germanin gave credit to the FST pilot who crashed his jammed hoverhelo in a dense forest to make approaching it complicated. The sergeant chose not to rappel directly over the crash to avoid any incoming fire. Instead, he and his squad stalked their way to the hoverhelo. To make matters more difficult, two unidentified people had bailed out of the hoverhelo on the way down, their orange parachutes opening against a dark green forest. This required Germanin to split his squad into three teams of four, meaning fewer people to press the assault on the crash site.

He flicked his fingers forward and his three teammates advanced. The hoverhelo's fires glowed a brilliant orange, encasing the dark gray ship. The sergeant didn't know if anyone would still be alive in the conflagration, but he knew FST people possessed some hardcore survival skills.

"Ready for flash-bangs?" asked Germanin. "On three... one, two, three, fire!"

Four rounds of stun grenades arced towards the disabled hoverhelo and exploded in spectacular yellow sparks and white smoke.

"Move in!" shouted Germanin in his helmet. A chatter of sharp sounds soon erupted.

"Taking fire," yelled Roger. "Returning fire!"

"Tango down!" shouted Wendy who pivoted to another orange flash. "Tango down!"

"Tango down!" repeated the sergeant as he watched a private security aide fall backwards, his gun shooting upwards in an arc.

"Clear!" Roger approached the smashed cockpit.

Wendy rounded the tail of the flaming hoverhelo while Judy cleared the treeline. "Clear!" they called out in unison.

"All clear!" confirmed Germanin. He scanned around and saw the three private security specialists lying motionless on the forest floor. No signs of the executive, which means he or she must have bailed before the crash. Capture of any FST executive at large now rested with Germanin's two other four-member squads somewhere back in the forest.

―――――――

Corporal Susie Wong took her time to advance, hiding herself behind large tree trunks. Her Wexcan body armor could stop small bullets and knives, but Far Space Travels' hired security specialists often carried ammo capable of penetrating body armor.

Sergeant Germanin informed her that the crash site had yielded no one of importance, which meant that whoever had bailed could be a top-level FST executive. Corporal Leonard led the second squad searching for the other bailer… no luck so far. The good news? It would be four S.W.A.T. teams against one since the pilots saw only two parachutes. However, the dropship's software could not identify the bailers. They could be hired guns, FST executives, or decoys.

"Give yourself up!" shouted Susie on her helmet's speakerphone. "We have you outnumbered and outgunned. Save yourself from getting shot!" Sometimes a little intimidation worked wonders. A shot rang out and her helmet's visor used a flashing red circle to zoom in on the source somewhere to the right, among the tree trunks.

"Surrender or you will be shot!" barked Susie. "Drop the gun and approach me with your hands up."

"Flash-bang out!" barked Susie's teammate, Hiron, before firing a grenade into the trees. A series of yellow sparks and puffs of smoke billowed from the dense thicket. "Advancing."

"Advancing!" shouted Millard.

Paul leveled his assault rifle at the smoke. "Covering!"

Susie shouted the same as she aimed her rifle from behind her tree. "I see him! I see him! Hands up, don't move! Don't you move!"

"I got his gun!" yelled Millard. "It's him. Positive ID. We got the CIO."

The FST outer space Chief Intelligence Officer? Susie couldn't believe her good luck. *Not an imposter? No bodyguards? Is this for real?*

She walked towards the scene and observed Hiron handcuffing the CIO, face flat in the dirt.

"He was armed with this." Millard presented a Bulkin 10mm pistol, grip first, to the Corporal. The 10mm bullets wouldn't penetrate the squad's Wexcan body armor. Still, most FST executives were suspected to be unarmed.

"Stand him up. Turn him around." Corporal Wong wanted to confirm the identification of their fugitive. He stood before her with a disgusted scowl of squinted eyes and pouted lips amid a dirt-smeared face.

"What's your name?" asked Susie.

"You know who I am! Can't your helmet recognize me?" Indeed, Susie's helmet visor confirmed a 98% positive facial recognition match to Far Space Travels' Chief Intelligence Officer, Joon Hiksan Yu.

Paul opened a wallet confiscated during his search of the CIO. "It's him." He held up a family picture of Yu with his bonny brunette wife and two young kids, boy and girl, in the sunny park, smiling during happier times.

Finally… Suzie nodded. "You're under arrest on charges of smuggling illegal weapons, firing on government law enforcement, and obstruction of justice." Susie went on to read Mr. Yu his rights before switching to the headquarters channel on her headset. "Chase over, Agent Weath. FST's CIO arrested with positive identification."

Lisa Weath and her agents erupted in cheers. Never in a million years did they think they would nab a real FST executive. More good news came in two minutes later, as the other fugitive turned out to be FST's Public Relations director, who surrendered on the spot in the forest because it was difficult for her to run in heels, a fur coat, and skirt suit after freeing herself from her parachute. Unarmed, she offered no resistance to Corporal Leonard's small squad. In one hoverhelo, *two* FST executives out of seven were apprehended in a matter of minutes by Sergeant Germanin's squad. His squad also managed to capture a wounded pilot, who might provide a treasure trove of information as to the secret FST hideaway locations and stealth capabilities of the hoverhelos. News spread quickly around the globe, capturing the attention of the world's governments. In a matter of minutes, they joined the hunt for the remaining FST executives, deploying additional spy satellites and resources.

Planet Orhon

Robots? We obliterated robots? Sergeant Radison cautiously stepped over the smoldering shards of twisted metal and wire. A robot's smoking severed arm here, a twisted leg there, bits and pieces of metal everywhere. The team did manage to salvage some of the robots' M-92A3 laser rifles, shattered into quarters and halves.

Riza's effective close air support didn't kill any humans, only drones. This rescue mission—a farce! Suspicion, bewilderment, and anger converged on Radison's team simultaneously. They'd risked their lives against a bunch of programmed robots. Any trace evidence of an FST motive was likely destroyed by Riza's fire support.

"So you think the *Vesty's* crew was comprised of robots?" asked Lisa from the *Abigail Lenten* over Sergeant Radison's helmet link.

"Not really," replied Radison. "These don't appear to be your normal run-of-the-mill crew-serving robots. These look more like battle drones, active during the flight and not stored away in some shipping container. I'm thinking these robots decided to save themselves like hired shipboard guards or independent contractors. It's highly unusual for robots to use escape pods unless they're of an extremely sophisticated and high-valued design. In other words, we obliterated hundreds of millions of dollars of technology here." Radison paused and surveyed the smoldering dirt. Perhaps the broken metal limbs and sheared guns could provide some trace back to the source. "We'll gather the remnants and see if we can find a responsible party."

"Copy that," replied Lisa. *Using battle robots to guard fifty M-781A3 hovertanks would make sense. When the Vesty's engines blew, they made a dash for the escape pods to save themselves. So, the plot thickens…* Lisa sent a communication to all search parties to beware of armed and hostile battle robots in the escape pods.

Earth, 4 P.M. Central Standard Time (CST)

Aboard his zooming stealth hoverhelo, GinHaou Lumging, Chief Executive Officer of Far Space Travels, stared at his private security aide as he absorbed the bad news of the apprehension of two of his outer-space branch executives. He knew his CIO would not talk, but his Public Relations director was a softie. Prod her and she might squeal. Worst of all, rumors indicated that U.S. Global S.W.A.T. had also captured one of the stealth pilots. GinHaou knew that the hired private security specialists would go down fighting. They were hardcore… but the hoverhelo pilots? He had no illusions that they would fight to the last man to protect their clients, even though they were supposed to be armed with a knife and pistol.

"Are we secure?" GinHaou asked his security specialist.

"Pretty sure," the specialist replied, but he offered the butt of a handgun to mask his discomfort.

GinHaou glared at the weapon. He didn't think it would come down to him having to arm himself. U.S. Global S.W.A.T. maintained a reputation of being elite, but that seemed unproven until recently. FST's pursuers were just names on a screen, little more than bumbling, goose-chasing fools that couldn't pinpoint a fleeing FST stealth hoverhelo even if it zoomed past their faces. Were the arrests of the CIO and PR Director blind luck or skillful hunting? He gingerly reached for the handgun, took it, and tucked it into his waistband. Then he asked for something he felt more accustomed to—his expensive Samurai katana, a weapon he trained with repeatedly. The private security aide brought the katana and GinHaou rested it against his lap.

The hoverhelo banked sharply to the left and the CEO heard the *boom-boom-boom* of countermeasures being fired.

"What's happening?" snapped GinHaou.

"We're being jammed!" shouted the pilot. "I have a visual. It's a S.W.A.T. dropship."

"*What?*" barked the security aide and GinHaou in unison. How was it possible that, with all the stealth and electronic masking—technology years ahead of anything the governments had—a S.W.A.T. dropship just happened to pick them up on sensors? Was it a new radar capability, a new sensor, or that blind luck working against FST's executives?

"Lose them," commanded GinHaou, "and get us out of here!"

"Trying to, sir," said the copilot, "but they're on us tight."

"Flank speed," ordered the pilot. "Outrun them!"

"They're jamming our engines." The copilot punched some buttons, to no avail. "We're losing power. We're going down!"

"Releasing countermeasures!" The pilot punched an orange button and the thunderous eruption of flares and chaff ejecting from the rear slightly shook the hoverhelo.

Far Space Travels sure makes beautiful hoverhelos, thought Sergeant Laura Blackwell as she stood behind her pilots' chairs. The FST hoverhelos locked their rotating rotor blades so that at high speed, they flew more like jets, the rotors acting as fixed wings.

"This one seems fancier," commented the copilot. "Could be someone very important inside."

"Keep the laser-lock on. I don't want to lose them," ordered Blackwell.

"Their jamming's pretty intense. We're compensating with our new software countermeasures."

"Bring it down gently," said Blackwell. "I want whoever's inside alive."

"Jamming engines," said the copilot. "They're losing power."

"They're releasing a lot of countermeasures." The pilot banked the S.W.A.T. dropship smartly around smoke clouds, flares, and blossoms of silvery chaff.

"They have us!" screeched the private security aide. "Do you want to bail?"

"Here? Now?" snapped GinHaou. *Is he insane? The CEO of Far Space Travels jumping out of a jammed hoverhelo?* "No!"

"Brace for impact!" the pilot warned. "Buckle up. We're going down!"

The security aide nodded to his four teammates. "Arm up." As they readied their weapons, the aide leaned towards the CEO. "We'll defend you, sir. Just tell us where you want to go." GinHaou nodded, seeing the treetops appear in the curved cockpit glass.

"Brace for impact!" the pilot repeated, shaking his stick to no avail. "We're going down hard."

The sound of wood splintering, followed by booms and scraping sounds, resonated for a few seconds before a huge thud threw anything unsecured into the air. Guns separated from hands and loose gear scattered. GinHaou saw the pilots disappear in a mess of limbs, leaves, and dirt. He didn't feel any remorse; they served their purpose. Time to get off this wreck and make a break for it into the woods.

Four of the five private security specialists were mobile. One of them moaned in the dropship with two broken legs, as he'd had no seat available to buckle in. GinHaou unfastened his seatbelt, grabbed the wounded guard's assault rifle, wished him well, and exited the craft.

"Into the trees," rasped the lead security aide. "Follow me."

"Hover right here! Right here!" ordered Sergeant Blackwell. "Ropes out now!"

The dropship flared and ropes descended, followed by twelve S.W.A.T. officers.

"Go! Go! Go! Get them!" commanded Blackwell. Flash-bang grenades arced into the trees, where they exploded with billowing puffs of white smoke and series of sparkling yellow flashes.

"Contact!"

"Taking fire!" The *brap-brap* of shots sounded from ahead.

"Return fire! Return fire!" shouted Blackwell as her team pressed the assault.

"Tango down!"

"More flash-bangs out!" shouted the corporal, and seven grenades arced into the air, landing generally in the same spot.

Blackwell waved her team forward. "Press the assault! Move in!" Four flashes erupted from the trees and twelve S.W.A.T. guns zeroed in on them.

"Tango down!"

"Tango down!"

Blackwell came face-to-face with a lone security guard and… *is that the CEO?* Both appeared alert and menacing, despite their repeated exposure to the grenades. Blackwell acted quickly and shot the bodyguard's and GinHaou's assault rifles to pieces. The stunned bodyguard merely stood there, staring at his shattered weapon, before Blackwell knocked him on the head with the butt of her assault rifle. He went down cold.

GinHaou roared, and Blackwell saw something thin and shiny. Her training took over and she raised her rifle in a defensive move. The katana clanged against blackened stamped steel.

"Har!" yelled GinHaou, swinging down.

Blackwell parried, batting the blade away to her left. She backed away and stood in a classic defensive stance. GinHaou, now alone, paused.

"Who are you?" asked the CEO. Her slim, curvy armor revealed a female, but the CEO probably wanted to know how old or young his possible captor was. "Remove your helmet and let me see you!"

Normally, Blackwell didn't obey orders from criminals. However, with twelve against one, she relented and removed her armored helmet and tossed it to a team member. She flashed a confident smile at GinHaou and her eyes shone with pride. "Ready to surrender, Mr. CEO?"

"Screw you!" snapped GinHaou, angling his katana before him. Blackwell eyed the butt of a handgun protruding from the Asian man's waist.

With a grin, she waved an arm toward her team before setting the safety on her rifle. "I got this. Your move, Mr. CEO... or you could be smart and surrender."

GinHaou Lumging looked around. Twelve imposing S.W.A.T. soldiers stood in a rough semicircle backing their sergeant. Most had their rifles trained on him, although a few had their guns pointed down. His gaze settled on Blackwell.

"I have an arrest to make," she said casually. "You decide how you want me to do it. I suggest you drop your weapons and surrender peacefully. You have nowhere to run. You know this won't end in your favor."

GinHaou's face twisted in disgust. If he had his private security in full force, this S.W.A.T. team wouldn't be talking on their terms.

The CEO lunged and Blackwell met his blade with her rifle. GinHaou swung again and Blackwell batted the blade to one side. The CEO roared and swung repeatedly. The sergeant countered expertly until she saw an opening, and the butt of her rifle smacked the CEO flat in the face, knocking him down, but not out. She swung her rifle again and it cracked at his fist, sending the katana flying out of reach in the dirt.

"Arrest him."

Four S.W.A.T. officers approached the beaten CEO as Blackwell read him his rights. She then contacted Agent Weath. "We've waited a long time to say this. Mission accomplished, we have Far Space Travels' top man, GinHaou Lumging. Four FST security agents down, zero casualties to Blue Force."

Cheers erupted aboard the *Abigail Lenten*. Lisa Weath found herself embraced by several of her fellow agents as tears welled up in their eyes.

One of the rookies let out a deep breath. "Wow, we actually got them."

"Yes, we did." Agent Weath grinned. "It just happened. Who knew that my two other criminal cases were connected to the *Vesty?*"

TAKE A CUE FROM THE CANINE
By Phil Giunta

Huddled inside the cramped compartment of the roll top desk, Joel flinched as the beagle scratched and pawed at the antique wood slats. "Rusty, no." He ran a soothing hand over the dog's belly. "It's gonna be okay. We just need to be quiet for a little longer."

Joel knew his best friend was not only scared, but probably still in pain. Resting his head against the hard surface, Joel tried to ignore his own set of freshly inflicted bruises.

A liquid lunch had cost Uncle Larry yet another job, sparking his worst whiskey-fueled rampage in months. Joel's attempts to calm him had been rewarded with the usual beating, but the confrontation had turned life-threatening after Larry kicked Rusty across the living room and pulled out a sawed-off shotgun from beneath the couch. When he'd stood up too quickly and toppled backward—blasting a hole in the ceiling—Joel snatched up Rusty and fled across the yard to the garage.

Ten minutes had passed since then. *Maybe he's too wasted to come after us.*

The slamming of a door told him otherwise.

"Get out here, boy! You and that damn dog ain't nothin' but a burden to me. If it wasn't for takin' care of you, I could've—" the crack of wood

followed by the shatter of glass told Joel that his uncle was stumbling along the far side of the garage.

"Damn it! Look what you made me do. I was gonna sell that. Sonna bitch. You'll pay for—" Larry drew in a sharp breath and launched into a bout of violent coughing. Joel closed his eyes, hoping the bastard would die on the spot. "You... make me hunt for you in here, boy, and... swear to God... you'll join your mother."

The heavy footfalls of Larry's work boots drew near until a shadow passed along the thin band of stark white light beneath the tambour door, inches from boy and dog. The shadow halted. Joel hugged Rusty close and counted the seconds by the throbbing in his temples. *Keep walking... Please, keep walking.*

Finally, the shadow disappeared. Joel allowed nearly a full minute to pass before risking a sigh. His relief was short-lived. With a yelp, Rusty shoved his snout into the narrow gap. The flexible door creaked and groaned against the pressure.

Somewhere in the garage, boot soles scraped against concrete. "You think you're so smart."

A thundercrack rocked the desk. Rusty howled and thrashed in the compartment. It had been a warning shot. There was no sense hiding any longer. Joel imagined himself lying in a pool of his own blood before the night was over. *But maybe Rusty can get away.* Reaching over the terrified dog, Joel slipped his fingers under the door and lifted it slowly, expecting to be greeted by the twin barrels of a sawed-off shotgun.

As Rusty skittered off the desk to the floor, Joel shielded his eyes and ravenously inhaled the cool, fresh air. When his vision adjusted, there was no shotgun in his face. No Uncle Larry. No garage.

Instead, Joel gazed at a distant horizon dominated by the undulating waves of a vast sea that sparkled beneath the hazy glow of a setting sun. All of this was revealed through three enormous arched windows that spanned floor to ceiling directly across the room.

Joel unfolded himself from the compartment and sat on the edge of the desk, taking in the strange surroundings. Nearly every inch of wall space was consumed by bookcases fully stocked with hardcovers and paperbacks. To his left, Rusty had curled up on one of two high-backed chairs facing a blazing brick fireplace. Joel nearly ordered him off but thought better of it. *If he's comfortable there, he'll stay out of trouble.* Off to his right, a softly ticking grandfather clock stood between two mahogany wood doors that led to parts unknown.

Yet it was the view beyond the windows that captivated Joel. As he approached them, he realized that he was on the second floor of—wherever this was—and that the ocean lay far below a grassy plateau mottled with trees and teeming with wild animals of every variety. Sprightly primates scaled branches with graceful aplomb, while giraffes leisurely gnawed on tree tops. Below them, a group of pandas rolled and frolicked among scurrying foxes and stolid rhinos as a family of elephants lumbered by. Among this perplexing menagerie, there stood no fences or barricades of any kind.

"What is this place?" Joel muttered.

"An animal sanctuary, of course."

Joel whirled at the unfamiliar voice, his gaze darting around the room until he noticed the steady puffs of smoke rising from the closest of the two high-backed chairs. From his vantage point, it was impossible to see the occupant, but rather than approach the stranger, Joel kept his distance. He hurried across the room to the other chair where Rusty remained firmly entrenched. At the sight of Joel, the recumbent beagle's brown and white tail tapped a gleeful tattoo against the upholstered seat.

"Man's best friend." Joel folded his arms. "You could've warned me someone else was here." He motioned for the dog to move. "Let's go, off the furniture."

"He seems content where he is." In the other chair, a middle-aged man leaned forward and removed a curled ebony pipe from beneath an enormous handlebar mustache, made even more striking by the fact that there was no other hair on his head. "No need for apprehension, young man. You're safe here. This is a sanctuary of life. Take a cue from your canine and relax. I'm Finley, the caretaker, at your service."

Joel sat on the arm of the chair, but his arms remained folded across his chest. "I'm Joel. This is Rusty."

"Welcome to my home."

"You *live* here?"

Finley nodded. "Along with my wife and innumerable creatures of land, sea, and air."

"How large is this sanctuary?"

"As large as it needs to be."

"What does that mean?"

"You'd have to see it for yourself."

"I'm not even sure how we got here."

Finley waved a pipe toward the desk behind them. "You crawled out of my roll top. That's a first, even for this place. The question is, how did you get in there?"

"When we climbed in, the desk was in my uncle's garage. We were hiding from him."

"Hiding from your uncle? Why?"

"He was trying to kill us." Joel lowered his gaze. "He's an angry drunk and I'm usually his punching bag, but this time, he had a gun."

Finley took a long draw from his pipe. "Where are your parents?"

"My father walked out when I was six. My mother died of cancer about a year ago."

"I'm sorry."

"Whatever."

Finley rose from his chair and straightened the hem of his maroon turtleneck over the top of his jeans. He walked to the window and gazed out at the plateau. "So, you saved not only yourself, but your dog as well."

Joel knelt down in front of Rusty. "What else would I do? He's the only friend I have."

"What else indeed." Finley grinned. "How old are you, if I may ask?"

"Fifteen."

"Going on thirty, but then I suppose that's to be expected given your circumstances." Finley glanced at the grandfather clock. "Would you like a tour of the sanctuary before it gets dark?"

"Is it safe to bring Rusty?"

"Of course. There's no aggression among our animals. Come along."

As Finley led the way toward the door, Joel pointed to several framed degrees and certificates on the wall above the desk. "You're a veterinarian."

"I was. Been retired for some time. This place is my life now… in a manner of speaking."

"I'd like to work with animals someday."

Finley merely smiled and took another draw from his pipe.

———

"Rusty, stay close." Standing at the edge of the plateau, Joel marveled as the sun began melting into the horizon, painting clouds and sea alike in a deep, rippling orange. To a city boy who had rarely seen an open space larger than an empty parking lot, it might as well have been the edge of the world. "I've never been to the ocean before, and I've never seen most of the animals here, except on TV."

During their tour, Finley had shown Joel dozens of species and habitats, from placid snow monkeys soaking in steaming hot springs to mountain goats scaling sheer rock walls hundreds of feet high. Now, as squawking seagulls circled and dropped out of sight, Joel peered down at a beach covered with marine life. Curious seals waddled and bounced between barking sea lions and whistling walruses while the fins of porpoises, sharks, and orcas occasionally surfaced beyond the shoreline.

Joel turned to Finley standing far off to his left. "How did you manage to get all these animals here?"

"Oh, I did nothing. They all end up here eventually. Some by air, others by water," Finley pointed his pipe toward the sky far off to the right, "and the rest take a more fabled route."

Joel followed his gaze to a long, shallow arch that extended from a low-hanging cloud near the horizon to a point somewhere behind a dense tree line on the far side of the plateau. *How did I miss that?* Shielding his eyes against the ocean's glare revealed that the arch was a bridge across which thousands of animals of every size and shape marched toward the sanctuary grounds. So focused was Joel on the approaching stampede, that it took him a moment longer to notice the various *colors* of the bridge. "Is that...?"

Finley nodded. "Welcome to the sanctuary at the end of the rainbow bridge."

"No, but... that means you're... that Rusty and I..." Joel closed his eyes and dropped to his knees. *That wasn't a warning shot.* "Oh, God, no." When he opened his eyes again, Rusty stood before him. With a whimper, the dog cocked his head to one side.

"I'm sorry." Joel leaned forward, resting his head against Rusty's. "I was trying to save you. I'm so sorry."

Finley lowered himself to the ground beside boy and dog. "Listen to me, Joel. You're both going to be fine."

"How can you say that?"

"Because this is paradise. You and Rusty will never again know pain, abuse, or fear—only peace and happiness. Besides, you said you wanted to work with animals. Now's your chance."

"To do what?" Joel sat back and wiped his eyes. Rusty stretched out beside him.

"Well, the wild ones need little attention from us," Finley waved his pipe toward the rainbow bridge, "but the others that cross over are house pets, like Rusty, and the purpose of the sanctuary is to reunite them with their human companions when the time comes. That's what my wife and I do as caretakers."

"Yeah, but why me? Why did I end up here?"

Finley shrugged. "You were chosen, as my wife and I were. You risked your life to save Rusty. Regardless of the outcome, I believe it was that unconditional love that brought you to us. Besides, we could use the help and there's plenty of room in the house. What do you say?"

Joel thought for a moment. "I think I'll take a cue from my canine." He patted the beagle's side. "What do you say, boy? Think you'd be happy here for eternity?"

Rusty's tail thumped the ground as he let out an eager yap.

"Yeah, me too." He looked at Finley. "One condition. Can I see my mother again?"

"As I said," the caretaker gazed beyond Joel, "reunions are our specialty."

Joel glanced over his shoulder at the woman strolling toward them across the plateau. "Finley," his voice cracked, "we got a deal."

THE HORROR OF THE MIST
By April Welles

That night in late summer will remain with me until I die. The horrifying event happened just over a year ago and its effects still linger…

———

"C'mon, dude. I want to get home," Keith complained. "It's getting dark and we're still on the road. We've got a nine-hour drive back after we make this delivery." He was usually in a hurry, but he was one of my best friends, so it didn't bother me much.

In fact, we'd known each other for almost eight years, nearly as long as we worked for the company. Normally, Keith and I each traveled solo—delivering packages and parcels throughout the Bay Area and Sacramento—but when the company would get large crates that needed to be delivered farther away, they would send two drivers. Each took a turn behind the wheel while the other slept.

This time, Keith and I were delivering to someone in the Southern California desert. It wasn't our first time, but what made this job challenging was that it wasn't in any of the towns. We were to deliver a piece of what I took to be photographic equipment to a residential location in the middle of nowhere—or so I thought.

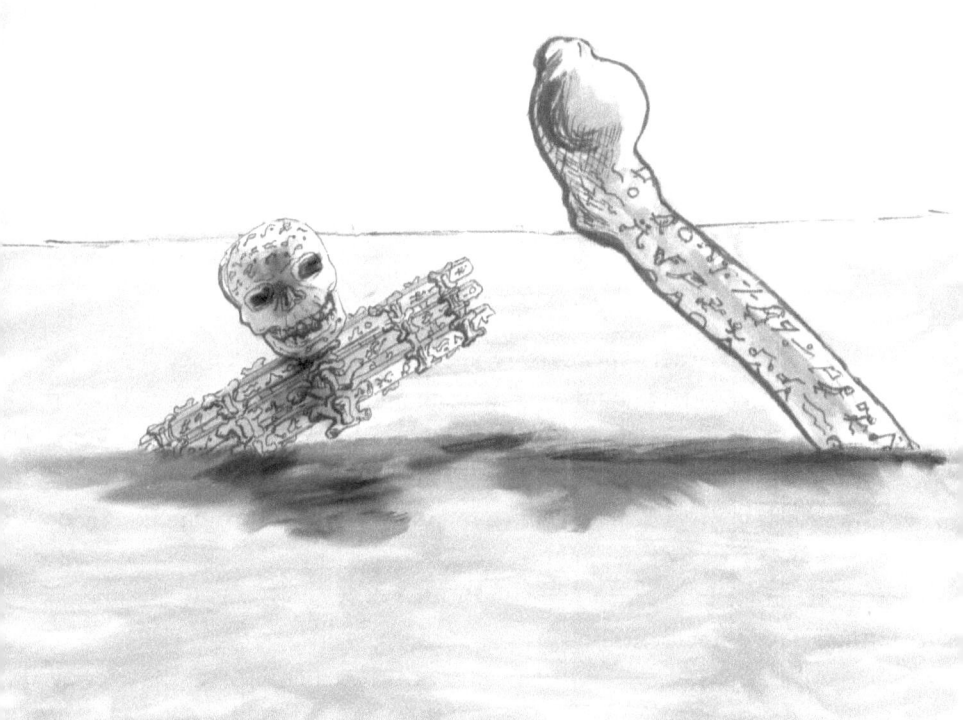

"Yo, man. Chill. I'm doing the best I can. I don't know this area. Do you?" I tossed a mock glare his way. Hell, I wanted to get home too, but we were from the Bay Area and didn't know Death Valley well.

"I want to be home before Amanda's birthday," Keith whined.

"Right. How old will she be again?" I knew, but I wanted to keep his mind off the drive. "Seventeen?"

"Wha-? Ha! No." He chuckled. Then, beaming, "Lucky thirteen. You're coming to her party, right?" He looked at me, eyes filled with hope.

Keith's parties were always something to behold and not always in a good way. I've been to a few of them, only to leave about a half hour later. Keith would always call me a wuss for it, but his parties were too raucous and silly, like frat parties but with married people. Honestly, they're not my scene, but he was my friend, so I always put in an appearance.

I have to admit, though, that he adored his daughter, and the parties he threw for her were usually fun.

"Sure, I'm coming to her birthday," I assured him. "What are you going to do this year, bunnies and balloons?"

"Naw, at her age she doesn't want to have a 'silly kiddie party' as she calls them. She wants something more mature. So I told her I'd hire strippers and serve beer." His guffaw pelted my ears, but I smiled and laughed.

"Of course, her reply was, 'Ew. Dad!' and Karyn slapped me in the back of the head." I could see the scene playing in front of my eyes and laughed even harder.

"Anyway, it's going to be a great party. Amanda will be pleased." Keith jostled in his seat and stared out the window for a moment. "Hey, I think that's our exit coming up."

He grabbed the map with our printed directions from the dashboard and stabbed it with his finger.

"Yep. This is the one. Get off at this exit, then turn left over the freeway, and continue on for twelve miles."

I'd driven about twenty minutes when my odometer said we'd arrived at the twelve-mile mark. Off to my left was the only opening in a dilapidated, weathered wooden fence. It looked like it could be a driveway, but I later discovered that the actual driveway was another 500 yards ahead. The only identification was a number nailed to one of the fence posts.

I now regret not driving that extra 500 yards and keeping us safe from the nightmare.

I turned left onto the old, bumpy road and continued on for half an hour. After another twenty minutes, what could be scarcely identified as a road disappeared and became flat desert. The sun was setting, and we were both beginning to worry.

"What do the instructions say?" I asked. "This is getting weird."

Keith grabbed the sheet. "Well, according to this, we're to drive for thirty-five minutes from the main road until we see the house."

"Damn. This guy likes his privacy, doesn't he?" I turned on the headlights as night was encroaching fast. "How long have we been driving? It has to have been at least thirty-five minutes."

"Forty-seven, according to my watch. It's almost eight o'clock." The lines in Keith's face matched the worry I felt. "We should have seen it by now."

The road was long gone. I continued as straight as I could considering the terrain, but there was no denying we were lost. Then, I saw something.

I slowed to a stop and turned off the headlights.

"What're you doing?" Keith asked anxiously.

"I saw something off to our right. Look there." I leaned over and pointed out his window toward a yellowish glow about a quarter mile away. I turned the wheel and made for it, using only the van's running lights so I could follow the glow. The van bucked and jolted in a way that told me we were definitely traveling off-road.

"Stop!" Keith cried.

I slammed on the brakes and we skidded to a halt. Thinking we were about to hit a coyote or something I looked around.

"What? What did you see?"

"We need to stop here." Fear laced his voice.

"What? Why? We're almost there. We drop this off and we can head home."

"Let's just go home now. Or at least to a nearby motel. I saw one just off the highway. We'll deliver it tomorrow."

"Man, you know we can't do that. We have to deliver it tonight or we get in trouble. Let's just go and get it done." I grabbed the shifter and put it in drive.

He grabbed my shifter hand. "No!"

"Keith, man. What's up?" I stared into his pleading, fear-filled eyes.

"I don't know, but that glow isn't safe. I can feel it. We have to get the hell out of here." By the meager light filling the cab from outside, I could see that he was starting to tear up.

"Okay. I'll tell you what. We'll walk over to that dune up ahead. I'll prove to you it's the house, then we can make the delivery. Even if it's not the right house, we can get directions from them." I shared a smile that seemed to relax him a little.

He agreed and, after turning off the engine and pocketing the keys, I led the way to the dune. The light undulated, almost danced, and soon we were at the peak of the dune looking down. What I saw surprised me at first. It was a bonfire. There were no structures of any kind in sight. Surrounding the fire were seven large stones about thigh high and a number of people dancing around just beyond them.

Actually, they were not dancing so much as gesticulating wildly in a circle.

From our distance, I couldn't make out any details save that they moved erratically, as though inebriated puppeteers were yanking their strings. Crouching, leaping, flailing, and whooping were all I could make out.

I was curious. Keith was nervous.

"Don't go down there, please," he moaned. "I just want to be back for Amanda's birthday."

"I won't let them know we're here. I just want to get a little closer to see what I can make out." Though I did feel a twinge of fear, I didn't yet share the same dread that Keith felt. Nevertheless, I approached cautiously so as to avoid startling them.

That's when I heard the beating of a drum. Its strange, non-rhythmic pounding made me uneasy. Edging closer, I could see the dancers more clearly. They were nude, male and female, and extremely grotesque. Their features appeared Native American, yet each was stooped and deformed with much paler, albino-like skin.

"C'mon Keith," I whispered. "Let's get closer. I want to hear what they're saying."

"No, dude." his voice quivered. "These guys are freaks. We need to leave *now*."

A tremendous sense of dread washed over me as I listened to the revelers' droning, frightening chant. I can't remember it, thankfully. There's only one phrase I recall from that night, but I won't share it yet.

As the chanting continued, a young girl was brought from the shadows at the opposite side of the bonfire. She appeared to be in her early teens—perhaps thirteen—and definitely out of place among these people.

Her young, healthy, Caucasian appearance was in direct contrast to that of her captors. She was pretty. Her auburn hair billowed excitedly as she entered the halo of light, though there was no breeze I could feel. Her naked body was painted with swirling designs in an unearthly bluish color. The patterns almost seemed to glow.

She walked as if in a dream state, guided along by two of the dancers.

"Oh, God, dude. What the hell is going on?" The panic in Keith's strained whisper was unmistakable. "What are we gonna do? She can't be older than my Amanda."

I managed to creep even closer to the outer edge of the ceremony, about 15 feet beyond the light of the bonfire.

"Dude!" Keith scrambled. "Wait for me." I could hear him shuffling along the ground behind me.

The revelers, dancing and gyrating and slithering through the sand, became faster and fiercer the closer she was brought to the fire. As they frolicked in the sand, I observed that some of them seemed to actually bathe themselves with it.

"Hey, Kev." Keith whispered. "Look over there. See that guy?" He pointed to a figure dressed in bones that were painted a variety of swirling colors. He wore a headdress that appeared to be a crown of rib bones capped by a small human skull. In one raised hand, he gripped a grotesquely shaped, blob-like idol made of silver while with his other, he waved an intricately carved leg bone. He seemed to be a shaman. He chanted a string of guttural words, rising in pitch until it became a frenzied scream. The only word I could make out at the time was "*shadanu*."

With a splintering *crack*!, the sky ripped apart. A massive hole appeared nearly a hundred feet above our heads, shimmering with an array of colors. Some were indescribable.

A florescent blue mist flowed out from the void. As it descended cautiously toward the bonfire, I got the impression of intelligence. The moment it touched the flames, an incredible flash of pure white light exploded with silent fury, blowing sand and dirt in all directions, covering us in a coat of dust.

Wiping my eyes, I looked again at the scene of debauchery. The fire was gone, but the mist continued pouring down, glowing with an intensity equal to a Hunter's Moon.

The shaman said something unintelligible to the revelers holding the girl and they lead her near the edge of the mist. With a gentle nudge, they pushed her in.

As if waking from a nightmare, a terrified, ghastly shriek erupted from her lips as the mist enveloped her. The girl's flesh began to dissolve, and her hair melted down her slowly liquefying body, only to disappear before reaching the ground.

"Amanda!" Keith wailed over her pitiful screams.

The shaman whirled to face us. His albino skin reflected the blue hue of the mist. His face seemed mutilated. One deformed eye was set higher than the other, and his nose never really seemed to have grown from his face. His mouth was by far the most disgusting. His teeth protruded at such odd angles that he couldn't even close his mouth completely, causing a nauseating amount of saliva to ooze forth.

"Oh God! Oh God! Oh God!" Keith's gaze locked on the child. Clutching the sides of his head, he collapsed to the ground and writhed helplessly in the sand.

"Keith!" I shouted. "It's not Amanda! Keith!" But he couldn't seem to hear me.

It was then I noticed the shaman flailing his arms in our direction and blurting something incomprehensible to his subhuman compatriots until he became aware of something happening behind him. Hollering in pain, he spun, revealing a back covered with fresh boils and burns.

"*Dum'n g'kai cho-sa Shadanu!*" He began shouting hysterically at the mist, waving the leg bone. He chanted over and over, as though trying to gain control of it or send it back.

That phrase remained seared in my mind. I had the feeling that it might save my life someday.

Fearing for our lives, I panicked, leaped up, and within two large strides reached the priest and shoved him—bursting his fetid boils all over my hands—-into the acidic mist which hungrily enveloped him. His screams rose in a cacophony of agonizing ecstasy mixed with demonic laughter. At this point, Keith seemed to be completely lost. His wailing broke into one long, anguished scream, as though his mind had shut down to protect him.

The revelers that didn't try to rescue their shaman, attempted to scramble away. Those that were covered with paint were snatched with ethereal tentacles and yanked into the mist.

Other worshipers who were covered with layers of dust, however, found themselves being wrapped in now violet-colored tentacles dissolving them from the inside out as smaller, intricate, tendrils thrust themselves into their nostrils and open mouths.

"Keith! Cover yourself with sand!" He didn't hear me. He was still writhing and screaming, kicking up sand and dirt all around him. Looking past him, I noticed a multitude of acidic tentacles snaking their way toward us. I knew I didn't have much time. I threw myself onto the ground and covered myself with more earth, hoping that Keith would be okay.

Face down, I clenched my eyes and mouth shut. Dirt filled my nostrils as I inhaled one last breath to fill my lungs and curled into a tight fetal position just as the mist settled over my head and around my body.

I knew, somehow, that it was alive. A force, a hunger. I could hear it in my mind. Not actual words, but a desire to get inside and consume everything. My heart pounded in my chest, and for a long minute, I kept my fingers pinching my nostrils and held my breath.

Moments ticked away until, just as quickly as it started, the tingling ceased.

I heard Keith babble deliriously next to me, but I was too afraid to open my eyes. What if the tendrils were waiting for that? Fear kept me paralyzed. My pulse slammed in my temples. My chest burned in abject protest, but I couldn't hold my breath any longer. I expected never to wake again. I exhaled, coughing up sand and dust before passing out.

I don't know how long I was unconscious. I awoke to warmth on my skin. Slowly, I opened my eyes to the blind intensity of the sun.

Ignoring my aching joints, I turned toward Keith. He sat, slowly rocking back-and-forth, eyes wide open and mumbling incoherently.

I struggled to my feet, shaded my eyes, and surveyed the area.

I flinched at the sight of the shaman's twisted skeleton, his crown laying close by, screaming eternally at me. Beside him was the strangely carved leg bone. With unexpected impulse, I picked it up. The silver blob-like idol, though, was gone. I searched the entire site but found only the other cult members' skeletons laying in various poses of agony, some with skin stretched like leather. Mummified.

I walked over to Keith and said gently, "C'mon, man. Let's go home."

He shot to his feet. "No! I can't leave Amanda here!" Tears flowed down his face.

I walked past the stone circle toward the remains of the fire, where I found her small skeleton pleading, it seemed to me, for help. I went to the van. Grabbed the tire iron. Popped off a hubcap. Dug a grave away from that blasphemous site and gently placed her in.

After I finished, I used the tire iron to smash up the henge to ensure, hopefully, that this profane rite could never happen again.

I walked back to Keith, who was standing at the small grave, sobbing. "Amanda..."

"Keith," I said softly. "Let's go home. Karyn and Amanda are there waiting for you." I guided him into the van and eventually found our way back to the highway.

He was catatonic all the way home.

I never bothered to deliver the crate. Someone else did that later.

I visit Keith in the hospital as often as I can. His mind never recovered from that night. He just sits in his wheelchair, staring out the window, gibbering. Sometimes, when Amanda visits with Karyn, he becomes hysterical, holding her and fending off anyone who tries to get near. But the nurses just inject him with a sedative and abandon him to dwell in his nightmare.

I, myself, was not unaffected by the ordeal.

Whenever a fog rolls in now, I become anxious, and clutch the strangely carved leg bone, repeating those words burned into my brain by the shaman: "*Dum'n g'kai cho-sa Shadanu*". It's the only way I know to keep the horror of the mist from coming again.

Who knows what other untold terrors lurk just beyond the sight of man?

GIRLFRIEND IN THE BASEMENT
By Michael Critzer

Robert and Vanessa returned from their honeymoon of scenic views and tropical "morning afters" to an out-of-town airport and a two-hour drive home. They arrived to find news vans parked before their lemon-yellow bungalow. Vanessa's mother shooed at cameramen standing in the tulip beds, as her father, still spattered with lemon-yellow paint, led the bewildered couple inside to shut out the crowd. Two men waited in the living room. One wore a dark suit, while the other held a dolly containing a long wooden crate with *Tigris Industries* stamped on the top.

The man with the suit stood and extended his hand. "Robert Slater?"

"Yes?" Robert said, keeping his arms around Vanessa.

"Mr. Slater, I represent Lilly Adams."

Something dropped in Robert's throat. He felt Vanessa stiffen against him.

"I'm afraid Miss Adams has taken some rather unorthodox measures." The man avoided the couple's gaze as he spoke. "She was recently diagnosed with a rare and fatal heart condition—so rare, in fact, that it attracted the interest of an overseas research facility. Tigris Industries has pioneered new breakthroughs in cryonic stasis. It's still a fuzzy area

according to law and jurisdictions. Suffice it to say, she was able to qualify for Tigris's services. Now typically, her body would be preserved until such time as medical science can find a cure for her condition. Miss Adams complicated matters, however, with a revised will and advance directive. As far as her estate is concerned, she's considered deceased, but she still has the rights of a patient in her current condition."

Vanessa traded her husband's side for her father's, leaving the sweat against Robert's ribs to cool in her absence.

"What does this have to do with me?" Robert asked. He looked at Vanessa. "I haven't spoken with Lilly in over a year."

"In Miss Adams's will, she left her preserved body to you." The man gestured to the wooden crate. "Which makes you responsible for her care as a patient."

Vanessa buried her head in her father's shoulder.

"Her advance directive," the man continued, "states that she is to be revived only in the event that you divorce your wife and sign a form of intent to wed Miss Adams."

"I'm taking you home," Vanessa's father said, turning her toward the door.

But when it opened to the eager faces of reporters, Vanessa made a sharp turn. "No. That's what she wants." She walked over to the wooden crate. "But she's not going to get it." She looked at the man holding the dolly. "Put her in the basement."

"I'll need a power source, ma'am," the man answered.

"I said, in the basement."

———

Headlines like LIFE, DEATH, OR NONE OF THE ABOVE? and DID GOD CREATE MAN TO BE VEGETABLE? were tossed on Robert and Vanessa's doorstep each morning. The phone rang constantly with talk show producers, eager to exploit the "Macabre Love Triangle." The constant messages from lawyers and special-interest groups overwhelmed Robert. Though it moved things along when Vanessa's father stepped in, bringing his lawyer and clear-headed advice. Robert felt like a child watching adults clean up his mess.

Vanessa's raging didn't help. "I swear to God, I'm going to take a sledge hammer and smash her frozen little face in!"

"I'm just as angry as you are," Robert said. "But what can we do?"

"Are you? You seem to be handling it just fine. Wife upstairs and girlfriend in the basement, what's there for you to be upset about?"

"That's not fair," he answered, too weary to continue the argument. Vanessa knew the danger they were in as well as he did—religious and social organizations threatening to sue over human rights and healthcare violations, while their legal liability was yet to be determined—but she wasn't happy, it seemed, unless Robert was squirming. His protection of the chamber, checking the meter on the box daily and rigging a backup generator, was all evidence of the torch he still carried for his ex-girlfriend. Why couldn't Vanessa understand? The shame that tugged at his core, every time he turned on the television or caught a reporter peeking through the curtains, brought him nothing but resentment for clingy, neurotic Lilly.

He'd never even dated Lilly all that long. After three weeks of mostly sex and a weekend "monthiversary" at a buddy's timeshare, she started talking about what they would name their kids and asking if he minded being confirmed Orthodox for her mother's sake. He'd backed off fast, and the breakup lasted longer than the relationship. "Why so sudden?" she'd asked, unable to accept it. He'd started declining her requests to talk "just one more time," and eventually ignored her altogether. She had never gone more than a week, though, without leaving him a message and even sending him a card on each following "monthiversary."

When he'd begun dating Vanessa, Lily's obsession took a dark turn. She'd made silent phone calls to Vanessa's house, to see if Robert was there, and left wilted bouquets on her doorstep with notes like "He'll soon be over you, too." Vanessa had been convinced that Robert still saw Lilly occasionally. Why else would his ex be so persistent? Nothing short of a diamond ring would prove his commitment to Vanessa. Finally, when they'd announced their engagement, Lilly seemed to get the message and stopped all contact with them both. Robert felt foolish now, reading Lilly's name next to his in the papers. She'd never given up.

Not until the tech's first monthly visit did Robert see Lilly in her current state. As the drop cloth fell, lightning struck down the back of Robert's neck. Lilly rested upright against a gray foam substance in her glass casket, making her body appear to float. She was naked except for thin strips of linen draped across her chest and pelvis, for accurate readings, the technician explained, though Robert suspected Lilly's flare for seduction. Her closed eyes and naturally pale skin added to the death-like appearance, especially in contrast to the black waves of hair that rolled down and around her shoulders. She would have looked peaceful except for the harsh, industrial light provided by a green electric coil twisting around the inside of the chamber.

The court "understood the strain" that the situation placed on Robert and Vanessa. "It is likely," the judge proclaimed, "that Miss Adams had tragically gone undiagnosed for mental illness. Her obsession with Mr. Slater and inability to make rational decisions regarding her health and well-being seem to prove as much. But now, we'll never know." He stalled then with some harsh words for Tigris Industries before giving his verdict: "Though laws are now specified to prevent another such occurrence, in this case it is wise to err on the side of life and protect Miss Adams in her current state." He made eye contact with Robert. "Yet we must respect the conditions of her Do Not Resuscitate, lest the court set a dangerous precedent." So much for the court's understanding.

Vanessa didn't speak for the entire drive home. When they parked in the garage, Robert had to jog after her into the house. As he suspected, she trotted downstairs. "Crazy bitch!" she screamed, hurling her purse at the stasis chamber.

Robert half-expected Lilly's eyes to open. They didn't, but when he looked back to Vanessa, she was popping the top from a paint can they had used to accent their bedroom.

"Stay there, then," Vanessa continued. "Rot in your little display case, while our life goes on around you." She wrenched her elbow away from Robert's grip. "But no one's going to pay any attention to you." She swung the can toward the chamber, and a red, plasmatic mass bloomed through the air to splatter the glass over Lilly's forehead and ooze down the casing above her body.

"Oh God, Vanessa," Robert said. "You have to stop. You heard the judge."

Vanessa turned the cold fury in her eyes onto her husband. "You don't have to look at her to read the meter," she said, before walking upstairs.

Robert spent the rest of the evening cleaning the glass, gliding his hands back and forth above the quiet contours of Lilly's body.

From then on, Vanessa avoided the basement. Robert did the laundry, stored each season's clothes, and did all he could to anticipate and redirect his wife's plummeting mood when she dwelt on their predicament. He still had to check the chamber's meter daily and escort the technician on each monthly visit, yet as the headlines and reporters faded, Vanessa seemed to pretend that their marriage was nothing out of the ordinary. Though she stopped speaking of her husband's girlfriend in the basement, she grew quiet if he added "only" to his "I love you."

Still, she began cooking his favorite meals and even showed a renewed interest in sex. Robert didn't know what to make of it until she took to humming lullabies and browsing baby clothes at yard sales. He didn't think they were ready for a child, but he received such frightening peeks behind her serenity when he tried to discuss waiting. "You just want me to remain alone," she said. "What am I supposed to do while you're downstairs with your whore? You can't give me an honest marriage, and now you refuse me this?" Then she became so warm when he gave in.

"This will change everything. You'll see. We need a part of us in living flesh to bring us back together. I love you enough to want this. Don't you?" It was an escape for her, he knew. He wondered what effect his charge in the basement was having on his wife's own mental health.

———

Sometimes, when Vanessa fell asleep, Robert would creep downstairs, pull back the door of the crate, and stare at the shrine that Lilly had made of herself for him. She was like an enchanted photograph, an hourglass body frozen in time while Vanessa's body ballooned with child. With each visit to the one part of the house that was solely his own, he developed an affinity for his lovely mute companion. When he was alone in the house, he spoke to her in the glow of devotion cast on her memory by the chamber's backlighting. Soon she became a different person from the trouble-making ex-girlfriend, not even a person at all, really. The girl in the basement became an angel, saving his sanity from the storm that constantly ebbed and flowed upstairs. He divulged his fears and hopes, and after a verbal onslaught of Vanessa's hormones, he would circle the convex chamber glass and masturbate to a new perspective.

———

As their grandson Jeremy slept in the maternity ward, Vanessa's parents offered to cover the cost of storing the stasis chamber in a hospital's research wing. No child should grow up around such a thing. Vanessa laughed through tears at the generous offer, and Robert knew better than to dissent. But as he held his son, a weight pulled at the joy in his chest. He had no desire to leave Vanessa for Lilly, but losing his time alone with the still life downstairs felt like losing the last secret part of himself. He would be nothing more than what was already laid bare for all to judge and command.

He disguised his fear and desperation as concern for his family's welfare. What if something happened to the chamber? He was still liable, no matter what kind of contract for care and protection he signed with a hospital. And what would become of his new family if he were to be prosecuted? In the end, he had to settle for storing the chamber locally, with visitation rights to ensure its upkeep.

Though the room was private, machines of all sorts were set to monitor, so his visits had to remain chaste. The fluorescent hospital lighting cast his reflection onto the glass above Lilly, and from a distance, the sight of them encased together brought a sense of order to Robert's universe. Then he'd step closer and see the lines around his eyes and the gray around his temples, hovering there above Lilly's forever perfect flesh. He shied away, lest his mortality tarnish her eternal devotion. He might have stopped his visits altogether if not for the way the nurses treated him, with no condescension or reproachful stares. Perhaps it was the conditioning of their job, but they treated him with the same sympathy and respect they might give a grieving husband. He felt solid and surefooted walking down the white corridors, past the smiles of powder blue cherubs and mint green seraphs, as he came to mourn at Lilly's living grave.

Jeremy was a natural in Little League, and Vanessa was his eager groupie, dancing in the stands and bringing water to the dugout. Robert bowed out of the spectacle as often as possible. He was Jeremy's father, but Jeremy was Vanessa's child. Robert's wife had become a mother, and they rarely spoke if not about the boy. He tried to form his own bond with his son over *Treasure Island*, video games, and chocolate bars, but Jeremy didn't have the attention span and Vanessa placed a ban on junk food and too much screen time. She preferred Jeremy outside with her, playing in the yard while she sunbathed beside the long-dead flowerbeds.

The passing of Vanessa's father only exacerbated the situation. Jeremy became her twelve-year-old nurse and confidant in grief while Robert handled the business end with his mother-in-law. Going over the finances, he saw an opportunity for self-serving chivalry and offered to take over care of Lilly's chamber once again, to ease the strain on the widow's fixed income. Vanessa was on too many depression and anxiety prescriptions to care. Robert wasn't even sure if she'd understood him when he told her, but there was the matter of what to tell Jeremy. How much did he already know?

While Vanessa slept off a Xanax one evening, Robert took his son for a drive. He tried to find the right introduction. He hadn't spoken about Lilly in so long that the words were too deep to find. As they browsed a convenience store, it occurred to Robert that the candy bar Jeremy had picked up on his way to the magazines was the first willful act of rebellion he'd seen his son take against Vanessa, and he did it openly before his father. Robert felt they had come to an unspoken understanding.

Yet what could he say of Lilly? How could a twelve-year-old boy understand even a fraction of the subterfuge between men and women, what they needed from—and loathed about—each other? Yet maybe Vanessa's coddling and chastising had already taught Jeremy more than most boys his age. Robert didn't say anything, but bought his son the *Penthouse* the boy had been hovering in front of and said, "Keep it from your mother."

———

When Jeremy left home, Robert moved into the basement, listening to Vanessa's footsteps, the incoherent warble of her phone calls, and all her ups and downs muffled through the floor. He was sure she'd taken a lover. Their attempts to remain secret brought a wry grin to his lips, the lighter-than-usual footsteps, the loud-then-hushed man's voice, as though Robert would care. Let her have her transient passion, he thought. True ecstasy lay in the glowing chamber set upright at the foot of his bed. It could never be held on this side of life.

What would become of Lilly after Robert's death had never been determined. Lilly hadn't provided for that eventuality in her directive, and the courts shied away from the value judgment the decision would imply. Robert had considered leaving the glass tomb and its living occupant to Jeremy. As the Adult Films Award-winning director of *Beach Blanket M.I.L.Fs I, II,* and *III,* his son might appreciate the conversation piece. But the thought of people gathered around his private treasure, appraising her, projecting their own emotions and desires onto her, thickened Robert's blood with indignation.

———————

Robert kept no mirrors in his downstairs home. The image of his age was sacrilege next to Lilly's beauty. He fantasized about waking her up, but to see himself in her eyes after all that time would be to see himself dying. Still, he asked the technician in roundabout ways what was involved in the process. The chamber would awaken her if the seal on the glass were broken, yet it wasn't safe to do so outside the Tigris facility, without regulators to keep her returning heartbeat steady.

Robert dreamed about the development of some rejuvenating technology that could return him to the age he had been when he returned from his honeymoon. He'd long since decided that her heart never had any fatal condition, other than the pieces he'd left it in. It was all part of her glorious plan. He sometimes wished he'd left Vanessa that very moment and revived the beauty who had sacrificed everything for him. But as the fantasy played out in his mind, he knew Lilly would only have become another Vanessa. He was in love with the eternity of the maiden before him, but he couldn't live forever—so neither could she.

———————

Four people came to Robert's funeral—the Tigris technician who had discovered the bodies, a retired nurse from the research hospital, and Jeremy, who arrived late with his girl of the month. Vanessa refused to attend, too livid over being questioned in a homicide investigation. The priest lamented the loss of both lives and said poignant things about reaping what we sow, forgiveness, and how all things happen for a reason. But none could imagine Robert's reason for opening Lilly's chamber, climbing inside, and then resealing the airtight lock.

CONNECTING VINES
By Sean Druelinger

October 22nd, 1983 14:26

My name is Lt. Colonel Richard Vines. I am a United States Air Force pilot—call sign "Wicked"—with fifteen years of service to my country. I come from a long line of pilots in my family. Today, I'm test-flying an F-4D Phantom jet fighter, over the skies of New Jersey, going 650 mph. My mission was to simulate a ground attack and stress the aircraft, but now the ground is rushing at me, spinning in front of my cockpit.

I am about to die.

Five minutes earlier

"Tower Control to Debon 91," blared in my headset as I level off at 4,000 feet.

"This is Debon 91," I replied.

"Your airway is clear. Wicked, that you?"

"Debon 91" was just my mission ID. The tower controller had recognized my voice.

"That's affirmative."

"Proceed to Range 40 Mike."

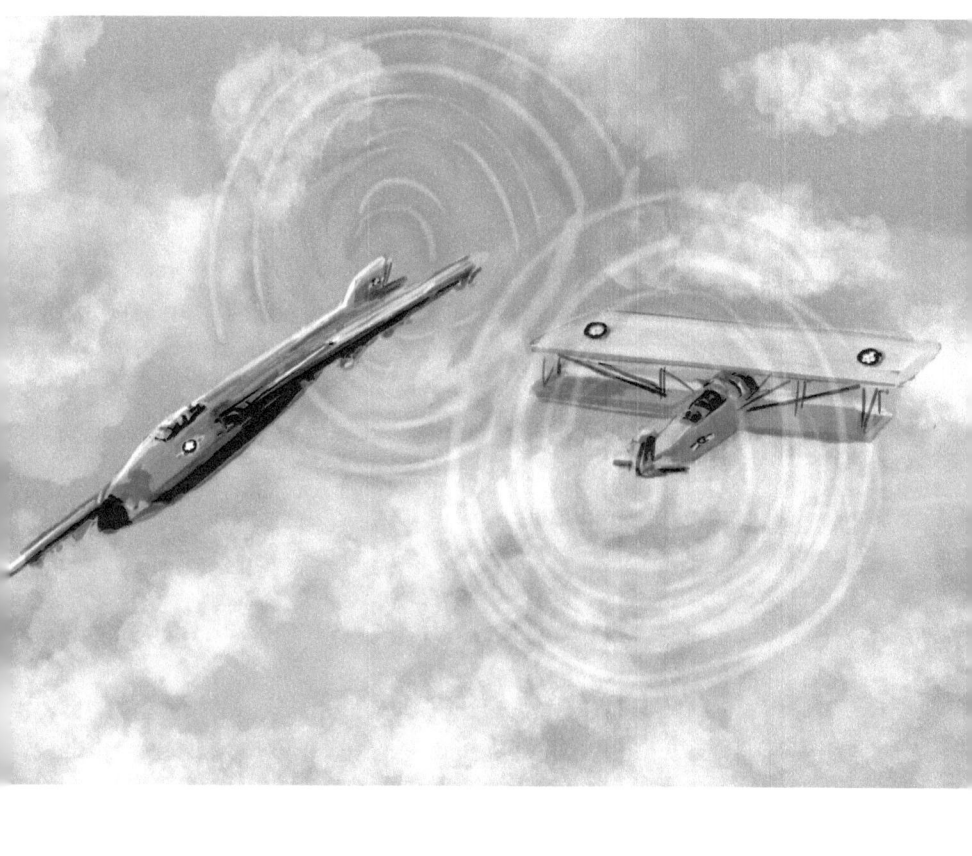

"I am parallel to the pipe." I banked my aircraft to the right to enter the imaginary pathway into the bombing range known as "the pipe." My plane began its gentle swoop towards the imaginary target.

I depressed my transmitter. "Tower, this is Wicked."

A *BANG!* was followed by a series of rumbles. The phrase "Houston, we have a problem" entered my mind, but any whimsical notions ended when my plane started barrel-rolling like a corkscrew. Thirty thousand pounds of aluminum and wiring, and I didn't have any way of slowing its roll.

I uttered my last words to the tower. "Mayday! Mayday! Mayday!"

I was losing power. Lights flashed on my panel and, in my headset, a high-pitched whine fought a loud, oscillating buzz. I suspected the culprit—a hydraulics failure in the aileron on the right wing. If it were stuck in the "down" position, there was no possible way to stop the roll from the cockpit. I'd barrel across the Garden State until I hit the ground.

I knew I had to eject, but I had to eject upward, not sideways or—*God no!*—down towards the ground.

My insides felt like they were surging outward as I worked on timing the roll so I could eject. "You can do this," I muttered to myself, teeth chattering. "You'll bail out and land in time to make happy hour at the O-Club."

That was bullshit, I knew. I'd seen the videos. No one walks away from ejections intact. Something's broken, or something's thrown, always. I'd be lucky to walk away at all.

It was now or never. I grabbed the eject handles above my head. Just reaching up was harder than expected, but I got my fingers around the grips. I hesitated. I didn't want to do it. It felt like failure. But I *had* to. Pull the handles and the canopy will blow off. I'd be catapulted at fourteen times the force of gravity into the air, hopefully far away from my aircraft.

Pull them now. Now!

I was starting to black out. Death seemed imminent. I shook myself awake, feeling a jolt of adrenaline.

I have to time this. Have to time this... Have to... time this...

I let go of the ejection handles, deciding at that moment to not fling my body out of the cockpit like a human artillery shell. I clenched my eyes shut and began to feel at peace, as if I were relaxed in a hot tub. I opened my eyes to find that the aircraft was decelerating. The revolutions were slow and pleasant. I felt as if they were warm and friendly, like rolling on soft grass. The earth below was scenic and calm. My instruments, however, did not agree with my senses. They told me that this plane was doomed and I should have ejected 5 seconds ago. Maybe I was just processing everything faster, but it was almost comical that I could make out every detail, every building, tree, and bush. I even saw a biplane in the distance, coming right at me.

What the hell's a biplane doing up here and why is it matching my jet's movements? The biplane was a Stearman, to be exact. I was looking at a 50-year-old plane, moving toward me at the pace of a parade float. *Why is everything so slow?* The ground revolved like a Catherine wheel. My instruments twitched lethargically, all in a bad direction, but at least I could read them. I gazed up at the Stearman again and blinked. *Is that a real biplane? Is there an airshow nearby? Are we really on a collision course?* Whatever it was, I appeared to be even more screwed than I was a minute ago.

Instead of dying on impact with the ground, or breaking my damned legs in a botched ejection, I was going to check out early, slammed head on into another aircraft—all at the speed of a lawn tractor.

This prop from *The Great Waldo Pepper* spun lazily counterclockwise as it approached. My vision was so clear I could make out the pilot's face. He looked as scared as I felt. He should have been. He was flying an aerodynamic soda can into a 30,000-pound jet.

I could no longer see the ground. Just... light. Bright light. I can't describe it any other way. The light was all around us. I wasn't even sure if we were both spinning any longer. His face looked familiar. His plane was upon me, slightly to my right. And then we weren't going to collide at all. His plane passed mine. I was going to live... for 30 more seconds, anyway. I was still riding an uncontrollable hunk of aluminum that had a date with the ground in about 60 seconds.

As he passed on the right, I saw and felt his wing hit the bottom of mine, freeing the stuck aileron. Then I lost sight of him. The light faded. I could see the horizon, sans spinning. I had roll back. I was flying level. Everything was still going bananas in my cockpit, and I had no pitch or yaw, but I wasn't barrel rolling any longer.

Handles. Pull!

The canopy blew off, and I felt the blast of wind. My ejection seat catapulted me into the air, rockets firing full blast, carrying me away from my crippled jet. I clenched my teeth, trying not to pass out. As I cleared my jet, it appeared still powered, but on a 30-degree incline, heading towards the ground. Would I see it hit?

My seat fell away, and I felt my parachute open. *I'm going to live!* My breathing slowed.

I made it.

I flippin' made it!

I landed on my back in the middle of an empty field. I had ejected successfully and didn't have a scratch on me. Incredible! Maybe I would get that drink today after all.

———————

"More than a Feeling" is a great song by Boston, and it soothed my mental state as I took another sip of Genesee. My favorite bar was a dive, but it was *my* dive. I went there to decompress from a stressful day. Finally, after nearly two weeks, I had no place else to be. Apparently, they don't let you go immediately to the bar after you successfully eject. This was my first sip of beer since the day I landed in the cornfield.

I'd been hospitalized for precautionary measures for three days, psych-evaluated for five, and interviewed for three more. The rest of the days had involved a deluge of paperwork. The military loves its paperwork almost as much as it hates having a 2.5 million-dollar fighter jet sprinkled all over New Jersey. I shuddered to think about the cleanup of the farm, plus the cost to the military for 15 barbecued cows.

I'd had some fairly detailed conversations with a military counselor in whom I confided about the "strange weather disturbance." I just couldn't reveal that another plane had been involved—because I was starting to believe that it really hadn't.

I rocked slightly on my chair, remembering that day. When I pictured the spinning horizon and the rapid descent, I became a little nauseous. But I was really bothered by the slowing down of time and appearance of a *kamikaze* barnstormer.

Where did it come from? Where did it go? Did it crash? If it had, it would have made the papers, but the only coverage was about my plane. Had there been a second crash, it would have been mentioned.

Margot handed me another beer. She worked afternoons here and knew me by name. She was always nice to talk with. I think her real name was Diane, but she never answered to that. She looked like a Margot—even a little like Margot Kidder from the *Superman* films.

She had empathy and could tell when something was on my mind. She pulled out the chair across from me and sat on its edge, elbows on the table. "What's bothering you, Rich?"

No one called me Rich. It was usually "Richard" or "Colonel."

"Would you believe me if I said that, a month ago, I ejected from an aircraft?"

She furrowed her brow, then her face lit up as if she had just won a sweepstakes. "Are you the guy whose plane crashed into a farmer's house and killed all of his cows?"

"Well, I missed the house, and more cows lived than didn't. But yeah, that was me."

She pursed her lips. I think she was trying to hold back a laugh. She asked if I was okay and I assured her that I was fine.

We talked for most of an hour. I told her my story, using my hands to explain the laws of physics. I explained that I had no idea how my fighter jet could have malfunctioned so seriously and so unexpectedly. I left out the near collision with the biplane, the slowing of time, and the miracle of the Stearman tearing into my wing just enough to stabilize my jet.

Margot sat back and spoke about strange weather or maybe spirits or some type of occurrence she had read in *The Enquirer*. "It could have been angels, Rich. They look out for us. I've read stories about how they can bring us across time and space to help each other. Someone was looking out for you and sent that biplane."

I think she was being passive-aggressive in an attempt to expand my thoughts on the matter. Was she truly concerned? Maybe she was into the supernatural and trying to goad me into a conversation about it.

My thoughts were on that biplane. I'd learned that there was no airshow that day, and I knew that no civilian aircraft would have flown near a military base unless it had no radio or map or sense.

Then an idea struck. "Do you have a phone book around here?"

Margot paused for a second, and I could tell by the look on her face that she was only going to comply because I was a regular. After she vanished into the back, I heard boxes being shuffled. A few minutes later, Margot returned with the Yellow Pages and dropped it in front of me with a thud.

"They gonna let you fly again?" she asked.

"Why wouldn't they?"

She gave me a look that said, *"Are you kidding?"*

Suddenly, I had doubts myself.

Another customer came in and Margot left me alone with the Yellow Pages. I let my fingers do the walking and looked for small a private airfield. There were none, but there was an aircraft repair shop nearby. I figured it had to be close to an airfield, even if it wasn't listed.

I copied the number, then walked over to the pay phone.

After about fifteen rings, a gravelly voice answered the phone. "Hello?"

I asked if he was located near an airfield.

"Of course there's an airfield near my shop. How the hell do you think they get them here you dumb—"

I hung up the phone, more than a little angry and embarrassed. I asked Margot for some coffee to snap me out of my funk. After I felt the caffeine kick in, I was off to the mechanic's shop listed in the Yellow Pages. *I hope that geezer I spoke with is in a better mood by the time I get there.*

———

I pulled into the parking lot of the aircraft mechanic shop and was not encouraged by the condition of the place. Paint was peeling off the exterior walls, parts of an old mono wing WW2 plane were attached to the roof, and an old man sat atop a stool holding a phone in his lap. Behind the shop I noticed a cleared area large enough for a runway and figured that I'd found my mystery airfield. It had several small dilapidated hangars, a single strip of pavement covered in weeds, a small control tower, and some old vehicles parked along the sides of the airstrip.

I climbed out of my car and cleared my throat anxiously. The man on the stool looked up at me, squinting as though trying to focus.

"How's it going, General?" He saluted me with a socket wrench.

I checked my instinct to salute back. "Just a lowly Lieutenant Colonel."

"What can I do you for?"

"I'm looking for a biplane, a Stearman to be exact."

The old man stood and offered me his hand. I reflexively shook it, only to realize it was coated with engine grease.

"A Stearman, you say? Haven't seen one of those 'round here ever. Most of them old planes were military. Best I can tell you is that we used to buy old planes for parts." The mechanic paused. "But haven't bought any Stearman parts in about 18 years."

"This would have been a new plane," I offered. "Maybe one with some damage?"

"I would have noticed something like that. Nope, I'm afraid you're S.O.L." He chuckled. "But you're welcome to look around."

He turned back to his work, making it clear our conversation was over. I stood there for a moment before glancing around the hangar for a rag to wipe my hand.

"You know," the mechanic said. "Now that I think about it, I once grabbed some parts for an old motor I was working on. Got 'em from that old barn just beyond the runway. Maybe check there. I've never been all the way through it. Might get you closer."

I thought that was weird. What did he mean by "closer?" Did he know something about what happened to me? Did he even know he'd said something odd?

I started back to my car when a feeling hit me. I was suddenly disoriented, like I had been while I was trying to eject and saw that biplane.

Shaking my head, I took another two steps, then spotted it between the two aircraft sheds in front of me. It was a barn, about 200 yards away. Why was I surprised? The mechanic had told me there was an old barn and suggested that I explore it. So why did I feel that sense of shock, that numb, tingling dread that felt so much like the tingling I'd felt when that Stearman was bearing down on me?

Whatever it was, I *had* to see what was in that barn.

I could barely make out its shape. It was set back from the tarmac some 50 yards, sunk into a sea of grass. There was a lot of overgrowth, and I thought I could see the top of a tree growing through the roof. I guessed no one had been inside for decades and wondered how many species of wildlife might dwell within.

But no way was there a plane in there—not in that decaying hulk. Maybe in the days when Lindbergh crossed the Atlantic, but not since. And the 15-foot-high doors were not even wide enough for a plane to fit through.

So why was I wasting my time? Why was I here at all?

Because I'd made a test flight, just certifying a repair, when my aircraft shit the bed, and then a Stearman came flying right at me out of nowhere. At the time, I was damn well convinced, as I prepared to die, that he had flown across decades just to splatter me across the Jersey Shore, but maybe Margot was right about those angels.

I needed answers, and that creepy mechanic said that maybe this barn would bring me "closer" to them.

What the hell? It's worth a shot.

The doors were still on their rails, but overgrowth had damn-near jammed them shut. I began pulling them apart until I was about two minutes past realizing I was in no shape for such exertion, but managed to make a narrow gap between them. Now I could see inside, where shafts of sunlight stabbed through holes in the dilapidated roof, highlighting the warped, rotting planks of the floor. Heavenly beams?

I saw piles of debris, but no aircraft. I wedged my foot into the opening and levered with my leg, gaining just enough space to squeeze through.

It smelled as bad as it looked. The odor of decay, coupled with that of mold and stale, primordial ooze, assaulted my nose and made a getaway straight into my lungs. In the dimness, I saw a mass—dark, ominous. Moving? Didn't think so. Breathing? A sleeping bear? No. Just my imagination. I stepped carefully toward it, wary of upturned pitchforks, rotted floorboards, or unseen holes.

The mass was a tarp.

What was it covering?

I drew close, grateful for the honest smell of damp canvas amidst all the filthy smells around it. Instinctively, I blew at it to clear the dust before touching it.

There was no dust.

It was the *only* thing in the place that was clean. As my eyes adjusted to the darkness, I saw that there were numbers stamped on the tarp—a military serial number.

I licked my lips. My mouth was dry. The dust, maybe.

I grabbed the edge of the tarp and pulled, sluggishly but steadily, revealing the fuselage of an aircraft. More accurately, half an aircraft. Parts of the engine were still attached to the cockpit, while other parts were stacked on top of the hull.

I turned on my flashlight and aimed its beam at the cockpit, or what was left of it.

The plane looked like a Stearman, but I couldn't be sure without out a recognition manual. It was probably yellow at one time. But there was no way that this plane was in the air a month ago. This mound had been here for years, albeit with someone having changed the tarp at least once in the recent past. The plane's interior was falling apart—bolt heads rusted, seat upholstery and straps torn and rotting away, gauges long since broken. The padding that once lined the cockpit opening was gone.

There's no way in Hell this plane nearly collided with mine last month.

Disgusted, I dropped the tarp and shone my light around the rest of the barn. I almost missed it. I spun back and found a dingy yellow wing propped against the wall. I ran to it and after wiping off the dust, traced its lines with my hand. Its color was more vibrant than that of the fuselage. I encountered a rough spot, deep scratches. I shone my light over them, and a chill seized my spine.

The scratches were highlighted in a different color. Paint transfer. Grey *aircraft* paint. Specifically, the paint of *my* aircraft. Something tells me it is. It can't be true, but... it *is*.

How? The aircraft had been here for years and was non-functional. The wing looked newer, but it wasn't attached to anything. I supposed it *could* have been removed after it was stored here.

Was I crazy to think this was connected to my crash simply because there was a yellow wing—like the wing of the biplane that had grazed me—with grey paint transfer on it, hanging in this musty, old barn?

Curious to inspect the wing more closely, I decided to have a look at the underside. Biplane wings aren't particularly heavy. I pulled it away from the wall, shining my light behind it to check the condition of the underside.

There was something on the ground that had been obscured by the wing.

I recognized a satchel, like an old mail pouch. I snagged its shoulder strap and pulled it to me, then eased the wing back against the wall.

The bag contained a pair of goggles in surprisingly good shape and a small logbook. With the flashlight clenched in my teeth, I scanned the pages of the book, fanning them until I read the last entry. I read it again. And again.

I fell on my ass, stunned, lightheaded, nauseous. A sound from outside interrupted my fit of disbelief, the buzz of an approaching plane. *It's a damned airfield. Of course, there's a plane landing!*

But other than those facts—that I was at an airfield, that there was a plane overhead, that I was flat on my ass—I had no clue what to believe.

October 22nd 1933 14:38

Lt. Richard Vines had just landed his brand new Stearman—barely. He came down haphazardly after his aircraft sustained severe wing damage. He was shaken by what he'd just experienced, but he maintained his composure as he told one of the mechanics about the damage before pondering how to explain what had happened to the officers of his squadron. The experience he'd had was playing through his head as he walked towards the flight office. His CO was busy with some other matters and clearly was not going to talk to him any time soon. It was routine to write up the flight log and he felt like he should at least get that out of the way. He wanted to tell someone immediately about his experience but did not want to bear the embarrassment of having damaged government property. He had not one explanation for what he'd seen.

I'll just write my report and be done with it.

He entered the flight office and poured some coffee that had just been brewed. He usually had cream and sugar with his joe, but he forwent anything that would dilute his drink. He sat down and licked the tip of his pencil.

So how do I write this? Truth? Slight Truth? Complete fabrication? Hell, no one reads these things anyway.

Lt. Vines recorded the following in his flight log:

Ten minutes after takeoff, the left aileron of Stearman model YPT-5 was stuck in down position. The aircraft had no roll control and could not maintain level. While the plane began to experience the malfunction an unexplained cloud/light pattern swirled in front of me, blocking visibility of the horizon. As I entered into the cloud pattern, I encountered a large aircraft approaching mine (Color: Grey / Marked USA), no prop visible. The left wingtip of my Stearman collided with unknown aircraft, which impacted my stuck aileron allowing control to return. After collision, the cloud pattern evaporated. I immediately returned to base, making a hasty landing. I am declaring major damage to my aircraft. Details in damage report.

Lt. Richard Vines

THE FOREST FOR THE TREES
By Phil Giunta

The Swedish Province of Finland - Summer 1697

It was three o'clock in the morning when a crack of thunder tore Petrus from a fitful sleep. A distant flash of stark white revealed the slender silhouette of his wife, Ievukka, standing at the window. He slipped out of bed and moved beside her. For the third consecutive night, the heavens erupted with terrifying fury—but this time, the spectacle was accompanied by distant screams.

Together, husband and wife watched helplessly as roiling clouds hurled bolts of lightning and streaks of fire in a relentless assault on the farmlands outside of town.

Ievukka sighed and lowered her head. "It will be dawn in less than an hour. Later today, we can expect more survivors to make their way here… if there are any. I hope there's room in the church."

"Better for them to die tonight, by God's wrath, than to continue starving with the rest of us."

"Each attack draws closer to us." Ievukka turned to her husband. "I fear we may be next. We should leave, Petrus. Abandon this town and move south. I'm sure my brother and his family will come with us."

Petrus shook his head. "The famine is everywhere. There is nothing but starvation between here and Helsingfors. I've heard stories that it goes far beyond our borders. People have died by the thousands. Robbery and cannibalism are rampant. There is nowhere for us to go."

Ievukka turned back to the window. The firestorm ceased as quickly as it had begun. The clouds dispersed, the strident cries faded, and peace reclaimed the night. Both of them knew it was only a temporary respite. "I wonder how many died this time, less than the night before or more? What have we done to anger Him, Petrus? Is it not enough to turn the weather against us and destroy our crops for the past three years? Must He now send fire down upon our homes? This is not the mercy that Jesus preached."

Petrus had no response, for what mere mortal could understand the mind of God? He remained silent as he took Ievukka into his arms and kissed her forehead. "We must continue to pray. I have faith that the answers will be revealed."

In the darkness, Ievukka sobbed. "I fear the only answer God has for us is death."

————————

Saint Antero's church had fallen into disrepair over the past year and a half since the pastor and his wife died within days of each other after devouring one of their two Lapphunds. It was rumored that the remaining dog had begun feeding off their corpses before they were finally discovered. Such desperation was common during the famine, but the news had devastated Petrus and Ievukka nevertheless. They had been married at Saint Antero's three years before.

The church continued to serve as a central meeting place for the predominantly Lutheran community, especially during times of crisis. Since God had begun attacking the farms three nights ago—for what other explanation could there possibly be?—Saint Antero's also served as a shelter.

When Petrus and Ievukka arrived for the dawn prayer meeting, they heard angry, raised voices even before opening the door.

The center of the narthex was occupied by local farmers as well as several village residents. The men were engaged in heated arguments, shouting over one another while distraught wives tried to intervene and frightened children sobbed under the baptismal font. Petrus clenched his jaw against the stench of sweat and fear.

Around the room's perimeter, a dozen townsfolk leaned against the walls, observing the clamor with weary, drawn expressions. Among them were Ievukka's brother Urbanus, his wife Kaisa, and their 14-year-old daughter Kreeta. They were the last remaining members of Ievukka's family. The rest had succumbed to disease or starvation over the past three years.

Urbanus waved and motioned toward the doors.

"What's this about?" Petrus asked as he followed Urbanus and Ievukka outside.

Once the doors closed behind them, Urbanus exhaled in relief. "Apparently, when the Lord unleashed his fury over the past three nights, many people fled into the forest and have not been seen since."

"The forest surrounds us," Petrus said. "It goes on forever. It's easy to get lost."

"That's what I told them at the start of this discussion, but some of the farmers had a different explanation."

"Such as?"

"They think God has taken their family members."

"God has not taken anyone," a new voice called out. "At least, not your Christian God."

All heads turned as an old man approached from the road. The first things that struck Petrus were his leonine mane of stark white hair and a beard that flowed to the hem of his rust-orange waistcoat. He stopped several feet away, pointing at them with a knobby walking stick as weathered as the man himself. "The devil has our land in her grasp, and she is not working alone."

Petrus raised an eyebrow. "She? You're not referring to Satan."

"Christianity has demonized many of our old gods," the man said. "We should not be surprised if some of them take offense."

"So you don't believe in Christ? Which of the gods are you referring to, then? Perkele?"

"When you venture into the forest, you will find the truth." With that, the man sauntered off.

"If Perkele is still among the gods, why doesn't he help us?" Petrus called out. "Wasn't he also Ukko, the old god of weather and harvests?"

"Petrus, let it go," Ievukka said. "He's just a crazy old pagan."

Without stopping or turning, the man replied. "Why would Perkele help those who have cursed his name?"

The church door opened and Kaisa emerged. "Urbanus, Petrus, they're forming a search party to comb the forest for the missing. They're looking for volunteers among the men."

Urbanus shook his head. "We don't even have enough food to feed the people who are here. Even if we find anyone lost in the forest, we'd only bring them back to starve."

"When do they intend to start?" Petrus asked.

"Today until dusk," Kaisa replied, "and at least for the next day or two. The women have agreed to make bark bread to take along. They have seven men already."

"Make that eight," Petrus said.

Ievukka frowned.

"Just for today, I promise."

"It's a waste of time and energy," Urbanus grumbled. "We'll all be dead soon enough."

———————

A few hours later, the men fanned out through the forest in pairs, each agreeing to remain within earshot of the others. Petrus teamed up with Johannes, one of the most prominent farmers in the area. His oldest son had vanished into the forest during the second night's attack.

"You didn't lose anyone out here," the farmer said. "Why did you volunteer?"

"I just want to help."

"Given the circumstances, I guess you and Ievukka are glad you didn't have children."

Although Johannes was right, Petrus didn't want to admit it. To do so seemed callous. "We still plan to... someday... whenever this famine ends."

"If we survive that long," Johannes snarled. "Remember when the Markonnens lost their daughter last year?"

Petrus nodded.

"Did you know the rest of the family cooked and ate her after she died?"

Petrus felt the bile rise in his throat. After a moment, he regained his composure. "Maybe we should spread out, but stay within sight of each other."

Johannes nodded, his expression grim. "Good idea, but be careful. Something doesn't feel right."

Petrus snickered. "I think you took those stories too seriously back at the church—in between the yelling."

"Some of the others said that God is trying to kill us, but I disagreed. I don't think God has anything to do with this."

"I met a stranger earlier today who said the same thing. He seemed to think it had to do with the pagan gods like Perkele or some such nonsense."

"I don't know from pagan beliefs, but I will tell you that Jesus and the Heavenly Father would not turn the weather against us and destroy our crops. They would never allow children to starve to death only to be devoured by their parents. I've seen people degenerate into animals these past few years. We're a faithful community, Petrus. We didn't deserve this punishment. There's something more happening here, but what it is, I can't imagine."

As Petrus took in their surroundings, the old man's words came back to him. *When you venture into the forest, you'll find the truth.* He gripped the handle of the knife hanging from his belt. "I'm not certain I want to know."

It took less than fifteen minutes for Petrus to find himself completely alone. He turned in all directions, but Johannes was nowhere in sight.

Petrus called out to him, but there was no response. He shouted the names of the other men in the search party. The forest returned only silence—until something rustled the underbrush nearby. Petrus ducked behind the thick bole of a fallen tree and reached for his knife. *Maybe I've been listening to too many stories.*

"Remain perfectly still and silent." A woman's voice whispered from… where? It was at once soft, yet urgent enough to freeze Petrus in place. "Do not be afraid. You shall not be harmed."

Petrus watched in awe as several branches of varying thickness sprouted from the trunk of the dead tree and stretched over and around him. Within seconds, he was completely encased, with only thin gaps between branches through which he could see something else moving into view close to the ground.

At first, Petrus thought another branch was stretching out across the forest floor, until he realized that it was not stretching at all—it was slithering. The thickest snake he had ever seen stopped just beyond his timbered cage, its black scales mottled with a chain of red triangles from head to tail.

After a moment, its head and upper body rose from the ground. By the time it drew itself to its full height, it stood taller than Petrus. Its tail, twice as long as its upright section, propelled it forward slowly as it turned right and left in search of something—or someone.

Eventually, the creature lowered itself to the ground and slithered out of sight. Seconds later, the branches covering Petrus slowly retracted. He rolled away from the tree and scrambled to his feet.

"You are safe now," the voice said, "but I suggest remaining here for a few minutes longer to be certain."

Petrus spun around, looking for the voice. Finally, he backed up against a nearby pine tree for cover.

"Have you no respect for personal space?"

Petrus turned his head—to find a face peering at him from the bole of the tree.

"Greetings, I am Tellervo."

With a gasp, Petrus pushed away from the tree and stared at the face, struggling to wrap his mind around what his eyes were showing him.

"Do you speak," said Tellervo, "or am I wasting my breath on another of Ajatarra's mindless minions?"

Petrus drew himself to his full height and found his voice. "Of course I speak, I just never before encountered a tree that could."

"It does not. It merely serves as my conduit, as do all of the trees."

"Conduit?"

Tellervo sighed. "I communicate through the trees. I am a goddess of this forest, and you are?"

"Petrus." He nodded slowly. "I'm from the village nearby. Wait... Tellervo, daughter of Tapio and Meilikki. Yes, I've heard your name in stories."

"And here I am in the bark."

"How do I know you are not an agent of Satan?"

"Satan? Oh yes, the devil of your Christian faith. Do you always insult those who save your life? Perhaps I should have left you to the piru." Tellervo's face extended several inches from the tree. "Then you would have met the *real* devil soon after."

Petrus held up his hands. "Forgive me. It wasn't my intention to insult you. I've been through this forest many times and have never encountered the likes of you before."

"You never needed help from the likes of me before."

"I see. Thank you for your protection. What did you mean earlier when you mentioned Ajatarra's minions? Is she the devil you referred to?" Once again, Petrus was reminded of his bizarre encounter with the old man. *The devil has our land in her grasp...*

"Many of your kind who fled into the forest after the attacks were captured by her pirus and turned into mindless slaves for reasons we do not yet understand."

Petrus frowned. "Pirus. You mean demons... like that snake?"

"Yes. You learn quickly for a mortal. We've been able to save a few of your people from capture."

"We?"

"My entire family has intervened in defiance of Ajatarra," Tellervo explained, "but we've been unable to provide safe passage out of the forest for those we've rescued. So we've kept them hidden from her. Ajatarra's forces are growing. They have infiltrated nearly every mile of the forest that borders your villages."

"To what end?"

"As I said, I do not know."

Petrus dropped to his knees, clutching his stomach.

"Are you injured?"

He shook his head. "Hungry. If you *are* a goddess, you must know of the famine that began three years ago. More of my people starve to death every day. Now you tell me the devil is taking them for some dark purpose. God help us."

Around him, plants sprouted from the ground bearing various fruits including bilberry, lingonberry, bramble, and cloudberry—although some of these were out of season, all were perfectly shaped and lusciously ripe.

Petrus began plucking berries at random. Once his hands were full, he shoved the fruit into his mouth and closed his eyes, savoring the sweet flavors.

"Eat as much as you like," Tellervo said. "Those we rescued have been kept well fed with all of these and more."

Petrus swallowed and continued snapping up more of Tellervo's bounty. "Where are they now?"

"In a sanctuary of trees toward the southeast. It remains one of the few places untouched by Ajatarra."

"I'll need to find a way to explain all of this to my people. May I take these berries back to them?"

"Of course."

"Thank you." Petrus dumped the bark bread from his satchel and quickly filled it with Tellervo's bounty.

"It is good that you did not venture too deeply into the forest," Tellervo said. "I can still guide you out so as to avoid any further encounters with Ajatarra's demons."

As Petrus walked, Tellervo's visage disappeared and reappeared in various trees, leading him along a circuitous route. Along the way, he asked Tellervo why she and her family had returned to the forest.

"We never left," she replied. "As the new faith of Christianity spread amongst your people, they turned away from their belief in the ancient gods. As a result, some of our kind left Earth behind and returned to the nether world, but we of the forest remained as silent stewards. However, when we sensed that evil had returned, my family decided to once again take an active role in its protection."

"What will happen if Ajatarra discovers what you're doing?"

"She might burn this forest to the ground. Especially now that she has an ally more powerful than she."

"Who?"

"Hush. More pirus approach."

Petrus slipped behind a tree just in time to avoid detection by two enormous snakes gliding past. One of them held a prisoner, a young boy no more than ten. Petrus recognized him as the son of one of the farmers who had died last year. Although the boy's eyes were open, he was motionless, his body limp in the gripping jaws of the serpent.

Petrus slowly slipped his knife from its sheath and started forward, only to find a branch wrapped around his waist. It yanked him back to the tree and held him in place until the snakes were out of view.

Tellervo's face materialized in the bole of the tree just above his head. "Foolish. There was nothing you could have done for the boy. You might have succeeded in wounding one of pirus, but the other would surely have captured or killed you." She paused, her gaze drifting off into the distance. "Ajatarra's forces are once again gathering at the edge of the forest, at least thirty serpents. I can feel them slithering among the trees."

"You were telling me that she allied herself with someone," Petrus said.

"We have heard it through the vines that Perkele has joined forces with her."

"Perkele! Satan himself!"

"Lower your voice, mortal. You are not out of the woods yet. Your Christian leaders have done a fine job of maligning the ancient ones. Perkele was no devil. He was the god of the skies and of the harvest. Some called him Ukko, among other names. If he truly has returned, then he might be furious to discover that his name has become a profanity among your people. Still, I find it difficult to believe he would collude with the mother of all evil."

Petrus fell silent, trying to wrap his mind around all that he'd seen and heard since encountering Tellervo, but contemplation would need to wait. Sunlight vanished from the forest, drawing their attention to a sky quickly engulfed by ominous clouds. Thunder rumbled in the distance.

Petrus gazed up at the goddess. "Please tell me this storm will bring only rain."

"No matter what happens, Petrus, stay here. I shall protect you."

He shook his head. "This isn't right. It always happens just before dawn."

"Who can predict the devil?"

Petrus looked west, toward the edge of the forest and his village beyond. "Ievukka…"

Then the world exploded.

———————

Petrus ran toward the edge of the forest, weaving through a maze of birch trees—until he tripped over an exposed root and landed face first. For a moment, he lay prone, the wind knocked out of him. As he caught his breath, a frigid breeze carried the stench of burning wood.

"Petrus, stop." Tellervo gazed down at him from the broad, gnarled hulk of an ancient yew. "I cannot protect you if you run."

Ignoring her, Petrus peered through the trees at the conflagration that had once been his village. The blaze served as a terrifying backdrop to the chaos unfolding around him. Several bolts of lightning struck just beyond the forest, their flashes of pale white revealing frantic silhouettes of people and demons darting in all directions. Petrus flinched as raging thunder shook the forest floor, momentarily muffling the shouts and screams that seemed to come from everywhere.

"Don't worry about me," he said finally. "Protect them!"

With that, he pushed himself off the ground and bolted toward the fray.

"Petrus!" Tellervo's pleading shouts were drowned in the mayhem.

When he was nearly clear of the forest, he rounded a cluster of towering pine trees just as two familiar figures rushed past. "Urbanus! Kaisa!"

The couple slid to a halt. Urbanus pointed toward the sky. "Petrus, God is unleashing his wrath upon us! We must take refuge."

"No! Don't go any further. The forest is dangerous."

"More so than out there?"

"Where is Ievukka?" Petrus said.

"We were separated," Kaisa replied. "She and Kreeta were ahead of us... somewhere."

As she spoke, a massive green and yellow snake uncoiled from a thick branch just above their heads. Its gaping maw descended toward Kaisa.

Petrus drew his knife. "Behind you!"

Urbanus yanked Kaisa away just as the serpent lunged—directly into the path of a spear that impaled its head and pinned it against the tree. Kaisa yelped as the rest of the creature's limp form unfurled and dropped to the ground in a crumpled heap.

Urbanus nudged its tail with his boot. "It's taller than a man and nearly as wide! It could have swallowed any one of us whole."

"He's a little one," a new voice called out. "Be glad you didn't encounter one of the beasts that Petrus saw earlier."

Everyone turned as the old man from the church approached with a grin. He pulled the spear out of the tree and dropped the tip, letting the snake's head slide off. "Good to see I still have my throwing arm."

"How did you know my name?" Petrus said. "For that matter, who are you?"

"I am known as Väinämöinen. As to how I know your name, I overheard it at the church earlier. By the way, I'm afraid that's the only building still standing in your village. I advise we regroup there quickly before more of Ajatarra's demons arrive."

Together, all four hurried out of the forest. The assault from the heavens had ceased, and the sky was now clear save for the billowing smoke from fires that had consumed most of the village.

In the narthex of St. Antero's, they sat in silence after Petrus imparted his experiences with Tellervo and the demons. Urbanus refused to believe a word of it while his wife quietly wept.

Now, Petrus leaned his head back against the wall and pondered his next move. He recalled the lifeless body of the boy in the jaws of the snake. Could his wife be enduring the same fate right now? Was she being carried off to whatever version of Hell lay deep in the forest? He looked over at Kaisa, huddled in the arms of her husband and knew they were wondering the same about their daughter.

"We have to go back into the forest," Urbanus said finally. "We need to find Kreeta."

"Is that so?" Väinämöinen raised an eyebrow. "Was it not you who, just earlier today, considered it a waste of time and energy to go searching for those who went missing? They're just going to starve to death anyway. Of course, I suppose it's different when it's one of your own."

"Why are you here, old man?" Urbanus snapped. "Where do you come from and what business is this of yours?"

"Urbanus." Petrus held up a hand. "He saved our lives back there."

"I simply offer my help," Väinämöinen said, "and from the looks of things, you could use it."

Kaisa touched her husband's arm and Urbanus lowered his gaze to the floor.

"We'll return to the forest at daybreak tomorrow." Petrus stood and patted his satchel. "I have some food to sustain us tonight and I know how to get more once we're in there. First, we'll need weapons. I suggest we spend the rest of today searching the abandoned farms for axes, sickles, knives, anything. We'll sleep here in the church tonight."

"And pray for Kreeta and Ievukka," Kaisa added.

Väinämöinen nodded and looked from one to the other in turn. "You now know what awaits you in the forest. It is almost certain that your loved ones have already fallen prey to Ajatarra's demons. The chances of finding them grow slimmer with each passing hour. What's more, we'll be grossly outnumbered. Are you certain you want to do this?"

Petrus nodded. "The devil herself couldn't keep me away."

Just after dawn the following morning, the group skulked among the trees, weapons in hand. In addition to his knife, Petrus had found an axe at one of the farms, while Urbanus now carried a sickle and Kaisa, a scythe. Väinämöinen had managed to conjure up a longsword, which now dangled from his belt in a well-worn leather scabbard.

"Petrus, where exactly did you see this... *goddess*?" Urbanus whispered.

"As I said, in the trees."

Everyone peered up into the branches and toward the treetops—all but Väinämöinen.

"No, here." Petrus tapped a nearby birch, just above eye level. "Her face appeared in the trunk and she spoke to me."

Kaisa was deadpan. "You had a conversation with a tree?"

"No, he had a conversation with a goddess," a voice replied from behind them. "Do I really need to explain all of that again?"

All heads turned to see the face of Tellervo materialize in the curling bark of a lone alder.

Petrus stepped around a gaping Urbanus. Of his three companions, only Väinämöinen appeared unfazed at the sight of a talking tree. "I'm relieved to see you again, goddess."

"Why have you returned, Petrus? It is too dangerous here. The pirus are still patrolling the forest. They captured many of your people yesterday."

"Were you able to save any?"

"Some, yes."

"A woman nearly as tall as I with reddish blonde hair possibly running with a shorter girl?"

Tellervo frowned. "Not that I recall, Petrus. I am sorry, but there is a chance they were rescued by my mother or father and are being ushered to the sanctuary as we speak."

"Can you take us to this sanctuary?" Väinämöinen said.

"It would have been easier in yesterday's chaos, but in the stillness now, it will be challenging to avoid detection. So many demons are still slithering about looking for stragglers."

"But it can be done."

"It's a three-day journey. Follow me, and do not deviate from the path."

Several hours into their trek, Tellervo warned of two demons approaching, each carrying human victims. As the group ducked behind nearby trees and undergrowth, Urbanus whispered, "We should let them pass, then attack from behind."

"Unwise," Tellervo said. "There are six others within earshot. You would be quickly outnumbered. We must continue moving. Undoubtedly, we'll encounter more of the same until we're clear of Ajatarra's territory. Wait here while I determine the safest—"

Tellervo's eyes widened as she looked beyond Petrus. All heads turned at the sound of leaves crunching underfoot. Something was moving among the trees. Everyone fell silent, weapons raised in anticipation. After a moment, the newcomer stepped into view just twenty feet away.

Kaisa covered her mouth to stifle a gasp. Kreeta stood before them, hair disheveled, clothes filthy and torn. She stared directly at her parents with a vacant expression as if they were strangers.

Urbanus charged toward her, but Väinämöinen pulled him back. "No. Ajatarra knows we're here. She's trying to draw us out. It's no coincidence that your daughter happens to be here when there are a half dozen pirus close by."

"How do you know it's a trap?" Petrus said.

"Because there are two serpents lying in wait," Tellervo says. "One is hiding in the underbrush behind that line of birch trees off to the right, and the other is still far off but closing in behind the girl."

"The four of us should be able to defeat two demons—" Petrus turned to Väinämöinen, but the old man was gone. "Damn fool, where did he go?"

Kreeta cried out, turning toward a tangle of wild shrubs where Väinämöinen stood over a dead snake, cleaved in half. He wiped the blade of his sword on a nearby birch. "Demon filth." He returned the sword to its scabbard and approached the girl.

Kaisa and Urbanus ran to their daughter.

"Whatever you do, hurry," Tellervo warned.

Kaisa hugged her daughter. "You're safe now."

"Of course I am, for Ajatarra is always with me."

Slowly, Kaisa pulled back, eyes wide. "She has become a witch."

Väinämöinen stepped up, placed his hands on either side of Kreeta's face, and spoke with a serene voice. "What is Ajatarra's purpose here, child? Why does she attack the villages and harvest mortals from the forest?"

"She is raising an army to wage war against the Christian god."

Väinämöinen shook his head. "She's wasting her time. Mortals cannot kill gods."

"We will not remain trapped in our corporeal forms for much longer," Kreeta explained. "When Ajatarra's forces are amassed, we shall gather as one and abandon our earthly bodies. Our immortal souls will follow Ajatarra and Perkele to war."

"Perkele would not ally himself with the mother of evil."

"Believe what you will. It is happening. You cannot stop us."

"Hear my voice, Kreeta. Throw off the cloak of evil that clouds your thoughts and blinds you from the light."

Kreeta struggled to pull away from Väinämöinen's grasp, but her gaze remained fixed on his.

"Hold her steady," he snapped. Urbanus dropped his sickle and embraced his daughter, pinning her arms to her sides as Väinämöinen continued. "Let my voice guide you out of the darkness, child."

Kreeta jerked her head back. "No."

"Four more pirus are closing in," Tellervo warned.

"Be ready to fight, Petrus," Väinämöinen said as Kreeta began trembling. "Let Ajatarra's poison flow from your mind, Kreeta. Release it from your heart."

"No," She croaked. Tears streaked her face. Then, "Help me…"

"You are stronger than Ajatarra! Follow my voice to the light. Reach out to me, child. Your mother and father are here with arms open. They are here with me in the light."

Kreeta reached up and clutched his forearms, her face taut. "She's in my head."

Väinämöinen smiled. "Not anymore."

With that, Kreeta collapsed—

———————

—and Ajatarra screamed.

Her momentary anguish echoed through the vast cave in the northern forest. She cradled her head in her hands until the pain subsided.

"What happened?"

Ajatarra twisted her serpent waist to find Perkele approaching from behind her. Although he was nearly seven feet tall, Ajatarra took pleasure in the fact that he still had to look up to address her. When she drew herself to her full height, her bare breasts were always at eye level to him. This amused her, and Ajatarra often flaunted herself in an attempt to make him uncomfortable, for she knew Perkele found her repulsive. While one side of her face was reptilian, the rest of her upper body was human in appearance, supported by a snake's tail of emerald green, over eight feet in length.

Nevertheless, it seemed his anger with the mortals surpassed his revulsion at the thought of joining forces with her, for it had been Perkele who initiated the firestorms that drove the mortals into the forest.

"Something unexpected," she hissed. "One of my mortals has been awakened by an old friend of yours—Väinämöinen."

"Where?"

"In the southern forest. It doesn't matter. The girl was expendable, but Väinämöinen had help from the forest gods."

"Perhaps it's time to put your army of entranced mortals to the test."

Just then, two pirus entered the cave, each with a human captive clutched in its jaws. They lowered their prisoners gently to the floor and hovered over them.

"And when one mortal is lost, two shall rise to take its place." Ajatarra smiled running, her forked tongue over her fangs.

She approached the closest prisoner, paralyzed from the piru's bite. She reached down and lifted him off the ground by his waistcoat. She lowered her head to whisper in the man's ear. "Perhaps, in your thoughts, you are praying to your precious Christ to save you. Let me assure you, he will be of no help to you here. As of today, you worship me, obey me, adore me. Your life shall be mine." She flicked her forked tongue around his ear. "I must admit, mortals are delicious."

She tore open his shirt and buried her fangs in his chest. After a moment, she pulled back, lips covered in blood. In her grasp, the man began convulsing with increasing violence. With a grin, she released him and watched in delight as he writhed and squirmed on the floor. Finally, his seizure abated, and the man lay in a fetal position, moaning softly.

"Rise," Ajatarra commanded.

The man stood, his expression blank.

"Speak."

"My life for you," the man said.

Ajatarra stroked his face with a clawed finger. "Perkele, when I am finished with the other prisoner, we will take my army south and destroy Väinämöinen. I shall then convert whatever mortals he managed to rescue."

"What of the tree gods?"

"Once we're finished, feel free to rain down fire from the sky and burn the forest as you did the villages. Then, finally, we shall move against the Christian God."

———

As Kaisa knelt and cradled her daughter, Urbanus retrieved his sickle and faced Väinämöinen. "What have you done to my daughter?"

The old man smiled thinly. "She will awaken momentarily and be completely free of Ajatarra's influence."

Petrus turned to Tellervo. "Where are those four demons you mentioned?"

"They are already upon us."

Abruptly, Väinämöinen spun and hurled his spear. At first, Petrus saw no target, until a blue and red snake leapt from behind a stretch of overgrown weeds. The weapon found its mark in the creature's belly. It landed several feet from Petrus, contorting its body until the spear shook loose. He raised his axe as the snake turned toward him, but was saved the trouble when Tellervo drove several sharpened branches into the beast's head.

Another piru reared up behind Urbanus and lunged. He dove to one side and slashed his sickle into its tail. The serpent shrieked and curled back on itself, catching Urbanus by a thigh and dragging him along the ground—until he buried the point of his weapon into its eye. The snake dropped him just before losing its head to Väinämöinen's sword.

"There are two more!" Petrus shouted.

Tellervo's face emerged from a pair of inosculated birch trees to his left. "Not anymore."

Petrus followed her gaze to the ground where two snakes lay, each with a narrow length of silver birch shoved down its throat. "Thank you, Tellervo."

Her face rotated to face him. "I am Mielikki. Tellervo is my daughter. She is still over there."

Petrus turned to his right. Tellervo smiled. Mother and daughter looked almost exactly alike. He nodded to Mielikki. "My humblest apologies and gratitude, and may I say that your daughter has saved my life at least twice in as many days. My name is Petrus. He gestured toward the others. "These are members of my family, Urbanus and Kaisa, their daughter Kreeta, and this is—"

"Väinämöinen," Mielikki smiled. "I did not know you had returned."

Petrus looked from one to the other. "You know each other?"

Väinämöinen grinned. "Since ages past, before the first mortal stepped foot on this soil." He reached out and placed a gentle hand on a branch of the intertwined birches. "I have missed you and your family. Your daughter has been an invaluable guide. How is your husband these days?"

"Tapio is well and keeping watch over the sanctuary where the rescued mortals are gathered," Mielikki said.

Petrus stared at the old man, his head filling with questions. Was he a god, too? His name was not familiar from the old legends, but then Petrus knew there were gaps in his knowledge of pagan myths. It was not a subject the Lutheran church encouraged.

He shot a sidelong glance at Tellervo. "Did you know?"

She shook her head, and the rest of the tree with it. "I only met him once and it was eons ago."

"I see your voice has not lost its magic," Mielikki said, looking past Väinämöinen.

Petrus followed her gaze to Kreeta, who was now awake and sitting up. He walked over and hunched down beside her. "How are you feeling, Kreeta?"

"Dizzy, and a bit nauseated."

"That, too, shall pass," Väinämöinen assured her.

Petrus placed a hand on Kreeta's shoulder. "Do you remember what happened to Ievukka?"

"She's alive, but under the spell of Ajatarra like so many of our people."

"I can put an end to that," Väinämöinen said, "if we can find them."

"*You* can find them... without us," Urbanus said. "I just got my daughter back and I won't risk losing her again, or my wife." He glanced at Petrus. "I'm sorry."

"Ievukka's your sister," Petrus seethed.

"And she would agree with me. I'm taking my family out of this unholy place."

"To where? Our homes were burned to the ground."

"Enough!" Mielikki said. "We should continue a bit further south before more pirus arrive. It will be dark in a few hours and far too dangerous to travel. Whoever wishes to leave can do so in the morning. I shall go on ahead and grow a shelter for the night. Tellervo will guide you there."

"Are you a god like the others?"

"It's hardly my place to tell you what to believe, Petrus."

Surrounded by a wide, circular wall of slim silver birch trees, the group sat around a fire in the center of the shelter. All around them, berries and mushrooms grew ripe for picking. Outside, mother and daughter goddesses stood watch.

"But exorcising demons is a power reserved only for Jesus and his apostles."

Väinämöinen tossed a few more dry branches into the fire. "All I can tell you is that I'm known for having an exceptionally persuasive voice. I simply use it to the best of my ability."

"I see," Petrus said. "This is difficult for us. We were taught that there is only one God."

Väinämöinen nodded. "I am aware."

"Is that why you've all returned?" Urbanus said. "To prove our religion as false and reassert your reign over us?"

The old man shook his head. "We're only here to stop Ajatarra and hopefully send her to Tuonela where she belongs."

Kaisa frowned. "Tuonela?"

"The realm of the dead."

Everyone stared at Väinämöinen for a moment before exchanging awkward glances with one another.

"Please don't think us ungrateful," Kaisa said finally, "but why are you helping us?" She waved toward the trees. "And by you, I mean—"

"All of us *pagan* gods?" Väinämöinen smiled. "This land was our domain for eons and to it we pledged our stewardship. Your ancestors worshipped us, yes, but also relied upon us for protection and, at times, their very survival. We provided for them when needed. We're not about to abandon our duty now, even if your faith in us has... drifted away."

"What about Perkele?" Petrus said. "If he is not the devil, then why has he allied himself with Ajatarra? Why would the god of the sky and harvest curse us with famine and then send fire down upon us from the heavens to burn our homes and drive us into a demon-infested forest?"

"It is not the work of Perkele."

"But Tellervo said—"

"There are many trickster demons in the forest. If left unchecked, who knows what havoc they could unleash?"

"Then where is Perkele?"

Väinämöinen turned his gaze to the fire and sighed. "That, I do not know."

The following morning, Tellervo informed Urbanus and his family of the fishing villages along the Gulf of Bothnia that remained untouched by Perkele.

"I will lead you there and provide plenty of food along the way," Tellervo assured them. "Enough to make an offering to the villagers when you arrive. They may be more willing to take you in."

"Say nothing of what you experienced here," Mielikki warned. "Else you run the risk of them killing you as pagans. Tell them only that you are fleeing the attack on your village."

"No matter what happens," Petrus added, "warn everyone you encounter to remain out of the forest until I return."

"And if you do not return?" Kaisa said.

"Please be careful," Mielikki continued. "There is a risk you could find yourselves quickly outnumbered by pirus."

"Perhaps I can even the odds," an unfamiliar voice called from above. All eyes turned to a grey owl perched atop one of the birch trees. As it swooped down to the forest floor, its body undulated and stretched. In a matter of seconds, the feathers on its massive wings retracted into lithe, human arms, while those on its body extended into a flowing silver gown, and the bare feet of a young woman gracefully touched ground.

Petrus stared at her yellow eyes as she approached. *Will the marvels never cease?*

Väinämöinen smiled. "Tuulikki. I was wondering when you'd arrive."

"I've been here for quite some time, hovering overhead."

"What news do you bring, daughter?" Mielikki said.

"Ajatarra and Perkele are assembling their army. They are on their way here with intent to kill Väinämöinen and take the mortals from the sanctuary."

"She's delusional," Väinämöinen turned to Petrus, "but if she is bringing her beguiled army to us, your wife will likely be among them."

"Will you be able to save her as you did Kreeta?"

"I intend to save them all, Petrus."

"You have a plan then."

Väinämöinen paused. "Of course, I… *will*… by the time we reach the sanctuary."

Tuulikki turned to Urbanus. "I would be happy to escort you and your family safely out of the forest. Tellervo's talents would be best utilized against Ajatarra's forces."

"In that case," Tellervo chimed in, "you should depart as soon as possible and take advantage of the daylight. It's two days to the coast."

Urbanus nodded. With a thin smile, he placed a hand on Petrus's shoulder. "Find my sister. Bring her back to us."

Petrus embraced each of his family members in turn. "May God protect all of you from the demons."

"Do not worry," Tuulikki interjected. "We will."

All eyes turned to the goddess—and the six gray wolves surrounding her. With a smile, she spread her arms. "As I said, perhaps I can even the odds."

———

For Petrus and Väinämöinen, the first day's journey passed mostly in silence for fear of attracting more pirus. By nightfall, however, Mielikki announced that they had passed beyond Ajatarra's territory. Another small shelter was constructed and this time, Tellervo and her mother joined Petrus and Väinämöinen near the fire.

"Tell me, Petrus," Väinämöinen began. "What was your life like before the famine?"

"Quiet… uneventful. I was raised on a farm, but when I was very young, I learned carpentry from my uncle and eventually became a journeyman under a master who happened to be Ievukka's father."

"And so romance bloomed?" Tellervo said as white kielos—lilies of the valley—sprouted from the ground around them.

Petrus laughed as he plucked a cluster of flowers. "Yes, romance bloomed. Ievukka and I were married a year later. I built our house in the village and we talked about starting a family." He twirled the stem between his thumb and forefinger. "That first spring, most of our crops were ruined by weeks of frost that continued well into spring, but we persevered with our reserves and what little we harvested at the end of the summer. Everyone thought it was just a fluke; that the next season would produce the bounty we'd been blessed with in years past."

Petrus tossed the flower into the fire. "That was three years and seven hundred deaths ago. Maybe more. I lost count. We slaughtered every animal for food—cattle, horses, dogs, cats. When they were gone, we went for days without food, or subsisted on bark bread. We ventured into the forest to pick what berries the frost hadn't destroyed and hunted what we could, but it was never enough to feed everyone.

"And after surviving for this long, my wife is taken from me by the devil in the blink of an eye. It... can't end this way."

"I assure you, it shall not."

Petrus looked up at Väinämöinen, but the voice that had spoken was not his. It was deeper and far more ominous.

"Do not be alarmed," Mielikki said. "My husband takes some getting used to."

Tapio... Petrus stood, turning slowly in search of the god's face among the surrounding birches. "Which tree is he speaking from?"

"All of them."

"Wife of mine," Tapio bellowed. "Are you and Tellervo escorting yet more wayward wretches to our sanctuary?"

Väinämöinen rose to his feet. "I beg your pardon you old, brittle, petrified, overgrown shrub!"

Petrus felt every muscle tense. "Väinämöinen, what are you—?"

"How dare you speak to me in—wait a minute. I know that voice..." Tapio paused. "Väinämöinen! You ancient, shriveled, prune-faced excuse for a wizard!"

"Well, you're not as senile as I expected."

"Who could forget such a hideous countenance as yours?"

Afraid to move, Petrus shifted his gaze to Mielikki.

She rolled her eyes. "Men." Then, to Tapio, "As if you didn't know Väinämöinen had returned the moment he stepped foot in the forest."

"Woman, why must you spoil our fun?" Tapio grumbled. "That old buzzard and I have not seen each other in centuries. This is almost like a family reunion."

"Complete with a few unwanted relatives," Väinämöinen added.

"Ajatarra, yes." Tapio lowered his voice to a mild rumble. "I'm not certain what to do about her, and can you actually believe that Perkele is involved with that beast?"

"No, but I have some ideas about that. When we arrive at the sanctuary tomorrow, let us discuss it."

"I look forward to seeing you and that ridiculous beard of yours. It's even longer than I remembered, like an angry little gnome."

"And I cannot wait to set my gaze upon your cracked, peeling, caterpillar-infested bark."

"How I have missed our intelligent discourses of old, Väinämöinen. Rest well tonight, and may your decrepit bones not turn to dust in your sleep."

After a few moments of silence, Petrus finally worked up the nerve to speak. "So, you have some ideas about how to stop Ajatarra?"

"I said I would have a plan by the time we reach the sanctuary."

"We're getting closer to the sanctuary."

"And I am getting closer to having a plan."

———————

By midday, Petrus and Väinämöinen reached the sanctuary. It was far more than merely a larger version of the shelters that Mielikki and Tellervo had provided over the last few days. At least a thousand birch trees formed a dense perimeter wall that enclosed an area nearly the size of Petrus's entire village.

As they approached, two of the trees parted, allowing Petrus and Väinämöinen entrance to a structure that was like some ancient cathedral of nature. Petrus noted the vaulted roof, at least twenty feet high and comprised of intertwined branches that extended from all of the surrounding trees. Gaps of varying sizes throughout the intricate filigree permitted generous sunlight.

Several people sat around fires, while others lay in beds framed in thick branches and padded with leaves and straw. All told, Petrus counted about three dozen people, all familiar faces and none of them appeared to be starving. As expected, fruits and vegetables grew within reach all throughout the sanctuary.

As the newcomers made their way to one of the closest fires, several people waved and called to Petrus. A pair of strong hands gripped his shoulders and spun him around. It was Johannes, the farmer with whom Petrus had been paired during the search party a few days ago.

"Petrus!" He smiled. "I thought you were taken by one of the giant snakes."

"Very nearly, but I had some help."

"Yes, from these *pagan* creatures," Johannes grumbled.

"Careful," Väinämöinen warned. "The walls have ears."

"And they did save our lives," Petrus added, "but we have a larger problem."

By now, the others had gathered around and were listening intently.

"If you thought the few snakes you saw before were frightening, there are more coming, as well as members of our families who have fallen under the spell of Ajatarra."

"Yes, we were told as much by the talking trees," a woman said. "Most of us didn't believe them."

Väinämöinen excused himself and wandered off to speak to Tapio, leaving Petrus to impart the details of his experiences in the forest, beginning with his encounter with Tellervo. All the while, eyes widened, jaws dropped, and heads shook.

"So, please," Petrus concluded, "show some measure of respect to those trying to help us. I realize their very existence is contrary to our Christian faith, but the Lord works in ways we cannot always understand."

There were grumbles and murmurs among his audience, but eventually, they agreed.

One of the farmers stepped forward from the back of the group. "So, how do we fight this army of snakes? We have no weapons."

"You will have weapons by tomorrow morning," Väinämöinen replied as he rejoined Petrus. "Axes, swords, shields—enough for all of you."

"And how do we exorcise the devil out of our people?" a woman asked.

Väinämöinen grinned. "Leave that to me."

———

After dusk, Petrus took Väinämöinen aside. "With respect, where are we going to find these weapons you promised?"

"From a place few mortals have ever seen. Are you up for a brief jaunt?"

"How far?"

"We're already there."

Around them, the sanctuary dissolved from view, leaving them alone in impenetrable darkness. Petrus tensed at the sound of hammering, metal against metal, from somewhere deep in the forest. Over Väinämöinen's shoulder, the glow of a small, distant fire illuminated the trunks of nearby trees.

"Who is that?"

"An old friend." Väinämöinen led the way through the thicket until they emerged in a clearing to find a tall, muscular man with a full, dark beard hammering a length of thin metal atop an anvil. It took a moment for Petrus to realize it was the blade of a sword. Several feet away, a fire blazed in a large stone enclosure. Two men in the background worked a massive bellows.

As Petrus looked around, his gaze settled on a cache of weapons strewn about the ground and lying against trees—swords, axes, shields.

"You've been busy," Väinämöinen called out.

The man didn't bother to look up. "I was expecting you."

"Of course you were."

Petrus turned to Väinämöinen. "Who is he?"

The man stopped hammering and held up the sword as he approached Petrus. "I was once known to your people as Ilmarinen."

Petrus opened his mouth, but words failed him immediately. Then, "Eternal Blacksmith, Forger of the Universe…"

Väinämöinen glared at him. "How is it that you knew his name immediately, but not mine?"

"Who can forget the Craftsman of the Heavens?"

Ilmarinen exchanged a brief glance with Väinämöinen before turning his attention to Petrus. "You flatter me, mortal. Do you not fear blaspheming your Christian God?"

This time, Petrus could think of nothing to say.

"You came here for weapons," Ilmarinen continued, "to fight the evil consuming your forest, destroying your crops, and possessing your people." He waved a hand toward the collection around them. "Yours for the taking."

"Thank you, but if you are... *Jumala*," Petrus said. "If you are the one *true* God, you could rid us of Ajatarra and Perkele with a mere thought—"

"Perkele?"

"I have been told that he has allied himself with Ajatarra, but I have only seen the attacks from the sky as proof."

Väinämöinen cleared his throat. Ilmarinen merely stared at Petrus for a moment.

"Will you help us?" Petrus said.

"What is it your Christian leaders say? God helps those who help themselves? I am giving you the tools so that you can do the work."

"Are you the one true God?"

"I cannot tell you what to believe, Petrus. You must come to such conclusions on your own, for gods only have power so long as there are those who believe in them. Once people forget, or deliberately turn their backs, their gods become impotent, no more than characters in a fairytale. Before this tribulation ends, you must decide where your faith lies."

Ilmarinen turned to Väinämöinen. "You will accompany the mortals into battle?"

"Yes. What say you to these rumors of Perkele's involvement with Ajatarra?"

"As you well know, Väinämöinen, when it comes to the devil, nothing is what it seems. The truth will be revealed when you confront the queen of serpents." Then, to Petrus, "Mortal, collect your weapons and prepare your people for a battle that will be waged as much in their hearts and minds as in the forest. Regardless of the outcome, you and I shall meet again."

With that, Ilmarinen and his forge vanished. Petrus and Väinämöinen found themselves in the center of the sanctuary, weapons scattered at their feet. Around them, people stopped and stared before cautiously approaching. As they began picking through the piles of swords, axes, and shields—some with trepidation, others with zeal—Petrus began to fear the days ahead. A disorganized, frightened mob of farmers and peasants against a legion of monsters determined to destroy God.

And who leads us? A mysterious old pagan and a family of forest creatures. Have I lost my faith in Christ? Petrus stepped away from the crowd as Väinämöinen distributed the weapons. "Get a feel for them tonight, but do not injure yourselves," he instructed. "Tomorrow I shall begin training you on basic fighting techniques. Remember, we will be combating beasts, not people."

Yet here they are, gods that had been demonized by the Christian church, working and fighting beside us to save our lives and rid our land of the devil. Petrus longed for Ievukka at his side. To tell her all that he had seen and experienced. She often put his mind at ease with thoughtful words of serene wisdom. He imagined himself speaking to her now. *Could it be, my love, that Väinämöinen and these stewards of the forest were agents of Jumala, the one true God? Maybe He took the form of Ilmarinen simply as a way of communicating with me and providing these weapons. Surely, He would not have brought us this far only to let us die in battle or become mindless slaves to the devil. That would make no sense, would it, Ievukka?*

You needed weapons to fight the devil and God provided, Ievukka replied in his imagination. *Overcome this challenge, and we shall face the rest once we are back in each other's arms…*

Petrus leaned against the wall of the sanctuary and peered up through a gap in the natural latticework of the arched roof. A single, bright star was visible and Petrus locked onto it, knowing that somewhere in the forest, Ievukka was under that same star and drawing nearer every minute, though she was not of her own mind. *You were right, my love. We should have fled the village that night. We should have traveled south to the shores of the bay. We would still be together. I am so sorry…*

Yelps and shouts from the opposite corner of the sanctuary jarred Petrus from his dark musings. He looked up just in time to see a gap in the wall of the sanctuary seal itself behind an approaching gray wolf. It sauntered toward one of the fires and emerged a second later as Tuulikki.

Petrus pushed off the wall and made his way over to her, as did Väinämöinen, who spoke up first. "What news have you brought us, my dear?"

"What of my family?" Petrus chimed in.

"Safely escorted to one of the fishing villages where they were welcomed as refugees from the north," Tuulikki explained. "Apparently, news of Perkele's attacks has spread throughout the province."

"Any difficulties along the way?" Väinämöinen said.

Tuulikki shook her head. "Our journey was free of incident, much to the chagrin of my wolves. We were looking forward to eliminating more of the serpents. Upon leaving Petrus's family, I ventured north for a bit of reconnaissance. Ajatarra and her army are moving swiftly and without rest. I estimate they will be here in two days."

Väinämöinen nodded. "What about their numbers?"

"About two dozen pirus and just over two hundred mortals armed with crude clubs and axes." Tuulikki looked around the sanctuary. "Although from the looks of things, you managed to gather quite a cache of weapons while I was gone."

"A gift from Ilmarinen. What of Perkele? Did you see him with Ajatarra?"

"We saw someone who looked and sounded like Perkele, but certainly did not conduct himself as befitting the god of thunder. He was like a callow youth, subordinating himself to her. Ajatarra was clearly in charge."

Väinämöinen sighed and leaned against the shaft of his spear. Do gods become weary, discouraged? To Petrus, Väinämöinen appeared to be both. "That is not the Perkele I know. All of the atrocities attributed to him as of late are completely out of character. My instincts tell me that not everything is as it appears. Either Ajatarra is being duped or all of us are. The truth will reveal itself in two days."

She ran a gentle hand along the still form of the snake, caressing the dry, brittle flesh until she touched the crusted blood surrounding the fatal wound. Ajatarra lifted her hand and peered at the dull gray scales that clung to her fingertips. "My children... I will see Väinämöinen lose his life for this." She shifted her gaze to the other slaughtered serpents scattered about the clearing. Her sights settled on two with birch trees protruding from their throats. "As will the forest gods, when we burn this place to the ground."

"As you wish," Perkele said, standing at a respectful distance behind her. "In the meantime, we've been moving without respite for nearly four days. The mortals require rest and sustenance. They will not be of much use—"

Ajatarra whirled on him. "Let them eat snake!"

Their gazes remain locked for several seconds, one furious, the other impassive, yet neither wavering. Finally, Ajatarra drew back. "Soon, they'll all be dead anyway, and we will lead their immortal souls into battle against the very god for whom they abandoned us. Perkele, the most powerful of us all—whose name has been reduced to a profanity by decree of this new Christian faith—why do you care about the welfare of these insects when they turned their backs—"

"Ajatarra..."

She fell silent at the whispered sound of her name. "Did you hear that?"

Perkele grabbed her by the hair and yanked her head back as he raised the blade of his axe to her throat. "I heard only your incessant and redundant chiding, of which I have had more than enough. Going forward, you would do well to mind your forked tongue when speaking to me, or you might find yourself joining your late children." He lowered the weapon and released her head with a shove.

Ajatarra raised a hand, claws pointed toward his eyes. "Don't ever threaten me. Remember it was you who sought me out and proposed this alliance when—"

"Ajatarra..."

She turned away from Perkele, unfurling her tail and pushing her body to its full height.

"What is wrong with you?" Perkele snarled.

She held up a hand and closed her eyes, remaining silent for nearly a full minute. Then, "We are close to their precious sanctuary. Less than a day away."

"How do you know that?"

"I can hear them. Their voices carry through the trees. Yes, they mention my name and yours. They speak of Väinämöinen and someone named Petrus, but I cannot determine precisely what they are saying. It is a cacophony of voices all talking over one another."

She opened her eyes and glanced at the army of humans standing around the clearing, staring at her with vapid expressions. "We keep moving. The mortals have had enough rest. They will share a final meal when we overtake the sanctuary."

———

On that second morning, Petrus was jarred awake by the sound of Väinämöinen's voice. As he sat up, Petrus realized that the old wizard was not speaking to him, but to the entire sanctuary. Confused faces turned in every direction, searching for the source of the announcement.

Petrus tilted his head toward the wall of trees beside him. Slowly, he moved along the perimeter, pausing every so often to listen. The birch trees were talking—all of them. Through them, Väinämöinen revealed his plan to defeat Ajatarra. No sooner had he finished speaking than two of the trees parted and Väinämöinen stepped into the sanctuary to stand beside Petrus.

"That certainly got everyone's attention," Petrus said.

"I had a little help from Tapio."

"Speaking of which, where is our family of forest gods this morning?"

"Out in the wild, ensuring that Ajatarra is guided directly here."

"Far be it from me to question the plans of gods, but the thought of allowing this sanctuary to be invaded by the devil and her horde of giant snakes is unsettling at best."

"I understand," Väinämöinen nodded, "but you must have faith, Petrus. If all goes well, more than one unpleasant surprise shall befall the queen of serpents, and your wife will be back in your arms before the day's end."

By that evening, Ajatarra stared up at the walls of the sanctuary listening to the voices of those within—heated discussions, innocuous conversations, nervous laughter, words of hope and fear.

"This feels like a trap," Perkele said. "Where are the forest gods? Where is Väinämöinen? Is no one keeping watch?"

"For a god of thunder, you sound worried," Ajatarra replied. "What can they possibly do to stop us? Remember, find Väinämöinen first. Kill him before he has a chance to utter a word." She stretched her arms out to her sides, fingers spread wide. In response, her pirus dispersed, slithering silently away to take up positions along the front wall of the sanctuary. A small contingent of mortals formed a line behind each of the demons. Once all columns were in place, Ajatarra dropped her arms. In unison, the snakes lunged forward, jaws and tails tearing out birch trees two at a time, creating gaps in the wall. Seconds later, Ajatarra's forces stormed through—and abruptly stopped.

The sanctuary was empty.

Ajatarra and Perkele exchanged puzzled glances.

"And yet I still hear voices," Perkele said, "as if they were standing before us."

Actually, there was only one voice speaking now, and it was Väinämöinen's. "Mortals, hear me. Let my voice guide you out of the darkness. Let Ajatarra's poison flow from your minds. Release it from your hearts."

"It's coming from the trees themselves!" Ajatarra cried out. "Perkele! Burn this place!"

Above them, storm clouds gathered from all edges of the forest. Lightning streaked across the sky, followed by explosions of thunder.

"You are stronger than the mother of evil!" Väinämöinen continued. All around Ajatarra, the mortals began wincing and groaning. Some began hyperventilating. "Follow my voice to the light. Reach out to me. Your mothers and fathers, sisters and brothers, await you with arms and hearts open. They are here in the light." Crying out, the mortals dropped their weapons and fell to their knees, weeping.

"Perkele! Why do you delay?" Ajatarra shouted. "Rain fire and lightning down on this place!"

He glanced up at the angry roiling clouds and shook his head. "That is not my doing. I believe we have finally awakened the old man."

"What do you mean? *You* are Perkele, you are Ukko! Who can be mightier?"

Perkele lowered his gaze with a smirk, his face stretching and contorting. Blue eyes darkened to black marbles and his complexion faded to a sickly green.

Ajatarra glowered at him. "Lempo… I thought you were long dead."

The demon shrugged. "You know me, old girl, I'm a survivor and still as capricious as ever. It's been fun playing this part, but my loyalties always shift with the prevailing wind and it seems this storm is coming for you. So, fare thee well, hideous one!"

"You bastard, I created you! I can destroy you!"

With a cackle, Lempo turned to flee. The lightning bolt that struck him left little more than a blackened, twisted heap. In his place stood a man bedecked in radiant, golden armor. He drove his sword into the charred form of what had once been Ajatarra's most infamous trickster. It crumbled into a pile of ashes.

"No one impersonates me." Perkele's bass voice resonated throughout the forest. He pointed his weapon at Ajatarra. "You do not belong here. Your place is in Tuonela."

Ajatarra flickered her tail, scooping up two axes and tossing them in the air. She caught one in each hand and advanced on Perkele. "Then bring your lightning and fire down upon me and send me there yourself."

Her pirus moved in close, forming a circle around the two combatants, but Perkele's furious gaze remained fixed on their queen.

"I need no magic to defeat you, witch. As for Tuonela, I shall personally escort you!"

As their blades clashed, chaos erupted in the sanctuary.

"Now!" Väinämöinen shouted. With Petrus at his side, he raced toward the ring of serpents, followed by three dozen farmers and tradesmen wielding weapons provided by Ilmarinen. They barreled into the snakes, slashing and stabbing. Those no longer under Ajatarra's influence either scrambled to the edges of the sanctuary or retrieved their weapons and joined the fight.

After felling his first demon, Petrus ducked away from the battle and peered into the throng of bodies. "Ievukka!"

At first, there was no response. *She must be here.* He cried out again.

"Petrus!"

He whirled to his right just in time to see his wife slice open the belly of a green and copper beast, its forked tongue dangling from its mouth as it collapsed.

Husband and wife started toward one another at a dead run—then Ievukka was gone. Petrus stumbled to a halt, staring up at his wife screaming and struggling in the jaws of one of the largest serpents he had ever encountered.

With a roar, Petrus hurled his axe toward the back of its head. Though the weapon missed its intended mark, the blade buried itself in the center of one of the diamond patterns along the snake's back. The creature hardly flinched—until four wolves surrounded the beast and pounced, sinking teeth and claws into its flesh.

Petrus retrieved a discarded sword from the ground and charged ahead. When he reached striking distance, he leapt and plunged the blade into the thrashing mass of gray and tan. The monster whipped its head to one side, flinging Ievukka toward the sanctuary wall. The sudden motion knocked Petrus to the ground. He rolled away as the serpent followed, enervated by the wolves' relentless assault. As they disengaged, one of the wolves turned and nodded to Petrus before returning to the battle, leaving the snake to bleed out.

Peering up toward the sanctuary wall, Petrus noticed Ievukka being lowered gingerly to the ground in a cradle of branches.

By the time husband and wife were face to face, they were both in tears.

"I was caught in a tree," Ievukka said.

"Actually you were caught *by* a tree." Tellervo winked at them from high above.

Petrus smiled in spite of himself. "Thank you, my friend."

Ievukka leapt from the cradle into her husband's waiting arms. "Petrus, I don't understand what's happening here."

He placed a hand on the side of her face and kissed her.

"I'll just be… over there," Tellervo said. "Killing snakes."

When their lips parted, Petrus spoke first, words tumbling out in a rush. "I promise I'll explain everything when this is over. I'm so sorry I went into the forest that day with the search party. I should have stayed with you."

Ievukka shook her head. "Don't blame yourself. You were trying to do the right thing. You're with me now and the devil no longer controls me. That's all that matters."

"I shall not leave your side."

"You two!" Väinämöinen called.

Petrus and Ievukka glanced up just as the god thrust his sword into the eye of a black piru. "Fight now, love later!"

They stood, weapons at ready, but most of the creatures had already been dispatched by the mob. All eyes turned to the center of the sanctuary where Ajatarra, having lost an axe and a hand, was swinging the other wildly at Perkele. The god of thunder deftly blocked each strike. With a strident howl, Ajatarra whipped her tail forward and swept his legs out from under him. Perkele crashed to the ground as Ajatarra moved in for the kill—until the bloody point of a spear emerged from between her breasts.

For several seconds, she did not move as her breathing became labored. She arched her back and turned her face to the sky, releasing a final, shrill scream before life fled her body. With eyes and mouth wide open, Ajatarra dropped her axe and toppled forward, meeting Perkele's blade with her throat. Her body struck the ground a moment before her head.

Perkele removed his helmet and exchanged a nod with Väinämöinen. "Nice throw, brother."

"Ilmarinen," Petrus blurted. "It cannot be."

As everyone looked on, Perkele—or Ilmarinen?—retrieved Ajatarra's head and moved toward her body. "I shall dispose of this. Väinämöinen, you and the forest gods will see to the mortals?"

Väinämöinen bowed his head.

Just as he had arrived, the god of thunder vanished in a blinding burst of white light. By the time Petrus's vision cleared, Perkele and Ajatarra were gone, along with all of her slain pirus.

In the silence that followed, those still standing exchanged wary glances.

"Is it over?" someone asked finally.

"The battle is won," Tapio replied, his voice resonating from every corner of the sanctuary. "Ajatarra has been defeated."

Shoulders slumped and weapons dropped to the ground with thuds and clangs. Some cried as they embraced one another, friends and families reuniting at long last. Others wept as they knelt before the fallen.

"Where do we go from here?" Ievukka asked.

Petrus pulled her close and kissed her on the forehead, but his thoughts were beyond the forest. *Now we return home to starve.*

At the request of the survivors, the dead had been buried at one end of the sanctuary with the help of Tapio and his family. The forest gods had shifted the earth, carving out two rows of individual graves spaced evenly apart.

"I am deeply sorry for those you lost today, Petrus," Tellervo said. "Especially considering the suffering your people have endured for so long."

Petrus nodded solemnly. "We have won a war against an unthinkable evil, but I fear the desolation that still awaits my people. One more season without crops will make us wish we had all died swiftly in this forest."

"You don't honestly think we would have brought you this far only to abandon you?" Väinämöinen placed a gentle hand on Ievukka's shoulder. "Might I borrow your husband for a few minutes, my dear? There is someone who would like to speak with him."

She flashed a bemused smile. "By all means."

Väinämöinen motioned for Petrus to precede him.

"Where are we going?" Petrus asked, but the old man merely waved a gnarled hand to keep moving. As they stepped beyond the boundaries of the sanctuary, Petrus turned. "Who wants to speak to—oh."

Both Väinämöinen and the sanctuary were gone. Once again, Petrus faced the forge of Ilmarinen, but this time, he did so alone. The Eternal Craftsman stood with his back to Petrus, lightly tapping on something atop a long wooden table. The deity's imposing form blocked Petrus's view of the object.

Without looking up, Ilmarinen spoke. "I once told you that God helps those who help themselves. You and your people fought well. Come closer, Petrus."

As Petrus approached, Ilmarinen stepped aside and gestured toward a gold dome about four feet around. The walls of the dome were perhaps ten inches tall. The object stood on three legs spaced at equal distances around its perimeter. Petrus was not certain if it glowed with its own light or merely reflected the lambent flames of the nearby fire.

"What is it?"

"It is the Sampo, a device that Väinämöinen once tricked me into creating for someone eons ago. That's a long story, but suffice it to say that once he realized the error of his ways, Väinämöinen helped me recover it."

Petrus was even more confused, if that were possible. "A device? What does it do?"

"It brings prosperity to whomever possesses it. With the Sampo, you could become rich beyond your widest desires. Gold, precious gems, dominion over man and country as far as the eye can see. Name your desire and it shall be yours."

"I wish only that this famine come to an end, that our crops thrive this coming season, and that no more of my neighbors starve to death." Petrus paused. Then, "I only wish to feed my people."

Ilmarinen smiled. "Väinämöinen chose wisely. For you are indeed a rock, Petrus, and to you I entrust my final gift to my people. The Sampo is now yours. Take it with you. You need merely to lay your hands upon it and think about what you want most. From now on, every harvest shall be bountiful throughout the land. Your people will rebuild and become stronger than ever."

"I do not know how to thank you."

"I ask only that you never forget. My kin and I are no longer relevant in the presence of this new god whose name is spreading to nearly all corners of the world like a fire through a forest. We must accept that change is inevitable and be content to fade into the brume of antiquity."

"I promise that I shall never forget," Petrus assured him, "nor cease believing in you. It saddens me that you're leaving us."

"Perhaps someday, centuries from now, all of the ancient pantheons of this Earth shall return to see if your people are willing to believe in us again."

As he finished speaking, Ilmarinen and his forge faded into the night. Beyond the walls of the sanctuary, Petrus turned to Väinämöinen. "I didn't have the temerity to ask if he and Perkele were one and the same."

Väinämöinen shrugged. "Ilmarinen, Perkele, Ukko. Is not your Christian god also known by many names?"

Petrus nodded. "True. This experience has certainly opened my mind."

Väinämöinen nodded toward the Sampo now sitting on the ground before them, pulsing with its own inner flame. "And that will open your world to even more possibilities than you ever imagined. Ilmarinen has placed great trust in you. I know you won't let him down, or your people. They look upon you as a leader now."

Petrus knelt down and placed a tentative finger upon the dome's surface. It was comfortably warm to the touch. With a deep breath, he spread both hands over its dome and closed his eyes.

One Year Later

It was three o'clock in the morning when a piercing cry tore Petrus from a restful slumber. He turned his head to glance at the empty space beside him in bed. Sitting up, he caught sight of Ievukka standing at the window, silhouetted in the pallid light of the full moon. Petrus slipped out of bed to stand behind his wife, embracing her and their newborn daughter nestled in her arms.

"It will be dawn in less than hour," Ievukka whispered, "and then she will be baptized. Eliisa Anniki Tellervo Tuulikki Koivisto."

"Perhaps it's best not to mention Tellervo and Tuulikki to the new minister. He might not take well to pagan names. Those will be our little secret."

"Like the Sampo?"

Petrus nodded. "It's too dangerous a device to reveal. It could be made into a dreadful weapon. Ilmarinen entrusted it to me and I shall do what I must to honor His trust. Our crops are abundant again and our village is beginning to thrive. Let the other survivors and our new neighbors praise their god."

"While we praise the Gods."

Petrus smiled and nuzzled Ievukka. "That will also be our little secret."

ABOUT THE AUTHORS

Known as Renfield to his friends and family—yes, really—DANIEL PATRICK CORCORAN lives in Baltimore, Maryland with his wife and house rabbits. Renfield is a familiar face at the Maryland convention scene and can usually be found taking to the stage in one form or another. When not busy turning beloved genres on their ears, he is sometimes seen wandering the streets dressed as Krampus or Schnabelperchten as a celebrant of all holiday traditions. Daniel's vampire comedy tale, "Apartment Hunting," and science fiction adventure, "The Hard Place," were published in *Somewhere in the Middle of Eternity* and *Elsewhere in the Middle of Eternity*, respectively.

MICHAEL CRITZER is the creator and writer of the graphic novel *Tales from the Stacks* and the author of *Heroic Inspirations*, an exploration of superhero stories and the life lessons we can draw from them. His short fiction appears in a number of literary magazines and genre anthologies. As a cultural studies scholar, he has presented at academic conferences on the cultural and psychological roles superheroes play in our society. To that end, he is the Professor Geek and the Catholic Bible Geek behind the so named YouTube channels. He teaches writing, rhetoric and American literature in Central Virginia. Find out more at MichaelCritzer.com and subscribe to him on YouTube at Professor Geek and Catholic Bible Geek. Follow him on Twitter @MichaelCritzer and at @Geek_Catholic and on Instagram @MichaelCritzer.

SEAN DRUELINGER is a newcomer whose main body of work has been with game design for Lock 'n Load Publishing. He is a native of Maryland, an armed services veteran, and an avid history fan with a love of all things *Twilight Zone*. "Connecting Vines" is his first story ever published.

JULIE FEEDON is originally from Scranton, PA, but has been living in the Lehigh Valley since 1986. She is a specialist in the sales support department of a large capital medical supply company. Her hobbies include writing, painting, and crochet. She is also a certified Jane Austen junkie. Next to her daughter and husband, she loves the beach most dear.

Twitter: @Julie101670

Instagram: @JulieLibraArt

PHIL GIUNTA enjoys crafting powerful fiction that changes lives and inspires readers. His novels include the paranormal mysteries *Testing the Prisoner, By Your Side,* and *Like Mother, Like Daughters.* His short stories appear in such anthologies as *A Plague of Shadows, Beach Nights, Beach Pulp,* the *ReDeus* mythology series, and the *Middle of Eternity* speculative fiction series, which he created and edited for Firebringer Press. As a member of the Greater Lehigh Valley Writers Group, Phil also penned stories and essays for *Write Here, Write Now, The Write Connections,* and *Rewriting the Past,* three of the group's annual anthologies.

Phil is currently working on the second draft of a science fiction novel while plotting his triumphant escape from the pressures of corporate America where he has been imprisoned for over twenty-five years. Visit Phil's website at: www.philgiunta.com. Find him on Facebook: @writerphilgiunta and Twitter: @philgiunta71

CHRISTOPHER D. OCHS dove into writing in 2014 with his epic fantasy, *Pindlebryth of Lenland.* His latest work is a collection of mirthful macabre short stories, *If I Can't Sleep, You Can't Sleep.* He's currently looking for a home for his YA urban fantasy, *My Friend Jackson.* He continues to write the gamut from short fiction to novels in the veins of myth and legend, paranormal, horror, and the occasional sci-fi—all in the hope to reassure himself that his life is normal.

Chris has too many interests outside of writing for his own damn good. With previous careers in physics, electrical engineering and QA—along with his incessant dabblings as a CGI graphic artist, classical organist, voice talent on radio, video and anime conventions—it's a wonder he can remember to pay the dog and feed his bills. Wait, what?

Follow CDO's antics:
www.ChristopherDOchs.com
www.facebook.com/Christopher.D.Ochs
ChristopherDOchs.wordpress.com.

PETER ONG is a Freelance Writer based in California, USA with a bachelor's degree in Technical Writing/Graphic Design and a master's degree in Business. He writes for defense, maritime, and emergency vehicle publications and also for product and travel reviews and blog websites.

BART PALAMARO is author of several published short stories and one published novel, *The Other Side of Time*, and *The Fate of U-1055*, its free prequel. All are pretty much in the SF genre. Almost everything Bart read growing up was SF or fantasy. Even *Horatio Hornblower* is a form of SF to a 20th Century kid.

Recently, he's taking a side trip into the paranormal, with a shapeshifter subculture living and prospering while indistinguishable from anyone else in our own world. *In the Teeth of the Problem* and *In the Eye of the Beholder* are due for publication in 2020. Who knows, he may commit fantasy one of these days.

Bart is also TechGuru for the Greater Lehigh Valley Writers Group, riding herd on the web site and various other techie stuff we do. For fun and profit, he edits and formats books for self-publishers, both print and ebook. He also does book covers.

SUSANNA REILLY has been enthusiastic about writing since she was named first runner-up in a story writing contest at the age of 11. For many years writing took a backseat to school, work, and motherhood, but the fire stayed alive. It was stoked in the late 1990's and early 2000's when she joined a science fiction fan club that published an annual fanzine. Although the fanzine sold less than 30 copies per year (mostly to friends and family of the authors), the joy of writing stories in her favorite sci-fi universes kept her going. Susanna's first professional publication came in 2013 when her short story "To Protect and to Serve" was included in the Main Line Writers Group's first anthology *Unclaimed Baggage: Voice sof the Main Line Writers Group*. She subsequently published two stories ("Form and Substance" and "Perchance to Dream") in the 2014 anthology *Somewhere in the Middle of Eternity* and one story ("Tree of Love") in the 2016 anthology *Elsewhere in the Middle of Eternity*.

STUART S. ROTH lives in the Philadelphia, PA area. His work has appeared in anthologies for Pseudoscope Publishing, Prometheus Radio Theatre, and prior editions of Firebringer's *Middle of Eternity* Series. He has recently completed a novel entitled *Myomria* and is shopping it for publication. For freelance work, Stuart can be contacted at stuartroth42@ gmail.com. He also takes criticism good or bad and loves to hear from readers.

APRIL WELLES spent much of her life moving from city to city. No one place was home. During her travels later in life, she felt the desire to write, strong during high school, return. She found herself drawn to the diversity of writing within different genres and the possibilities within each.

April's most recent paraterrestrial horror tale, "Terror in Agradeb," was published in the anthology *Elsewhere in the Middle of Eternity* in 2016. Her previous stories can be found in the anthology magazines *Fantasy Times: Issue 1*, *Fantasy Times: Issue 2*, and *Pure Fantasy and Sci-Fi: Issue 2*. April's first paraterrestrial horror novelette *The House on the Cliff*, was published in *Pure Fantasy and Sci-Fi*, issue 2.

She enjoys creating, writing, building models, and DeLoreans. April and her cat reside in the paradise of the Pacific Northwest, where they have beautiful views of the mountains and trees.

April can be found on Facebook (aprilnikita.welles) and Amazon Author Central.

STEVEN HOWELL WILSON created the Mark Time and Parsec Award-winning podcast series The Arbiter Chronicles, as well as authoring *Taken Liberty* and several other novels and novellas in the Arbiters universe. His other works include the novel *Peace Lord of the Red Planet*, short stories for Crazy 8 Press's ReDeus series, and contributions to Sequart Press's Star Wars essay collections. Most recently, Steve has branched out into historical fiction, with his first effort appearing in *Hobnail and Other Frontier Stories* from Five Star Press. He has written for DC Comics and Starlog, and is publisher for Firebringer Press. He blogs often, if not regularly, at www.StevenHWilson.com.

LANCE WOODS's first script was a one-page episode of the *Batman* TV series (he was 7), which ultimately led him to become the creator/writer of *SuperHuman Times* (http://www.superhumantimes.com) for Prometheus Radio Theatre in 2006. The podcast series inspired his first book, *Heroic Park: A SuperHuman Times Novel*, published by Firebringer Press in 2012.

Lance's short stories include "The Gravest Show Unearthed" in the anthology *Elsewhere in the Middle of Eternity* (Firebringer Press, 2016) and "Dead Air" in the anthology *Somewhere in the Middle of Eternity* (Firebringer Press, 2014).

Additionally, he has had two comedy-mysteries—*Breeding Will Tell* and *Murder Case*—produced by the Baltimore Playwrights Festival and has written for more than 25 years in areas of the comic-book industry he doesn't like to talk about on his own time. When he isn't daydreaming about writing under the palm trees of Orlando, he lives with his family in a situation comedy format outside of Baltimore.

ABOUT THE ARTISTS

LAURA INGLIS is a freelance artist based in Western Maryland. She's created art for more than 50 licensed trading card sets including *Batman*, *Doctor Who*, *Star Trek*, and *Transformers*. She is also the cover artist for several novels from Firebringer Press including *By Your Side* and *Like Mother, Like Daughters* and has worked with RustyInk on assorted comic book projects. You can follow her on Twitter or Instagram as WandringRebel or on Facebook as The Art of Laura Inglis.

TIM MARRON is a professional graphic artist and illustrator working mainly out of DC for a Naval contracting company. He has been featured as an artist on books by Steven Wilson and Emily Bentz, as well as in several tabletop strategy games published by Lock 'n Load publishing. In his artwork, Tim draws inspiration largely from video games such as the *Metal Gear* franchise, *Mass Effect*, and in particular, *Warframe*. Tim lives in Maryland with his wife and 3 cats.

Known in many circles as "The Ornament Guy," MICHAEL RIEHL has earned a following for his amazing and much sought-after hand painted ornaments featuring characters, ships, and vehicles from film and television. Mike has become a staple at many SF and horror conventions such as Shore Leave, Monster Mania, and Chiller Theatre. Some of his most famous customers include LeVar Burton, Brent Spiner, Richard Herd, and other celebrities. Between Thanksgiving and Christmas, Michael's extraordinary display of ornaments can be admired at the popular Christkindlmarkt in Bethlehem, PA.

CHEYENNE-AUTUMN CHRISTINE REILLY is a student at Northern Vermont University studying Animation/Illustration and English Writing. This is her first publication of art and she does freelance commission work.

www.ingramcontent.com/pod-product-compliance
Lightning Source LLC
Chambersburg PA
CBHW020436030726
47495CB00006B/1826